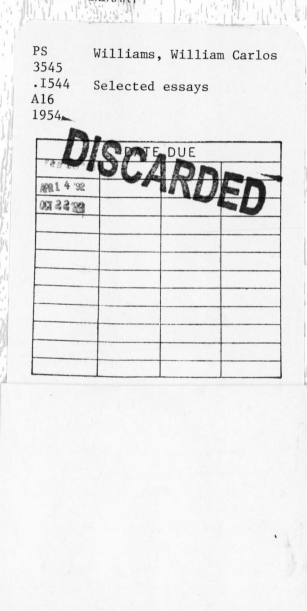

Selected Essays of William Carlos Williams

To the memory of "Uncle" Billy Abbott

the first English teacher

who ever gave me an

A

By William Carlos Williams

† *City Lights Books*

SELECTED ESSAYS OF
WILLIAM CARLOS WILLIAMS

A NEW DIRECTIONS BOOK

Copyright 1931, 1936, 1938, 1939, 1940, 1942, 1944, 1946, 1948, 1949, 1951, 1954, by William Carlos Williams.

Library of Congress Catalog Card Number: 54-7815
(ISBN: 0-8112-0235-6)

Acknowledgment is here made to the following publications in which some of the essays included in this volume first appeared: *Transition, The Symposium, Contact, Twice A Year, North American Review, The Kenyon Review, The Sewanee Review, Furioso, Now, View, Wake, Yale Poetry Review, Poetry, Quarterly Review of Literature, The New York Times, The Yale Literary Magazine, Art News* and *Origin*. The song, *Button Up Your Overcoat*, is used by permission and is Copyright 1928, by De Sylva, Brown and Henderson, Inc., New York, N.Y.

First published by Random House in 1954.
First published as New Directions Paperbook 273 in 1969.
Published simultaneously in Canada by George J. McLeod, Ltd., Toronto

Manufactured in the United States of America.

New Directions Books are published for James Laughlin
by New Directions Publishing Corporation,
80 Eighth Avenue, New York 10011.

FIFTH PRINTING

Contents

Contents

Preface

WHEN I AWOKE, that first morning, in my small dormitory room at the University of Pennsylvania where I had gone to study medicine, it was to the sound of music. It came from the room next to my own. It was good music, good piano music. I was too homesick and timid to do anything about it but greedily to drink it in. But when after a few days I could stand it no longer, I got out my fiddle and answered it.

The effect was instantaneous. The young man whom I had not yet even seen knocked on my door and when admitted turned out to be a student who was delighted to find a fellow music lover so close at hand. His name was Van Cleve, far advanced in his art over anything I could pretend to.

Discovering, as we talked, that I was no musician but kept a notebook in which from time to time I jotted down my poems and other thoughts, he immediately became interested. With excitement in his voice he told me of one of his classmates, an extraordinary fellow, also a poet, whom he offered to produce for me. Thus my years of patient if unsuccessful plodding at the fiddle were about to pay off.

I agreed to meet this young poet and with no more ado my new friend went into a neighboring building and came back with him in tow. He came willingly enough when told that a fellow poet had sent out a call for him. Thus I met Ezra Pound and began a friendship that has lasted unabated for the past half-century. He was my first major acquaintance among the writers.

There was a group of young men and women centering about Ezra Pound in those days who were important to me.

At the same time, my mind was tough and not easily carried away by the opinions of others. I was a good listener but enjoyed most to take home what I had heard to chew it over and to accept it only when I had made up my mind. I was not easily moved.

There was also the world of my ancestral background, the West Indies and Colonial America which led me to look at writing with very different eyes from any to be found about Philadelphia. Then there was what I came to learn about French and Spanish literature, not from books but from hearsay from my mother and father since Spanish and French also were languages frequently spoken at home.

This resulted in a certain cast of mind which made me want, after I had looked at the world about me, to form opinions which demanded to be heard. My religious training was, as they used to say, liberal. That also contributed its quota. I remember E. J. Luce, a cantankerous lawyer, who used to read selections from Kant's *Critique of Pure Reason* to our Sunday School class.

My opinions, from this background, grew to be as broad as the background itself. That, as far as I could tell, was the thing as a growing young American that I should treasure and add to as I went along. I had not yet come to the conviction: It is not what you say that matters but the manner in which you say it; there lies the secret of the ages.

I read everything that was handy on my father's bookshelves, including the *Principles of Philosophy* by Herbert Spencer. But I have never studied anything for long. Pleasure was what I wanted from my reading. And as I went along, the thing which gave me the most pleasure, the most thrills of a superior sort, was the poem. I still have a copy of Palgrave's *Golden Treasury of English Verse*, very much worn around the binding, dating from those days. I knew it from cover to cover. But modern poetry, what there was of it, and especially the free verse of Walt Whitman, opened my eyes.

Poetry is a dangerous subject for a boy to fool with, for

the dreams of the race are involved in it. The impractical dreams of men least able to advise those just reaching adult-hood were my constant diet. I was caught up by the fascina-tion of it and forgot the warning—for my father warned me to give poetry a wide berth. But I knew best what was good for me.

The trace of these beginnings remains in all I have said subsequently on the subject of verse—because it is principally about the poem that I have written critically in my life. All the emotion that is involved in the making and defining of a poem is brought out. It shows how much I am involved and how my judgment has been twisted in the defense of what I have wanted to defend.

We are a half-mad race, and what we say is not to be trusted.

Into this morass of feeling began to be born an idea. It wasn't at first much of an idea and didn't come in a burst of revelation. It was a gradual conviction that writing, and es-pecially verse, has parts precisely as the human body has also of which it is made up and if a man is to know it, it behooves him to become familiar with those parts.

That took the whole field out of the realm of the emotions for their own sakes and made it a study of means to an end. Such a move was risky—it seemed to involve a contradiction in terms. If the emotions do not control the poem, what in Heaven's name does? The answer is the mind, which drives and selects among them as though they were a pack of trained hounds. Not that I was up to the task that I had chosen for myself, but at least, win or lose, I saw the way that lay ahead. Or rather I did not see it at all but was convinced that the way, a way, was there had I the ability to find it.

Meanwhile I went on writing my poems. I had better say, constructing my poems. For I soon discovered that there were certain rules, certain new rules, that I became enmeshed in before I had gone far, which I had to master. These were ancient rules, profoundly true but long since all but forgotten. They were overgrown with weeds like ruined masonry. Present teaching had very little to do with them, but that they existed I had no doubts; it remained only for me to rediscover them. A new country, unencumbered by the debris of the ages, offered me this opportunity. I seized it with alacrity, knowing beforehand that I should have much assistance in finding my way through such a wilderness.

I speak as if writing poetry were my sole concern and indeed it is finally so. For as far as I know all writing starts and ends with the poem. When I write a short story it might better have been a poem, and for an essay there is nothing so fine as a definition or defense of the art which deals with the poetic principle.

Consequently in this selection of my prose essays, addresses, prefaces and reviews is to be found much that relates to the poet and his poem as well as much that relates to the allied arts. The painters especially have been prominent among my friends. In fact I almost became a painter, as my mother had been before me, and had it not been that it was easier to transport a manuscript than a wet canvas, the balance might have been tilted the other way.

In Philadelphia when I was a medical student I used to go on Sunday afternoons to the second-story room of a house on North 34th Street and sit with a dirty little old man in whose company I was transported to a colloquy with the angels. He would have a commission to complete, a pastoral scene in oils, a few cows standing or lying down in a meadow, for which he was well-known among the lesser dealers. Smoking a pipe as he painted, he hardly disturbed himself as I entered, other than to indicate where fresh brushes were to be found and to pick up a few random objects and place them in a favorable light near where he would be working. He gave me no instructions more than to nod his head in approval when he thought I had done well. Meanwhile he went on with his work.

My friend Charley Demuth I met in Philadelphia when I

was at school there. It was over a dish of prunes, we used to say, at Mrs. Chain's boarding house. I tried to bring him together with my dormitory companion Ezra Pound, but nothing came of it.

And once also in those days I journeyed out to Bryn Mawr to see the future poetess Hilda Doolittle in a performance of a May Day frolic on the green, and Marianne Moore was there, but I did not know her then.

During those years I lived with my parents in the house where my younger brother was born. I shall always remember the arguments I had with my father about the dining-room table, over whatever was uppermost in the news or our thoughts at the time. I loved my father but never forgave him for remaining, in spite of everything we could say against it, a British subject. It had much to do with my sometimes violent partisanship toward America. Not that we discussed this openly—it would have been better for us both if we had—but it was, I am sure, always at the back of our thoughts. He was not easily worsted, and to gain a point in a controversy whenever one came up was all I could do.

Our arguments were prolonged and sometimes bitter. Often the point at issue was immaterial, but the training I got in how to maintain myself under fire was invaluable. It has stood me in good stead through the years. What worth attaches to my critical judgment owes itself, perhaps, to those attacks and defenses. They went on for years.

All this was before I had begun to write or at least had written anything I have since wanted to keep. And now I am engaged in writing this potpourri of a preface to a book, a collection of the prose pieces which I have from time to time, more or less at random, sometimes on the spur of the moment, composed.

I cannot vouch for the opinions offered, for they represent a span of years during which I do not pretend to have had any but those largely in flux. In general, nevertheless, I have thought always to remain conscious of what I was about and to shape the writing after that which had, as time passed, become more clear to me. I kept trying to look ahead, as if it were through a mist with which I was surrounded. Granted my interest in writing, to make the poets particularly more accepted in what they say, I wanted to reinterpret them and relate them to the world. This ranged from an early admiration for the poems of Maxwell Bodenheim, to a concern for a formal yet liberally measured line; the poems of Mr. Eliot and all that they implied, to the designs of *The Pisan Cantos*.

I knew and loved Marsden Hartley. I knew and still know and love Marianne Moore. I knew and admired Gertrude Stein. I knew Kay Boyle when she was young. I knew the wonderful Ford Madox Ford and learned much from him. I knew James and Nora Joyce; he was a gentle person. Once, E. E. Cummings came to see me, in 1928 when my wife was in Europe, and admired a litter of kittens which I had playing in the back yard. I knew the painter Gleizes, the internationalist Marcel Duchamp and laughed with the rest admiringly before his "Nude Descending a Staircase." Charles Sheeler was an intimate of mine, and William Zorach was a fellow actor in one of Alfred Kreymborg's plays. I knew also Djuna Barnes, Mina Loy and the Baroness Elsa von Freytag Loringhoven. There were also Margaret Anderson and Jane Heap.

Time is a storm in which we are all lost. Only inside the convolutions of the storm itself shall we find our directions —whether we measure by the latest phenomena of Dada or make our computations after the archeological findings of a Frobenius whose researches in Algeria carried him back 500,-000 years to the shores of a great lake that existed there then. The clouds are racing across the sky. Today they are coming from the northeast. It will be cold and rainy for us even though it be June. I shall never forget when I heard Frobenius lecture once in New York limping about the platform on his badly set broken leg. He told us that he had been a weakling as a boy, he had a bad heart and had been advised to find a profession which would not entail a life of much physical effort, and so he went into the most difficult and exhausting work he could have selected for himself: archeological research in a tropical mountain region—and survived and grew stronger with the years till he became an old man. Thus it is all a matter of luck and determination what will happen to you.

As Frobenius saw and spoke of the evening, a mere war with its deaths and mutilations makes only an imperceptible mark on the processes of time. The processes of art are far more lasting. The least stroke with a stone ax is far more permanent and that itself is only relatively permanent so that the movements of Dada after all represent a greater truth. So that when we say, Long live dada! we are praising that which has already, in some one of its phases, long since outlived the pyramids.

What then of a life such as mine? I say that Chaucer, Villon and Whitman were contemporaries of mind with whom I am constantly in touch—through the art of writing. They are worthy rivals—whom I am proud and have been proud to honor as I can. And if I cannot find a way to surpass them I will not at least write in a lesser mode and stop trying. For to honor them I cannot do less.

I have passed through various phases with their imitations of imitations of that which seemed popular at the time. But I agree with Elizabeth Bowen that a masterpiece is only a mark to surpass. The processes of art, to keep alive, must always challenge the unknown and go where the most uncertainty lies. So that beauty when it is found, as it rarely is, shall have a touch of the marvelous about it, the unknown. If it were not so, it would be the end of beauty. Masterpieces are only beautiful in a tragic sense, like a starfish lying stretched dead on the beach in the sun.

What I have recorded here concerns these and many others whose names appear in the text, so that it is not necessary to make special note of them. Some of them are already half-forgot. Many I am still happy to number among my friends.

They represent a world from which the inexorable processes of time have not made, as yet, any final selections for remembrance. One or two may very well be heard from in the coming years. It would be a satisfaction to know that their names and something of what they did had been recorded here.

June 17, 1954

Prologue to Kora in Hell *

The Return of the Sun

Her voice was like rose-fragrance waltzing in the wind.
She seemed a shadow, stained with shadow colors,
Swimming through waves of sunlight . . .

1918

THE SOLE precedent I can find for the broken style of my prologue is *Longinus on the Sublime* and that one far-fetched.

When my mother was in Rome on that rare journey for-ever to be remembered, she lived in a small pension near the Pincio Gardens. The place had been chosen by my brother as one notably easy of access, being in a quarter free from confusion of traffic, on a street close to the park, and further-more the tram to the American Academy passed at the cor-ner. Yet never did my mother go out but she was in fear of being lost. By turning to the left when she should have turned right, actually she did once manage to go so far astray that it was nearly an hour before she extricated herself from the strangeness of every new vista and found a landmark.

There has always been a disreputable man of picturesque personality associated with this lady. Their relations have been marked by the most rollicking spirit of comradeship. Now it has been William, former sailor in Admiral Dewey's fleet at Manila, then Tom O'Rourck who has come to her to do odd jobs and to be cared for more or less when drunk or ill, their Penelope. William would fall from the grape arbor much to my mother's amusement and delight and to his blus-tering discomfiture or he would stagger to the back door nearly unconscious from bad whiskey. There she would serve him with very hot and very strong coffee, then put him to scrubbing the kitchen floor, into his sudsy pail pouring half a bottle of ammonia which would make the man gasp and water at the eyes as he worked and became sober.

She has always been incapable of learning from benefit or disaster. If a man cheat her she will remember that man with a violence that I have seldom seen equaled, but so far as that could have an influence on her judgment of the next man or woman, she might be living in Eden. And indeed she is, an impoverished, ravished Eden but one indestructible as the imagination itself. Whatever is before her is sufficient to itself and so to be valued. Her meat though more delicate in fiber is of a kind with that of Villon and La Grosse Margot:

Vente, gresle, gelle, j'ai mon pain cuit!

Carl Sandburg sings a Negro cotton picker's song of the boll weevil. Verse after verse tells what they would do to the insect. They propose to place it in the sand, in hot ashes, in the river, and other unlikely places but the boll weevil's refrain is always: "That'll be ma HOME! That'll be ma HOOME!"

My mother is given over to frequent periods of great depression being as I believe by nature the most light-hearted thing in the world. But there comes a grotesque turn to her talk, a macabre anecdote concerning some dream, a passionate statement about death, which elevates her mood without marring it, sometimes in a most startling way.

Looking out at our parlor window one day I said to her: "We see all the shows from here, don't we, all the weddings and funerals?" (They had been preparing a funeral across the street, the undertaker was just putting on his overcoat.) She replied: "Funny profession that, burying the dead people. I should think they wouldn't have any delusions of life left." W.—Oh yes, it's merely a profession. M.—Hm. And how they study it! They say sometimes people look terrible and they come and make them look fine. They push things into their mouths! (Realistic gesture) W.—Mama! M.—Yes, when they haven't any teeth.

By some such dark turn at the end she raises her story out of the commonplace: "Look at that chair, look at it! [The plasterers had just left.] If Mrs. J. or Mrs. D. saw that they would have a fit." W.—Call them in, maybe it will kill them. M.—But they're not near as bad as that woman, you know, her husband was in the chorus—has a little daughter Helen. Mrs. B., yes. She once wanted to take rooms here. I didn't want her. They told me: 'Mrs. Williams, I heard you're going to have Mrs. B. *She* is particular.' She said so herself. Oh no! Once she burnt all her face painting under the sink.

Thus, seeing the thing itself without forethought or afterthought but with great intensity of perception, my mother loses her bearings or associates with some disreputable person or translates a dark mood. She is a creature of great imagination. I might say this is her sole remaining quality. She is a despoiled, molted castaway but by this power she still breaks life between her fingers.

Once when I was taking lunch with Walter Arensberg at a small place on 63rd Street I asked him if he could state what the more modern painters were about, those roughly classed at that time as "cubists": Gleizes, Man Ray, Demuth, Duchamp—all of whom were then in the city. He replied by saying that the only way man differed from every other creature was in his ability to improvise novelty and, since the pictorial artist was under discussion, anything in paint that is truly new, truly a fresh creation, is good art. Thus, according to Duchamp, who was Arensberg's champion at the time, a stained-glass window that had fallen out and lay more or less together on the ground was of far greater interest than the thing conventionally composed *in situ*.

We returned to Arensberg's sumptuous studio where he gave further point to his remarks by showing me what appeared to be the original of Duchamp's famous "Nude Descending a Staircase." But this, he went on to say, is a full-sized photographic print of the first picture with many new touches by Duchamp himself and so by the technique of its manufacture as by other means it is a novelty!

Led on by these enthusiasms Arensberg has been an indefatigable worker for the yearly salon of the Society of Independent Artists, Inc. I remember the warmth of his description of a pilgrimage to the home of that old Boston hermit who, watched over by a forbidding landlady (evidently in his pay), paints the cigar-box-cover-like nudes upon whose fingers he presses actual rings with glass jewels from the five-and-ten-cent store.

I wish Arensberg had my opportunity for prying into jaded households where the paintings of Mama's and Papa's flowertime still hang on the walls. I propose that Arensberg be commissioned by the Independent Artists to scour the country for the abortive paintings of those men and women who without master or method have evolved perhaps two or three unusual creations in their early years. I would start the collection with a painting I have by a little Englishwoman, A. E. Kerr, 1906, that in its unearthly gaiety of flowers and sobriety of design possesses exactly that strange freshness a spring day approaches without attaining, an expansion of April, a thing this poor woman found too costly for her possession—she could not swallow it as the Negroes do diamonds in the mines. Carefully selected, these queer products might be housed to good effect in some unpretentious exhibition chamber across the city from the Metropolitan Museum of Art. In the anteroom could be hung perhaps photographs of prehistoric rock-paintings and etchings on horn: galloping bisons and stags, the hind feet of which have been caught by the artist in such a position that from that time until the invention of the camera obscura, a matter of six thousand years or more, no one on earth had again depicted that most delicate and expressive posture of running.

The amusing controversy between Arensberg and Duchamp on one side, and the rest of the hanging committee on the other as to whether the porcelain urinal was to be admitted to the Palace Exhibition of 1917 as a representative piece of American sculpture, should not be allowed to slide into oblivion.

One day Duchamp decided that his composition for that day would be the first thing that struck his eye in the first hardware store he should enter. It turned out to be a pickax which he bought and set up in his studio. This was his composition. Together with Mina Loy and a few others Duchamp and Arensberg brought out the paper, *The Blind Man*, to which Robert Carlton Brown, with his vision of suicide by diving from a high window of the Singer Building, contributed a few poems.

In contradistinction to their South, Marianne Moore's statement to me at the Chatham parsonage one afternoon— my wife and I were just on the point of leaving—sets up a North: My work has come to have just one quality of value in it: I will not touch or have to do with those things which I detest. In this austerity of mood she finds sufficient freedom for the play she chooses.

Of all those writing poetry in America at the time she was here Marianne Moore was the only one Mina Loy feared. By divergent virtues these two women have achieved freshness of presentation, novelty, freedom, break with banality.

When Margaret Anderson published my first improvisations Ezra Pound wrote me one of his hurried letters in which he urged me to give some hint by which the reader of good will might come at my intention.

Before Ezra's permanent residence in London, on one of his trips to America—brought on I think by an attack of jaundice—he was glancing through some book of my father's. "It is not necessary," he said, "to read everything in a book in order to speak intelligently of it. Don't tell everybody I said so," he added.

During this same visit my father and he had been reading and discussing poetry together. Pound has always liked my father. "I of course like your old man and I have drunk his Goldwasser." They were hot for an argument that day. My parent had been holding forth in downright sentences upon my own "idle nonsense" when he turned and became equally vehement concerning something Ezra had written: what in heaven's name Ezra meant by "jewels" in a verse that had come between them. These jewels,—rubies, sapphires, ame-thysts and whatnot, Pound went on to explain with great de-termination and care, were the backs of books as they stood on a man's shelf. "But why in heaven's name don't you say so then?" was my father's triumphant and crushing rejoinder.

The letter:

. . . God knows I have to work hard enough to escape, not *prop-agande*, but getting centered in *propagande*. And America? What the h—l do you a blooming foreigner know about the place. Your *père* only penetrated the edge, and you've never been west of Upper Darby, or the Maunchunk switchback.

Would H., with the swirl of the prairie wind in her underwear, or the Virile Sandburg recognize you, an effete easterner as a REAL American? INCONCEIVABLE!!!!!

My dear boy you have never felt the woop of the PEEraries. You have never seen the projecting and protuberant Mts. of the SIerra Nevada. WOT can you know of the country?

You have the naive credulity of a Co.Clare emigrant. But I (*der grosse Ich*) have the virus, the bacillus of the land in my blood, for nearly three bleating centuries.

(Bloody snob. 'eave a brick at 'im!!!) . . .

I was very glad to see your wholly incoherent unamerican poems in the L.R.

Of course Sandburg will tell you that you miss the "big drifts," and Bodenheim will object to your not being sufficiently deca-dent.

You thank your bloomin gawd you've got enough Spanish blood to muddy up your mind, and prevent the current Ameri-can ideation from going through it like a blighted colander.

The thing that saves your work is opacity, and don't forget it. Opacity is NOT an American quality. Fizz, swish, gabble, and verbiage, these are *echt americanisch*.

And alas, alas, poor old Masters. Look at Oct. *Poetry*.

Let me indulge the American habit of quotation:

"Si le cosmopolitisme littéraire gagnait encore et qu'il réussit à éteindre ce que les différences de race ont allumé de haine de sang parmi les hommes, j'y verrais un gain pour la civilisation et pour l'humanité tout entière. . . .

"L'amour excessif d'une patrie a pour immédiat corollaire l'horreur des patries étrangères. Non seulement on craint de quitter la jupe de sa maman, d'aller voir comment vivent les autres hommes, de se mêler à leur luttes, de partager leurs travaux, non seulement on reste chez soi, mais on finit par fermer sa porte.

"Cette folie gagne certains littérateurs et le même professeur, en sortant d'expliquer le Cid ou Don Juan, rédige de gracieuses injures contre Ibsen et l'influence, hélas, trop illusoire, de son oeuvre, pourtant toute de lumière et de beauté." et cetera. Lie down and compose yourself.

I like to think of the Greeks as setting out for the colonies in Sicily and the Italian peninsula. The Greek temperament lent itself to a certain symmetrical sculptural phase and to a fat poetical balance of line that produced important work but I like better the Greeks setting their backs to Athens. The ferment was always richer in Rome, the dispersive explosion was always nearer, the influence carried further and remained hot longer. Hellenism, especially the modern sort, is too staid, too chilly, too little fecundative to impregnate my world.

Hilda Doolittle before she began to write poetry or at least before she began to show it to anyone would say: "You're not satisfied with me, are you Billy? There's something lacking, isn't there?" When I was with her my feet always seemed to be sticking to the ground while she would be walking on the tips of the grass stems.

Ten years later as assistant editor of the *Egoist* she refers to my long poem, "March," which thanks to her own and her husband's friendly attentions finally appeared there in a purified form:

14 *Aug.* 1916

Dear Bill:—

I trust you will not hate me for wanting to delete from your poem all the flippancies. The reason I want to do this is that the beautiful lines are so very beautiful—so in the tone and spirit of your *Postlude*—(which to me stands, a Nike, supreme among your poems). I think there is *real* beauty—and real beauty is a rare and sacred thing in this generation—in all the pyramid, Ashur-ban-i-pal bits and in the Fiesole and in the wind at the very last.

I don't know what you think but I consider this business of writing a very sacred thing! —I think you have the "spark"—am sure of it, and when you speak *direct* are a poet. I feel in the hey-ding-ding touch running through your poem a derivative tendency which, to me, is not *you*—not your very self. It is as if you were *ashamed* of your Spirit, ashamed of your inspiration!—as if you mocked at your own song. It's very well to *mock* at yourself —it is a spiritual sin to mock at your inspiration—

Hilda

Oh well, all this might be very disquieting were it not that "sacred" has lately been discovered to apply to a point of arrest where stabilization has gone on past the time. There is nothing sacred about literature, it is damned from one end to the other. There is nothing in literature but change and change is mockery. I'll write whatever I damn please, whenever I damn please and as I damn please and it'll be good if the authentic spirit of change is on it.

But in any case H. D. misses the entire intent of what I am doing no matter how just her remarks concerning that particular poem happen to have been. The hey-ding-ding touch *was* derivative, but it filled a gap that I did not know how better to fill at the time. It might be said that that touch is the prototype of the improvisations.

It is to the inventive imagination we look for deliverance from every other misfortune as from the desolation of a flat

Hellenic perfection of style. What good then to turn to art from the atavistic religionists, from a science doing slavery service upon gas engines, from a philosophy tangled in a miserable sort of dialect that means nothing if the full power of initiative be denied at the beginning by a lot of baying and snapping scholiasts? If the inventive imagination must look, as I think, to the field of art for its richest discoveries today it will best make its way by compass and follow no path.

But before any material progress can be accomplished there must be someone to draw a discriminating line between true and false values.

The true value is that peculiarity which gives an object a character by itself. The associational or sentimental value is the false. Its imposition is due to lack of imagination, to an easy lateral sliding. The attention has been held too rigid on the one plane instead of following a more flexible, jagged resort. It is to loosen the attention, my attention since I occupy part of the field, that I write these improvisations. Here I clash with Wallace Stevens.

The imagination goes from one thing to another. Given many things of nearly totally divergent natures but possessing one-thousandth part of a quality in common, provided that be new, distinguished, these things belong in an imaginative category and not in a gross natural array. To me this is the gist of the whole matter. It is easy to fall under the spell of a certain mode, especially if it be remote of origin, leaving thus certain of its members essential to a reconstruction of its significance permanently lost in an impenetrable mist of time. But the thing that stands eternally in the way of really good writing is always one: the virtual impossibility of lifting to the imagination those things which lie under the direct scrutiny of the senses, close to the nose. It is this difficulty that sets a value upon all works of art and makes them a necessity. The senses witnessing what is immediately before them in detail see a finality which they cling to in despair, not knowing which way to turn. Thus the so-called natural or scientific array becomes fixed, the walking devil of modern life. He who even nicks the solidity of this apparition does a piece of work superior to that of Hercules when he cleaned the Augean stables.

Stevens' letter applies really to my book of poems, *Al Que Quiere* (which means, by the way, "To Him Who Wants It") but the criticism he makes of that holds good for each of the improvisations if not for the *oeuvre* as a whole.

It begins with a postscript in the upper left hand corner: "I think, after all, I should rather send this than not, although it is quarrelsomely full of my own ideas of discipline."

April 9

My dear Williams:

.   .   .   .

What strikes me most about the poems themselves is their casual character. . . . Personally I have a distaste for miscellany. It is one of the reasons I do not bother about a book myself.

[*Wallace Stevens is a fine gentleman whom Cannell likened to a Pennsylvania Dutchman who has suddenly become aware of his habits and taken to "society" in self-defense. He is always immaculately dressed. I don't know why I should always associate him in my mind with an imaginary image I have of Ford Madox Ford.*]

. . . My idea is that in order to carry a thing to the extreme necessity to convey it one has to stick to it; . . . Given a fixed point of view, realistic, imagistic or what you will, everything adjusts itself to that point of view; the process of adjustment is a world in flux, as it should be for a poet. But to fidget with points of view leads always to new beginnings and incessant new beginnings lead to sterility.

(This sounds like Sir Roger de Coverley)

A single manner
or mood thoroughly matured and exploited is that fresh thing . . . etc.

One has to keep looking for poetry as Renoir looked for colors in old walls, woodwork and so on.

Your place is

—among children
Leaping around a dead dog.

A book of that would feed the hungry . . .

Well a book of poems is a damned serious affair. I am only objecting that a book that contains your particular quality should contain anything else and suggesting that if the quality were carried to a communicable extreme, in intensity and volume, etc. . . . I see it all over the book, in your landscapes and portraits, but dissipated and obscured. Bouquets for brides and Spencerian compliments for poets . . . There are a very few men who have anything native in them or for whose work I'd give a Bolshevik ruble. . . . But I think your tantrums not half mad enough.

[*I am not quite clear about the last sentence but I presume he means that I do not push my advantage through to an overwhelming decision. What would you have me do with my Circe, Stevens, now that I have double-crossed her game, marry her? It is not what Odysseus did.*]

I return Pound's letter . . . observe how in everything he does he proceeds with the greatest positiveness, etc.

Wallace Stevens

I wish that I might here set down my "Vortex" after the fashion of London, 1913, stating how little it means to me whether I live here, there or elsewhere or succeed in this, that or the other so long as I can keep my mind free from the trammels of literature, beating down every attack of its *retiarii* with my *mirmillones*. But the time is past.

I thought at first to adjoin to each improvisation a more or less opaque commentary. But the mechanical interference that would result makes this inadvisable. Instead I have placed some of them in the preface where without losing their original intention (see reference numerals at the beginning of each) they relieve the later text and also add their weight to my present fragmentary argument.

V. No. 2. By the brokenness of his composition the poet makes himself master of a certain weapon which he could possess himself of in no other way. The speed of the emotions is sometimes such that thrashing about in a thin exaltation or despair many matters are touched but not held, more often broken by the contact.

II. No. 3. The instability of these improvisations would seem such that they must inevitably crumble under the attention and become particles of a wind that falters. It would appear to the unready that the fiber of the thing is a thin jelly. It would be these same fools who would deny touch cords to the wind because they cannot split a storm endwise and wrap it upon spools. The virtue of strength lies not in the grossness of the fiber but in the fiber itself. Thus a poem is tough by no quality it borrows from a logical recital of events nor from the events themselves but solely from that attenuated power which draws perhaps many broken things into a dance giving them thus a full being.

It is seldom that anything but the most elementary communications can be exchanged one with another. There are in reality only two or three reasons generally accepted as the causes of action. No matter what the motive it will seldom happen that true knowledge of it will be anything more than vaguely divined by some one person, some half a person whose intimacy has perhaps been cultivated over the whole of a lifetime. We live in bags. This is due to the gross fiber of all action. By action itself almost nothing can be imparted. The world of action is a world of stones.

XV. No. 1. Bla! Bla! Bla! Heavy talk is talk that waits upon a deed. Talk is servile that is set to inform. Words with the bloom on them run before the imagination like the saeter girls before Peer Gynt. It is talk with the patina of whim upon it makes action a bootlicker. So nowadays poets spit upon rhyme and rhetoric.

The stream of things having composed itself into wiry strands that move in one fixed direction, the poet in desperation turns at right angles and cuts across current with startling results to his hangdog mood.

XI. No. 2. In France, the country of Rabelais, they know that the world is not made up entirely of virgins. They do not deny virtue to the rest because of that. Each age has its perfections but the praise differs. It is only stupid when the praise of the gross and the transformed would be minted in unfit terms such as suit nothing but youth's sweetness and frailty. It is necessary to know that laughter is the reverse of aspiration. So they laugh well in France, at Coquelin and the *Petoman*. Their girls, also, thrive upon the love-making they get, so much so that the world runs to Paris for that reason.

XII. No. 2B. It is chuckleheaded to desire a way through every difficulty. Surely one might even communicate with the dead—and lose his taste for truffles. Because snails are slimy when alive and because slime is associated (erroneously) with filth, the fool is convinced that snails are detestable when, as it is proven every day, fried in butter with chopped parsley upon them, they are delicious. This is both sides of the question: the slave and the despoiled of his senses are one. But to weigh a difficulty and to turn it aside without being wrecked upon a destructive solution bespeaks an imagination of force sufficient to transcend action. The difficulty has thus been solved by ascent to a higher plane. It is energy of the imagination alone that cannot be laid aside.

Rich as are the gifts of the imagination bitterness of world's loss is not replaced thereby. On the contrary it is intensified, resembling thus possession itself. But he who has no power of the imagination cannot even know the full of his injury.

VIII. No. 3. Those who permit their senses to be despoiled of the things under their noses by stories of all manner of things removed and unattainable are of frail imagination. Idiots, it is true nothing is possessed save by dint of that vigorous conception of its perfections which is the imagination's special province but neither is anything possessed which is not extant. A frail imagination, unequal to the tasks before it, is easily led astray.

IV. No. 2. Although it is a quality of the imagination that it seeks to place together those things which have a common relationship, yet the coining of similes is a pastime of very low order, depending as it does upon a nearly vegetable coincidence. Much more keen is that power which discovers in things those inimitable particles of dissimilarity to all other things which are the peculiar perfections of the thing in question.

But this loose linking of one thing with another has effects of a destructive power little to be guessed at: all manner of things are thrown out of key so that it approaches the impossible to arrive at an understanding of anything. All is confusion, yet it comes from a hidden desire for the dance, a lust of the imagination, a will to accord two instruments in a duet.

But one does not attempt by the ingenuity of the joiner to blend the tones of the oboe with the violin. On the contrary the perfections of the two instruments are emphasized by the joiner; no means is neglected to give to each the full color of its perfections. It is only the music of the instruments which is joined and that not by the woodworker but by the composer, by virtue of the imagination.

On this level of the imagination all things and ages meet in fellowship. Thus only can they, peculiar and perfect, find their release. This is the beneficent power of the imagination.

Age and youth are great flatterers. Brooding on each other's obvious psychology neither dares tell the other outright what manifestly is the truth: your world is poison. Each is secure in his own perfections. Monsieur Eichorn used to have a most atrocious body odor while the odor of some girls is a pleasure to the nostril. Each quality in each person or age, rightly valued, would mean the freeing of that age to its own delights of action or repose. Now an evil odor can be pursued with praiseworthy ardor leading to great natural activity whereas a flowery skinned virgin may and no doubt often does allow herself to fall into destructive habits of neglect.

XIII. No. 3. A poet witnessing the chicory flower and re-alizing its virtues of form and color so constructs his praise of it as to borrow no particle from right or left. He gives his poem over to the flower and its plant themselves, that they may benefit by those cooling winds of the imagination which thus returned upon them will refresh them at their task of saving the world. But what does it mean, remarked his friends?

VII. *Coda*. It would be better than depriving birds of their song to call them all nightingales. So it would be better than to have a world stript of poetry to provide men with some sort of eyeglasses by which they should be unable to read any verse but sonnets. But fortunately although there are many sorts of fools, just as there are many birds which sing and many sorts of poems, there is no need to please them.

All schoolmasters are fools. Thinking to build in the young the foundations of knowledge they let slip their minds that the blocks are of gray mist bedded upon the wind. Those who will taste of the wind himself have a mark in their eyes by virtue of which they bring their masters to nothing.

All things brought under the hand of the possessor crum-ble to nothingness. Not only that: He who possesses a child if he cling to it inordinately becomes childlike, whereas, with a twist of the imagination, himself may rise into com-radeship with the grave and beautiful presences of antiquity. But some have the power to free, say a young matron pur-suing her infant, from her own possessions, making her kin to Yang Kuei-fei because of a haunting loveliness that clings about her knees, impeding her progress as she takes up her matronly pursuit.

As to the sun what is he, save for his light, more than the earth is: the same mass of metals, a mere shadow? But the winged dawn is the very essence of the sun's self, a thing cold, vitreous, a virtue that precedes the body which it drags after it.

The features of a landscape take their position in the imagination and are related more to their own kind there than to the country and season which has held them hitherto as a basket holds vegetables mixed with fruit.

VI. No. 1. A fish swimming in a pond, were his back white and his belly green, would be easily perceived from above by hawks against the dark depths of water and from below by larger fish against the penetrant light of the sky. But since his belly is white and his back green he swims about in safety. Observing this barren truth and discerning at once its slavish application to the exercises of the mind, a young man, who has been sitting for some time in contemplation at the edge of a lake, rejects with scorn the parochial deductions of history and as scornfully asserts his defiance.

XIV. No. 3. The barriers which keep the feet from the dance are the same which in a dream paralyze the effort to escape and hold us powerless in the track of some murderous pursuer. Pant and struggle but you cannot move. The birth of the imagination is like waking from a nightmare. Never does the night seem so beneficent.

The raw beauty of ignorance that lies like an opal mist over the west coast of the Atlantic, beginning at the Grand Banks and extending into the recesses of our brains—the children, the married, the unmarried—clings especially about the eyes and the throats of our girls and boys. Of a Sunday afternoon a girl sits before a mechanical piano and, working it with her hands and feet, opens her mouth and sings to the music—a popular tune, ragtime. It is a serenade. I have seen a young Frenchman lean above the piano and looking down speak gently and wonderingly to one of our girls singing such a serenade. She did not seem aware of what she was singing and he smiled an occult but thoroughly bewildered smile —as of a man waiting for a fog to lift, meanwhile lost in admiration of its enveloping beauty—fragments of architecture, a street opening and closing, a mysterious glow of sunshine.

VIII. No. 1. A man of note upon examining the poems of his friend and finding there nothing related to his immediate understanding laughingly remarked: After all, literature is communication while you, my friend, I am afraid, in attempting to do something striking, are in danger of achieving mere preciosity.——But inasmuch as the fields of the mind are vast and little explored, the poet was inclined only to smile and to take note of that hardening infirmity of the imagination which seems to endow its victim with great solidity and rapidity of judgment. But he thought to himself: And yet of what other thing is greatness composed than a power to annihilate half-truths for a thousandth part of accurate understanding. Later life has its perfections as well as that bough-bending time of the mind's florescence with which I am so discursively taken.

I have discovered that the thrill of first love passes! It even becomes the backbone of a sordid sort of religion if not assisted in passing. I knew a man who kept a candle burning before a girl's portrait day and night for a year—then jilted her, pawned her off on a friend. I have been reasonably frank about my erotics with my wife. I have never or seldom said, my dear I love you, when I would rather say: My dear, I wish you were in Tierra del Fuego. I have discovered by scrupulous attention to this detail and by certain allied experiments that we can continue from time to time to elaborate relationships quite equal in quality, if not greatly superior, to that surrounding our wedding. In fact, the best we have enjoyed of love together has come after the most thorough destruction or harvesting of that which has gone before. Periods of barrenness have intervened, periods comparable to the prison music in *Fidelio* or to any of Beethoven's pianissimo transition passages. It is at these times our formal relations have teetered on the edge of a debacle to be followed, as our imaginations have permitted, by a new growth of passionate attachment dissimilar in every member to that which has gone before.

It is in the continual and violent refreshing of the idea that
love and good writing have their security.

Alfred Kreymborg is primarily a musician, at best an in-
novator of musical phrase:

> We have no dishes
> to eat our meals from.
> We have no dishes
> to eat our meals from
> because we have no dishes
> to eat our meals from
>
> .   .   .   .
>
> We need no dishes
> to eat our meals from,
> we have fingers
> to eat our meals from.

Kreymborg's idea of poetry is a transforming music that
has much to do with tawdry things.

Few people know how to read Kreymborg. There is no
modern poet who suffers more from a bastard sentimental
appreciation. It is hard to get his things from the page. I have
heard him say he has often thought in despair of marking his
verse into measures as music is marked. Oh, well—

The man has a bare irony, the gift of rhythm and *Others.*
I smile to think of Alfred stealing the stamps from the envelopes sent for return of mss., to the *Others* office! The best
thing that could happen for the good of poetry in the United
States today would be for someone to give Alfred Kreymborg a hundred thousand dollars. In his mind there is the determination for freedom brought into relief by a crabbedness
of temper that makes him peculiarly able to value what is
being done here. Whether he is bull enough for the work I
am not certain, but that he can find his way that I know.

A somewhat petulant English college friend of my brother's once remarked that Britons make the best policemen the

world has ever witnessed. I agree with him. It is silly to go into a puckersnatch because some brass-button-minded nincompoop in Kensington flies off the handle and speaks openly about our United States prize poems. This Mr. Jepson— "Anyone who has heard Mr. J. read Homer and discourse on Catullus would recognize his fitness as a judge and respecter of poetry"—this is Ezra!—this champion of the right is not half a fool. His epithets and phrases—slipshod, rank bad workmanship of a man who has shirked his job, lumbering fakement, cumbrous artificiality, maundering dribble, rancid as *Ben Hur*—are in the main well-merited. And besides, he comes out with one fairly lipped cornet blast: the only distinctive U. S. contributions to the arts have been ragtime and buck-dancing.

Nothing is good save the new. If a thing have novelty it stands intrinsically beside every other work of artistic excellence. If it have not that, no loveliness or heroic proportion or grand manner will save it. It will not be saved above all by an attenuated intellectuality.

But all U. S. verse is not bad according to Mr. J., there is T. S. Eliot and his "Love Song of J. Alfred Prufrock."

But our prize poems are especially to be damned not because of superficial bad workmanship, but because they are rehash, repetition—just as Eliot's more exquisite work is rehash, repetition in another way of Verlaine, Baudelaire, Maeterlinck—conscious or unconscious—just as there were Pound's early paraphrases from Yeats and his constant later cribbing from the Renaissance, Provence and the modern French: Men content with the connotations of their masters.

It is convenient to have fixed standards of comparison: All antiquity! And there is always some everlasting Polonius of Kensington forever to rate highly his eternal Eliot. It is because Eliot is a subtle conformist. It tickles the palate of this archbishop of procurers to a lecherous antiquity to hold up Prufrock as a New World type. Prufrock, the nibbler at sophistication, endemic in every capital, the not quite (because he refuses to turn his back), is "the soul of that modern land," the United States!

> Blue undershirts,
> Upon a line,
> It is not necessary to say to you
> Anything about it—

I cannot question Eliot's observation. Prufrock is a masterly portrait of the man just below the summit, but the type is universal; the model in his case might be Mr. J.

No. The New World is Montezuma or, since he was stoned to death in a parley, Guatemozin who had the city of Mexico leveled over him before he was taken.

For the rest, there is no man even though he dare who can make beauty his own and "so at last live," at least there is no man better situated for that achievement than another. As Prufrock longed for his silly lady, so Kensington longs for its Hardanger dairymaid. By a mere twist of the imagination, if Prufrock only knew it, the whole world can be inverted (why else are there wars?) and the mermaids be set warbling to whoever will listen to them. Seesaw and blindman's buff converted into a sort of football.

But the summit of United States achievement, according to Mr. J.—who can discourse on Catullus—is that very beautiful poem of Eliot's, "La Figlia Que Piange": just the right amount of everything drained through, etc., etc., etc., etc., the rhythm delicately studied and—IT CONFORMS! *ergo,* here we have "the very fine flower of the finest spirit of the United States."

Examined closely this poem reveals a highly refined distillation. Added to the already "faithless" formula of yesterday we have a conscious simplicity:

Simple and faithless as a smile and shake of the hand.

The perfection of that line is beyond cavil. Yet, in the last

stanza, this paradigm, this very fine flower of U. S. art is
warped out of alignment, obscured in meaning even to the
point of an absolute unintelligibility by the inevitable straining after a rhyme, the very cleverness with which this straining is covered being a sinister token in itself.

And I wonder how they should have been together!

So we have no choice but to accept the work of this fumbling conjurer.

Upon the Jepson filet Eliot balances his mushroom. It is the
latest touch from the literary cuisine, it adds to the pleasant
outlook from the club window. If to do this, if to be a Whis-
tler at best, in the art of poetry, is to reach the height of
poetic expression then Ezra and Eliot have approached it and
tant pis for the rest of us.

The Adobe Indian hag sings her lullaby:

> The beetle is blind
> The beetle is blind
> The beetle is blind
> The beetle is blind, etc., etc.

and Kandinsky in his, *Ueber das Geistige in der Kunst*, sets
down the following axioms for the artist:

> Every artist has to express himself.
> Every artist has to express his epoch.
> Every artist has to express the pure and eternal
>   qualities of the art of all men.

So we have the fish and the bait, but the last rule holds three
hooks at once—not for the fish, however.

I do not overlook De Gourmont's plea for a meeting of the
nations, but I do believe that when they meet Paris will be
more than slightly abashed to find parodies of the middle
ages, Dante and *langue d'oc* foisted upon it as the best in

United States poetry. Even Eliot, who is too fine an artist to allow himself to be exploited by a blockheaded grammaticaster, turns recently toward "one definite false note" in his quatrains, which more nearly approach America than ever "La Figlia Que Piange" did. Ezra Pound is a Boscan who has met his Navagiero.

One day Ezra and I were walking down a back lane in Wyncote. I contended for bread, he for caviar. I became hot. He, with fine discretion, exclaimed: "Let us drop it. We will never agree, or come to an agreement." He spoke then like a Frenchman, which is one who discerns.

Imagine an international congress of poets at Paris or Versailles, Remy de Gourmont (now dead) presiding, poets all speaking five languages fluently. Ezra stands up to represent U. S. verse and De Gourmont sits down smiling. Ezra begins by reading "La Figlia Que Piange." It would be a pretty pastime to gather into a mental basket the fruits of that reading from the minds of the ten Frenchmen present; their impressions of the sort of United States that very fine flower was picked from. After this Kreymborg might push his way to the front and read "Jack's House."

E. P. is the best enemy United States verse has. He is interested, passionately interested—even if he doesn't know what he is talking about. But of course he does know what he is talking about. He does not, however, know everything, not by more than half. The accordances of which Americans have the parts and the colors but not the completions before them pass beyond the attempts of his thought. It is a middle-aging blight of the imagination.

I praise those who have the wit and courage, and the conventionality, to go direct toward their vision of perfection in an objective world where the signposts are clearly marked, viz., to London. But confine them in hell for their paretic assumption that there is no alternative but their own groove.

Dear fat Stevens, thawing out so beautifully at forty! I was one day irately damning those who run to London when

Stevens caught me up with his mild: "But where in the world will you have them run to?"

Nothing that I should write touching poetry would be complete without Maxwell Bodenheim in it, even had he not said that the *Improvisations* were "perfect," the best things I had ever done; for that I place him, Janus, first and last.

Bodenheim pretends to hate most people, including Pound and Kreymborg, but that he really goes to this trouble I cannot imagine. He seems rather to me to have the virtue of self-absorption so fully developed that hate is made impossible. Due to this, also, he is an unbelievable physical stoic. I know of no one who lives so completely in his pretenses as Bogie does. Having formulated his world neither toothache nor the misery to which his indolence reduces him can make head against the force of his imagination. Because of this he remains for me a heroic figure, which, after all, is quite apart from the stuff he writes and which only concerns him. He is an Isaiah of the butterflies.

Bogie was the young and fairly well acclaimed genius when he came to New York four years ago. He pretended to have fallen in Chicago and to have sprained his shoulder. The joint was done up in a proper Sayre's dressing and there really looked to be a bona-fide injury. Of course he couldn't find any work to do with one hand so we all chipped in. It lasted a month! During that time Bogie spent a week at my house at no small inconvenience to Florence, who had two babies on her hands just then. When he left I expressed my pleasure at having had his company. "Yes," he replied, "I think you have profited by my visit." The statement impressed me by its simple accuracy as well as by the evidence it bore of that fullness of the imagination which had held the man in its tide while we had been together.

Charley Demuth once told me that he did not like the taste of liquor, for which he was thankful, but that he found the effect it had on his mind to be delightful. Of course Li Po is reported to have written his best verse supported in the arms of the Emperor's attendants and with a dancing girl to hold his tablet. He was also a great poet. Wine is merely the latch-string.

The virtue of it all is in an opening of the doors, though some rooms of course will be empty, a break with banality, the continual hardening which habit enforces. There is nothing left in me but the virtue of curiosity. Demuth puts in. The poet should be forever at the ship's prow.

An acrobat seldom learns really a new trick, but he must exercise continually to keep his joints free. When I made this discovery it started rings in my memory that keep following one after the other to this day.

I have placed the following *Improvisations* in groups, somewhat after the A.B.A. formula, that one may support the other, clarifying or enforcing perhaps the other's intention.

The arrangement of the notes, each following its poem and separated from it by a ruled line, is borrowed from a small volume of Metastasio, *Varie Poesie Dell' Abate Pietro Metastasio*, Venice, 1795.

September 1, 1918

Comment

Contact I, 1921

IN ANSWER to all criticisms we find the first issue of *Contact* perfect, the first truly representative American magazine of art yet published.

I should like to make St. Francis of Assisi the patron saint of the United States, because he loved the animals. The birds came to him not for wheat but to hear him preach. Even the fish heard him.

The columns of the trees in his forests were a lesson to him; he looked up between them and mingled with the animals as an equal.

How then are we to love France? There young men of daring and intelligence move into the arts as naturally as our brood moves through football into business. If we are to love or to know France, or any France, or any country it will be through the mature expression of these men in whom France has physically realized herself for better or worse. In their mastery of the art of expression France is expressed. There alone France exists in a mode capable of serving for international exchange. We may buy their pictures but money has a cat's mask. Or it wears the blank face of armies.

But in the arts the features appear full of movement and passion. France becomes a man with whom we can talk.

What then? A patron saint is one thing but in the intercommunications of art there should be something more than conversations between men on the one hand and beasts on the other. The farmer, weary of his cows, is glad when a neighbor hails him. If men are to meet and love and understand each other it must be as equals. Nor will it serve, when our good saint turns his back, for the monkey to take up the Bible and pretend to read from it while the lion roars and the ass brays.

In the work of James Joyce the underlying fact which has impressed me is that by the form of his thought he has forced the reader into a new and special frame of mind favorable to the receipt of his disclosure. By his manner of putting down the words it is discovered that he is following some un-apparent sequence quite apart from the usual syntactical one. That is of course the power behind all good writing but Joyce has removed so many staid encumbrances that his method comes like stroke of sunlight today. He forces me, before I can follow him, to separate the words from the printed page, to take them up into a world where the imagi-nation is at play and where the words are no more than titles under the illustrations. It is a reaffirmation of the forever-sought freedom of truth from usage. It is the modern world emerging among the living ancients by paying attention to the immediacy of its own contact; a classical method.

And in proportion as a man has bestirred himself to be-come awake to his own locality he will perceive more and more of what is disclosed and find himself in a position to make the necessary translations. The disclosures will then and only then come to him as reality, as joy, as release. For these men communicate with each other and strive to invent new devices. But he who does not know his own world, in whatever confused form it may be, must either stupidly fail to learn from foreign work or stupidly swallow it without knowing how to judge of its essential value. Descending each his own branch man and man reach finally a common trunk of understanding.

The only possible way that St. Francis could be on equal footing with the animals was through the word of God which he preached with fervent breath of understanding. Here was a common stem where all were one and from which every paired characteristic branched. It is the main body of art to which we must return again and again. Nor do

I think it is especially recorded that St. Francis tried to make the sparrows Christians. When the service was over each beast returned to his former habits.

America is far behind France or Ireland in an indigenous art. If there is no genius who can make a sermon of understanding deep enough and gentleness of sufficient catholicity to include all our animals, birds and fishes than those who must write, those who will create their own imaginative world as best they can with what they have, those who would meet the best in Europe with invention of their own must go down into the trunk of art, which is their word of God, where conversation can take place.

In France there are special reasons for every phase of an art. Americans are still too prone to admire and to copy the very thing which should not be copied, the thing which is French or Irish alone, the thing which is the result of special local conditions of thought and circumstance. And on the other hand, Marduk! we fail to learn anything at all. Yes, I prefer the man who will be influenced a trifle indiscriminately by the new, I prefer Ford Madox Ford to Wells. I prefer him to the man who is too solid. It is a common language we are seeking, a common language in which art itself is our St. Francis, we all meanwhile retaining our devotional character of Wolf, Sheep and Bear.

We, *Contact*, aim to emphasize the local phase of the game of writing. We realize that it is emphasis only which is our business. We want to give all our energy to the setting up of new vigors of artistic perception, invention and expression in the United States. Only by slow growth, consciously fostered to the point of enthusiasm, will American work of the quality of Marianne Moore's best poetry come to the fore of intelligent attention and the ignorance which has made America an artistic desert be somewhat dissipated. We lack interchange of ideas in our country more than we lack foreign precept. Every effort should be made, we feel, to develop among our serious writers a sense of mutual contact first of all. To this also we are devoted.

A Matisse

A Novelette and Other Prose, 1921–1931

ON THE french grass, in that room on Fifth Ave., lay that woman who had never seen my own poor land. The dust and noise of Paris had fallen from her with the dress and underwear and shoes and stockings which she had just put aside to lie bathing in the sun. So too she lay in the sunlight of the man's easy attention. His eye and the sun had made day over her. She gave herself to them both for there was nothing to be told. Nothing is to be told to the sun at noonday. A violet clump before her belly mentioned that it was spring. A locomotive could be heard whistling beyond the hill. There was nothing to be told. Her body was neither classic nor whatever it might be supposed. There she lay and her curving torso and thighs were close upon the grass and violets.

So he painted her. The sun had entered his head in the color of sprays of flaming palm leaves. They had been walking for an hour or so after leaving the train. They were hot. She had chosen the place to rest and he had painted her resting, with interest in the place she had chosen.

It had been a lovely day in the air. —What pleasant women are these girls of ours! When they have worn clothes and take them off it is with an effect of having performed a small duty. They return to the sun with a gesture of accomplishment. —Here she lay in this spot today not like Diana or Aphrodite but with better proof than they of regard for the place she was in. She rested and he painted her.

It was the first of summer. Bare as was his mind of interest in anything save the fullness of his knowledge, into which her simple body entered as into the eye of the sun himself, so he painted her. So she came to America.

30

No man in my country has seen a woman naked and painted her as if he knew anything except that she was naked. No woman in my country is naked except at night.

In the french sun, on the french grass in a room on Fifth Ave., a french girl lies and smiles at the sun without seeing us.

Contact II, 1921

Yours, O Youth

Contact III, 1921

It is DIFFICULT, apparently, to make clear that in stating contact with experience, as evidenced in a man's work, to be the essential quality in literature, we do not mean to state and have never stated that *Contact* is literature. Neither have we stated or implied that *Contact* ensures everything written under its influence to be literature. We have definitely declined to start a school; and must we repeat, how many times? our refusal to be responsible for teaching anyone how to write.

We have said simply and as frequently as possible and with as many apt illustrations as we could muster that contact with experience is essential to good writing or, let us say, literature. We have said this in the conviction that contact always implies a local definition of effort with a consequent taking on of certain colors from the locality by the experience, and these colors or sensual values of whatever sort are the only realities in writing or, as may be said, the essential quality in literature. We have even given what seem to be definite exceptions to the rule: unattached intelligence (the Jewish sphere), virtuosity (Russian violinists). But apparently we do not work in a fluid medium.

We have not stated that an American in order to be an American must shut his mind in a corncrib and let the rest of the world go hang. We see no advantage in being ill-informed when one might be well-informed. We see every advantage to a man in up-to-date information made his own through experience of its significance in his own environment. This is knowledge. Spurious information is that which is unrelated to the contacts of experience. Out of it literature is NOT made. Except——

There are those who have a taste for words and ideas, like the Jews, and who are able to appraise them, themselves remaining wholly detached from the affair. But actually these figures too, if they are of any importance, deal wholly with the real literary values defined above. It is to say that the cooks too may be artists and that they are known first by their choice of potatoes. It is only to prove that these men (De Gourmount) supported by the basic pyramid of tradition are the proof of its foundation. These do not show the intelligence to be a disease. They prove only the existence of a structure of sufficient reality to bear all fevers without catastrophe. True historians, they are the infamous Papas of us all. But what of it? They are there and we are here. It is a battle arrayed, a battle that must be in the end yours. O Youth, yours!

To which the hounds will set up a baying: Verbiage! very pretty but show us work of the quality of that which you condemn.

If "immediate" in the following sentence is taken to mean a man's objective world at some one moment of perception we agree that "the artist is (not) limited to the range of his *immediate* contact with the objective world." We agree moreover that "his material is vast and comprehensive: it is influenced by every sentient moment; it is the aggregate of all those experiences which have taken form in his imagination." We take pleasure in giving the rest of Mr. Craven's paragraph: "Were it not for the immeasurable mass of adaptable form stored in the mind, art would be a shallow and poverty-stricken affair."

Yet the artist is limited to the range of his contact with the objective world. True, in begetting his poem he takes parts from the imagination but it is simply that working among stored memories his mind has drawn parallels, completed progressions, transferred units from one category to another, clipped here, modified there. But it is inconceivable that, no matter how circuitously, contact with an immediate objective world of actual experience has not been rigorously maintained. By "artist" is meant nearly this thing alone.

But if by the use of "immediate" as underscored above it is implied that an artist is not limited to his direct contacts with certain definite environmental conditions through which alone he can know other "outside" worlds—in that case, one continues the search for an American critic.

Of any work the important thing to ask is: What are its contacts? One may almost say there is nothing else of importance to be asked. There will be established thereby—what? A color; something in any case ponderable in the experience of other men.

What is it I see in Rex Slinkard's letters? Surely not what Harriet Monroe saw: another untrained enthusiasm stabbing emptiness and achieving—what might have been expected. In these letters there is evidence of the man's critical attitude toward his art of painting; for this reason they have a distinct literary value. As criticism they present the unironic, the unbent vision of youth. And in this case it is a full release without sacrifice of intelligence. There is an abundance of fresh color but presented without the savage backbite of a Degas using pinks and blues. It is all very young, this man's writing about his painting; it is what I recognize as in some measure definitely and singularly American.

This same quality was the secret of Pound's early success in London with his *Personae*. God help me for suggesting such a thing.

The American critical attitude! it is that we are seeking to establish. It is young. It is not necessarily inexpert, as the hollow wits would have us believe, but it is necessarily young. There is no long chain of sophistication to engage us, "part of it crawling, part of it about to crawl, part of it torpid in its lair." Our processes are for the moment chaotic but they have the distinct advantage of being able to claim no place of rest save immediacy.

Not that Americans today can be anything less than citizens of the world; but being inclined to run off to London and Paris it is inexplicable that in every case they have forgotten or not known that the experience of native local contacts, which they take with them, is the only thing that can give that differentiated quality of presentation to their work which at first enriches their new sphere and later alone might carry them far as creative artists in the continental hurly-burly. Pound ran to Europe in a hurry. It is understandable. But he had not sufficient ground to stand on for more than perhaps two years. He stayed fifteen. Rereading his first book of poems it is easy to see why he was successful. It was the naive warmth of the wilderness—no matter how presented. But in the end they played Wilson with him.

Unfortunately for the arts here, intelligence and training have nearly always forced a man out of the country. Cut off from the dominant of their early established sensory backgrounds these expatriates go a typical and but slightly variable course thereafter.

The few among us who might write well in any generation, however they will be trained, fear to believe that in writing it will be exactly as it has been in other spheres on inventive activity, that the project has not grown until precedent has been rendered secondary to necessity or completely ignored. It has been by paying naked attention first to the thing itself that American plumbing, American shoes, American bridges, indexing systems, locomotives, printing presses, city buildings, farm implements and a thousand other things have become notable in the world. Yet we are timid in believing that in the arts discovery and invention will take the same course. And there is no reason why they should unless our writers have the inventive intelligence of our engineers and cobblers.

Can Princess White Deer train herself to reach a distinguished perfection in her dancing without losing her environmental individuality. In short can she avoid becoming a Russian. Every American activity in the arts is a phase of this problem.

Of course the lady in question will probably remain a mediocrity but should she prove a genius it will be discovered to have been because she consciously noted and turned to her advantage the detail of her local contacts. She would do well to study the masters. The master is he whom one may approach without prostituting himself. It is because in the masters' work all things go back to the ground. But the thing that continually baffles men is that this ground is a peculiarity. May I suggest again that *Contact* has not been devised as a means to teach anyone how to write.

Kenneth Burke's Laforgue article in the present issue of *Contact* gives me the sense of an American critical attitude working with foreign material. It is this milligram of radium that I have been seeking. Hearing others mention Laforgue I have never been tempted to read him. But from Burke I begin to feel myself in another atmosphere more congenial to my sense. I begin to feel that there is in Laforgue a something, a very simple and direct thing, without which his ironic talent would have gone for nothing. It is his clear use of sensation. It is a building upon the basis of what is observed, what is proved, what is of value to the man in the welter as he found it, and a rigid exclusion of everything else. It makes the efforts of an Eliot to "escape the influence of Laforgue" most silly. Why escape influences unless one has imitated the wrong thing?

Burke at least makes me feel, more than any writing at me from abroad can do, that Laforgue existed and was a real person. This ability on Burke's part lies not only in his intimate knowledge of everything Laforgue has written but in his knowledge of my world. He, Burke, is of my own environment and he has found the writings of Laforgue greatly applicable to it. Therefore Burke has written criticism. And feeling this to be true I say criticism must be first in contact with the world for which it is intended. That contact alone can give it life, reality. Nothing from abroad would have the reality for me that native writing of the same quality would have. Eliot or Pound might say to me today: "Read Laforgue!" I might even be tempted to read because I had respect for their intelligence. But their words could not tempt me, force me, accompany me into the reading. I object to appreciative articles on foreign work being written at me from Europe. The environment gets into the writing every time and it is inimical to me. I resent the feel I get from such exercises.

Criticism must originate in the environment it is intended for if it is to be of fullest value. Laforgue in America is not the same man he is in France. Our appreciation recreates him for our special world if it is genuine. His ability to exist under universal conditions is the proof of his genius. Burke has taken what he wanted from the master in order to satisfy his own needs and his needs are the product of his world.

This illustrates again what we mean by contact. The quotation at the end of Burke's present article is a well-nigh perfect example of our attitude. Laforgue here tells how he has taken what he finds most suitable to his own wants, what at least he has, and made it *the* thing. It is what the man of force will always do. He can't do anything else either in America or out of it. It is scarcely a matter of the will. It is fate. We are here under certain general conditions, run from them they remain the same. Together they form the only unity we possess. On this basis alone can we afford dispersion of efforts, the modern individualistic dispersion. We can afford it under no other condition.

The Writers of the American Revolution

("*Nothing of note in Parliament, except one slight day on the American Taxes.*"—*Horace Walpole*)

Not previously published

JAMES OTIS, a criminal lawyer in Boston and a Harvard graduate, was one of the foremost in America, prior to 1770, in advancing the legality of colonial resistance to the coercive methods of the British Parliament. His speech against the Writs of Assistance in 1761 is comparable to that of Patrick Henry in the Virginia Convention of Richmond in 1775. Otis, declares John Adams, was a flame of fire. He had an enthusiasm for ideas and a nervous, forceful expression. He took the ground that the various state constitutions under grants from the English sovereigns justified the Colonies in their refusal to submit to some of the phases of direct Parliamentary control. With his speeches the campaign leading to an open breach between the two countries may be said formally to have begun.

"Government is a conditional compact between king and people . . . A violation of the covenant by either party discharges the other from its obligations.". . . "An act (of Parliament) against the Constitution is void.". . . In these thirty words Patrick Henry and James Otis substituted common law for the divine origin of British Legislative supremacy— held in England for centuries, tho' not applied since the time of Cromwell.

But the mere legality of the question was too narrow a bounds for the difference in fundamental viewpoints involved. The struggle went deeper than that. As Otis wearied in the attack others took his place. Practically put in the words of Tom Paine—"A greater absurdity cannot be conceived of, than three millions of people running to their sea-coast every time a ship arrives from London, to know what portion of liberty they should enjoy."—

A great many causes, mainly economic in nature, served to foment the American Revolution. But underneath, there was a real revolution of thought, hereditary to America but new to the rest of the world of that time which was striving for supremacy. When the economic forces had developed to a pitch inviting action, this crystallized to give a solid character to the conflict of arms which ensued. It was an actual revolution of ideas. It supported the ablest minds among the Colonies through the hardships, the blunders, the treasons of the war years to follow, toward a clearly defined end: a new world reconstituted on an abler pattern than had been known theretofore.

The gist of it was human liberty, that is, the right to self-determination in matters involving local affairs as well as conscience. It was opposed by the classic sense of a central, arbitrary authority—in London. Small matter that John Locke had been its earlier sponsor; in America the movement remained alive. It constituted a revolution of the most profound and far-reaching significance, though at the time its objectives proved to be largely unattainable. It almost made conscious, and did succeed in doing so for a while, the basic meaning of America as a positive factor in world thought, the one considerable contribution of the New World to political reasoning: an actual democracy.

It was a period of political speculation, marked by sober and intelligent realism.

At first there had been no real thought of separation from England but the colonists, as "freemen," demanded merely their just rights before the law. They insisted only that they must settle their accounts with Parliament as equals, but to this England would not accede. John Dickinson, leader of the moderate men, through his *Letters from a Farmer in Philadelphia* (1768) pled for temperance. To the Colonies, hoping against all evidence for reconciliation, these letters were soothing. Well aware of the gulf opening up before him Dickinson prayed that it might close up again of its own accord.

Meanwhile, with Boston the spearhead in the rising resentment against British tyranny there began to emerge the figure of Samuel Adams, the Man of the Town Meeting, as they called him and later, the Father of the American Revolution.

A second cousin of John Adams and like Otis a Harvard graduate, Samuel Adams came into nationwide note as a radical in 1771. He grew up in the spirit of the times. His father, greatly interested in public affairs, to his house came many lively spirits to discuss the issues then paramount. But the boy's mother was of a totally different sort, the stern religious tradition of New England. The son, hearing the discussion about his father's table and at the same time taking it all to heart with the intensity bred of his mother, became a violent and uncompromising advocate of the American cause. A mind, it is said, resembling in its rebellious firmness that of Martin Luther.

It is hard to tell just when Samuel Adams first made up his mind as to the necessity of a separation between the Colonies and England. It seems rather that his stand was for an uncompromising insistence upon American *rights* even to the point, if it must come, of a separation. And in the meantime to fight with every means at his command against "tyranny" and to prepare for the outcome which he saw to be inevitable.

"He first came into wider prominence at the beginning of the Stamp Act episode, when, as author of Boston's instructions to its representatives in the General Court of Massachusetts, he urged strenuous opposition to taxation by act of Parliament," according to the *Encyclopaedia Britannica*. Adams took a prominent position in the revolutionary councils in which he advised against any sort of compromise. Many of the Massachusetts revolutionary documents, including the famous "Massachusetts Resolves" and the circular letter to the legislatures of the other Colonies, are from his pen. Indeed there can be no question that he was one of the first American political writers to deny the legislative power of Parliament and to desire and advocate separation from the mother country. The *Britannica* continues:

To promote the ends he had in view Adams suggested non-importation, instituted the Boston Committees of Correspondence, urged that a Continental Congress be called and wrote a vast number of articles for the newspapers, especially the Boston *Gazette*, over a multitude of signatures. He was in fact one of the most voluminous and influential political writers of his time. . . . He is considered to have done more than any other one man, in the years immediately preceding the War of Independence, to mold and direct public opinion in his community. . . .

During the intense excitement following the shooting of members of a mob, in Boston, by British soldiers whom they had been molesting, it was Adams who was quick to brand the incident the "Boston Massacre." And it was Adams who skillfully secured the removal of the soldiers from the town to a fort in the harbor. He also managed the proceedings of the "Boston Tea Party," and later he was leader in the opposition to the Boston Port bill. One of the main objectives of the expedition sent out by the Governor, General Thomas Gage, to Lexington and Concord, April 18–19, 1775, was the capture of Adams and John Hancock who at the time were rumored to be spending the night in a farmhouse on the Concord Road. Paul Revere notified them of their plight and they were enabled to escape. When General Gage issued his proclamation of pardon the following July, he excepted these two, whose offenses, he said, were "of too flagitious a nature to admit of any other consideration than condign punishment."

Adams strove for harmony among the several Colonies in the common cause. And later served on the Massachusetts Committee of Safety which virtually took over the government of the several Colonies until the legislatures could be organized. It was through the agency of this committee that the news of Lexington and Concord was carried throughout the other Colonies, the courier passing through New York on the 23rd and the news reaching Charleston by boat six days later.

It was November 2, 1772, that Adams made his famous motion for a Committee of Correspondence in Massachusetts to consist of twenty-one members. There were not more than three hundred at these meetings, and many, being satisfied with conditions as they existed, were opposed, but Adams carried out his design. Committees of Correspondence had existed in Philadelphia since 1744 that the town might keep in touch with its agents in London. But Adams broadened the scope of them to serve between the Colonies to spread information and prepare means for defense against "the common enemy." Adams made these committees which were soon formed in all the states the direct instruments of the revolution. Their business was transacted in secret.

Prior to that his means of action had been the town meeting. The authorities tried their best to abolish such gatherings on the basis of their legality. Adams fought back and won.

Adams would write: "Committee of Correspondence of Boston—to that of Roxbury—on movements of armed troops —invitation to come to Faneuil Hall on Thursday next at three o'clock, joyntly to consult on this alarming occasion." He wrote of the arrival of fifty tons of saltpeter at Egg Harbor. "Sail cloth at Baltimore—"

Another letter: Oct. 21, . . . ending:

We are far from desiring that the connection between Britain and America should be broken. *Esto Perpetua*, is our ardent wish; but upon terms only of Equal Liberty. If we cannot establish an agreement upon these terms, let us leave it to another wiser Generation. But it may be worth consideration that the work is more likely to be well done, at a time when Ideas and its importance are strongly in men's minds. There's danger that these Ideas will hereafter grow faint and languid. Our Posterity may be accustomed to bear the Yoke & Being inured to Servility they may even bow the shoulder to the burden. It can never be expected that a people, however *numerous*, will form and execute a wise plan to perpetuate their Liberty, when they have lost the Spirit and feeling of it.—

P.S. It is the request of the Committee that the Contents of this letter be not made publick lest our Common Enemies should counteract and prevent its design.

[signed]   T. Cushing,   S. Adams,   W. Heath.

There followed shortly after this the "Massachusetts Resolves" signed by the full subcommittee:

Resolutions of the Town of Boston: Nov. 5, 1773

Whereas it appears by an act of the British Parliament passed in the last sessions, that the East India Company are by the said Act allowed to export their Teas to America, in such quantities as the Lord of the Treasury shall judge proper: and some People with an evil intent to amuse the People, and others thro' inattention to the true design of the Act, have so construed the same, as that the Tribute of three Pence on every Pound of Tea is not to be enacted by the detestable Task Master there—upon the due consideration thereof.

Resolved, That the sense of the Town cannot be better expressed on this occasion, than in the words of certain Judicious Resolves lately entered into by our worthy Brethren of the Citizens of Philadelphia—wherefore,

Resolved, That the disposal of their own property is the Inherent Right of Freemen; that there can be no property in that which another can of right take from us without our consent; that the Claim of Parliament to tax America, is in other words a claim of right to lay contributions on us at pleasure—

2d That the Duty imposed by Parliament upon Tea landed in

America, is a tax on the Americans, or levying contributions on them without their consent—

3d That the express purpose for which the tax is levied on the Americans, namely for the support of Government, the Administration of Justice, and the defence of His Majesty's Dominions in America, has a direct tendency to render Assemblies useless. and to introduce Arbitrary Government and Slavery—

4th That a virtuous and steady opposition to the Ministerial Plan of governing America, is absolutely necessary to preserve even a shadow of liberty, and is the duty which every Freeman in America owes to his Country, to himself and to his Posterity——

5th That the Resolutions lately come by the East India Company, to send out their teas to America subject to the payment of Duties on its being landed here, is an open attempt to enforce the Ministerial Plan, and a violent attack upon the Liberties of America——

6th That it is the Duty of every American to oppose this attempt——

7th That whoever shall directly or indirectly countenance this attempt or in any wise aid or abet in unloading, receiving or vending the Tea sent or to be sent out by the East India Company while it remains subject to the payment of a duty here is an enemy to America——

8th That a Committee be immediately chosen to wait on those Gentlemen, who it is reported are appointed by the East India Company to receive and sell said Tea, and to request them, from a regard to their own characters and the peace and good order of this Town and Province, immediately to resign their appointments.

The three million inhabitants of the eastern American coastline from Maine to Georgia were thrown into a state of violent turmoil by the events culminating at Lexington and Concord. It was natural that letters should reflect this condition.

It was inevitable that the writers of the American Revolution should be for the most part the patriots, those who by their writing served as instigators and coadjutors of the military. They were of all types, diplomats, ministers of the gospel, and some, like Washington, soldiers as well. Such men as Franklin the urbanity of whose prose style, acceptable to the French Court, played its part in winning the French to America as an ally—Tom Paine, Freneau, Jefferson. They were not unopposed. But the Tory element whose weapon was in the main virulent satire produced no such works as the patriot.

Add to these a few anonymous figures, or lesser lights, the composers of the various state constitutions, the stray recorders of individual experiences: *A Narrative of Colonel Ethan Allen's Captivity* (1779), another *The Old Jersey Captive, or A Narrative of the Captivity of Thomas Andros*. Andros was a farmer's boy from Connecticut who was confined on the *Old Jersey* prison ship, but escaped. "Disease and death" he says, "were wrought into her very timbers."

And there were the writings of such men as Hector St. John de Crèvecoeur and William Bartram.

Crèvecoeur was a Tory but scarcely in the bitter sense common to the time. His *Letters from an American Farmer* is one of the most extraordinary books of this period—as he is one of the most original and powerful writers of the era of the Revolution. A cultivated Norman gentleman, after serving with Montcalm at Quebec, Crèvecoeur lived for a number of years in the Colonies, traveled widely, took an American wife and established himself on a pleasant farm. Crèvecoeur was deeply infused with the current French philosophy and, as a humanitarian and nature lover, observed with considerable acuteness the growth of a new type of society in the western wilderness.

In the midst of alarms, Crèvecoeur cries out, "I am a lover of peace, what must I do . . . I was happy before this unfortunate Revolution. I feel that I am no longer so; therefore I regret the change."

A kindred spirit was William Bartram, son of the well-known botanist, John Bartram, who was brought up in his father's botanical garden in Philadelphia. In April, 1773, he set forth on extensive travels through the southeastern frontier, a botanizing trip that extended to nearly five years. The result was *The Travels of William Bartram*, published in Philadelphia in 1791 and a year later in London. It was read by Coleridge who pronounced it the last book "written in the spirit of the old travelers." A gentle, kindly spirit, William Bartram was a man to have delighted Crèvecoeur and to have shared the enthusiasms of Jefferson.

Philip Freneau, a classmate at Princeton of James Madison and Hugh Henry Breckenridge, later a sea captain, became known in his own time as the chief gadfly of the Tories. He was far more than this. In him more, perhaps, than in any other writer of the Revolution, is shown the violence of the times. For Freneau saw the Revolution with much the same eyes as S. Adams and, later, Jefferson, giving himself largely to the cause but to do so slighted a noteworthy literary talent, a romantic poet.

He was a man of strong contrasts from whose pen came equally, cutting satire against the enemies of America and at the same time lovely romantic verse, one entirely separate from the other. In his poems, "The Wild Honeysuckle," "The House of Night," a gentle precursor of the supernatural in American literature which was to follow, "The Indian Burying Ground," Freneau touches the still unworked, vast theme of American nature.

But the sweetness and conventional beauty of his poems, putting him among the earliest of the new tradition, disappeared in his service to the cause. Passionate for the complete Revolution, Freneau, like Adams, wrote endless abuse of England and the British leaders. But in the end he turned against Washington also as the one more than any other who had subverted the cause of that Democracy for which he had uncompromisingly given himself. As Jefferson's secretary in the postwar years Freneau excoriated Washington to the bitter end in his newspaper editorials. And it was Freneau who said, that if ever a man had debauched a country, it was this country and George Washington was the man.

For the Revolution began to change its character with the difficulties of the military campaign and the necessary, but not universally approved, appointment of Washington as American Dictator during the severe winter of 1777–78. The college men, Adams and Freneau, had great difficulty to see with the same eyes as the wealthy farmer and one time backwoodsman from Virginia whose whole life had been worn into the mold of the difficulties before him.

A split was inevitable, a compromise if the union was to live at all. But the uncompromising Democrats who had fought for the full play of their ideas merely turned from one enemy to what they conceived as another. Freneau was one of them.

John Trumbull, of the famous Hartford School, the Connecticut Wits, Joel Barlow, Lemuel Hopkins, David Humphreys, Timothy Dwight, they were a small school who after the war issued from time to time *The Echo* "printed at the Porcupine Press by Pasquin Petronius." Of Barlow it is said he was "fond of an endless flow of pentameter between covers of embossed leather." Nevertheless they added, if to the increase of dullness, a certain urbanity to the letters of the time.

And there was also the child prodigy, the first of her kind in America, Phyllis Wheateley Peters, a Negro slave who at the age of twelve wrote in the manner of Pope, her *Poems on Various Subjects Religious and Moral*.

But if the patriots and their descendants have laughed at the sharp couplets of Freneau and Trumbull, it is profitable to recall that the most virulent and relentless of these satirists was a Tory, the Reverend Jonathan Odell of New Jersey. Odell cracks his whip about the head of the atrocious traitor Washington to the meanest tattered heel. He damns unwearyingly the dirty reptiles, the poltroons, the shirtless, shoeless gangs that will not celebrate the King's birthday. "These rats who nestle in the lion's den." They tracked him down but he hid in a friend's house and escaped.

Then there appeared, from England, a rebel, one of the greatest pamphleteers the English race has produced. His influence in America was enormous. A Quaker, his *Common Sense*, published early in 1776, some fourteen months after his arrival in America, presented vividly to the mass mind the advantages of independence and very likely hastened the formal action of the Congress a few months later.

"These are the times that try men's hearts," etc.

At the same time that it sent Mr. Dickinson's petition for a redress of grievances to London, Congress also decided to raise a Continental army to assist Massachusetts in driving the British forces out of Boston of which army it appointed, as Commander-in-Chief, George Washington, Esq.; and in justification of these measures published a Declaration of Causes and Necessity of Taking up Arms:

Our cause is just. Our union is perfect. Our internal resources are great, and, if necessary, foreign assistance is undoubtedly obtainable. . . . Fortified with these animating reflections, we . . . declare that . . . the arms we have been compelled by our enemies to assume, we will . . . employ for the preservation of our liberties, being with one mind resolved we die freemen rather than live slaves. . . . We have not raised armies with ambitious designs of separating from Great Britain. . . . We shall lay them down when hostilities shall cease on the part of the aggressors. . . . etc. etc. In Reconciliation on war.

Those were the early days but with the tremendous difficulties of the campaigns, the untrained soldiers, unskillful officers, the defeats and disappointments, Biglow, a traitor in Franklin's own office in Paris, notifying the British of ships sailing with supplies for America—but most of all with the short enlistments in the army, the desertions, the indifference of those who expected a short campaign and deserted to return quickly to their farms—Washington with the whole burden on his shoulders was having great difficulty to hold out.

In his many letters Washington, as a writer, assailed Congress with his complaints. It was no longer the same man who in the Virginia House of Burgesses had stood up and made his pithy offer: I will arm a thousand men, subsist them at my own expense and march at their head to the relief of Boston. —That was all. A split in the American front was occurring. Those who were at all costs striving to keep the army together and to win battles on the one side, with men like S. Adams, Freneau and some others largely opposing them. The mind of the Commander-in-Chief was greatly troubled. He doubted the success of the national cause. His letters are voluminous and often desperate.

Even the lifelong friendship between two such men as Washington and Jefferson was ultimately to be brought to a close by a rift in ideas the seeds of which had been sown during the Revolution. Jefferson took over and brought to their highest fruition the basic democratic philosophy which had first inspired S. Adams. As a writer, Jefferson was of great service to America by the lofty turn of phrase which gave weight and dignity to the outstanding public documents which he drafted, the first of which being the Declaration of Independence. By this he wished to be remembered.

Jefferson produced no outstanding work but, as with so many others of the period, for his full effect should be read in his letters. Deeply interested in the land, he was opposed by Alexander Hamilton, the industrialist, who led the country during the ensuing years to financial stability but at the cost of much that had been envisioned during the early years of the Revolution. But, though defeated, Jefferson still left his principles indelibly impressed on the growing nation by his inspired words.

A committee had been appointed to prepare a formal declaration setting forth the circumstances and motives which might justify them, in the judgment of mankind, in taking this momentous step toward independence. The committee had many meetings to discuss the matter, and, when the main points had been agreed upon, John Adams and Thomas Jefferson were instructed to "draw them up in form and clothe them in a proper dress." Many years afterward, in 1822, John Adams related as accurately as he could, the conversation which took place when these two met to perform the task assigned them. "Jefferson proposed to me to make the draught. I said, 'I will not.' 'You should do it.' 'Oh! no.' 'Why will you not? You ought to do it.' 'I will not.' 'Why?' 'Reasons enough.' 'What can be your reasons?' 'Reason first—You are a Virginian, and a Virginian ought to appear at the head of this business. Reason second—I am obnoxious, suspected and unpopular. You are much otherwise. Reason third—You can write ten times better than I can.' 'Well!' said Jefferson, 'if you are decided I will do as well as I can.' "

The general tenor of what Jefferson had to say is well illustrated by the following excerpt:

We hold these truths to be self-evident: that all men are created equal, that they are endowed by their Creator with certain unalienable rights, that among these are Life, Liberty and the pursuit of Happiness. That to secure these rights, Governments are instituted among Men, deriving their just powers from the consent of the governed. That, whenever any Form of Government becomes destructive of these ends, it is the Right of the People to alter or to abolish it, and to institute new Government, laying its foundation on such principles and organizing its powers in such form, as to them shall seem most likely to effect their Safety and Happiness.

Meanwhile Washington was struggling to keep his army together, begging Congress to aid, to abolish the militia system and to conscript the necessary means or, as he pointedly remarked, "Very soon I shall have to dismiss one half of the army to bring the other half back." And against whom should he be speaking but S. Adams, a bitter opponent. To James Warren, Adams wrote: "A standing army, however necessary it may be at some time, is always dangerous to the liberties of the people—soldiers are apt to consider themselves a Body distinct from the rest of the People. They have their arms always in their hands.—" Thus many times Washington was near to being thwarted by those who failed to see the dangers self-apparent to a man of action.

The Revolution came to an end. With the adoption of the Constitution which grew out of a compromise between the states on practical grounds in order to secure a union, the extreme objectives of such men as S. Adams, Paine and Freneau as well as Jefferson came practically to an end. All became confirmed enemies of George Washington as a result. The Federalist Party perpetuated the resulting feud under Hamilton's guidance whereas the Republican-Democratic Party adopted the older revolutionary spirit under Jefferson. S. Adams took this as his own. But under the dual theory of government by opposing parties the full weight of the early reasoning became lost, one party largely neutralizing the other and laying the field open to the opportunist form of political control which followed.

But one of the most effective writers of the Revolution remained unswayed by these political considerations. He was Baron von Steuben, trained in the army of Frederick the Great of Prussia, who had come to America to offer his aid to the struggling colonists.

At Valley Forge when winter interrupted military operations, Steuben commenced to prepare a complete book of regulations for the army. It is a manual, which under the title, *Regulations for the Order and Discipline of the Troops of the United States*, embodies in twenty-five chapters everything necessary in connection with troops, their weapons, exercises, marching, camping, maneuvering, signal service, inspection, aid and treatment of the sick and wounded. With this invaluable book, known in the army as "Steuben's Regulations" or "The Blue Book," the officers of the American Army received for the first time a clear and definite guide for the performance of their duties.

That Steuben, in composing this manual, did not merely copy the regulations of the Prussian Army, but followed his own ideas, is clearly shown by the fact that he created an entirely new military organization, the light infantry, unknown before. In Europe with its broad fields the armies were used to fighting in compact masses. In America with its more broken terrain and thick forests new conditions had arisen making the use of the solid phalanx often impractical as could not have been better shown than in the costly example of Braddock's defeat some years earlier. Taking into consideration the thick forests and the habits of the solitary settlers, used to frequent skirmishes with the Indians, accustomed to fight singly, relying entirely on their own judgment and best abilities—taking these facts into consideration, Steuben instructed the light infantry to fight in a scattered manner—so great a success that it became a standing institution in the American Army—introduced by Frederick the Great for his own, a token of appreciation which Steuben greatly appreciated.

A commentator of the time says, "I have seen the Baron and his assistants seven long hours inspecting a brigade of three small regiments. Everything had to be accounted for. Even the sick were brought out on cots. Uniforms, arms, equipment of all kinds were minutely examined. The kit supplied for each man was unrolled and each article in it counted. Nothing escaped notice. And if anything whatsoever was amiss or unaccounted for, a definite reason for its condition or absence must have been given."

As a result, at the last inspection of the main army, whereas in early times five thousand muskets beyond the actual number of the muster had to be supplied and never sufficient to guard against the waste that occurred, at the last inspection of the main army, only three muskets were deficient and those accounted for.

It was to Steuben's drilling and careful instructions that Washington owed in great part the success of his engagement at Monmouth when, as described by eyewitnesses, the troops deployed under fire with the perfection of movement one would have expected on the drill field—the first time such a thing had occurred in the experience of the American Army.

The same for Anthony Wayne's attack at Stony Point. It required twelve maneuvers to produce a shot with the musket at that time. But Steuben drilled them in the use of the bayonet so that the troops under Wayne's orders marched up to the British breastworks without a shot being fired and with such *élan* that the occupants were completely taken by surprise and made captive almost before they knew it. As one of the officers said afterward, for the first time American soldiers acted as if the bayonet was of some use other than to roast a steak on.

In what regard the "Blue Book" was held by the army appeared from the "Creed," adopted by the officers of the American Army in 1782 at Verplanck's Point (across the Hudson from Stony Point). It reads as follows:

We believe that there is a great First Cause by whose almighty will we are framed; and that our business here is to obey the orders of our superiors. We believe that every soldier who does his duty will be happy here, and that every such one who dies in battle, will be happy hereafter. We believe that George Washington is the only fit man in the world to head the American Army. We believe that Nathaniel Green was born a general. We believe that the evacuation of Ticonderoga was one of those strokes which stamp the man who dares to strike them, with everlasting fame. We believe that Baron Steuben has made us soldiers. And that he is capable of forming the whole world into a solid column, and displaying it from the center. We believe in his Blue Book. We believe in General Knox and his artillery. And we believe in our bayonets. Amen!

1925

Shakespeare

Not previously published

THE SPECIAL circumstance which uniquely unlocked Shakespeare's imagination and at the same time made him, forced him, to write, since no one writes if he doesn't have to, is worth knowing. It kept him at it, through thirty-five plays, for life in spite of business worries, twins and a number other human cares. It is worth knowing for critical reasons relative to the poems and plays, for the light it throws on them increasing a latter-day enjoyment, but it is still more valuable for the light his plays throw upon the dark places of all imaginations by which, cramped, one still lives or would live.

And this second reason for ascertaining the force of Shakespeare's imagination is the more valuable since it must have been his own reason for valuing the plays at all. They cannot have been anything but of the most vital importance to him himself in his conception of living without his thinking of himself as a rather long-drawn-out sort of lying person. And he didn't think that, by the critical solidity of the plays themselves. Yet he went on doing the same thing all his life, over and over again, like a person who needs to reaffirm something to himself in order to keep believing it; a kind of weakness, in a sense. The matter kept turning over afresh, from start to finish. His imagination kept him continually oscillating—or vacillating, as one may choose to look at it.

This is the sort of person who lives in one place, having no need to move his carcass in order to keep alive. It is the imagination that travels: Pattern of the more serious interval between the serious travel of being born and dying. How shall a man rival that journey in this world or see anything really

new here by throwing himself about—except in the imagination? Yet by about that measure men are known as the strong
and the weak—within limits of the intelligence.

Studies blight the imagination, inevitably. No knowledge
kills it. To vary between knowing and feeling is the artist's
purgatory, living in which he keeps alive by losing his life, in
a brutal sense, and losing it by making "plays," objects, realities which he has to abandon to make another, and another—
perfectly blank to him as soon as they are completed.

1927

George Antheil and the Cantilène Critics

A Note on the First Performance of Antheil's Music in New York City (April 10th, 1927)

A Novelette and Other Prose, 1921–1931

EVERY MAJOR musical critic of New York reacted unintelligently to Antheil's first presentation of his compositions in Carnegie Hall last April. I do not mean that they reacted stupidly, for they were shrewd in listening to and sensing the immediate expressions of feeling among certain of the audience rather than to have paid attention to what was going on within the limits of the musical problem itself confronting them. I mean they found nowhere in their minds an apposite thing to say musically about the object for criticism, or nothing of importance, so that their "columns" in the papers the next morning were totally blank to a person seeking musical information concerning the event. They completely failed to place, musically, what had gone on.

Of Antheil they said, of course, a great deal. Small, ill-mannered, silly, they were. But what of that if they had actually heard anything even to defame. Naturally, they claimed that they had heard nothing, which was probably quite true. Certainly, I did not seek to have them favor Antheil. I really did not. But I did expect their criticism to be about music. I did expect them to say at least somewhere what the works might have been about even if they were failures. It is their inability even to come in contact with the problem and not their unfavorable comments which disturbed me.

For music is changing in character today as it has always done. Where is it going? Did Antheil's work cast any light on that? No answer. And why? No answer. Was the work seeking a track and what track and why, if it did not attain it, why did it not do so? No answer. All they wrote was fillgap, and dirty fillgap too, some of it, showing their nervousness under stress of the occasion—always the result of failure to focus.

I say they were dirty since having nothing else in their heads they must attack Antheil in the qualities of his person saying catty things of his press-agenting, his appearance on the stage, etc., etc. This in New York, the musical center of America. They described the noises at the back of the auditorium and counted (later to lie about it) the number of people who, overborne by the avalanche of sound, walked out. The critics had time for that.

I myself remember one lantern-jawed young gentleman somewhat resembling the pictures we used to see of Alfred Dreyfus, who rose to his feet in the middle of the parquet seats during the long ringing of the electric bells in the "Ballet Mécanique," and shaking his head like a tormented young bull, stumbled blindly out over the feet beyond him whilst his lady smilingly and protestingly followed after. I can understand the unhappiness, even the madness, of such a defeat. He was stuck and ran off bellowing. But neither this sort of thing, nor even its frozen counterpart, is musical criticism and offers no escape from the dilemma of making apposite comment when the mind is empty.

As a fact, the audience stayed almost to a person until the end of the concert, even applauding wildly at the success of the final "Jazz" Symphony. Who has a right to say what was in their minds as Lawrence Gilman offered to do; or to interpret their reactions in the mass from the noise of a few disturbers? No one who uses his mind musically, surely. For myself, I am sure that many a one went away from Carnegie Hall thinking hard of what had been performed before him. It is to present one of these thoughts, or possible thoughts that I am writing. Not praise, not senseless derogations but—what could one, not being a musical critic, really, think about that music?

One thing Gilman did say was that in respect of "canti-lène" Antheil was deficient. Now that is something at any rate. It means roughly that a hat is not much like a banana unless we try to make it so, which was quite patently not Antheil's purpose. Or most likely "cantilène" was not one of the qualities Antheil was after.

But just why does a critic pick out just this detail of style for comment? Perhaps because when among listeners to music the wearying body fails in its following of the mind it drags all down more and more to that, asking to be rocked, "inspired" as they say. But there is an operation for that. But the alert mind outspreads the dull song, goes any way it can from point to point, brokenly if it must.

But the habitual music writers having mentioned this and some other "flaws" in Antheil's work (without respecting the critic's function to inquire why) the way is at least opened for a note on the facts of the case. I, too, saw the empty phrases, the failure to come up to a grand summary of the age in the climaxes and the "childish" rhythms. This requires depth in a critic, I wonder if anyone missed those things. And the resemblance of some of the tonality to Schönberg. And the "Jazz" Symphony not being epic must, of course, be flat, not being lyric it must of course be trite, though if ever there were anything more exquisitely lyric of present-day "new world" than the saxophone cadenza in that symphony, surely I have never heard it.

The question, I think, resolves itself to this, as always with contemporaneous criticism: Shall we (from our free *fau-teuil*) knock a man down as hard as we can whenever we are given an unpoliced (by opinion) opportunity, hitting him personally when we have nothing to say about his music? Or do we perhaps find in the music something we wish to hold up (or to condemn) in particular that it may (or may not) go on to develop into that unique thing of vast importance "the future of music"? I think there is something in Antheil that should be saved.

For myself I am willing to let most of the works performed at the concert remain out of the discussion or to say very little of them. To bring such work up to the mind at a single hearing is most difficult. And the music is hard. I am not a trained critic. Hardest of all for me was the quartet where Gilman says Antheil resembles Schönberg. I do not know. Perhaps that's the trouble, maybe that's where he needs to work hardest. Men do have to work, even to be critics. Yet in the quartet the allegro–andante oscillation was a most welcome innovation not at all to be condemned because of its simplicity, which Gilman does without the faintest reason. But to cry out that this "is not music" is simply futile. "It's all wrong, it's all wrong," kept repeating the woman back of me. Of course it is. We are not used to it, therefore, it must be so. But we are not quite yet dead. Everything new must be wrong at first since there is always a moment when the living new supplants that which has been and still is right and is thus sure to be wrong in transit, or until it is seen that that which was right is dead.

I myself have but one bit of observation worth anything to present: Here is Carnegie Hall. You have heard something of the great Beethoven and it has been charming, masterful in its power over the mind. We have been alleviated, strengthened against life—the enemy—by it. We go out of Carnegie into the subway and we can for a moment withstand the assault of that noise, failingly! as the strength of the music dies. Such has been its strength to enclose us that we may even feel its benediction a week long.

But as we came from Antheil's "Ballet Mécanique" a woman of our party, herself a musician, made this remark: "The subway seems sweet after that." "Good," I replied and went on to consider what evidences there were in myself in explanation of her remark. And this is what I noted. I felt that noise, the unrelated noise of life such as this in the subway had not been battened out as would have been the case with Beethoven still warm in the mind but it had actually been mastered, subjugated. Antheil had taken this hated thing life and rigged himself into power over it by his music. The offense had not been held, cooled, varnished over but annihilated and life itself made thereby triumphant. This is an important difference. By hearing Antheil's music, seemingly so much noise, when I actually came upon noise in reality, I found that I had gone up over it.

1927

Notes in Diary Form

Not previously published

10/23/27   I WILL make a big, serious portrait of my time. The brown and creamwhite block of Mexican onyx has a poorly executed replica of the Aztec calendar on one of its dicefacets the central circle being a broadnosed face with projected hanging tongue the sun perhaps though why the tongue is out I do not know unless to taste or gasp in the heat, its own heat, to say it's hot and is the sun. Puebla, Mexico, Calendario Azteca, four words are roughly engraved in the four corners where the circle leaves spaces on the square diceface this is America some years after the original, the art of writing is to do work so excellent that by its excellence it repels all idiots but idiots are like leaves and excellence of any sort is a tree when the leaves fall the tree is naked and the wind thrashes it till it howls it cannot get a book published it can only get poems into certain magazines that are suppressed because because waving waving waving waving waving waving tic tack tic tock tadick there is not excellence without the vibrant rhythm of a poem and poems are small and tied and gasping, they eat gasoline, they all ate gasoline and died, they died of—there is a hole in the wood and all I say brings to mind the rock shingles of Cherbourg, on the new houses they have put cheap tile which overlaps but the old roofs had flat stone sides steep but of stones fitted together and that is love there is no portrait without that has not turned to prose love is my hero who does not live, a man, but speaks of it every day

What is he saying? That love was never made for man and woman to crack between them and so he loves and loves his

62

sons and loves as he pleases. But there is a great law over him which—is as it is. The wind blowing, the mud spots on the polished surface, the face reflected in the glass which as you advance the features disappear leaving only the hat and as you draw back the features return, the tip of the nose, the projection over the eyebrows, the cheekbones and the bulge of the lips the chin last.

I remember, she said, we had little silver plaques with a chain on it to hang over the necks of the bottles, whisky, brandy or whatever it was. And a box of some kind of wood, not for the kitchen but a pretty box. Inside it was lined with something like yes, pewter, all inside and there was a cover of metal too with a little knob on it, all inside the wooden box. You would open the outer cover and inside was the lid. When you would take that off you would see the tea with a silver spoon for taking it out. But now, here are the roses—three opening. Out of love. For she loves them and so they are there. They are not a picture. Holbein never saw pink thorns in such a light. Nor did Masaccio. The petals are delicate, it is a question if they will open at all and not drop, loosing at one edge and falling tomorrow all in a heap. All around the roses there is today, machinery leaning upon the stem, an aeroplane is upon one leaf where a worm lies curled. Soppy it seems and enormous, it seems to hold up the sky for it has no size at all. We eat beside it—beside the three roses that she loves. And an oak tree grows out of my shoulders. Its roots are my arms and my legs. The air is a field. Yellow and red grass are writing their signature everywhere.

10/27   And Coolidge said let there be imitation brass filigree fire fenders behind insured plateglass windows and yellow pine booths with the molasses-candygrain in the wood instead of the oldtime cake-like whitepine boards always cut thick their faces! the white porcelain trough is no doubt made of some certain blanched clay baked and glazed but

how they do it, how they shape it soft and have it hold its
shape for the oven I don't know nor how the cloth is woven,
the gray and the black with the orange and green strips
wound together diagonally across the grain artificial pneu-
mothorax their faces! the stripe of shadow along the pave-
ment edge, the brownstone steeple low among the office
buildings dark windows with a white wooden cross upon
them, lights like fuchsias, lights like bleeding hearts lights like
columbines, cherry-red danger and applegreen safety. Any
hat in this window $2.00 barred windows, wavy opaque
glass, a block of brownstone at the edge of the sidewalk
crudely stippled on top for a footstep to a carriage lights
with sharp bright spikes, stick out round them their faces!
STOP in black letters surrounded by a red glow, letters with
each bulb a seed in the shaft of the L of the A lights on the
river streaking the restless water lights upon pools of rain-
water by the roadside a great pool of light full of overhang-
ing sparks into whose lower edge a house looms its center
marked by one yellow window-bright their faces!

10/28   born, September 15, 1927, 2nd child, wt. 6 lbs. 2 ozs.
The hero is Dolores Marie Pischak, the place Fairfield, in my
own state, my own county, its largest city, my own time.
This is her portrait: O future worlds, this is her portrait—
order be God damned. Fairfield is the place where the Octo-
ber marigolds go over into the empty lot with dead grass like
Polish children's hair and the nauseous, the stupefying monotony of decency is dead, unkindled even by art or anything—dead: by God because Fairfield is alive, coming
strong. Oh blessed love you are here in this golden air, this
honey and dew sunshine, ambering the houses to jewels. Order—is dead. Here a goose flaps his wings by a fence, a white
goose, women talk from second-story windows to a neighbor
on the ground, the tops of the straggling backyard poplars
have been left with a tail of twigs and on the bare trunk a
pulley with a line in it is tied. A cop whizzes by on his sidecar
cycle, the bank to the river is cinders where dry leaves drift.

The cinders are eating forward over the green grass below, closer and closer to the river bank, children are in the gutters violently at play over a dam of mud, old women with seamed faces lean on the crooked front gates. Where is Pischak's place? I don't know. I tink it's up there at the corner. What you want?—

Here one drinks good beer. Don't tell my husband. I stopped there yesterday, really good. I was practically alone, yes.

Some streets paved, some dirt down the center. A Jew has a clothing store and looks at you wondering what he can sell. And you feel he has these people sized up. A nasty feeling. Unattached. When he gets his he'll burn it up and clear out in a day. And they do not suspect how nicely he has measured them. They need stuff. He sells it. Who's that guy I wonder. Never seen him around here before. Looks like a doctor.

That's the feeling of Fairfield. An old farmhouse in long tangled trees, leaning over it. A dell with a pretty stream in it below the little garden and fifty feet beyond, the board fence of the Ajax Aniline Dye Works with red and purple refuse dribbling out ragged and oily under the lower fence boards. No house is like another. Small, wooden, a garden at the back, all ruined by the year. Man leaning smoking from a window. And the dirt, dry dust. No grass, or grass in patches, hedged with sticks and a line of cord or wire or grass, a jewel, a garden embanked, all in a twenty-foot square, crowded with incident, a small terrace of begonias, a sanded path, pinks, roses in a dozen rococo beds.

Knock and walk in: The bar. Not a soul. In the back room the kitchen. Immaculate, the enameled table featured. The mother nursing her from a nearly empty breast. She lies and sucks. Black hair, penciled down the top flat and silky smooth, the palmsized face asleep, the mother at a point of vantage where under an inside window raised two inches she can govern the street entrance.

Who's that?

A woman. Oh that old woman from next door.

The father, young, energetic, enormous. Unsmiling, big headed, a nervous twitch to his head and a momentary intense squint to his eyes. She watches the door. He is in shirt sleeves. Restless, goes in and out. Talks fast, manages the old woman begging help for a bruised hand. A man who might be a general or president of a corporation, or president of the states. Runs a bootleg saloon. Great!

This is the world. Here one breathes and the dignity of man holds on. "Here I shall live. Why not now? Why do I wait?"

Katharin, 9, sheepish, shy—adoring in response to gentleness so that her eyes almost weep for sentimental gratitude, has jaundice, leans on his knee. Follows him with her eyes. Her hair is straight and blond.

On the main river road, a gray board fence over which a grove of trees stick up. Oaks, maples, poplars and old fruit trees. Belmont Park, Magyar Home. For rent for picnics. Peace is here—rest, assurance, life hangs on.

Oh, blessed love, among insults, brawls, yelling, kicks, brutality—here the old dignity of life holds on—defying the law, defying monotony.

She lies in her mother's arms and sucks. The dream passes over her, dirt streets, a white goose flapping its wings and passes. Boys, wrestling, kicking a half-inflated football. A gray motheaten squirrel pauses at a picket fence where tomato vines, almost spent, hang on stakes.

Oh, blessed love—the dream engulfs her. She opens her eyes on the troubled bosom of the mother who is nursing the babe and watching the door. And watching the eye of the man. Talking English, a stream of Magyar, Polish what? to the tall man coming and going.

Oh, blessed love where are you there, pleasure driven out, order triumphant, one house like another, grass cut to pay lovelessly. Bored we turn to cars to take us to "the country" to "nature" to breathe her good air. Jesus Christ. To nature.

It's about time, for most of us. She is holding the baby. Her eye under the window, watching. Her hair is bobbed half-short. It stands straight down about her ears. You, you sit and have it waved and ordered. Fine. I'm glad of it. And nothing to do but play cards and whisper. Jesus Christ. Whisper of the high-school girl that had a baby and how smart her mama was to pretend in a flash of genius that it was hers. Jesus Christ. Or let us take a run up to the White Mountains or Lake Mohonk.

And so order, seclusion, the good of it all.

But in Fairfield men are peaceful and do as they please—and learn the necessity and the profit of order—and Dolores Marie Pischak was born.

10/28   a flash of juncos in the field of gray locust saplings with a white sun powdery upon them and a large rusty can wedged in the crotch of one of them, for the winter, human fruit, and on the polished straws of the dead grass a scroll of crimson paper—not yet rained on

11/1   INTRODUCTION
in almost all verse you read, mine or anybody's else, the figures used and the general impression of the things spoken of is vague "you could say it better in prose" especially good prose, say the prose of Hemingway. The truth of the object is somehow hazed over, dulled. So nobody would go to see a play in verse if

the salvias, the rusty hydrangeas, the ragged cannas

there's too often no observation in it, in poetry. It is a soft second light of dreaming. The sagas were not like that they seem to have been made on the spot. The little Greek I have read—and in translation—is not like that. Marlow, Chaucer, el Cid, Shakespeare where he is homely, uncultured, a shrewd guesser is not like that. Where he puts it over about some woman he knew or a prince or Falstaff. The good poetry is where the vividness comes up "true" like in prose but better. That's poetry. Dante was wrestling with Italian, his vividness comes from his escape from Latin. Don Quixote. I don't know about the Russians or the French.

> and the late, high growing red rose
> it is their time
> of a small garden

poetry should strive for nothing else, this vividness alone, *per se*, for itself. The realization of this has its own internal fire that is "like" nothing. Therefore the bastardy of the simile. That thing, the vividness which is poetry by itself, makes the poem. There is no need to explain or compare. Make it and it *is* a poem. This is modern, not the saga. There are no sagas—only trees now, animals, engines: There's that.

11/1 I won't have to powder my nose tonight 'cause Billie's gonna take me home in his car—

The perfect type of the man of action is the suicide.

11/8 Out of her childhood she remembered, as one might remember Charlie Wordsworth's print shop in the rear of Bagellons, the hinged paperknife, the colored posters of horses (I'll bet it was for the races at Clifton where the High School now stands). Once Pop made a big kite, five feet tall maybe, with the horses' heads in the middle and it flew and I couldn't hold it without help. They fastened it to a post of the back porch at nightfall, real rope they had on it, and in the morning it was still there. She remembered the day the old man painted the mirror back of the bar: He took off his coat and laid the brushes and pans from his bag on one of the barroom tables. No one else was there but Jake who sat with his head in his hands except when someone came in for something or to telephone. Then he'd unlock the inside door and sit down again watching the old man. It was a big mirror.

First he painted in a river coming in over from the door and curving down greenywhite nearly the whole length of it and very wide to fall in a falls into the edge of another river that ran all along the bottom all the way across, only a little of the water to be seen. Then he put in a blue sky all across the top with white clouds in it and under them a row of brown hills coming down to the upper river banks. Green trees he made with a big brush, just daubing it on, some of it even up top over the hills on the clouds, the trunks of the trees to be put in later. But down below, under the top river and all down the right side where it curved down to the falls he painted in the trunks first like narrow dark brown bottles. Then he drew in the houses, with white sides, three of them near the falls. "A good place to fish," Jake said. The roofs were red. On the other side of the falls, between the two rivers, the houses were brown, two of them on brown hills with trees all among them. Then, after the paint of the rivers was dry, he began to paint in little boats, above and below—She never saw the work finished, for the saloon had been sold and they moved away. The last thing she saw him do was paint in the boats, "Look out that boat up there don't go over those falls," Jake said. The rivers were painted flat on the glass, wonderful rivers where she wanted to be. Someday she wanted to go to that place and see it. Like the song she remembered in school and she always wanted them to sing when you could ask what song you wanted sung, "Come again soon and you shall hear sung the tale of those green little islands." She always wanted to hear the rest of it but there was never any more. They moved away.

11/11   A cat licking herself solves most of the problems of infection. We wash too much and finally it kills us.

11/13   SHAKESPEARE
By writing he escaped from the world into the natural world of his mind. The unemployable world of his fine head

was unnaturally useless in the gross exterior of his day—or any day. By writing he made this active. He melted himself into that grossness, and colored it with his powers. The proof that he was right and they passing, being that he continues always and naturally while their artificiality destroyed them. A man unable to employ himself in his world.

Therefore his seriousness and his accuracies, because it was not his play but the drama of his life. It is his anonymity that is baffling to nitwits and so they want to find an involved explanation—to defeat the plainness of the evidence.

When he speaks of fools he is one; when of kings he is one, doubly so in misfortune.

He is a woman, a pimp, a Prince Hal—

Such a man is a prime borrower and standardizer—No inventor. He lives because he sinks back, does not go forward, sinks back into the mass—

He is Hamlet plainer than a theory—and in everything.

You can't buy a life again after it's gone, that's the way I mean.

He drinks awful bad and he beat me up every single month while I was carrying this baby, pretty nearly every week.

(Shakespeare) a man stirred alive, all round *not* minus the intelligence but the intelligence subjugated—by misfortune in this case maybe—subjugated to the instinctive whole as it must be, but not minus it as in almost everything—not by cupidity that blights an island literature—but round, round, a round world *E pur si muove. That* has never sunk into literature as it has into geography, cosmology. Literature is still medieval, formal, dogmatic, the scholars, the obstinate rationalists—

These things are easy and obvious but it is not easy to formulate them, and it is still harder to put them down briefly. Yet it must be possible since I have done it here and there.

Such must be the future: penetrant and simple—minus the scaffolding of the academic, which is a "lie" in that it is inessential to the purpose as to design.

This will do away with the stupidity of little children at school, which is the incubus of modern life—and the defense of the economists and modern rationalists of literature. To keep them drilled.

The difficulty of modern styles is made by the fragmentary stupidity of modern life, its lacunae of sense, loups, perversions of instinct, blankets, amputations, fulsomeness of instruction and multiplications of inanity. To avoid this, accuracy is driven to a hard road. To be plain is to be subverted since every term must be forged new, every word is tricked out of meaning, hanging with as many cheap traps as an altar.

The only human value of anything, writing included, is intense vision of the facts.

God—sure if it means sense. "God" is poetic for the unobtainable. Sense is hard to get but it can be got. Certainly that destroys "God," it destroys everything that interferes with simple clarity of apprehension.

11/16   The art of writing is all but lost (not the science which comes afterward and depends completely on the first) it is to make the stores of the mind available to the pen— Wide! That which locks up the mind is vicious.

Mr. Seraphim: They hate me. Police Protection. She was a flaming type of stupidity and its resourceful manner under Police Protection—the only normal: a type. One of the few places where the truth (demeaned) clings on.

11/24   If genius is profuse, never ending—stuck in the middle of a work is—the wrong track. Genius is the track, seen. Once seen it is impossible to keep from it. The superficial definitions, such as "genius is industry, genius is hard work," etc. are nonsense. It is to see the track, to smell it out, to know it inevitable—sense sticking out all round feeling, feeling, seeing—hearing touching. The rest is pure gravity (the earth pull).

Creations:—they are situations of the soul (Lear, Harpagon, Oedipus Rex, Electra) but so closely (subjectively) identified with life that they become people. They are off-shoots of an intensely simple mind. It is no matter what we think, no matter what we are.

The drama is the identification of the character with the man himself (Shakespeare—and his sphere of knowledge, close to him). As it flares in himself the drama is completed and the back kick of it is the other characters, created as the reflex of the first, so the dramatist "lives," himself in his world. A poem is a soliloquy without the "living" in the world. So the dramatist "lives" the character. But to labor over the "construction" over the "technique" is to defeat, to tie up the drama itself. One cannot live after a prearranged pattern, it is all simply dead.

This is the thing (obvious and simple) that except through genius makes the theater a corpse. To intensely realize identity makes it live (borrowing stealing the form by feeling it —as an uninformed man must). A play is this primary realization coming up to intensity and then fading (futilely) in self. This *is* the technique, the unlearnable, it is the *natural* drama, which can't imagine situations in any other way than in association with the flesh—till it becomes living, it is so personal to a nothing, a nobody.

The painfully scrupulous verisimilitude which honesty affects drill, disciplines defeats its own ends in—

To be nothing and unaffected by the results, to unlock, and to flow (They believe that when they have the mold of technique made perfect without a leak in it that the mind will be *drilled* to flow there whereas the mind is locked the more tightly the more perfect the technique is forged) (or it may flow, disencumbered by what it has learned, become unconscious, provided the technique becomes mechanical, goes out of the mind and so the mind (now it has been cut for life in this pattern)) can devote itself to that just as if it had learned it imitatively or not at all.

To be nothing and unaffected by the results, to unlock and flow, uncolored, smooth, carelessly—not cling to the unsolvable lumps of personality (yourself and your concessions, poems) concretions—

12/2   The first snow was a white sand that made the white rocks seem red.

The police are "the soldiers of the Duke." The great old names: Gaynor, Healy—

12/9   Imagine a family of four grown men, one in bed with a sore throat, one with fresh plaster dust on his pants, one who played baseball all last summer and one holding the basin, four young men and no women but the mother with smallpox scars marring the bridge and the end of her nose and dinner on the table, oil and meat bits and cuts of green peppers, the range giving out a heat for coats on the backs of the chairs to dry in.

Fairfield: Peoples Loan and Service, Money to Loan: and a young man carrying a bowling ball in a khaki canvas case. The Midland and a fern in the window before the inner oak and cut-glass screen. House and sign painting in all its branches. Fairfield Bowling and Billiard Academy. Architect John Gabrone Architect, U. S. Post Office, Fairfield, N. J. Branch. Commercial Barber Shop. The New Cigarette Three Castles. Real Estate and Insurance. Motor Vehicle Agency. Commercial Lunch. Fairfield Home Laundry, soft water washing.

12/18   Here by the watertank and the stone, mottled granite, big as a rhinocerous head—cracked on one side—Damn families. My grandfather was a business man, you know. He kept the ice house in Mayaguez. They imported the ice. He kept it and sold it. My grandmother, my mother's mother, would make syrups, strawberry and like that. He would sell them also. But his half-brother Henriquez, there's plenty of that in my family, would go there, to the ice house, and drink all day long without paying anything, until the man my grandfather had there complained. "You know Henriquez comes and drinks five or six glasses of syrup and never pays anything." He did that. Just drank, lived at the house, took anything he pleased. That's how, as my mother says, she came to know Manuel Henriquez, her half-cousin, better than she did her own brother. My brother was in Paris studying. When Krug told my mother she must send for him, that there was nothing left, she wrote. He answered her that he would sweep the streets of Paris rather than leave. She would send him money she made on her little business. Sometimes, he told us afterward, he would keep a sou in his pocket two weeks so as not to say he hadn't any money. The students helped each other. Barclay, an Englishman, was one of his best friends. He helped him."

That's why my own mother's education ended abruptly. Sometimes she would copy out letters for my grandmother, child that she was, to send to Paris. When her brother returned a doctor he himself sent her to Paris to study painting. But he married and he began to have children and he never collected any money—he had a wife too. So finally he sent for my mother to go back to Santo Domingo where they were living then. Mother cried for three days then she had to go and leave it all. When she got there her brother told her about his friend, Blackwell. A fine fellow, the best in the world "*pero no es musicante*." Blackwell was in the States at the time of my mother's return from Paris having his teeth fixed.

When a little child would be bothersome they would tell her to go ask the maid for a little piece of *ten te aya*.

When my brother was happy he would sing, walking up and down kicking out his feet: *Si j'étais roi de Bayaussi-e, tu serais reine-e par ma foi!* You made me think right away of him.

A Note on the Recent Work of James Joyce

transition, 1927

A SUBTITLE to any thesis on contemporary reputations might well be: How truth fares among us today. I see no other approach, at least, to the difficulties on modern literary styles than to endeavor to find what truth lies in them. Not in the matter of the writing but in the style. For style is the substance of writing which gives it its worth as literature.

But how is truth concerned in a thing seemingly so ghost-like over words as style? We may at least attempt to say what we have found untrue of it. To a style is often applied the word "beautiful"; and "Beauty is truth, truth beauty," said Keats; "that is all ye know and all ye need to know." By saying this Keats showed what I take to have been a typical conviction of his time consonant with Byron's intentions toward life and Goethe's praise of Byron. But today we have reinspected that premise and rejected it by saying that if beauty is truth and since we cannot get along without truth, then beauty is a useless term and one to be dispensed with. Here is a location for our attack; we have discarded beauty; at its best it seems truth incompletely realized. Styles can no longer be described as beautiful.

In fact it would not be stretching the point to describe all modern styles in their grand limits as ways through a staleness of beauty to tell the truth anew. The beauty that clings to any really new work is beauty only in the minds of those who do not fully realize the significance. Thus tentatively, James Joyce's style may be described, I think, as truth through the breakup of beautiful words.

If to achieve truth we work with words purely, as a writer must, and all the words are dead or beautiful, how then shall we succeed any better than might a philosopher with dead abstractions? or their configurations? One may sense something of the difficulties by reading a page of Gertrude Stein where none of the words is beautiful. There must be something new done with the words. Leave beauty out or, conceivably, one might begin again, one might break them up to let the staleness out of them as Joyce, I think, has done. This is, of course, not all that he does nor even a major part of what he does, but it is nevertheless important.

In Joyce it began not without malice I imagine. And continued, no doubt, with a private end in view, as might be the case with any of us. Joyce, the catholic Irishman, began with English, a full-dressed English which it must have been his delight to unEnglish until it should be humanely Catholic, never at least sentimental. This is purely my imagination of a possible animus. And again a broken language cannot have been less than affectionately fostered since it affords him a relief from blockheaded tormentors. Admirably, of course, Joyce has written his words to face neither customs officials nor church dignitaries, Catholic or Protestant, but the clean features of the intelligence. Having so suffered from the dirtiness of men's minds—their mixed ideas, that is—suffered to the point of a possible suppression of all he puts upon paper, there is a humane, even a divine truth in his appeal to us through a style such as his present one which leaves nothing out. Much that he must say and cannot get said without his brokenness he gets down fully with it. But this is, again, merely a fancy. It is nothing and I put it down to show that it is nothing, things that have very little general value.

We are confronted not by reasons for its occurrence in Joyce's writings but by his style. Not by its accidental or sentimental reasons but its truth. What does it signify? Has he gone backward since *Ulysses?* Hish-hash all of it?

To my taste Joyce has not gone back but forward since *Ulysses*. I find his style richer, more able in its function of unabridged commentary upon the human soul, the function surely of all styles. But within this function what we are after will be that certain bent which is peculiar to Joyce and which gives him his value. It is not that the world is round nor even flat, but that it might well today be catholic; and as a corollary, that Joyce himself is today the ablest protagonist before the intelligence of that way of thinking. Such to my mind is the truth of his style. It is a priestly style and Joyce is himself a priest. If this be true to find out just what a priest of best intelligence intends would be what Joyce by his style intends. Joyce is obviously a catholic Irishman writing english, his style shows it and that is, less obviously, its virtue.

A profitable beginning to going further is to note the kinship between Joyce and Rabelais. Every day Joyce's style more and more resembles that of the old master, the old catholic and the old priest. It would be rash to accuse Joyce of copying Rabelais. Much more likely is it that the styles are similar because they have been similarly fathered.

Take what is most obviously on the surface in both of them, their obscenity. Shall we object to Joyce's filth? Very well, but first answer how else will you have him tell the truth. From my own experience I am perfectly willing to venture that Joyce's style has been forced upon him, in this respect at least, by the facts, and that here he has understated rather than overstated the realistic conditions which compel him. One might even go on to say that in this respect of obscenity all other present styles seem lying beside his. Let his words be men and women; in no other way could so much humanity walk the streets save in such hiding clothes. Or put it the other way: in no other way could the naked truth hidden from us upon the streets in clothes be disclosed to us in a way that we could bear or even recognize save as Joyce by his style discloses it. We should praise his humanity and not object feebly to his fullness, liars that we are. It would be impossible for Joyce to be truthful and accurate to his understanding by any other style.

This it is, let us presume, to be a catholic of the world, or so Joyce has impressed me by his style. They say Joyce fears that were he to return to Ireland it would be seen to that they excommunicate him. I cannot believe such foolishness. They are wiser than that in the church today. Joyce writes and holds his place, I would assure them, solely by the extreme brilliance of his catholicism.

And all this is no more than a reflection of the truth about Rabelais now common property. He was not at all the fat-headed debauchee we used to think him, gross, guffawing vulgarly, but a priest "sensitized" to all such grossness. Else his style would not have assured his lasting out a year.

Joyce is to be discovered a catholic in his style then in something because of its divine humanity. Down, down it goes from priesthood into the slime as the church goes. The Catholic Church has always been unclean in its fingers and aloof in the head. Joyce's style consonant with this has nowhere the inhumanity of the scientific or protestant or pagan essayist. There is nowhere the coldly dressed formal language, the correct collar of such gentlemen seeking perhaps an english reputation.

Joyce discloses the X-ray eyes of the confessional, we see among the clothes, witnessing the stripped back and loins the naked soul. Thoughtfully the priest under the constant eyes of God looks in. He, jowl to jowl with the sinner, is seen by God in all his ways. This is Joyce. To please God it is that he must look through the clothes. And therefore the privacy of the confessional; he must, so to speak, cover the ache and the sores from the world's desecrating eye with a kindly bandage. Yet he must tell the truth, before God.

Joyce has carried his writing this far: he has compared us his reader with God. He has laid it out clean for us, the filth the diseased parts as a priest might do before the Maker. I am speaking of his style. I am referring to his broken words the universality of his growing language which is no longer english. His language, much like parts of Rabelais, has no faculties of place. Joyce uses German, French, Italian, Latin, Irish, anything. Time and space do not exist, it is all one in the eyes of God—and man.

Being catholic in mind, to blatantly espouse the church, that is the superficial thing to do. The sensible thing is to risk excommunication by stupidity if it come to that in order to tell the truth. Therefore I rate Joyce far above such men as G. K. Chesterton, that tailor, or even Cocteau, if he has turned catholic as I have heard, though in the case of the latter it chimes well with his acknowledged cleverness to be anachronistic.

And why should we fear, as do so many protestants, that all the world turn Romanist? What in that conglomerate is out of date would even there be finally corrected by the sovereign power of the intelligence than which nothing is greater including as it must at work the instincts and emotions, that is the round brain and not the flat one. And this is once more Joyce's style.

To sum up, to me the writings of James Joyce, the new work appearing in *transition*, are perfectly clear and full of great interest in form and content. It even seems odd to me now that anyone used to seeing men and women dressed on the street and in rooms as we all do should find his style anything but obvious. If there is a difficulty it is this: whether he is writing to give us (of men and women) the aspect we are most used to or whether he is stripping from them the "military and civil dress" to give them to us in their unholy (or holy) and disreputable skins. I am inclined to think he leans more to the humaner way.

A Point for American Criticism

transition, 1929

IT IS regrettable that Rebecca West's article in *The Bookman*, New York, for September should have appeared in the United States. It puts both James Joyce and ourselves in a bad light.

It begins with relish—carefully defined to remove false implications. It is Paris, there is a pigeon bridging the rue de l'Odéon, Rebecca West has found two lines of a double quatrain in a book of Joyce's—*Pomes Penyeach*—which she has come from purchasing. "Suspicions had been confirmed. What was cloudy was now solid. In those eight lines he had ceased to belong to that vast army of our enemies, the facts we do not comprehend; he had passed over and become one of our friends, one of those who have yielded up an account of their nature, who do not keep back a secret which one day may act like a bomb on each theory of the universe that we have built for our defense.

"For really, I reflected . . . Mr. James Joyce is a great man who is entirely without taste."

She enters then upon a long account of a game of boules played upon a highway in Provence to the constant interruption of passing vehicles, its points like those scored by the sentimental artist. *Shock*. Finishing with an image of a great umbrella pine and the statement of the purpose of the nonsentimental artist, as determined and exclusive as the tree's intention of becoming a tree. Very fine. Examples: *La Princesse de Clèves, Adolphe* . . . She speaks of the bad example of Mr. Arnold Bennett's *The Pretty Lady*, of Katherine Mansfield's weaknesses, the sentimentality of Charles

Dickens, implying at the same time the nonsentimental successes of Tchekov. She compares the content of the younger American expressionist writers to that of *East Lynne*.

She states that, "Seduced by the use of a heterodox technique Joyce believes himself to be a wholly emancipated writer." Quite untrue. This is one of her characteristic pronouncements.

"But the sentimental artist (Joyce) is becoming nothing."

She criticizes the drawing of Stephen Dedalus, "He rolls his eyes, he wobbles on his base with suffering, like a Guido Reni . . . a consequence of Mr. Joyce's sentimental habit of using his writing as a means for gratifying certain compulsions under which he labors, without making the first effort towards lifting them over the threshold that divides life from art." She objects to his use of obscene words on the same grounds.

"There is working here a narcissism, a compulsion to make a self-image with an eye to the approval of others."

"This is not to say that he does not write beautiful prose." She refers to the scene of the young men bathing, in the early part of *Ulysses*, and to the evocations of Marion Bloom, "the great mother." But that does not alter the fact that James Joyce is safe only when he stays within tradition, a path prepared by Latin poetry.

Following are detailed descriptions of Joyce's short stories: "A Sad Case" and "The Dead," from *Dubliners*. "These two stories alone should explain why we rank James Joyce as a major writer." Early work.

Nevertheless, there are two colossal fingerprints left by literary incompetence on *Ulysses*. First, the reasonlessness of the close parallelism between *Ulysses* and the *Odyssey* which Rebecca West finds execrable, since the theme of *Ulysses* is essentially Manichean and opposed to everything that is Greek. She asks, in effect, what the devil is served by these analogies? But, Bloom being in Ireland a wanderer as Odysseus was a wanderer—she quite forgets that ten lines further on she herself answers herself as to the appropriateness of the parallel: "When one looks at the works of art recovered from the city of Khochu, which are our first intimations of what Manicheanism, functioning as orthodoxy, produced other than what we have gleaned from the reports of its enemies, one is amazed by the way that though the externals of Greek are faithfully borrowed and respectfully super-imposed on more Oriental forms, the admission that there is a fundamental disharmony in nature causes it to create effects totally different from anything which we could possibly experience on account of Greek art." And why not? Could anything be more illuminating than such a contrast? Could Joyce have chosen a better way to say exactly what he means?

The other "colossal fingerprint" occurs in the scene in the Lying-In Hospital: "The imitations of Bunyan and Sterne completely disprove all that is alleged concerning the quality of Stephen's mind . . . even allowing for the increasing cloudiness of drunkenness." Possibly. But think of the "colossal" slip of Ibsen in the first scene, Act Four of *Peer Gynt*, the Frenchman, the Englishman, the German and the Swede on the southwest coast of Morocco, as dull a piece of bully-ragging as one could find anywhere in a work of genius. To speak of "colossal incompetence" over lapses of this sort—one need note only the word "colossal."

Now for line after line she goes on proving that sentences originate before words. It is a pretty exposition. She brings in cats, wild animals and babies. But what in God's name it has to do with any intention Joyce has had, not even after three full paragraphs totaling a page of double columns and small print, is she able to make clear; any relation, that is, beyond her own erroneous, intolerant assumption of Joyce's purpose.

In this way, she makes her points, some of them valid, some not so good. I have not attempted to sum them all. She goes at the work with a will and an enviable ability for exposition. But all she says must be thrown out of account as beside the question.

Here is the very thing most inimical to all that is forward-looking in literature, going to pieces of its own fragility, English criticism in a moment of overextension come all loose underneath. Here it is proving itself inadequate to hold a really first-rate modern moment, hanging as it must still be with gross imperfections.

I saw Rebecca West straining toward some insistence she could not quite achieve so that she appeared wholly off balance. The evidences of exaggeration and nervousness are in such things as the exhilaration at the start, the suspiciously lyric dove, the bold but unsupported pronouncements recurring through the text. But especially it appeared in the initial step of the logic, the stress upon the two lines of the little poem which would cast a searchlight of significance over all that goes before and comes after them. "The most stupendous," "colossal," etc., etc. There is the table-pounding of the "right, by Jove" attitude, the ex-cathedra "this is so." Ending finally in the summary verdict that because of his sentimental defects Joyce must be, is, in fact, debarred from the privilege of launching a technical advance in literary form; that he is great only as a conventional writer in a tradition, that of Latin poetry; the rest gibberish—nonsense.

It means just that Joyce, firing from Paris, has outranged English criticism completely and that R. W., with fair skill, is penning not so much an attack on Joyce—whom she tremendously admires—but a defense, a defense littered by a dire necessity to save all that she loves and represents, lest what he had done may "one day act like a bomb on each theory of the universe that we have built for our defense": all accountable to an inadequacy of critical resource in a respectable orthodoxy.

British criticism, like any other, is built upon the exigencies of the local literary structure and relates primarily thereto. Afterward it may turn to the appraisal of heterodox and foreign works. But if these are in nature disruptive to the first, the criticism will be found to be (first) defensive, to preserve its origins. Only when an acknowledged break has been forced upon it can any criticism mend itself in a way to go up into a more commanding position. Rebecca West is solely defensive in what she says of Joyce. Within the tradition lies "perfection," the Sacred Grove, a study of Dryden. Outside is imperfection and formative chaos.

It is quite impossible for British critical orthodoxy (R. W. its spokesman) to say that Joyce's imperfections are of inconsequence, in view of something else larger. For if it (she) does so, it invalidates its own major pretense to being an inclusive whole made up of mutually related parts. It can only say this is within, that is outside the pale.

We recognize its inviolable methods. But once having said that, we must step beyond it, to follow Joyce. It is able, it is erudite, it is ill-tempered and correct—due to its limited size and the opportunity offered thereby for measurement and thorough exploration.

Rebecca West cannot take Joyce, as a whole, into the body of English literature for fear of the destructive force of such an act. She must dodge and be clever and find fault and praise. She can only acknowledge genius and defect, she cannot acknowledge an essential relationship between the genius and the defect. She cannot say that on the basis of Joyce's effort, the defect is a consequence of the genius which, to gain way, has superseded the restrictions of the orthodox field. She cannot say that it is the break that has released the genius—and that the defects are stigmata of the break. She cannot link the two as an indissoluble whole—but she must put defect to the right, genius to the left, British criticism in the center, where it is wholly forced; a thorough imposition.

Joyce does offend in taste. Joyce is sentimental in his handling of his material. He does deform his drawing and allow defective characterizations to creep in. But this does not at all debar him from making valid technical innovations in literary form, as R. W. must say it does. Both are due to the suddenness, the leap of a new force.

It is all to an American just the English viewpoint, an old basis, without further capacity for extension and nearly ready to be discarded forever. Nearly.

Forward is the new. It will not be blamed. It will not force itself into what amounts to paralyzing restrictions. It cannot be correct. It hasn't time. It has that which is beyond measurement, which renders measurement a falsification, since the energy is showing itself as recrudescent, the measurement being the aftermath of each new outburst.

Joyce has broken through and drags his defects with him, a thing English criticism cannot tolerate.

But even so, Rebecca West does not always play the game, even within her own boundaries—it is the strain she is under. A descent to Freudian expedients of classification is in a literary discussion a mark of defeat. Here is a mixing of categories, a fault in logic—that is unimaginable in a person of orderly mind.

It has always been apparent to me that references to Freud —except as Freud—are in a literary discussion particularly out of place. But the use of Freudian arguments and classifications as critical staves is really too much. The reasons are simple. Freud like other psychologists uses the same material as literature but in another mode. To use the force of psychology in a category foreign to its devices is to betray the very essence of logic.

It must be patent that in any of the Freudian classifications a man may produce good writing. That is, it may be good or bad in any Freudian category. Comment if you like on Joyce's narcissism but what in the world has it to do with him as a writer? Of course it has, as far as prestige is concerned, but not as to writing—a division which R. W. seems anxious to make when she calls him a genius. But the expedient is convenient if we want to gain a spurious (psychologic, not literary) advantage for temporal purposes.

What Joyce is saying is a literary thing. It is a literary value he is forwarding. He is a writer. Will this never be understood? Perhaps he is fixed in his material and cannot change. It is of no consequence. The writing is, however, changing, the writing is active. It is in the writing that the power exists. Joyce is a literary man writing as he may—with as much affection from his material, his Freudian category as—Aesop from his hump or Scarron from his nerves. It is stupid, it is narrow British to think to use that against him.

The thing is, they want to stay safe, they do not want to give up something, so they enlist psychology to save them. But under it they miss the clear, actually the miraculous, benefits of literature itself. A silent flower opening out of the dung they dote on. They miss Joyce blossoming pure white above their heads. They are *literary* critics. That's what gets me.

Usually something has been disturbed, possibly outraged—so they search around, muck around in psychology for what *cause* to blame, instead of searching in the writing, in literature, for the *reason*. They shut the eyes, do nothing about the fact of the writing or cry "genius"—and avoid the issue. They forget that literature, like all other effects, by genius transcends the material, no matter what it is. That it, by itself, raises the thing that is to be observed into a rare field. I don't give a damn what Joyce happens by the chances of his life to be writing of, any more than I care about the termination of the story of Pantagruel and the Sibyl. Shock there if you wish.

And this is the opportunity of America! to see large, larger than England can.

An appearance of synchrony between American and English literature has made it seem, especially at certain times, as if English criticism could overlay the American strain as it does the English. This cannot be so. The differences are epochal. Every time American strength goes into a mold modeled after the English, it is wholly wasted. There is an American criticism that applies to American literature—all too unformed to speak of positively. This American thing it is that would better fit the Irish of Joyce.

Their duty is to conserve and explain in relation to established facts—that is all. We Americans ourselves must still rely on English models. But we must not be misled. We have to realize that an English dictum on any work is, for us, only an approximation. It exists only as an analogous appraisal, as far as we are concerned, to fill a lack on our part of actual value.

A fault-finding elucidation of Joyce's work gives Rebecca West a final satisfaction. This is what is meant by the term "insular." Surrounded, limited yet intact. It is the exact counterpart of the physical characteristic of England. They have attempted freedom but achieved only extension of insularity, for the central fear remains.

With hieratical assurance Rebecca West lays down her fiats about everything, rising to a transcendental ecstasy at last and the longing for a spiritual triumph and the life onward and upward forever. She is speaking, that is, of a life nearly at its end, just as a younger culture or one at its beginning, in full vigor, wishes for a fusion of the spirit with life as it exists here on earth in mud and slime today.

Truly her conception of the Shakespearean fool, to whom she likens Joyce's mental processes, is cloacal if anything could be so, with his japes and antics which so distress her thought, in that transcendental dream in which the spirit is triumphant—somewhere else. Whereas *here* is the only place where we know the spirit to exist at all, befouled as it is by lies. Joyce she sees as a "fool" dragging down the great and the good to his own foul level, making the high spirit "prove" its earthy baseness by lowering itself to laugh at low truth. "And that is why James Joyce is treated by this age with a respect which is more than the due of his competence: why

Pomes Penyeach had been sold to me in Sylvia Beach's book-shop as if it had been a saint's medal on the porch of West-minster Cathedral."

But the true significance of the fool is to consolidate life, to insist on its lowness, to knit it up, to correct a certain fatuousness in the round-table circle. Life is not to run off into dream but to remain one, from low to high. If you care to go so far, the fool is the premonition of the Russian Revolution, to modern revolutions in thought.

Whereas R. W.'s attitude is not noble, "an escape from the underground burrows of lust," but is bred of a terminal process of life that is ending, since in an old society, as in an old criticism, exhaustion takes place finally. Lear's fool, however, is far from what R. W. paints his genus to be, but is full of compassion. Joyce, where he stoops low, has in him all the signs of a beginning. It is a new literature, a new world, that he is undertaking.

Rebecca West, on the other hand, has no idea at all what literature is about. She speaks of transcendental tosh, of Freud, of Beethoven's *Fifth Symphony*, of anything that comes into her head, but she has not yet learned—though she professes to know the difference between art and life—the sentimental and the nonsentimental—that writing is made of words. And that in just this essential Joyce is making a technical advance which she is afraid to acknowledge—that is actually cutting away all England from under her.

But Joyce *knows*—in spite of every barrier—in and out, self and world. And he is purifying his effort (in a new work) which she calls gibberish.

Joyce is breaking with a culture older than England's when he goes into his greatest work. It is the spirit liberated to run through everything, that makes him insist on un-expurgated lines and will not brook the limitations which good taste would enforce. It is to break the limitations, not to conform to the taste that his spirit runs.

Naturally they strain to drag him back.

Here it is: he is going somewhere, they are going nowhere.

They are still looking back weighing (good enough); he is going on, carrying what he needs and what he can. What good is it, as far as literature is concerned, to have observed, felt the pangs of sorrow that Joyce is recognized, even by R. W., to feel if he is doing nothing about it—as literature? As *literature*. He is a writer broken-hearted over the world (stick to literature as his chosen symbol). Broken-hearted people do not bother about the place their tears are falling or the snot of their noses. As literature, Joyce is going on like French painters by painting, to find some way out of his sorrow—by *literary* means. (Stay within the figure which R. W. cannot do.) As a writer he is trying for new means. He is looking ahead to find if there be a way, a literary way (in his chosen category) to save the world—or call it (as a figure) to save the static, worn-out language.

Here Joyce has so far outstripped the criticism of Rebecca West that she seems a pervert. Here is his affinity for slang. Even if he has to lay waste the whole English structure. It is *that* the older critics smell and—they are afraid.

He is moving on relentlessly in his literary modes to find a way out. This is not an ordered advance of troops. Or it is one place only in the attack. The whole bulk of the antagonist looms above him to make him small. But the effect is tremendous.

To me Rebecca West's view seems incompatible with American appreciation, and though her observations appear mainly true, they seem narrow, inadequate, even provincial, certainly scared, protestant female—unsatisfactory. A little ill-natured, a little sliding; what might be termed typically British and should be detected as such from the American view, a criticism not quite legitimate, save for England where it may be proper due to national exigencies like the dementia of Wyndham Lewis.

Joyce maims words. Why? Because meanings have been dulled, then lost, then perverted by their connotations (which have grown over them) until their effect on the mind is no longer what it was when they were fresh, but grows rotten as *poi*—though we may get to like *poi*.

Meanings are perverted by time and chance—but kept perverted by academic observance and intention. At worst they are inactive and get only the static value of anything, which retains its shape but is dead. All words, all sense of being gone out of them. Or trained into them by the dull of the deadly minded. Joyce is restoring them.

Reading Joyce last night when my mind was fluid from fatigue, my eyes bulging and painful but my spirit jubilant following a successful termination of a fight between my two boys I had brought to an intelligent end—subverted and used to teach them tolerance—I saw!

Joyce has not changed his words beyond recognition. They remain to a quick eye the same. But many of the stultifying associations of the brutalized mind (brutalized by modern futility) have been lost in his process.

The words are freed to be understood again in an original, a fresh, delightful sense.

Lucid they do become. Plain, as they have not been for a lifetime, we see them.

In summary: Rebecca West makes (is made by) a mold; English criticism, a product of English literature. She states her case for art. It is an excellent digest but for a world panorama inadequate. She fails to fit Joyce to it. She calls him, therefore, "strange," not realizing his compulsions which are outside of her sphere. In support of this, she builds a case against him, using Freudian and other nonliterary weapons. She is clever, universal in her informational resorts. What is now left over—Joyce's true significance—his pure literary virtue—is for her "nonsense." Of literature and its modus showing that she knows nothing. America, offering an undeveloped but wider criticism, will take this opportunity to place an appreciation of Joyce on its proper basis.

The Simplicity of Disorder

A Novelette and Other Prose, 1921–1931

RING, RING, RING, RING! There's no end to the ringing of the damned. The bell rings to announce the illness of someone else. It rings today intimately in the warm house. That's your bread and butter.

Is the doctor in? (It used to ring.) What is it? (Out of the bedroom window.) My child has swallowed a mouse.—Tell him to swallow a cat then. Bam! This is the second paragraph of the second chapter of some writing on the influenza epidemic in the region of New York City, January 11, 1929. In the distance the buildings fail. The bluewhite searchlight-flare wheels over to the west every three minutes. Count. One.

The things—one thing I disliked about your book was that you said that sex is beautiful. Did I? I thought I had said the opposite. No, you said it somewhere.

She looked at me so queerly, so intently.

In this house you have to get up out of bed to get well. You can't stay in bed with that man around. Why I believe if he was going to my funeral he'd say to the hearse driver, Shake it up, I've got to get back to the office.

Touch it off. She tummy, tummy (count 'em) a delightful animal. Ode to a misty star.

And day comes in round the edges of the drawn shades staining the fluted curtains green and gray. January of squirrels' nests and the light returning. In the exposed tops of oaks the squirrels build—have built their round nests of leaves. At seven the sun is not yet up—from the night clubs—but his breath—his stain empurples. The stairs creak. The sliding doors rumble. The thermometer also is at seven.

Her nude pinkness and familiar sex in the icy air—just for a moment. And my own icy hands. And the bugle rests upright on its bell.

This is Mrs. Gladis, will you come down this morning, I've got two or three children sick. Trrrrrihg. Can you make a call this morning? I guess the half of the house is dying again. And the cat boxes the piece of crumpled paper over the floor.

Look out you don't get that twig in your eye. To direct, sanctify and govern. Not too often. A pink carnation. A sheaf of ferns. Two timeless daffodils. Two orange daisies. And three tilted, salmon-red and yellow, tulip cups. She stopped, holding her coat close and blinked her eyes—not knowing what else to do Sunday.

You see, dear, I pretend to be frivolous as a way of being courageous—as a sort of self-defense—but such is human nature—I'm hurt when you seem to believe it. Then, you must see, too, how I am always set to detect the slightest indication in your look or manner that you are getting tired of my friendship—and I try to have a sort of quick "getaway" ready. I'd hate to be "hard to get rid of"—and I'd never "die on your doorstep." And yet I know that your moods are variable, so I don't want to be too sensitive. Kind of complicated—isn't it?

I know it was all nonsense to blow off the other day—that was just nerves. I'm all right now. Don't believe a word I say about stunning men (with beards or without) or any of the nonsense I pull. Don't ever believe anything at all but my sincerity. I know my affection means something to you—I've seen it in your face—I know it when we are talking, together.

Yes, they are here. I couldn't imagine who had left them. I'll keep them for you in my desk.

I think these days when there is so little to believe in—when the old loyalties—God, country, and the hope of Heaven—aren't very real, we are more dependent than we should be on our friends. The only thing left to believe in—someone who seems beautiful.

You like to write about love—"sweet love"—but what is it? I don't know. I only know I care about you—and what happens to you. I shall for a good many years—perhaps always.

So believe in me, dear. It's the only thing I've ever asked of you.

Photographed feeding two she-goats with bulging udders in a Mary world. A smell of paint in the hospital. The color of dogs on a gray morning, minus their shadows. They seem shadows—silently running they stop before the slow, sinister advance of a greater dog, they cower and retreat. He selects one to sniff. Looking back the other draws away. Go tell the milkman to wait a minute, the doctor is here. He's getting so big now I have to put him in a pen. I just got a packing box (lined with white oilcloth).

These (in the snow) are the prints of the small birds' feet.

And nothing—opens the doors, inserts the key, presses the starting pedal, adjusts the throttle and the choker and backs out, downhill. Sees the barberry gouttes. Seize the steering wheel and turn it sharply to the left, the lilac twigs—that have lost prestige through the loss of plumage—scrape the left front fender sharply.

The tall red grass has lost its feathers too, bare stalks now, sharpened by the difficulty with the cold and the wind. The grapevines like rusty wire. The green hedge by the green signal light.

I don't know what I'd do if I had six. I'd be in an asylum or the electric chair. I'd kill 'em. *She Regained*. A short novel. Write going. Look to steer. Her ways, serious, alert, WINNING. The woolly back of a little trotting dog, his breath (her breath) standing out before him (her). The breath flittering from the other end of the cars. And now at eleven the sun is warming the air.

This house of red sandstone blocks has stood since 1797. The river is frozen overnight. The sumac clusters, snow caught in the berry red, are stiffly curled since summer. In the gutters, snow—a double pennant blue and white. And the heated air—over the car radiator the heated air dances. Dances.

In the house into which he had entered from the cold he saw a picture of autumn, a running stream, the yellow leaves. This surprised him—in January. And another picture nearby was an old man in a beard photographed before the needles of a pine tree. But what has all this to do with general ideas if it is not the essence. Time presses.

I'm going to get undressed and get into bed and read awhile—if you don't mind my being in your private sanctum. A quick look, all that has been strangled off. The poem *Paterson* must be finished. There *are* his thoughts.

Keep up your courage. Get through with this awful drive. There's no way out just now—unless you quit entirely—which seems hardly possible for the moment. It will end soon (in a few years) and then you must write day and night—or as you please forever after. I'll be thinking of you and wishing I could be near you.

The firemen—unlike the cops—have six silver buttons three each side down the slit at the back and bottom of their coats—of which the lining, as they walk, shows red.

This is the essence of literature. And the concrete replica of the Palazzo Vecchio cupid in the frozen fountain hugs still his dolphin. It was damned clever, making a diagnosis like that and saving a baby's life, worth more than any poem, *I* think. But I'll do anything you say—anything, only make up your mind.

Why?

Doctrinaire formula-worship—that is our real enemy. The rustle of her book is in his ear.

2   A BEAUTIFUL IDEA

It has the same effect—the epidemic—as clear thought. It is like the modern advent of an old category supplanting a stalemate of information. A world of irrelevancies in the doing of one thing. But the intense haste is raised, wholly unforeseen, to a higher power: the birth of a female baby (colored) under a mustard-colored ceiling, by a cracked wall, to a turkey wishbone, in the shivering cold.

This morning, eh, will you stop in to see Mamie Jefferson, eh, she's having pains, eh, quite often.

And they have added a new brick front to the old brick house, coming out to the sidewalk edge for a store. Writing should be like that, like the world, a criticism of ideas; a thought implied in trees, the storm grown vocal: One thing supplanting all things—the flu, summing all virtues. A lardy head—new bricks joined to the old—the corner of the street in a wind that's driven them all indoors.

Take the surrealists, take Soupault's *Les Dernières Nuits de Paris*, take—You think I take no interest in you? It is not so. I avoid your eye merely to avoid interruption. Gladly, were I able, would I serve you and listen to you talk of your sore toe. But, unless I apply myself to the minute—my life escapes me. You must pardon me. I love you as I hope that you will notice by all that I have done to make you comfortable. Talk is the most precious thing in the world. I know that and I will find a way to secure it for you also but my interest in writing is so violent an acid that with the other work, I must pare my life to the point of silence—though I hope surliness may never intervene—in order to get to the paper.—Take the work of Eric de Haulleville, in *transition*: Well, take it.

Want alone is what makes poverty tolerable, impressing unity and seriousness. And the old, aged, seventy-five-year-old woman: all she does is pray that she be taken. What makes you shake like that, Grandma? I don't know. The pain catches her. Thus the effect of poverty that makes it tolerable.

So the surrealists. So the enlivening scurry. So the injected birth of a black child breaking the simplicity to a patient—to the five bare eyes.

Language is in its January. How shall I say it? The surrealists are French. It appears to be to them to knock off every accretion from the stones of composition. To them it is a way to realize the classical excellence of language, so that it becomes writing again, and not an adjunct to science, philosophy and religion—is to make the words into sentences that will have a fantastic reality which is false.

By this the falseness of the piecemeal (when language is subservient to the sale of old clothes and ideas and the formulas for the synthetic manufacture of rubber) is made apparent and the triumphant of an old category that will liberate all ands and thes is—as you shall see.

Did the academicians but know it, it is the surrealists who have invented the living defense of literature, that will supplant science; and it is they who betray their trust by allowing the language to be enslaved by its enemies; the philosophers and the venders of manure and all who cry their wares in the street and put up signs: "House for sale."

Language, which is the hope of man, is by this enslaved, forced, raped, made a whore by the idea venders. It has always angered me that other classes of men write their books in words which they betray. How can a philosopher, who is not an artist, write philosophy in words? All he writes is a lie.

Surrealism does not lie. It is the single truth. It is an epidemic. It is. It is just words.

But it is French. It is *their* invention: one. That language is in constant revolution, constantly being covered, merded, stolen, slimed. Theirs.

It is in the kind that we should see it. In that diversity of the mind which is excellence, like a tree—one single tree it—French—it is surrealism. It is of that kind which is the actual.

There rested her bum. The heat lingers. In the moment of admiration, she leaned back her head and he saw up to her left nostril a THING, entangled in hairs. Oh, wipe out the stain. The memory lingers on. A delicate false balance. We see too much.

Theirs is a simplicity of phrase emphasizing the elusive reality of words. Mine is—hanging my coat in the closet in pink pants.

Take the enormous Joyce brandishing his classic symbols. Nothing could be further from Paris. Yet it is the one thing. And I'll say this for myself that in spite of obvious defects of learning I have never known differently.

Never known differently. It is this which, in all, is the one that from the viewpoint of intelligence criticizes religion as bad writing. Which is to state that Shakespeare, were he to be read aright, would have an identical relation to a pair of shoes—in the mind—that on paper distinguished his plays from a press dispatch.

This is the alphabet q w e r t y u i o p a e d f g h j k l z x c v b n m. The one extraordinary thing is that no one has yet taken the trouble to write it out fully. And what is a beautiful woman?

She is one.

Over and over again, she is one.

Look at her bare feet. You will see the effects of wearing shoes—unless she be used to going barefoot. Sometimes the toenails will be round, sometimes square and at others long. At the ankle the foot is joined to the leg. From here to the knee is usually sixteen inches. The knee is important. Let us describe the thigh of a beautiful woman. Most literature is now silent. The physiognomy of the joint between the torso and the thighs is as various as the faces of dogs. In literature the necessity for a constant freshness of praise—of words that will have a fresh distinction of cut, of tint, of texture— must be felt as one feels instantly a dereliction in the selection of covers for this joint. Other than that—The corner of the street became, not indifference, but a cold stone-edged place of the winds.

So all things enter into the singleness of the moment and the moment partakes of the diversity of all things. And so starting, stopping, alighting, climbing, sitting—a singleness lights the crocheted edge of the heavy white sheets in the

houses of the Umbrian peasants in Lyndhurst. n.j. And so it
makes her also one, combining them all in her composite necessity, doing all honor—as Joyce by one means honors surrealism and the others, him.

So she-building of all excellence is, in her single body,
beautiful; enforcing the mind by imperfections to a height.
Born again. Venus from the confused sea. Summing all the
virtues. Single. Excellence. Female.

What happened last night? I must never go to sleep before
you again.

Who shall say differently? Edison who invented the electric bulb—of which I have two in this room—is still alive.
And in self-defense—Jo. No, I mean. Where I am and what I
am, under the time that I am. Who shall say differently?

3   CONVERSATION AS DESIGN

By this singleness do you, my dear, become actually my
wife.

By design do you become bright, purely what you are
(and visible), not to bear me a message—but as a wife you
carry me the freshness of all women. There is no necessity
for witty fingers. The solidity of the pure lends itself by pure
design in which you are accomplished.

That would be a writing.

What's that?

In which the conversation was actual to the extent that it
would be pure design.

How?

Till death do us part.

Do you like it?

It is the one thing I admire in his drawings—since there is
nothing else.

When writing is not witty it is dull.

Take a guitar.

Nonsense.

Really. I wish I could believe that.

You are copying.

Always.

But that's not original nor is it design.

Purely.

Purely what?

Conversation of which there is none in novels and the news.

Oh, yes, there is.

Oh, no, there is not. It is something else. To be conversation, it must have only the effect of itself, not on him to whom it has a special meaning but as a dog or a store window——

For this we must be alone.

It must have no other purpose than the roundness and the color and the repetition of grapes in a bunch, such grapes as those of Juan Gris which are related more to a ship at sea than to the human tongue. As they are.

As you by becoming pure design have become real. In the singleness of this epidemic which is like the singleness of Juan Gris?

You are copied after all wives and all women but by the papers or a novel no one could possibly guess it. And just because the lack has never been described means nothing in the sense of it, or the uncertainty.

It takes writing such as unrelated passing on the street to rescue us for a design that alone affords conversation. Do you see?

What's your husband's job?

Let's see, what shall I say? he just drives cars.

He can't even vomit in the spittoon. It came from him from the front, from the sides, from the back. He didn't know what he was doing. Just like I don't know what is doing in Paris.

There is no conversation in marriage as there is none in a novel for it is all sold first.

What is pure in marriage unless it be the actual? And what

is actual if it rely on wit merely to outwit? In that surely there is no wit. Not even a cyclamen for the window.

By all means give him an enema and I'll be there as soon as I can.

And so you become actual.

I can't see that. It seems to me I become a copy.

Exactly, and so purely yourself, real. I really think I'd better examine you.

Come on, thrill of a lifetime.

Suddenly within fifteen minutes, everywhere in the town and in the whole section, a light drizzle fell upon the packed snow of the streets making the roads impossible, that's what I mean. Cars were caught everywhere without chains—by the swiftness. All were alike affected. It was as if at a signal the cars had been all deprived of their brakes.

Where is there any serious conversation in a novel?—except descriptions or nonsense that is not read—knowing; for that comparable to a discussion with an intelligent parent over the inevitability of "a mastoid" in an only son, where the *Streptococcus capsulatus* has been found in the ear in pure culture.

Since in a novel conversation is not actual (as you are) and never can be—but a pale reflection never can be real, as conversation or design.

But conversation in a novel can be pure design.

Yes, if it doesn't have to tell a story. That would be difficult: a novel that is pure design—like the paintings of Juan Gris.

That's what I like about the best writing of McNutt. It is actual. Thucydides. Remind the boy.

The trouble was that she was run down. You see, they made her an angel just before Christmas and she did quite a little running round in her bare feet and she's not used to that.

But the thing is that the actual sentences of conversation simply do not exist in literature—and can never do so; Since they have doffed their actuality: One thing, they could eat regularly.

Save in relation to a new interest.

There is damned little else to say: I regret the necessity of—forgotten what I was going to say.

But in the very room. What could I do? He wouldn't say anything but that he respected every hair on my head. He sat there in my room and said that. That he said sitting in the very room of the hotel. He pays no attention to me. Everything that you can imagine has long since taken place between a man and a woman.

The sparkles of red and yellow light in the wet ink of his script as he made notes rapidly delighted him.

If you don't be a husky around here, she said swinging her ten-year-old son over on his back, you don't get nowhere.

Eliot's Tivoli Underwear, he read on a tag sticking up over the edge of the boy's trousers. I do a little peddling, fruits and vegetables, two days a week, but there's too many in it. It's a shame what the workingman has to put up with, you can't save nothing.

Why do you write?

For relaxation, relief. To have nothing in my head—to freshen my eye by that till I see, smell, know and can reason and be.

1929

Caviar and Bread Again:

A Warning to the New Writer

THERE IS one major phase of modern poetry on which both critics and their begetters have gone astray. That is substance. So riled have the former been over the modern radical changes in technique that as far as any substance can be distilled out of what they have had to say such substance is thoroughly negligible. It ranges up and down from the squawks of such hens as Mencken and Cabell to the celluloid-ivory of the recent Eliot substitutions—though Eliot was at least once a poet and didn't merely quit at the beginning from deficient ability.

Cabell, at any rate, comes clean. He wipes out poetry itself as unworthy of the adult mind, an anachronism stamping a man as arrested in his growth. Yet it must be apparent to everyone that Cabell's work lacks just this: being worth at least a second reading; a decent poetic organization through lack of which it lies spineless where he dropped it.

But it is from the poet himself that the trouble really arises. We've heard enough of the cant that the artist is a born weakling, that his works are effects of a neurosis, sublimations, escapes from the brutal contact with life that he, poor chap, horribly fears. This has always been said, and Freud seemed to put the last nail in the coffin with his discoveries. But, as reported in the last number of *transition*, an abler man than Freud, Dr. C. G. Jung, has finally revealed the true state of affairs to be profoundly in favor of the poet. It is he, the poet, whose function it is, when the race has gone astray, to lead it—to destruction perhaps, but in any case, to lead it.

102

This he will not do by mere blather but by a magnificent organization of those materials his age has placed before him for his employment.

At the same time he usually invents a technique. Or he seems to do so. But really it is that he has been the fortunate one who has gathered all the threads together that have been spun for many centuries before him and woven them into his design.

What I am driving at is some kind of an estimate of what is going on today, some kind of estimate of the worth of modern poetry before condemning it for the lack of substance which strikes one in such a magazine as *Blues*.

The older poetry is worn out for us along with all new work which follows the older line. No amount of reinflation after Eliot's sorry fashion can help it. At most we can admire Eliot's distinguished use of sentences and words and the tenor of his mind, but as for substance—he is for us a cipher. We must invent, we must create out of the blankness about us, and we must do this by the use of new constructions.

And for this we cannot wait until—until—until Gabriel blow his horn. We must do it now—today. We must have the vessel ready when the gin is mixed. We've got to experiment with technique long before the final summative artist arrives and makes it necessary for men to begin inventing all over again.

On the poet devolves the most vital function of society: to recreate it—the collective world—in time of stress, in a new mode, fresh in every part, and so set the world working or dancing or murdering each other again, as it may be.

Instead of that—Lord, how serious it sounds!—let's play tiddlywinks with the syllables. And why not? It doesn't cost anything except the waste of a lot of otherwise no-good time. And yet we moderns expect people actually to read us—even to buy our magazines and pay for them with money. . . .

Experiment we must have, but it seems to me that a number of the younger writers have forgotten that writing doesn't mean just inventing new ways to say "So's your Old Man." I swear I myself can't make out for the life of me what many of them are talking about, and I have a will to understand them that they will not find in many another.

If you like Gertrude Stein, study her for her substance; she has it, no matter what the idle may say. The same for Ezra Pound, for James Joyce. It is substance that makes their work important. Technique is a part of it—new technique; technique is itself substance, as all artists must know; but it is the substance under that, forming that, giving it its reason for existence which must be the final answer and source of reliance.

We must listen to no blank-minded critic, without understanding, when it comes to what we shall do and how we shall do it; but we must realize that it is a world to which we are definitely articulating—or to which we might be, were we all able enough.

Excerpts from a Critical Sketch

A Draft of X X X Cantos by Ezra Pound

The Symposium, 1931

Poetry? Words: figments of the mind, of no real substance.
What more then is light? It is precisely a figment of the mind
* if the apprehension of it be our consideration.*
But it is an emanation consequent on microscopic action in the
* sun.*
Then words are the same, call the microscopic action which is
* their source 'Socrates' or what you will.*

THE *Cantos* have been in Pound's mind since 1908, at least: "that forty year epic"—(*Personae*, etc., etc.)

The poem begins after an image much resorted to by modern writers: the *Odyssey*, ever more pat to the times as time passes— (But it was Virgil who led Dante through the Inferno.)

The first *Canto* has to do with Odysseus' descent to the world of shadows. The effect in this case being qualified by Pound's use of a translation into our tongue of a sixteenth-century translation from the original Greek—thus making the *Odyssey* itself a link with which to hold together his theme. He uses a poem, words, modes that have been modified by use—not an idea. He uses the poem objectively.

The now hackneyed theme of the appearance of the aged Tiresias comes up as in the original text (probably) but is not stressed.

The thing that is felt is that the quick are moving among the dead—and the oarsmen "placed," the oarsmen who went down in the whirlpool chained to their rowing benches and were not saved.

It is the gone world of "history."

105

(Canto II)

Now the poet takes his place: hallucination or genius. The ship is stopped in mid-career, in mid-ocean. The youth beaten by the sailors into the ship's stern feels the God beside him (Acoetes' story). He chronicles the arrest of the vessel's on-rush:——

"Ship stock fast in seaswirl, . . ." etc., etc., etc.

As to the Greek quotations—knowing no Greek—I presume they mean something, probably something pertinent to the text—and that the author knows what they mean. . . . But in all salient places—Pound has clarified his out-land insertions with reasonable consistency. They are no particular matter save that they say, There were other times like ours—at the back of it all.

Pound has had the discernment to descry and the mind to grasp that the difficulties in which humanity finds itself need no phenomenal insight for their solution. Their cure is another matter, but that is no reason for a belief in a complicated mystery of approach fostered by those who wish nothing done, as it is no reason for a failure of the mind to function simply when dangerously confronted. Here is a theme: a closed mind which clings to its power—about which the intelligence beats seeking entrance. This is the basic theme of the *XXX Cantos*.

Reading them through consecutively, at one sitting (four hours) Pound's "faults" as a poet all center around his rancor against the malignant stupidity of a generation which polluted our rivers and would then, brightly, give ten or twenty or any imaginable number of millions of dollars as a fund toward the perpetuation of *Beauty*—in the form of a bequest to the New York Metropolitan Museum of Art.

"In America this crime has not been spread over a period of centuries, it has been done in the last twenty or twenty-five years, by the single generation, from fifteen to twenty-five years older than I am, who have held power through that slobbery period."

His versification has not as its objective (apparently) that of some contemporary verse of the best quality. It is patterned *still* after classic meters and so does often deform the natural order—though little and to a modified degree only (nor is his practice without advantages as a method). Pound does very definitely intend a modern speech—but wishes to save the excellences (well-worked-out forms) of the old, so leans to it overmuch.

A criticism of Pound's *Cantos* could not be better concerned, I think, than in considering them in relation to the principal move in imaginative writing today—that away from the word as a symbol toward the word as reality.

1) His words affect modernity with too much violence (at times)—a straining after slang effects, engendered by their effort to escape that which is their instinctive quality, a taking character from classic similes and modes. You cannot *easily* switch from Orteum to Peoria without violence (to the language). These images too greatly infest the *Cantos*, the words *cannot* escape being colored by them: 2) so too the form of the phrase—it affects a modern turn but is really bent to a classical beauty of image, so that in effect it often (though not always) mars the normal accent of speech. But not always: sometimes it is superbly done and Pound is always trying to overcome the difficulty.

Pound is humane in a like sense to that of the writer of the great cantos—without being in the least sentimental. He has been able to do this by paying attention first to his art, its difficulties, its opportunities: to language—as did Dante: to popular language—It is sheer stupidity to forget the primarily humane aspect of Dante's work in the rhapsodic swoon induced by his blinding technical, aesthetic and philosophic qualities.

All the thought and implications of thought are there in the words (in the minute character and relationships of the words—destroyed, avoided by . . .)—it is *that* I wish to say again and again—it is there in the technique and it is that that is the making or breaking of the work. It is that that one sees, feels. It is that that *is* the work of art—to be observed.

The means Pound has used for the realization of his effects —the poetry itself——:

It is beside the question to my mind to speak of Pound's versification as carefully and accurately measured—beyond all comparison——

Perhaps it is and if so, what of it?

That has nothing in it of value to recommend it. It is deeper than that. His excellence is that of the maker, not the measurer—I say he *is* a poet. This is in effect to have stepped beyond measure.

It is that the material is so molded that it is changed in *kind* from other statement. It is a *sort* beyond measure.

The measure is an inevitability, an unavoidable accessory after the fact. If one move, if one run, if one seize up a material—it cannot avoid having a measure, it cannot avoid a movement which clings to it—as the movement of a horse becomes a part of the rider also——

That is the way Pound's verse impresses me and why he can include pieces of prose and have them still part of a *poem*. It is incorporated in a movement of the intelligence which is special, beyond usual thought and action——

It partakes of a quality which makes the meter, the movement peculiar—unmeasurable (without a prior change of mind)——

It is that which is the evidence of invention. Pound's line is the movement of his thought, his concept of the whole——

As such, it has measure but not first to be picked at: certain realizable characteristics which may be looked at, evaluated more pointedly, then measured and "beautifully," "ideally," "correctly" pointed.

They (the lines) have a character that is parcel of the poem itself. (It is in the small make-up of the lines that the character of the poem definitely comes—and beyond which it cannot go.)

It is (in this case) a master meter that wishes to come of the classic but at the same time to be bent to and to incorporate the rhythm of modern speech.

This is or would be the height of excellence—the efflorescence of a rare mind—turned *to* the world.

It succeeds and not—it does and fails.

It is in the minutiae—in the minute organization of the words and their relationships in a composition that the seriousness and value of a work of writing exist—*not* in the sentiments, ideas, schemes portrayed.

It is here, furthermore, that creation takes place. It is not a plaster of thought applied.

The seriousness of a work of art, the belief the author has in it, is that he does generate in it—a solution in some sense of the continuous confusion and barrenness which life imposes in its mutations—(on him who will not create).

It is always necessary to create, to generate, or life, any "life," the life of art, stales and dies—it dies out from under, it ceases to exist—it is not captured merely by studied excellence——

We seek a language which will not be at least a deformation of speech as we know it—but will embody all the advantageous jumps, swiftnesses, colors, movements of the day——

—that will, at least, not exclude language as spoken—all language (present) as spoken.

Pound has attempted an ambitious use of language for serious thought without sequestration (the cloistering of words) —an acceptance—and by his fine ear attempted to tune them —excluding nothing.

He has by intention avoided (quite as much as if he had announced it) the camphorated words of what passes today for classical usage. And also the cracked up—the cracking up of words and natural word sequences in an effort toward synthesis—"synthesis," that is—and——

Pound finds the problem of new word use more difficult

than that—and correctly so, I believe; that generation is sub-tler, that such writers are "seeking in the wrong garbage can."

He is seeking to demonstrate the intelligence—as he be-lieves a poet must—by laboring with the material as it exists in speech and history. Doing that, he is attempting the true difficulty (though I am not here attacking the other slant on the theme).

It is not by a huge cracking up of language that you will build new work, he postulates (that is a confusion even when skilful—a true babel—onomatopoeia, a reversion, its most signal triumph), nor by use of an embalmed language, on the other hand. But by poetry—that will strike through words whipping them into a shape—clarity and motion: analysis: be they what they may.

Analysis. It is what all poets have done with the language about them.

> *Button up your overcoat*
> *When the wind blows free*
> *Take good care of yourself*
> *You belong to me.*

There's speech—fairly accurately. Caught alive, no doubt, and written down, put to a tune.

Pound has wanted to do the same to a heightened and pro-founder degree. He has chosen flawlessly where and what he will create.

How far has be succeeded? Generation, he says, as I in-terpret him, is analytical, it is not a mass fusion. Only super-ficially do the *Cantos* fuse the various temporal phases of the material Pound has chosen, into a synthesis. It is important to stress this for it is Pound's chief distinction in the *Cantos*—his personal point of departure from most that the modern is attempting. It is not by any means a synthesis, but a shot through all material—a true and somewhat old-fashioned analysis of his world.

It is still a Lenin striking through the mass, whipping it about, that engages his attention. That is the force Pound believes in. It is not a proletarian art——

He has succeeded against himself. He has had difficulties of training to overcome which he will not completely undo—in himself at least—if that were all.

But the words reveal it: white-gathered, sun-dazzle, rock-pool, god-sleight, sea-swirl, sea-break, vine-trunk, vine-must, pin-rack, glass-glint, wave-runs, salmon-pink, dew-haze, blue-shot, green-gold, green-ruddy, eye-glitter, blue-deep, wine-red, water-shift, rose-paleness, wave-cords, churn-stick.

We have, examining the work, successes—great ones—the first molds—clear cut, never turgid, not following the heated trivial—staying cold, "classical" but swift with a movement of thought.

It stands out from almost all other verse by a faceted quality that is not muzzy, painty, wet. It is a dry, clean use of words. Yet look at the words. They are themselves not dead. They have not been violated by "thinking." They have been used willingly by thought.

Imagistic use has entirely passed out of them, there is almost no use of simile, no allegory—the word has been used in its plain sense to represent a thing—remaining thus loose in its context—not gummy—(when at its best)—an objective unit in the design—but alive.

Pound has taken them up—if it may be risked—alertly, swiftly, but with feeling for the delicate living quality in them—not disinfecting, scraping them, but careful of the life. The result is that they stay living—and discreet.

Or almost. For beside living passages, there are places where he wrenches the words about for what "ought to be" their conformation.

That's no matter. He has taken up language and raised it to a height where it may stand—beside Artemis——

If that is not a purpose worthy of a poet and if Pound has not done it—then——

It isn't all, it's even (in a sense) a defect to want so much the Artemis thing. But Pound has lifted the language up as no one else has done—wherever he has lifted it—or whatever done to it in the lifting.

His defects (dey's good too) are due to his inability to surmount the American thing—or his ability to do so without physical success—if that be preferred.

The Work of Gertrude Stein

> "Would I had seen a white bear!
> (for how can I imagine it?)"

A Novelette and Other Prose, 1921–1931

LET IT BE granted that whatever is new in literature the germ of it will be found somewhere in the writings of other times; only the modern emphasis gives work a present distinction.

The necessity for this modern focus and the meaning of the changes involved are, however, another matter, the everlasting stumbling block to criticism. Here is a theme worth development in the case of Gertrude Stein—yet signally neglected.

Why in fact have we not heard more generally from American scholars upon the writings of Miss Stein? Is it lack of heart or ability or just that theirs is an enthusiasm which fades rapidly of its own nature before the risks of today?

The verbs auxiliary we are concerned in here, continued my father, are am; was; have; had; do; did; could; owe; make; made; suffer; shall; should; will; would; can; ought; used; or is wont . . . —or with these question added to them;—Is it? Was it? Will it be? . . . Or affirmatively . . . —Or chronologically . . . —Or hypothetically . . . —If it was? If it was not? What would follow?—If the French beat the English? If the Sun should go out of the Zodiac?

Now, by the right use and application of these, continued my father, in which a child's memory should be exercised, there is no one idea can enter the brain how barren soever, but a magazine of conceptions and conclusions may be drawn forth from it.—Didst thou ever see a white bear? cried my father, turning his head round to Trim, who stood at the back of his chair.—No, an' please your honour, replied the corporal.—But thou couldst discourse about one, Trim, said my father, in case of need?—How is

113

it possible, brother, quoth my Uncle Toby, if the corporal never saw one?—'Tis the fact I want, replied my father,—and the possibility of it as follows.

A white bear! Very well, Have I ever seen one? Might I ever have seen one? Am I ever to see one? Ought I ever to have seen one? Or can I ever see one?

Would I had seen a white bear! (for how can I imagine it?)

If I should see a white bear, what should I say? If I should never see a white bear, what then?

If I never have, can, must, or shall see a white bear alive; have I ever seen the skin of one? Did I ever see one painted?—described? Have I never dreamed of one?

Note how the words *alive, skin, painted, described, dreamed* come into the design of these sentences. The feeling is of words themselves, a curious immediate quality quite apart from their meaning, much as in music different notes are dropped, so to speak, into repeated chords one at a time, one after another—for themselves alone. Compare this with the same effects common in all that Stein does. See *Geography and Plays*, "They were both gay there." To continue——

Did my father, mother, uncle, aunt, brothers or sisters, ever see a white bear? What would they give? . . . How would they behave? How would the white bear have behaved? Is he wild? Tame? Terrible? Rough? Smooth?

Note the play upon *rough* and *smooth* (though it is not certain that this was intended), *rough* seeming to apply to the bear's deportment, *smooth* to surface, presumably the bear's coat. In any case the effect is that of a comparison relating primarily not to any qualities of the bear himself but to the words rough and smooth. And so to finish——

Is the white bear worth seeing?
Is there any sin in it?
Is it better than a black one?

In this manner ends Chapter 43 of *The Life and Opinions of Tristram Shandy*. The handling of the words and to some extent the imaginative quality of the sentence is a direct fore-runner of that which Gertrude Stein has woven today into a synthesis of its own. It will be plain, in fact, on close atten-tion, that Sterne exercises not only the play (or music) of sight, sense and sound contrast among the words themselves which Stein uses, but their grammatical play also—i.e. for, how, can I imagine it; did my . . . , what would, how would, compare Stein's "to have rivers; to halve rivers," etc. It would not be too much to say that Stein's development over a lifetime is anticipated completely with regard to sub-ject matter, sense and grammar—in Sterne.

Starting from scratch we get, possibly, thatch; just as they have always done in poetry.

Then they would try to connect it up by something like— The mice scratch, beneath the thatch.

Miss Stein does away with all that. The free-versists on the contrary used nothing else. They saved—The mice, under the . . . ,

It is simply the skeleton, the "formal" parts of writing, those that make form, that she has to do with, apart from the "burden" which they carry. The skeleton, important to ac-knowledge where confusion of all knowledge of the "soft parts" reigns as at the present day in all intellectual fields.

Stein's theme is writing. But in such a way as to be writing envisioned as the first concern of the moment, dragging be-hind it a dead weight of logical burdens, among them a dead criticism which broken through might be a gap by which endless other enterprises of the understanding should issue— for refreshment.

It is a revolution of some proportions that is contemplated, the exact nature of which may be no more than sketched here but whose basis is humanity in a relationship with literature hitherto little contemplated.

And at the same time it is a general attack on the scholastic viewpoint, that medieval remnant with whose effects from generation to generation literature has been infested to its lasting detriment. It is a break-away from that paralyzing vulgarity of logic for which the habits of science and philosophy coming over into literature (where they do not belong) are to blame.

It is this logicality as a basis for literary action which in Stein's case, for better or worse, has been wholly transcended.

She explains her own development in connection with *Tender Buttons* (1914). "It was my first conscious struggle with the problem of correlating sight, sound and sense, and eliminating rhythm;—now I am trying grammar and eliminating sight and sound" (*transition* No. 14, fall, 1928).

Having taken the words to her choice, to emphasize further what she has in mind she has completely unlinked them (in her most recent work) from their former relationships in the sentence. This was absolutely essential and unescapable. Each under the new arrangement has a quality of its own, but not conjoined to carry the burden science, philosophy and every higgledy-piggledy figment of law and order have been laying upon them in the past. They are like a crowd at Coney Island, let us say, seen from an airplane.

Whatever the value of Miss Stein's work may turn out finally to be, she has at least accomplished her purpose of getting down on paper this much that is decipherable. She has placed writing on a plane where it may deal unhampered with its own affairs, unburdened with scientific and philosophic lumber.

For after all, science and philosophy are today, in their effect upon the mind, little more than fetishes of unspeakable abhorrence. And it is through a subversion of the art of writing that their grip upon us has assumed its steel-like temper.

What are philosophers, scientists, religionists, they that have filled up literature with their pap? Writers, of a kind. Stein simply erases their stories, turns them off and does without them, their logic (founded merely on the limits of the perceptions) which is supposed to transcend the words, along with them. Stein denies it. The words, in writing, she discloses, transcend everything.

Movement (for which in a petty way logic is taken), the so-called search for truth and beauty, is for us the effect of a breakdown of the attention. But movement must not be confused with what we attach to it but, for the rescuing of the intelligence, must always be considered aimless, without progress.

This is the essence of all knowledge.

Bach might be an illustration of movement not suborned by a freight of purposed design, loaded upon it as in almost all later musical works; statement unmusical and unnecessary, Stein's "They lived very gay then" has much of the same quality of movement to be found in Bach—the composition of the words determining not the logic, not the "story," not the theme even, but the movement itself. As it happens, "They were both gay there" is as good as some of Bach's shorter figures.

Music could easily have a statement attached to each note in the manner of words, so that C natural might mean the sun, etc., and completely dull treatises be played—and even sciences finally expounded in tunes.

Either, we have been taught to think, the mind moves in a logical sequence to a definite end which is its goal, or it will embrace movement without goal other than movement itself for an end and hail "transition" only as supreme.

Take your choice, both resorts are an improper description of the mind in fullest play.

If the attention could envision the whole of writing, let us say, at one time, moving over it in swift and accurate pursuit of the modern imperative at the instant when it is most to the fore, something of what actually takes place under an optimum of intelligence could be observed. It is an alertness not to let go of a possibility of movement in our fearful bedazzlement with some concrete and fixed present. The goal is to keep a beleaguered line of understanding which has movement from breaking down and becoming a hole into which we sink decoratively to rest.

The goal has nothing to do with the silly function which logic, natural or otherwise, enforces. Yet it is a goal. It moves as the sense wearies, remains fresh, living. One is concerned with it as with anything pursued and not with the rush of air or the guts of the horse one is riding—save to a very minor degree.

Writing, like everything else, is much a question of refreshed interest. It is directed, not idly, but as most often happens (though not necessarily so) toward that point not to be predetermined where movement is blocked (by the end of logic perhaps). It is about these parts, if I am not mistaken, that Gertrude Stein will be found.

There remains to be explained the bewildering volume of what Miss Stein has written, the quantity of her work, its very apparent repetitiousness, its iteration, what I prefer to call its extension, the final clue to her meaning.

It is, of course, a progression (not a progress) beginning, conveniently, with "Melanctha" from *Three Lives*, and coming up to today.

How in a democracy, such as the United States, can writing which has to compete with excellence elsewhere and in other times remain in the field and be at once objective (true to fact) intellectually searching, subtle and instinct with powerful additions to our lives? It is impossible, without invention of some sort, for the very good reason that observation about us engenders the very opposite of what we seek: triviality, crassness and intellectual bankruptcy. And yet what we do see can in no way be excluded. Satire and flight are two possibilities but Miss Stein has chosen otherwise.

But if one remain in a place and reject satire, what then? To be democratic, local (in the sense of being attached with integrity to actual experience) Stein, or any other artist, must for subtlety ascend to a plane of almost abstract design to keep alive. To writing, then, as an art in itself. Yet what actually impinges on the senses must be rendered as it appears, by use of which, only, and under which, untouched, the significance has to be disclosed. It is one of the major problems of the artist.

"Melanctha" is a thrilling clinical record of the life of a colored woman in the present-day United States, told with directness and truth. It is without question one of the best bits of characterization produced in America. It is universally admired. This is where Stein began. But for Stein to tell a story of that sort, even with the utmost genius, was not enough under the conditions in which we live, since by the very nature of its composition such a story does violence to the larger scene which would be portrayed.

True, a certain way of delineating the scene is to take an individual like Melanctha and draw her carefully. But this is what happens. The more carefully the drawing is made, the greater the genius involved and the greater the interest that attaches, therefore, to the character as an individual, the more exceptional that character becomes in the mind of the reader and the less typical of the scene.

It was no use for Stein to go on with *Three Lives*. There that phase of the work had to end. See *Useful Knowledge*, the parts on the U.S.A.

Stein's pages have become like the United States viewed from an airplane—the same senseless repetitions, the endless multiplications of toneless words, with these she had to work.

No use for Stein to fly to Paris and forget it. The thing, the United States, the unmitigated stupidity, the drab tediousness of the democracy, the overwhelming number of the offensively ignorant, the dull nerve—is there in the artist's mind and cannot be escaped by taking a ship. She must resolve it if she can, if she is to be.

That must be the artist's articulation with existence.

Truly, the world is full of emotion—more or less—but it is

caught in bewilderment to a far more important degree. And the purpose of art, so far as it has any, is not at least to copy that, but lies in the resolution of difficulties to its own comprehensive organization of materials. And by so doing, in this case, rather than by copying, it takes its place as most human.

To deal with Melanctha, with characters of whomever it may be, the modern Dickens, is not therefore human. To write like that is not in the artist, to be human at all, since nothing is resolved, nothing is done to resolve the bewilderment which makes of emotion an inanity: That, is to overlook the gross instigation and with all subtlety to examine the object minutely for "the truth"—which if there is anything more commonly practiced or more stupid, I have yet to come upon it.

To be most useful to humanity, or to anything else for that matter, an art, writing, must stay art, not seeking to be science, philosophy, history, the humanities, or anything else it has been made to carry in the past. It is this enforcement which underlies Gertrude Stein's extension and progression to date.

Marianne Moore

A Novelette and Other Prose, 1921–1931

THE BEST WORK is always neglected and there is no critic among the older men who has cared to champion the newer names from outside the battle. The established critic will not read. So it is that the present writers must turn interpreters of their own work. Even those who enjoy modern work are not always intelligent, but often seem at a loss to know the white marks from the black. But modernism is distressing to many who would at least, due to the necessary appearance of disorder in all immediacy, be led to appreciation through critical study.

If one come with Miss Moore's work to some wary friend and say, "Everything is worthless but the best and this is the best," adding, "only with difficulty discerned" will he see anything, if he be at all well read, but destruction? From my experience he will be shocked and bewildered. He will perceive absolutely nothing except that his whole preconceived scheme of values has been ruined. And this is exactly what he should see, a break through all preconception of poetic form and mood and pace, a flaw, a crack in the bowl. It is this that one means when he says destruction and creation are simultaneous. But this is not easy to accept. Miss Moore, using the same material as all others before her, comes at it so effectively at a new angle as to throw out of fashion the classical conventional poetry to which one is used and puts her own and that about her in its place. The old stops are discarded. This must antagonize many. Furthermore, there is a multiplication, a quickening, a burrowing through, a blasting aside, a dynamization, a flight over—it is modern, but the critic must show that this is only to reveal an essential poetry

121

through the mass, as always, and with superlative effect in this case.

A course in mathematics would not be wasted on a poet, or a reader of poetry, if he remember no more from it than the geometric principle of the intersection of loci: from all angles lines converging and crossing establish points. He might carry it further and say in his imagination that apprehension perforates at places, through to understanding—as white is at the intersection of blue and green and yellow and red. It is this white light that is the background of all good work. Aware of this, one may read the Greeks or the Elizabethans or Sidney Lanier even Robert Bridges, and preserve interest, poise and enjoyment. He may visit Virginia or China, and when friends, eager to please, playfully lead him about for pockets of local color—he may go. Local color is not, as the parodists, the localists believe, an object of art. It is merely a variant serving to locate acme point of white penetration. The intensification of desire toward this purity is the modern variant. It is that which interests me most and seems most solid among the qualities I witness in my contemporaries; it is a quality present in much or even all that Miss Moore does.

Poems, like painting, can be interesting because of the subject with which they deal. The baby glove of a Pharaoh can be so presented as to bring tears to the eyes. And it need not be bad work because it has to do with a favorite cat dead. Poetry, rare and never willingly recognized, only its accidental colors make it tolerable to most. If it be of a red coloration, those who like red will follow and be led restfully astray. So it is with hymns, battle songs, love ditties, elegies. Humanity sees itself in them, it is familiar, the good placed attractively and the bad thrown into a counter light. This is inevitable. But in any anthology it will be found that men have been hard put to it at all times to tell which is poetry and which the impost. This is hard. The difficult thing to realize is that the thrust must go through to the white, at least somewhere.

Good modern work, far from being the fragmentary, neu-
rotic thing its disunderstanders think it, is nothing more than
work compelled by these conditions. It is a multiplication of
impulses that by their several flights, crossing at all eccentric
angles, might enlighten. As a phase, in its slightest beginning,
it is more a disc pierced here and there by light; it is really
distressingly broken up. But so does any attack seem at the
moment of engagement, multiple units crazy except when
viewed as a whole.

Surely there is no poetry so active as that of today, so unbound, so dangerous to the mass of mediocrity, if one should
understand it, so fleet, hard to capture, so delightful to pur-
sue. It is clarifying in its movements as a wild animal whose
walk corrects that of men. Who shall separate the good
Whitman from the bad, the dreadful New England maunder-
ers from the others, put air under and around the living and
leave the dead to fall dead? Who? None but poems, such as
Miss Moore's, their cleanliness, lack of cement, clarity, gentleness. It grows impossible for the eye to rest long upon the
object of the drawing. Here is an escape from the old dilemma. The unessential is put rapidly aside as the eye searches
between for illumination. Miss Moore undertakes in her
work to separate the poetry from the subject entirely—like
all the moderns. In this she has been rarely successful and this
is important.

Unlike the painters the poet has not resorted to distortions
or the abstract in form. Miss Moore accomplishes a like result by rapidity of movement. A poem such as "Marriage"
is an anthology of transit. It is a pleasure that can be held
firm only by moving rapidly from one thing to the next. It
gives the impression of a passage through. There is a distaste
for lingering, as in Emily Dickinson. As in Emily Dickinson
there is too a fastidious precision of thought where unrhymes
fill the purpose better than rhymes. There is a swiftness im-
paling beauty, but no impatience as in so much present-day
trouble with verse. It is a rapidity too swift for touch, a ser-

aphic quality, one might have said yesterday. There is, however, no breast that warms the bars of heaven: it is at most a swiftness that passes without repugnance from thing to thing.

The only help I ever got from Miss Moore toward the understanding of her verse was that she despised connectives. Any other assistance would have been an impoliteness, since she has always been sure of herself if not of others. The complete poem is there waiting: all the wit, the color, the constructive ability (not a particularly strong point that, however). And the quality of satisfaction gathered from reading her is that one may seek long in those exciting mazes sure of coming out at the right door in the end. There is nothing missing but the connectives.

The thought is compact, accurate and accurately planted. In fact, the garden, since it is a garden more than a statue, is found to be curiously of porcelain. It is the mythical, indestructible garden of pleasure, perhaps greatly pressed for space today, but there and intact, nevertheless.

I don't know where, except in modern poetry, this quality of the brittle, highly set-off porcelain garden exists and nowhere in modern work better than with Miss Moore. It is this chief beauty of today, this hard crest to nature, that makes the best present work with its "unnatural" appearance seem so thoroughly gratuitous, so difficult to explain, and so doubly a treasure of seclusion. It is the white of a clarity beyond the facts.

There is in the newer work a perfectly definite handling of the materials with a given intention to relate them in a certain way—a handling that is intensely, intentionally selective. There is a definite place where the matters of the day may meet if they choose or not, but if they assemble it must be there. There is no compromise. Miss Moore never falls from the place inhabited by poems. It is hard to give an illustration of this from her work because it is everywhere. One must be careful, though, not to understand this as a mystical support, a danger we are skirting safely, I hope, in our time.

Poe in his most-read first essay quotes Nathaniel Willis' poem "The Two Women," admiringly and in full, and one senses at once the reason: there is a quality to the feeling there that affected Poe tremendously. This mystical quality that endeared Poe to Father Tabb, the poet-priest, still seems to many the essence of poetry itself. It would be idle to name many who have been happily mystical and remained good poets: Poe, Blake, Francis Thompson, et cetera.

But what I wish to point is that there need be no stilled and archaic heaven, no ducking under religiosities to have poetry and to have it stand in its place beyond "nature." Poems have a separate existence uncompelled by nature or the supernatural. There is a "special" place which poems, as all works of art, must occupy, but it is quite definitely the same as that where bricks or colored threads are handled.

In painting, Ingres realized the essentiality of drawing and each perfect part seemed to float free from his work, by itself. There is much in this that applies beautifully to Miss Moore. It is perfect drawing that attains to a separate existence which might, if it please, be called mystical, but is in fact no more than the practicability of design.

To Miss Moore an apple remains an apple whether it be in Eden or the fruit bowl where it curls. But that would be hard to prove——

"dazzled by the apple."

The apple is left there, suspended. One is not made to feel that as an apple it has anything particularly to do with poetry or that as such it needs special treatment; one goes on. Because of this, the direct object does seem unaffected. It seems as free from the smears of mystery, as pliant, as "natural" as Venus on the wave. Because of this, her work is never indecorous as where nature is itself concerned. These are great virtues.

Without effort Miss Moore encounters the affairs which concern her as one would naturally in reading or upon a walk outdoors. She is not a Swinburne stumbling to music, but

one always finds her moving forward ably, in thought, un-
impeded by a rhythm. Her own rhythm is particularly revealing. It does not interfere with her progress; it is the
movement of the animal, it does not put itself first and ask the
other to follow.

Nor is "thought" the thing that she contends with. Miss
Moore uses the thought most interestingly and wonderfully
to my mind. I don't know but that this technical excellence
is one of the greatest pleasures I get from her. She occupies
the thought to its end, and goes on—without connectives.
To me this is thrilling. The essence is not broken, nothing is
injured. It is a kind hand to a merciless mind at home in the
thought as in the cruder image. In the best modern verse,
room has been made for the best of modern thought and Miss
Moore thinks straight.

Only the most modern work has attempted to do without
ex machina props of all sorts, without rhyme, assonance, the
feudal master beat, the excuse of "nature," of the spirit, mys-
ticism, religiosity, "love," "humor," "death." Work such as
Miss Moore's holds its bloom today not by using slang, not
by its moral abandon or puritanical steadfastness, but by the
aesthetic pleasure engendered where pure craftsmanship joins
hard surfaces skilfully.

Poetry has taken many disguises which by cross reading or
intense penetration it is possible to go through to the core.
Through intersection of loci their multiplicity may become
revelatory. The significance of much reading being that this
"thing" grow clearer, remain fresh, be more present to the
mind. To read more thoroughly than this is idleness; a common classroom absurdity.

One may agree tentatively with Glenway Wescott, that
there is a division taking place in America between a proletarian art, full of sincerities, on the one side and an aristocratic and ritualistic art on the other. One may agree, but it
is necessary to scrutinize such a statement carefully.

There cannot be two arts of poetry really. There is weight

and there is disencumberedness. There can be no schism, except that which has always existed between art and its approaches. There cannot be a proletarian art—even among savages. There is a proletarian taste. To have achieved an organization even of that is to have escaped it.

And to organize into a pattern is also, true enough, to "approach the conditions of a ritual." But here I would again go slow. I see only escape from the conditions of ritual in Miss Moore's work: a rush through wind if not toward some patent "end" at least away from pursuit, a pursuit perhaps by ritual. If from such a flight a ritual results it is more the care of those who follow than of the one who leads. "Ritual," too often to suit my ear, connotes a stereotyped mode of procedure from which pleasure has passed, whereas the poetry to which my attention clings, if it ever knew those conditions, is distinguished only as it leaves them behind.

It is at least amusing, in this connection, to quote from *Others,* Volume 1, Number 5, November 1915—quoted in turn from J. B. Kerfoot in *Life:* "Perhaps you are unfamiliar with this 'new poetry' that is called 'revolutionary.' It is the expression of democracy of feeling rebeling against an aristocracy of form."

> As if a death mask ever could replace
> Life's faulty excellence!

There are two elements essential to Miss Moore's scheme of composition, the hard and unaffected concept of the apple itself as an idea, then its edge-to-edge contact with the things which surround it—the coil of a snake, leaves at various depths, or as it may be; and without connectives unless it be poetry, the inevitable connective, if you will.

Marriage, through which thought does not penetrate, appeared to Miss Moore a legitimate object for art, an art that would not halt from using thought about it, however, as it might want to. Against marriage, "this institution, perhaps one should say enterprise"— Miss Moore launched her thought not to have it appear arsenaled as in a textbook on psychology, but to stay among apples and giraffes in a poem. The interstices for the light and not the interstitial web of the thought concerned her, or so it seems to me. Thus the material is as the handling: the thought, the word, the rhythm— all in the style. The effect is in the penetration of the light itself, how much, how little; the appearance of the luminous background.

Of marriage there is no solution in the poem and no attempt to make marriage beautiful or otherwise by "poetic" treatment. There is beauty and it is thoughtless, as marriage or a cave inhabited by the sounds and colors of waves, as in the time of prismatic color, as England with its baby rivers, as G. B. Shaw, or chanticleer, or a fish, or an elephant with its strictly practical appendages. All these things are inescapably caught in the beauty of Miss Moore's passage through them; they all have at least edges. This too is a quality that greatly pleases me: definite objects which give a clear contour to her force. Is it a flight, a symphony, a ghost, a mathematic? The usual evasion is to call them poems.

Miss Moore gets great pleasure from wiping soiled words or cutting them clean out, removing the aureoles that have been pasted about them or taking them bodily from greasy contexts. For the compositions which Miss Moore intends, each word should first stand crystal clear with no attachments; not even an aroma. As a cross light upon this, Miss Moore's personal dislike for flowers that have both a satisfying appearance and an odor of perfume is worth noticing. With Miss Moore a word is a word most when it is separated out by science, treated with acid to remove the smudges, washed, dried and placed right side up on a clean surface. Now one may say that this is a word. Now it may be used, and how?

It may be used not to smear it again with thinking (the attachments of thought) but in such a way that it will remain scrupulously itself, clean perfect, unnicked beside other

words in parade. There must be edges. This casts some light
I think on the simplicity of design in much of Miss Moore's
work. There must be recognizable edges against the ground
which cannot, as she might desire it, be left entirely white.
Prose would be all black, a complete black painted or etched
over, but solid.

There is almost no overlaying at all. The effect is of every
object sufficiently uncovered to be easily recognizable. This
simplicity, with the light coming through from between the
perfectly plain masses, is however extremely bewildering to
one who has been accustomed to look upon the usual "poem,"
the commonplace opaque board covered with vain curlicues.
They forget, those who would read Miss Moore aright, that
white circular discs grouped closely edge to edge upon a
dark table make black six-pointed stars.

The "useful result" is an accuracy to which this simplicity
of design greatly adds. The effect is for the effect to remain
"true"; nothing loses its identity because of the composition,
but the parts in their assembly remain quite as "natural" as
before they were gathered. There is no "sentiment"; the softening effect of word upon word is nil; everything is in the
style. To make this ten times evident is Miss Moore's constant
care. There seems to be almost too great a wish to be trans-
parent and it is here if anywhere that Miss Moore's later work
will show a change, I think.

The general effect is of a rise through the humanities, the
sciences, without evading "thought," through anything (if
not everything) of the best of modern life; taking whatever
there is as it comes, using it and leaving it drained of its
pleasure, but otherwise undamaged. Miss Moore does not
compromise science with poetry. In this again, she is ably
modern.

And from this clarity, this acid cleansing, this unblinking
willingness, her poems result, a true modern crystallization,
the fine essence of today which I have spoken of as the porcelain garden.

Or one will think a little of primitive masonry, the units unglued and as in the greatest early constructions unstandardized.

In such work as *Critics and Connoisseurs*, and *Poetry*, Miss Moore succeeds in having the "thing" which is her concern move freely, unencumbered by the images or the difficulties of thought. In such work there is no "suggestiveness," no tiresome "subtlety" of trend to be heavily followed, no painstaking refinement of sentiment. There is surely a choice evident in all her work, a very definite quality of choice in her material, a thinness perhaps, but a very welcome and no little surprising absence of moral tone. The choice being entirely natural and completely arbitrary is not in the least offensive, in fact it has been turned curiously to advantage throughout.

From what I have read it was in *Critics and Connoisseurs* that the successful method used later began first to appear: If a thought presents itself the force moves through it easily and completely: so the thought also has revealed the "thing" —that is all. The thought is used exactly as the apple, it is the same insoluble block. In Miss Moore's work the purely stated idea has an edge exactly like a fruit or a tree or a serpent.

To use anything: rhyme, thought, color, apple, verb—so as to illumine it, is the modern prerogative; a stintless inclusion. It is Miss Moore's success.

The diction, the phrase construction, is unaffected. To use a "poetic" inversion of language, or even such a special posture of speech, still discernible in Miss Moore's earlier work, is to confess an inability to have penetrated with poetry some crevice of understanding; that special things and special places are reserved for art, that it is unable, that it requires fostering. This is unbearable.

Poetry is not limited in that way. It need not say either

> Bound without
> Boundless within.

It has as little to do with the soul as with ermine robes or graveyards. It is not noble, sad, funny. It is poetry. It is free. It is escapeless. It goes where it will. It is in danger; escapes if it can.

This is new! The quality is not new, but the freedom is new, the unbridled leap.

The dangers are thereby multiplied—but the clarity increased. Nothing but the perfect and the clear.

Kenneth Burke

A Novelette and Other Prose, 1921–1931

WRITING IS MADE of words, of nothing else. These have a contour and complexion imposed upon them by the weather, by the shapes of men's lives in places. Their combined effect is not sculptural; by their characters they are joined to produce a meaning. This is termed good writing. By success with the words, the success of the composition is first realized.

Writing otherwise resolves itself into trite sentences of occasional grace, the idea becomes predominant, the craft becomes servile. Kenneth Burke is one of the few Americans who know what a success of good writing means—and some of the difficulties in the way of its achievement. His designs are difficult, possibly offensive, at times recondite.

From the shapes of men's lives imparted by the places where they have experience, good writing springs. One does not have to be uninformed, to consort with cows. One has to learn what the meaning of the local is, for universal purposes. The local is the only thing that is universal. Vide Juan Gris, "The only way to resemble the classics is to have no part in what we do come of them but to have it our own." The classic is the local fully realized, words marked by a place. With information, with understanding, with a knowledge of French, a knowledge of German, I do not hear Burke calling out, Good-bye New Jersey!— No place is important, words.

I know Burke would like to go to Paris if he could afford it. He doesn't have to listen to the dialect of some big Swede or other to paste up a novel. Words will come to him just as they come to them, but of a different order. Writing.

132

This is rather negative in the way of praise, but in a starving country one might as well at least talk of food. This will be at least important to American literature, though negatively, if there will ever be an American literature. And when there is, will it be important to French literature, English literature, and so finally to the world. There is no other way. Burke seems to me to be stalled in the right place. But that doesn't finish him.

For me, his life itself is a design, gives me a satisfaction enough, always from the viewpoint of an interest in writing. He is one of the rarest things in America: He lives here: he is married, has a family, a house, lives directly by writing without having much sold out.

Any cricket can inherit a million, sit in a library and cook up a complicated or crotchety style. Plenty of Americans who know the importance of the word, if it is French or British, can be taught to do smooth puttying. But damned few know it and know the reward and would rather work with the basic difficulty to what end is not apparent.

Kenneth Burke (and family, very important) found a place out in the country where they could live. That's all.

The White Oxen is a varied study, as any book where writing is the matter, must be. American beginning—in the sense of the work of Gertrude Stein, difficult to understand, as against, say the continuities of a De Maupassant. It is a group of short accounts, stories, more or less. They vary from true short stories to the ridiculousness of all short stories dissected out in readable pieces; writing gets the best of him, in the best of the book. "The Death of Tragedy" and "My Dear Mrs. Wurtlebach." "Then they were all gone. They had all gone ahead, leaving the log behind them, and the fresh rips in the ferns growing out of the rotten leaves. Wurtlebach had avoided the cow-flops, as well as the eyes of the girls."

The American Background

From "America and Alfred Stieglitz"

They saw birds with rusty breasts and called them robins. Thus, from the start, an America of which they could have had no inkling drove the first settlers upon their past. They retreated for warmth and reassurance to something previously familiar. But at a cost. For what they saw were not robins. They were thrushes only vaguely resembling the rosy, daintier English bird. Larger, stronger, and in the evening of a wilder, lovelier song, actually here was something the newcomers had never in their lives before encountered. Blur. Confusion. A bird that beats with his wings and slows himself with his tail in landing.

The example is slight but enough properly to incline the understanding. Strange and difficult, the new continent induced a torsion in the spirits of the first settlers, tearing them between the old and the new. And at once a split occurred in that impetus which should have carried them forward as one into the dangerous realities of the future.

They found that they had not only left England but that they had arrived somewhere else: at a place whose pressing reality demanded not only a tremendous bodily devotion but as well, and more importunately, great powers of adaptability, a complete reconstruction of their most intimate cultural make-up, to accord with the new conditions. The most hesitated and turned back in their hearts at the first glance.

Meanwhile, nostalgically, erroneously, a robin.

IT IS CONCEIVABLE that a new language might have sprung up with the new spectacle and the new conditions, but even genius, if it existed, did not make one. It was an inability of the mind to function in the face of overwhelming odds, a retreat to safety, an immediate defensive organization of

134

whatever sort against the wilderness. As an emergency, the
building up of such a front was necessary and understandable. But, if the falsity of the position is to be appreciated,
what they did must be understood to have been a temporary
expedient, permissible only while a new understanding was
building.

Thus two cultural elements were left battling for supremacy, one looking toward Europe, necessitous but retrograde
in its tendency—though not wholly so by any means—and
the other forward-looking but under a shadow from the first.
They constituted two great bands of effort, which it would
take a Titan to bring together and weld into one again.
Throughout the present chapter, the terms native and borrowed, related and unrelated, primary and secondary, will
be used interchangeably to designate these two opposed split-
offs from the full cultural force, and occasionally, in the same
vein, true and false.

The English settlers, on the northeast coast, were those
most concerned in this division of the attack, but it was they
who would establish the predominant mode and its consequences. Further south—and it is important to note that it
was to the south and in California, where the climate was
milder, that this bolder phase of the colonization had its brief
flowering—an attempt on a different scale was instituted.
Under the Spanish the sixteenth-century universities, bish-
oprics and works of a like order, constituted a project dia-
metrically opposed to what the English understood. What
they seemed to have in mind was no colony at all, but within
the folds of their religious hegemony an extension of Spain
herself to the westward. But the difficulties were too great,
too unimaginably novel to the grasp of their minds for them
to succeed.

From geographic, biologic, political and economic causes,
the Spanish conception ended in failure, and the slower,
colder, more practical plan of lesser scope out of northern
Europe prevailed. North America became, in great measure,

a colony of England, so to be regarded by the intellect and fashion of the day. While on the part of most of the colonists there would be a reciprocal attitude toward "home." The immediate cultural aspect, in dress, music, manners, soon developed a disdain for the local, as became a colony looking back toward fashion brought to it by its governors and copied in America wherever possible.

Nowhere is the antagonism of the times toward local initiative better shown than in *An Official Report on Virginia* (1671), by Governor Sir William Berkeley, when he wrote:

I thank God there are no free schools or printing, and I hope we shall not have these hundred years, for learning has brought disobedience, and heresy, and sects into the world, and printing has divulged them, and libels against the best government. God keep us from both.

Alongside all this, nevertheless, an enterprise neither Spanish nor English, nor colonial by any way of speaking save in its difficulty and poverty of manner, began widely to form, a new reference by which knowledge and understanding would one day readjust themselves to a changing world. It was America itself which put up its head from the start—to thrive in mode of life, in character of institutions, in household equipment, in the speech, though opposed with might and main everywhere from the official party both at home and abroad. Noah Webster spent a life here building the radically subversive thesis which his dictionary represents. But the same force began pushing its way forward in any number of other forms also. Necessity drove it ahead. Unorthodox, it ran beside the politer usages of the day, never, except in the moment of a threatened national catastrophe, the Revolution, to be given a general sanction.

It was a harsh world the first men had to face. He who has seen the hill coming up from the waterfront at Plymouth, changed though it be from all possible resemblance to the

poverty of that day, will have no trouble for all that in imag-
ining the bareness, the savage exposure, of those first isolated
buildings regularly laid out either side the one climbing
street. Merely to read the stone which commemorates the
fifty per cent death rate of that first winter is enough to fas-
ten the picture of tragedy on the mind. But just the bare
statement in the chronicles of the necessity the people were
under to bury their dead at night so as not to give the natives
knowledge of their rapidly diminishing numbers while they
waited for the ships to return, fastens the impression of terror and an alien mood toward the land upon the mind indelibly. And these things were repeated north and south in
a hundred other instances.

The land was from the first antagonistic. The purpose must
have been in major part not to be bound to it but to push
back its obstructions before the invading amenities—to drive
them before one. To force them back. That these trans-
planted men were at the same time pushing back a very necessary immediate knowledge of the land to be made theirs
and that indeed all that they possessed and should henceforth
be able to call their own was just this complexity of environment which killed them, could not become at once apparent.

Even the Revolution would prove anything but a united
movement toward self-realization on the part of America.
The colonists did not, except in their humbler parts, desire
separation from the mother country—not in the beginning,
at any rate. It took time for the national consciousness to
make itself known, and against heavy odds. The significance
of these old conflicts is often lost now, but valuable light
arises in them again and again throughout the annals. The
conflict existed strongly in the intimate nature of the Commander-in-Chief himself. He did not for more than a year
after the beginning of the Revolution think of his action as
anything but the protest of a loyal subject to his king. Not till
after bitterest realization of disappointed hopes did the full

force of the thing break heavily upon him. It caused Washington a wrench not only of the heart but of the understanding itself to drag himself away from England.

The two divergent forces were steadily at work, one drawing the inhabitants back to the accustomed with its appeals to loyalty and the love of comfort, the other prodding them to face very often the tortures of the damned, working a new way into a doubtful future, calling for faith, courage and carelessness of spirit. It was, be it noted, an inner tension, a cultural dilemma, which was the cause of this. As corroborating evidence of which, note further that it was Thomas Jefferson, a man of delicate and curiously balanced mentality, not a soldier, who envisioned and drafted the Declaration of Independence. And that it was a practical man of unusual sagacity, Benjamin Franklin, who was the most persistent and successful exponent of the project to take into native hands and to deal directly, by force, if necessary, with the world of their time.

Washington's unique place in the history is that of the blameless leader, the great emblem, almost the unconscious emblazonment of the cause. As a soldier he was merely a servant. The other outstanding figure was John Adams, representing the relic obstinacy of the original Pilgrims.

The war over, the true situation, raised into relief by patriotic fervor, would flatten out as before into the persistent struggle between the raw new and the graciousness of an imposed cultural design. England eliminated, those very ones who opposed her would fast take the leading place in the scheme from which she had been driven, renewing the old struggle at home. The fashionable would still be fashionable, and the unfashionable, unfashionable as before.

In this inevitable conflict of interests, Thomas Jefferson stands out as the sole individual who seems to have had a clear understanding of what was taking place. He did appear to see the two trends and to make a conscious effort to embrace them and to draw them together into a whole. But even for him, the disparity remained unbridgeable in his day. It was Jefferson who, when President, would walk to his office in the mud, out of principle, and walk home again ignoring the mud, as against the others who would ride. And at the same time it was Jefferson who, recognizing the imperious necessity for other loveliness to lay beside his own, such as it was, would inquire whether or not it might be possible, in securing a gardner, to get one who could at the same time play the flute. His home at Monticello, with its originality, good taste, with its distinctive local quality, is one of the few places where the two cultural strains approach in our history, where they consciously draw together. But Jefferson's idea would be sadly snowed under.

While it was destined that Jefferson should directly fail in propagating his cultural insights, it was at the same time the good fortune of Franklin indirectly to succeed.

Franklin, coming down from New England, saw things in a different way from that of Virginia. His talent, primarily technical, with the bearing which all technical matters have upon the immediate, took him quite apart from his will in the right direction. Though there seems always too much of the bumptious provincial in Franklin, he had the luck. For America has approached the cultural plateau from this necessitous technical side.

But with the beginners, facing difficulties, things did not go so well at first. America had to be before it could become effective—even in its own mind. Finding itself, as a democracy, unable to *take up* the moral and economic implications of its new conditions, which Jefferson lived and proposed, America slumped *back to* fashion on the one, favored, side, and, having slighted the difficult real, it fell back at the same time to unrelated, crazy rigidities and imbecilities of formal pattern, later to blossom as Dowieism, Billy-Sundayism, etc., etc., to say nothing of the older schisms over petty ritual of the same sort. Confusion, a leaderless mob, each wandering into a mire of its own—with perfect logic.

All this weight would one day have to be lifted in the final cultural pick-up still waiting—tremendous, neglected; a stone on the neck for the time being at least, it left Jefferson crushed.

When the first courageous drives toward a realistic occupation of America slackened, men like Boone, Crockett and Houston had to be accounted for. It is not hard to fabricate a melodramatic part for them. The hard thing to do is to make the understanding of what they were appear integral with the history, effective in a direct understanding, of what men have become today. Presented historically because of their picturesqueness or a legendary skill with a gun, actually the cultural place these men occupy is the significant one. And if it seems always easier to romanticize a thing than to understand it, it is so because very often it is more convenient to do so. Especially is this true when to romanticize a thing covers a significance which may be disturbing to a lying conscience.

For Boone, at least, was not a romantic, losing himself in the "mystery" of the forest. He was a technical genius of the woods, enjoying, in that respect, the admiration of the most skilful native craftsmen, who remained actually in awe of his sheer abilities and accomplishments. What was more cultured to him than the solitude of the trees? He was fiercely disdainful of the scrambling colonist, and ever more so as time went on.

The significance of Boone and of the others of his time and trade was that they abandoned touch with those along the coast, and their established references, and made contact with the intrinsic elements of an as yet unrealized material of which the new country was made. It is the actuality of their lives, and its tragic effect on them, which is illuminating.

All of them, when they did come back to the settlements, found themselves strangers. Houston, as late at Lincoln's time, lived apart from his neighbors, wearing a catskin vest, whittling a stick and thinking. But the reason underlying this similarity of action in all of them is not that they were out-moded but rather defeated in a curious way which baffled them. Only Jackson carried the crudeness of his origins suc-cessfully up to the top by the luck of battle, and for a short time only. And when he did, as Ezra Pound has recently pointed out, it was Jackson who, because of his basic culture, was able first to smell out the growing fault and attack the evidence of a wrong tack having been taken, the beginning raid on public moneys by private groups, which he turned back for a few years.

Such men, right thinking, but prey to isolation by the forces surrounding them, became themselves foreigners—in their own country. They were disarmed by the success of their softer-living neighbors, a success which can now be marked as the growing influence of the false cultural trend. Actually Boone was a genius, lamed by the gigantic newness which won him but into which he could not penetrate far enough—it was impossible. At least he signalized rightly what was to be done. Such men had no way of making their realizations vocal. They themselves became part of the an-tagonistic wilderness against which the coastal settlements were battling. Their sadness alone survives. Many of them could hardly read. Their speech became crude. Their man-ners sometimes offensive. It was the penalty they had to pay.

It was a curious anomaly. They in themselves had achieved a culture, an adjustment to the conditions about them, which was of the first order, and which, at the same time, oddly cut them off from the others.

Even Washington, during a lifetime, was subject to the same torsion, and was extremely backward in adjustment to the growing laxity of his time, by virtue, be it said, of the actuality of this same backwoods training, which in his case did not last long enough to hold him entirely in its narrow-ing grasp. Another evidence of his great shrewdness. But, at the pinch, it was this which later stood him in good stead, though it caused him, at the same time, endless suffering. It was powerful by its direct relation to actuality but remained heavily opposed by a more fashionable choice. Not he, but Roger Morris got the wealthy Mary Philipse.

It was precisely that which gave them their realistic grasp of situations and things which made these men unacceptable to their world of a rising cultural tide, gone astray, but of the sort which would predominate. Washington had all kinds of luck, quite apart from his character, to get through alive. He did manage to maintain himself intact, but only at the cost of a tremendous isolation, at a time of national stress which required the unique strength of moral base possessed by him, which came from a complexity of events in his birth and bringing up, and in which the others were lacking. But he was generously hated for it. All manner of intrigue dogged his steps in the attempt to break down his difficult standard.

His realization of what he was after came out one night when, on his way to West Point from Hartford, he passed through a small Connecticut town. The women and children came out with torches to cheer him and accompanied him a short distance on his way. This is the army, he said, that they will never conquer. It is easily conceivable that with less luck he could have been destroyed early, and the mud they threw at his carriage during his second term in the Presidency not have been counted among his laurels. He stood out because, like Boone, he stuck fast to facts which enforced his adherence above the glamour of an easier fortune. He was shrewd and powerful in other respects, but it was the unswerving moral integrity by which he clove to the actual conditions of his position which was at the bottom of his courage. It was the strength of a cultural adjustment of the first sort.

One is at liberty to guess what the pure American addition to world culture might have been if it had gone forward singly. But that is merely an academicism. Perhaps Tenochtitlan which Cortez destroyed held the key. That also is beside the point, except that Tenochtitlan with its curious brilliance may still legitimately be kept alive in thought not as something which *could* have been preserved but as something which was actual and was destroyed.

One might go on to develop the point from this that the American addition to world culture will always be the "new," in opposition to an "old" represented by Europe. But that isn't satisfactory. What it is actually is something much deeper: a relation to the immediate conditions of the matter in hand, and a determination to assert them in opposition to all intermediate authority. Deep in the pattern of the newcomers' minds was impressed that conflict between present reliance on the prevalent conditions of place and the overriding of an unrelated authority. It is that which, at its best, comes like the cut of a knife through old sophistry—but it requires the skilful wielding of a sharp knife. And this requires a trained hand.

Not that this direct drive toward the new is a phenomenon distinctively confined to America: it is the growing edge in every culture. But the difficulties encountered in settling the new ground did make it a clearer necessity in America—or should have done so—clearer than it could have been shown to be otherwise or elsewhere. To Americans the effort to appraise the real through the maze of a cut-off and imposed culture from Europe has been a vivid task, if very often too great for their realizations. Thus the new and the real, hard to come at, are synonymous.

The abler spirits among the pioneers cut themselves off from the old at once and set to work with a will directly to know what was about them. It set out helter-skelter. And, by God, it was. Besides, it couldn't wait. Crudely authentic, the bulk of a real culture was being built up from that point. The direct attack they instituted, shown in many cases by no other results than the characters of the men and women themselves, was in many cases at least within reach of the magnificent wish expressed in cries of wonder let out by Columbus' men on ,seeing the new world actually, for the first time, standing and running about before them.

At moments it flashes bewilderingly before people as reflected in the wild cries of the Paris crowds about Woodrow Wilson's carriage when he held up his hope of escape in 1918. But, unrealized in America itself, there too it slipped away again.

It isn't just to say that the acquisition of borrowed European culture was in itself a bad thing. It was, moreover, inevitable that it should be brought here. As inevitable as the buying of legislatures many years later in order that railroads might with the least possible delay be laid across the country. It is only unfortunate that this sort of thing should be taken to be virtue itself, a makeshift, really, in constant opposition to the work of those good minds which had the hardihood to do without it. The appurtenances of Europe came in with their language and habits, more finished than anything native could have been—that is, barring Indian workmanship and manner, which were of slight value in the East. As a matter of fact, these borrowed effects were better in quality than the native.

Samuel Butler's famous witticism, **O God, O Montreal!** is the sort of gibe the authentic crudeness had to weather at the start.

But while the men working toward the center were inventing their new tools of thought, welding their minds to new conformations with the situation as it existed, the men of the opposing force were in closer and closer touch with the Old World. By improvement of the means of transportation, the slow accumulation of goods, and the coming to the New World of more gentle types, these secured their hold more and more on the American cultural scene.

It was all right to say, as Poe did, speaking of writing, that we should cut ourselves loose from the lead strings of our British grandmama. He did so—to the confusion of critics even to the present day—but few could follow him. And Charles Dickens could well reply by his well-known attack on American manners—his vituperation salted by astonishment before a strangeness he could not explain. Wider and wider the two bands of effort drew apart, the division which must inevitably have taken place signalized by the two more or less definite parties in American politics. And it was foreordained that the cleverer, more united, and more numerous unrelated element—represented by the cities along the seaboard—should have the ascendancy.

After the Revolution there would be a constant gnawing away of the State which, under the powerful influence of Washington and his associates, had been constructed. There would be an accelerated dropping back to style and the unrelated importations. Boone's lands would be stolen away from him by aid of unscrupulous land speculators with influence in Congress, and he would go off to Spanish territory around St. Louis in disgust of his race. It was not "culture" of either sort, to be sure, which drove him out, but it was under the necessities, the conditions, under the skirts of the borrowed lack of attachment, that the agencies throve which were his undoing.

Nor is this solely an American difficulty. It is seen in such things as the steady decay of life in the Shetland Islands, while the Faroes, less favorably situated to the north, too far for exploitation by the London markets, have begun a regeneration under a rediscovered genius of place. A like impetus is behind the bombing by a young and patriotic Breton of the memorial celebrating the absorption of Brittany by a greater France. The attempt of an unrelated culture upon a realistic genius of place is deeply involved in these events, as in the undying movement to free Ireland.

But in America the struggle was brilliant and acute. It was also on a vaster scale.

Many of us, who should know better, are quick to brand Americans with the term "colonial" if in a moment of irritation some Yankee stands up and wants to wipe out, let us say, French painting. In a loud voice he lets go: We can paint as well—or intend shortly to do so—as them damned frogs. We'll show 'em.

But there is a more persuasive phase to the feeling from which such an outburst might arise. It is this: The chief reason for existence cannot be but in the devising of excellence (or in destroying it, for it would be senseless to destroy the worthless) which is in effect evidence of the approach of equals. And though it is profitable to milk a cow and to use its milk (as well as its manure) it is quite as profitable in another way to talk with a man of sense and novel experience and to propose and carry out with him cultural projects. Especially is this delightful, or of value, when that man's outlook and background are new to us—by that much more in a way to cast a light on old errors of judgment.

In poverty and danger America borrowed, where it could, a culture—or at least the warmth of it ad interim. But this, valuable for the moment and later also as an attribute of fashion and wealth, fixed itself upon the mind until, the realization of the actual, original necessity being largely forgotten, it even went so far that Americans themselves no longer believed in it.

Meanwhile an unrelated Hopi ceremonial—unrelated, that is, except to the sand, the corn, the birds, the beasts, the periodic drought, and the mountain sights and colors—was living in the farther West.

A servile copying of Europe, not Jefferson's, became the rule. And along with it a snobbism from which or from the effects of which very few escaped. The secondary split-off from what, but for fear, had been a single impetus, finally focused itself as personal wealth in America, important since it is wealth that controls the mobility of a nation. But dangerous since by its control it can isolate and so render real values, in effect, impotent.

So, being held as a prerogative, wealth, by the influence it wields, may become the chief cause of cultural stagnation. This has been the case in America. To support its own position it has sought to surround itself with the appurtenances of a finished culture which is of no direct significance in the new sphere. But by this emphasis such a culture of purchase, a culture in effigy, has become predominant. The harm is done. The primary cultural influence, embraced by the unfortunately impoverished native, came to a stop.

Wealth went on. The cities were its seat. By its centralization of money men flocked to them, leaving the already hard-pressed and often failing culture of immediate references still farther behind. The small cities and lesser communities involving nine-tenths of the population began to waste more and more. In many places life has actually disappeared— buildings being occupied only by chipmunks and porcupines. And these were once sources of energy, drained off by a cause not quite so simple as it has been imagined to be.

Certainly the trend must have been from poor land to good and from cheap lands toward the gold fields, the power sites, navigation centers, and the locations of natural resources of all sorts. Inevitably. One must accept the fact. But the pull exerted by tastes of a secondary order, involved in this rush to the cities, though unstoppable, may nevertheless be traced out and recorded. The cities had at least population and a quickened pulse, but in getting this, as in everything where the secondary culture predominates, the cost was severe. It involved the actual decay of the small community. And the decay of the small community was a primary cultural decay. It would seem as if the city has as its very being the raising of the cultural level, as if it were in the very stream of the great flow. Quite the opposite is true, unless the place of the city, as a sort of turntable and that only, be clearly realized.

The decay of the small community was an actual decay of culture; it was a sack by invisible troops, leaving destruction for which the gains—and they were considerable—did not compensate. It was a loss which degraded, which was compelled by circumstances but which posited a return to sources in some form later on. The inevitable destruction of the South during the Civil War was of this order. It was the overwhelming desire for an immediate realization of wealth, for escape from isolation which made wealth paramount and to be fought for, at any cost. Wealth meant, as it means to-day, the control of movement, mobility, the power to come and go at will. In small communities, being drained of wealth by the·demand for it in the cities, men died like rats caught in a trap. And their correctly aimed but crude and narrow beginnings died with them.

Take such a place as H——, Vermont, apart from the difficulties with the water supply—rotten and fallen into decay—inspiration, the full spirit, alone could ever have made it possible for men to live there. It is that something tremendously volatile and important has been withdrawn. Without attachment to an essential reality, nothing could have lived in these closed-off areas. And with it life can spring up in the very sand.

A related culture is a plant of such a sort. It spreads itself everywhere. But an unrelated culture is neither hardy nor prolific.

It was the reality of the small community which settled the territory in the first place, but from behind came the wave which blotted that out. And it was the culture of immediacy, the active strain, which has left every relic of value which survives today. It was a losing battle. Against an overwhelming mass superiority of wealth the struggles of a related culture grew still less and less. The very roots were being dried up.

Note well, that there is a hard law of the world which governs the emergence and disappearance of men as of communities and nations: To the victor belong the spoils. The cultural effects of America are governed by this as everything else is governed. Nothing is good because it is American, as nothing survives merely because it is authentic. The false may and often does supersede it. But the law is operative, like every other law, only under definite conditions. These may be ascertained and measured. All that is being said is that it must be realized that men are driven to their fates by the quality of their beliefs. And that in America this has been the success of the unrelated, borrowed, the would-be universal culture which the afterwave has run to or imposed on men to impoverish them, if it has not actually disenfranchised their intelligences.

As the force of the crude but related beginnings faded away, for without money to make them mobile they stagnated, it nevertheless had some successes. The most effective drive of local realization came, as mentioned above, in practical inventiveness. Crude, at first, necessitous, immediate, hand-to-mouth, that was the first test. There it could not afford to wait on anything. It had to be cut and go.

And wealth took the scene, representative of a sort of squatter spirit, irresponsible because unrelated to the territory it overran. And wealth, in this temper, grew to be intolerant to the beginning culture it replaced. It seems strange that this mobility should have aligned itself as it did and shown itself antagonistic to the locally related. But being secondary and psychologically inferior to the first, the cause for the antagonism is plainly discernible. This psychological inferiority of position is reflected in the sordidness of much that was tolerated by the rich as time went on, as so well pointed out by Lincoln Steffens, in order to maintain themselves in their position.

It was the new, American phase of that same rule of wealth which "had adapted and converted the vast sources of power in nature to its own use and convenience, and which has exploited and perverted the course of religion and philosophic thought since the dawn of civilization." Particularly vicious was this in a democracy with the history which had been America's, since it was just that, as the note was set, which the first white men had come here to escape.

And still, men flocked to the cities.

Against this heavy tide, the real cultural forms might take on an unconscious beauty of refinement in the lines of fast ships and, in more conscious form, the carved and painted figureheads of the ships themselves. It might produce glassware, such collectors' items as the wooden marriage chests of Pennsylvania workmanship, an architecture old and new, and many other things as well exemplified as anywhere by the furniture in white pine and other native woods built by the Shakers in their colonies along the New York–Connecticut border. Beautiful examples are these of what could be done by working in a related manner with the materials in hand; they are plastically the most truthful monuments to the sincerity of the motives that produced them that could well be imagined. Here was a sect, isolated by their beliefs, living in small self-sufficient communities, seeking to make what they needed out of what they had for the quiet and disciplined life they sought. It was a bigoted, small life, closing in of themselves for a purpose, but it was simple and inoffensive. All these qualities appear in the workmanship, a kind of gentle parable to the times. To no purpose. It was vitally necessary that wealth should accumulate. It did. It couldn't help it. The consequences were persistent and unfortunate. And the strategy of fashion, partisans of the colonial spirit, had to be to keep the locally related in a secondary place. They needed art and culture, and the art and culture they fostered, and paid for, major in quantity, overshadowed the often defective and ineffectual new.

And there it was. The insecurity all men felt in the predominance of this purchased culture, unrelated to the new conditions, made them rush for security in money all the more. With these consequences: the abandonment of the primary effort and the further and further concentration of population at the trade centers, the cities, and the steady depletion of the rural districts.

It is in character that Washington with his sense of reality had an instinct away from them to his "vine and fig tree"—though he shared equally with the others, it must be said, the common lust for money and the security it could buy.

Men went to the cities, correctly, not even for the cash directly so much as because of the growing spiritual impoverishment of the outlying districts, a breakdown which brought a moral breakdown in its train. How could it be otherwise? The actual, the necessity for dealing with a condition as it existed, seemed to become unnecessary because of mystical powers represented by money. Decay must, therefore, immediately have got in motion among the faculties which fastened the pioneer to his world.

And the agent serving this colossal appetite for wealth, what has come to be known as "the law," became in fact the index of the moral corruption of the time, actually not the law, but a professional class of law-breakers. In Lincoln Steffens' autobiography, the structure of this moral decay is laid bare in its childlike simplicity: the economic, the military, the political masters at the top—all who were in power swept up by the predominant, unrelated culture they had been practicing. It grew, a great snowball rolling them up together, minister and financier, senator and college teacher, woman and man, young and old—fashion and cash. But being unrelated, having no basis in the conditions of the place, it had to have power by other means, and it had to have it quickly.

Museums were founded. Country estates, operas founded. And in the "generosity" of their gifts this series of generations believed they offered an excuse for their actions. The baleful architecture of certain of the years might have made them think, but it appears not to have done so. Religion became a stencil which roused many a man to a pitch of hatred against the form and repetitious stupidity of it, that would never be eradicated from his nature thereafter.

But those, at the top, possessing cash, and so retaining their enviable mobility, relied on the lawyer-politician-officeholder or professional intermediary as the means to keep them there.

It is clear that the racketeer, the hired assassin, the confirmed perjurer, the non-office-holding boss, is the same person as the higher agent of the class holding the money, who by their cash in turn keep the whole range of false cultural agencies in line. Money being power and the power to move at will, it has always been the prime agent of decay in the world. But in America, whose resources made Golconda look like a copper penny, it would run, a fire through the grass, more wildly than anything the world had ever seen before. The organization of the underworld would be exactly the replica, the true picture, of the national government—until finally they fused actually into one in the early years of the century, unabashed.

Incredible, fairy-tale-like, even offensively perverse as it may seem, it is the fear, the cowardice, the inability before the new, which in America whipped the destructive false current on like a forest fire. And, though it is not easily to be believed, it is a sense of their inferior position which drove the early fortunes on to their exorbitant excesses.

A board of directors of a great national corporation which has been using a man's patent illegally for ten years owes him two million dollars in back royalties. He institutes suit against them. He, one man without money. But in this case there are incriminating letters on file in the Department of Justice. Now. These letters may be destroyed if someone in Washington can be fixed. The man may possibly be bluffed out of a realization of his aspirations, or a feeling of futility toward his quest may unhorse him. Or he may be murdered, if posible, "accidentally." There's the setup. And the law has devised for itself an immunity so that it may with perfect impunity "legally" serve not only the corporate ruler himself but his servants and imitators all down the line to the lowest crook, even to the point of such technical minutiae of upsetting a verdict as that one of the jurors is slightly hard of hearing.

And such instruments do, very certainly, hold the awed admiration of the sheep en masse, who wish they also could be sure of, be able to pay for, such a friend as the law in time of need.

The influence of a primary culture went on diminishing, save by moments through the work of a Whitman or a Poe; and there were clipper ships leading the race for trade around the world—and in the back yards of their masters and crews, a refined school of literary borrowers looking gracefully askance at Melville.

Andrew Jackson took up his battle with the banks, which by that time had gradually succeeded in diverting every nickel of the government's funds into their private coffers. And three-quarters of a century later, Woodrow Wilson would still be making statements relative to the menace to government of a vast and illusory credit power.

And still somewhat later, money was being consciously thrown away to known bankrupts, Brazil, Peru, and the German Reich, for the sole apparent purpose of impoverishing the region in which the bankers happened to maintain their traffic. Dizzily they conceded credits to allied corporate interests, at the same time calling small loans in order to pinch out the individual borrower, thus intrenching themselves in the monopoly and impoverishing the little man more and more till he should leave the field or take less and less in wages.

But this ascendancy of a secondary culture, secure in wealth, was gained not without results that were ludicrous as well as tragic. Wealth established museums, but it could not tell, it had to be told, what was good in them. Nor can it do anything with the treasures of the ages but stand by, while the primary forces employ them with taste, understanding, and, it may be finally, with power. There were the Boni de Castellanes, the tiara age of American opera, boxholders sleeping through the music or wondering what the hell it was all about, while the American composer, Ives, remained unknown.

And nowhere better than in the case of Ives is shown the typical effects of this neglect: witness phenomenally intelligent and original conceptions, never fully oriented and worked out for lack of the necessary orchestra to work with; recognition first abroad, but a recognition tempered by the palpable deficiencies in finish bred of the inimicable atmosphere in which the work of a lifetime was spent; effects on his character the product of a pitiless isolation, his designation as an eccentric—a typical American retort to the castigations genius ends by applying to its compatriots—and finally a retirement from the encounter with mountains of unfinished and half-finished projects, in which the young of the next generation find "marvelous bits," the work of a man "way ahead of Europe in his time."

At the same time a whole world of successful musicians is carefully quarreled over, as to this or that quality they do or do not possess or would possess—wholly second-rate, therefore not dangerous, and so acceptable to the ever-present villainy in power. As a postlude Ives's compositions are occasionally performed in cheap auditoriums to the real audiences, potentially at least appreciative—but too late.

It is not to be gathered from this that first-rate work would be set aside for inadequacies merely because of a name. Because a thing is American or related to the immediate conditions it is not therefore to be preferred to the finished product of another culture. One merely presumes that in a flight of the intelligence the actual body passes through various climates and zones of understanding which are variable. It does not simply arrive at the destination by virtue of wishes and good intentions. And in passing from one place to another it is changed by that which it encounters. It does not just go and encounter nothing. If it did, there would be no use in going, for it would be the same there as here. It is a question of give and take. If there is no equation, no comparable value to be set beside the first, adding or subtracting, multiplying or dividing, the thing stands alone and must stand impotent. America might produce work of value to Europe.

And on the other hand, one does not disguise one's poverty by enhancing one's appearance through the use of another's spiritual favors.

Even an Emerson did not entirely escape, his genius as a poet remaining too often circumscribed by a slightly hackneyed gentility. He did not relate himself so well to the underlying necessity as his style shows him to have been related to the style of the essayists of the older culture—running counter to a world exploding around him. Only at moments did his vigor break through. His formal thought did not set a sufficiently labile mold for his great vigor. It leads one to suspect that, but for this, he might have broken through to an astonishing brilliance actually close to him. He must have written essays of secondary importance, since the correlation of his effort was with the effulgence of other places and times whose direct connection with an actual he could not realize. The wrenchings of fate at his elbow, occupation with which would have put him beside the older efforts on a first-rate, if cruder, basis, he avoided or missed by rising superior to them into a world of thought which he believed to be universal only because he couldn't see whence it had arisen. It had a ground, all must, but it was not his, while his remained neglected.

He was a poet, in the making, lost. His spiritual assertions were intended to be basic, but they had not—and they have not today—the authenticity of Emily Dickinson's unrhymes. And she was of the same school, rebelliously.

It is impressive to experience the reflection of the American dearth in culture among women. Talk to her, to begin with, and see the panorama of her desires. Take the one who is tall, alert, and anonymous. They lead her to incompletions.

What is there for her to do outside a pioneer's lot, children, and the sentimentalization of the term "mother"? Loving her and watching her, one sees ghostly figures moving in that curious sexual brilliance. She will listen avidly to the talk of a province, a cultural continent, which men usually think to usurp to themselves. She will love only fully the man who takes her there, where she sees—a life fascinating to her.

They love best where the drink a man offers is of the rarest, and this is the mirror to be used.

But who can blame them for turning to Paris or Britain if they can? Or to someone with at least manners, if only professional manners, Hollywood brand or as it may be. Married, they look, stop, and wish for a paid dance partner. It is one more evidence, though a left-handed one, of the general lack. Is it perhaps a cultural lag in women—or an alertness to the cultural necessity about them by which, for their purposes, they search out the rare men? Mothers wish their sons to be instructed, as fathers that their daughters be beautiful.

On a broker's yacht, as a substitute, drunk in self-defense, what else is there to do but jump overboard?—and be found two days later in the surf—off Coney Island. They have at least experienced what is termed "action," a thorough trial of excitation of a sort. And this may be taken up out of arithmetic into algebra, seldom higher into any very interesting complications. Mostly dullness and the accidents common to all fillgap—the shells and casings to be towed out to sea and dumped.

What have we to offer compared to the effective friendship between Marcel Proust and the Comtesse de Noailles? A few selected suicides.

The ordinary, and I mean extremely ordinary, answer of what would pass for refinement, in the sense that metal is refined out of muck, is inaction with a taste for the draperies of thought. The basis of the impasse is ignored. But without an understanding of the structural difficulties underlying the anticipated pleasure, even poetry might as well be taken in the vulgar sense.

It is seldom realized that what has been borrowed has arisen in a direct necessity, just as the real culture of America must also arise there and that it had a person and a set of circumstances it was made to fit. It fits the new man under other conditions as any borrowed clothes might fit someone of a different weight or complexion from him for whom they were originally intended.

The burning need of a culture is not a choice to be made or not made, voluntarily, any more than it can be satisfied by loans. It has to be where it arises, or everything related to the life there ceases. It isn't a thing: it's an act. If it stands still, it is dead. It is the realization of the qualities of a place in relation to the life which occupies it; embracing everything involved, climate, geographic position, relative size, history, other cultures—as well as the character of its sands, flowers, minerals and the condition of knowledge within its borders. It is the act of lifting these things into an ordered and utilized whole which is culture. It isn't something left over afterward. That is the record only. The act is the thing. It can't be escaped or avoided if life is to go on. It is in the fullest sense that which is fit.

The thing that Americans never seem to see is that French painting, as an example of what is meant, is related to its own definite tradition, in its own environment and general history (which, it is true, we partly share), and which, when they have done with some one moment of it and have moved on to something else, they fatly sell where they can—to us, in short. And that American painting, to be of value, must have comparable relationships in its own tradition, thus *only* to attain classic proportions.

And as for the helpful critics, their cataractous eyes are filled with classic mud.

But you can't quite kill the love of the actual which underlies all American enjoyment. The stage-tricked, waylaid, cheated sucker will yet come to post. When the cheapness of commercial lying is penetrated and something for a moment shows true, grotesque perhaps also, it will always be that which Americans will find amusing: Wintergreen for President; Ben Blue standing indolently and in a storm of wild music making circles in the air with his finger to caricature the violent exertions of Russian dancing. Or as the orchestra plays, to start a fight which ends in the musicians, one and all, smashing their instruments over each other's heads. However, it is the *pathetic* charm of the cowboy which makes him attractive and of use to the movie scenario and the rodeo.

To many writers the great disappointment of the years just after the war was that Amy Lowell, while sensing the enterprise of a reawakened local consciousness, touched it so half-heartedly and did so little to signal plainly the objective. Much could have been accomplished by aid of what seemed to be her great prestige. Pound, defeated at home, did far better, in reverse, from abroad. The best Amy Lowell had to offer was to say, at ease, that the iron of poverty had better be sunk into the generation's hides, and they'd be the better for it, as witness Villon and some others. Very good. But that is no excuse for a failure fully to realize and to state the project and its conditions.

We have an excellent and highly endowed hospital in the metropolis for dogs and an attractive canine cemetery in the suburbs. There are capital yachts and private vessels for transoceanic travel, airplanes, and flying heroes, de luxe cars, princely estates in the West where liberal barbecues are the fashion, and in the East as well, museums, collections and the patronage of swanky Old Masters, horses, racing—Palm Beach and the abandon of an occasional war for profit: even expensive universities for the propagation of something that passes for the arts. But for the rapid pick-up of clear, immediately related thought (as far as the conscious realization of necessary cultural forms shall go), shove the iron into them.

The slow, foot-weary ascent goes on. And this painstaking construction from the ground up, this Alexander's bridge, does *not* imply lack of appreciation for the French by native artists handling their own materials, but on the contrary, the deepest appreciation for them and the marvels they have performed.

Witness again the extraordinary dullness and sloth of the official preceptors as represented, let's say, by the heads of the cultural departments, the English Departments in the lead, in the American universities. The tremendous opportunities under their noses have not attracted them. One would think that the Physics Department alone under the same roof might have given an inkling of the revolutions in theory and practice that had taken place during the last hundred years, the fundamental, immediate nature of the investigations necessary, on the ground, and that this would have started them thinking and into action. Instead, they have continued to mull over the old records, gallivanting back and forth upon the trodden-out tracks of past initiative, in a daze of subserviency and impotence.

Subserviency is the correct term; for the power of wealth, which by endowments makes the university and its faculty possible, at the same time keeps that power, by control of salaries and trustees' votes, in order to dictate what those who teach must and must not say. And the teachers submit to it. And thus the higher is suborned by the lower branch of the cultural split-off, another evidence of how the coercion is applied. The teachers must not venture. Thus they lie, except again in technological branches, the good fortune of those spiritual descendants of Ben Franklin, gelded.

In the same sense, for writers, the official magazines have been a positive plague.

The truly pathetic spectacle of Frank Munsey leaving his money, which he made by capitalizing writers, to the Metropolitan Museum of Art, while the difficulties of a local realization were so patently evident in the difficulty of getting

valuable books published, etc., etc., was a gesture to knock
'em cold. Maybe he had an idea that that was the best way to
dispose of the stuff, the best way to forward indigenous effort—by his contempt for it. In any case, Stieglitz didn't feel
that way—in his sphere. Realizing the fullness and color in
French painting—certainly one of the delights of the modern
world—he went directly to work, a real act of praise, by
striving to push forward something that would be or that
was comparable in America.

Over and over again it must be repeated: none can afford
to ignore, or to forget, or to fail to have seen, at least for the
single glance, the superb wealth of, say, a Morgan collection.
Its illuminated manuscripts alone, dating from the fifth century, must make us humble and raise our aspirations to the
heights. But neither can a region afford not to have lived.
It must be understood, while we are looking, that great art,
in all its significance and implications, in all its direct application to our moment, has used great wealth merely as an instrument, and that the life and vigor of every primary culture
is its real reason for being.

Those who appeared to have or did have the opportunity
to forward a true cultural effectiveness in America have too
often, backed by constituted authority, neglected it—being
content, if anything, to push their personal programs exclusively. While these others who had the vision lacked the
opportunity, through official neglect, to establish the basic
program.

Not Alfred Stieglitz. Using his own art, photography, he
still, by writing, by patronage, by propaganda and unstinted
friendship, carried the fullest load forward. The photographic camera and what it could do were peculiarly well
suited to a place where the immediate and the actual were
under official neglect. Stieglitz inaugurated an era based
solidly on a correct understanding of the cultural relationships; but the difficulties he encountered both from within
and without were colossal. He fought them clear-sightedly.

The effect of his life and work has been to bend together and fuse, against whatever resistance, the split forces of the two necessary cultural groups: (1) the local effort, well understood in defined detail and (2) the forces from the outside.

A 1 Pound Stein

WITH MY KNOWLEDGE and equipment, if someone should make me Professor of American in one of our better universities, I believe that within a month I could push our literature and in consequence our culture ahead at least twenty years. I would begin by expounding the lives and works of Ezra Pound and Gertrude Stein. I would present them as phases of the same thing. This would be amusing as well as instructive since the two detest each other so heartily. But with both at work upon a fundamental regeneration of thought in our language, to which each has added a noteworthy achievement during 1934, a similarity of purpose between them is easily demonstrable.

The presentation on the New York stage of Miss Stein's *Four Saints in Three Acts*, and the appearance of Pound's *Canto XXXVII* in *Poetry: A Magazine of Verse*, constitute a dual event of such importance that were our teaching places of any account whatever to the nation the authorities concerned would declare an immediate holiday in their departments of languages until their students had thoroughly familiarized themselves with the works in question.

The fact that they have not done so is proof of the national lack of culture, not to say our servility and blockheadedness.

To me Virgil Thomson's music is of doubtful aid to Stein's prose. It even shows up the major weakness in it, adding a consecutive interest which is often lacking there. But I'm not speaking of that now.

It's the disinfecting effect of the Stein manner or better said perhaps, its releasing force, that I wish to dwell upon.
162

It's this which gives a listener to the opera his laughs, it's the same thing which fascinates an attentive reader, especially if he knows something about the terrors of writing. The tremendous cultural revolution implied by this interior revolution of technique tickles the very heart and liver of a man, makes him feel good. Good, that is, if he isn't too damned tied to his favorite stupidities. That's why he laughs. His laugh is the first acknowledgment of liberation. He feels clean. He's had a bath. He has been in fact disinfected.

For everything we know and do is tied up with words, with the phrases words make, with the grammar which stultifies, the prose or poetical rhythms which bind us to our pet indolences and medievalisms. To Americans especially, those who no longer speak English, this is especially important. We need too often a burst of air in at the window of our prose. It is absolutely indispensable that we get this before we can even begin to think straight again. It's the words, the words we need to get back to, words washed clean. Until we get the power of thought back through a new minting of the words we are actually sunk. This is a moral question at base, surely but a technical one also and first.

But every time anyone today tries to use a word it's like trying to get a few nails out of an old box to fix something with. You have to smash and pull and straighten—and then what have you got? That's not too good a simile, similes never are. In writing you can never pull out the words from the broken wood. They carry everything over with them. Unless—

Stein has gone systematically to work smashing every connotation that words have ever had, in order to get them back clean. It can't be helped that it's been forgotten what words are made for. It can't be helped that the whole house has to come down. In fact the whole house has to come down. It's been proved over and over again. And it's got to come down because it has to be rebuilt. And it has to be rebuilt by unbound thinking. And unbound thinking has to be done with straight, sharp words. Call them nails to hold together the joints of the new architecture.

When in the middle of the music there is a pause and St. Plan says clearly, "The envelopes have been tied to all the fruit trees," or whatever the devil he does say, you see the trees, you see the envelopes and you don't see anything else.

It's nonsensical? So are you, only you don't know it. You can't know it without clean words. And you haven't any.

I don't care for the effect when the boys and girls stand belly to belly and say, "Thank you very much." That's not Stein, though it's good theatre.

And no man can say, and be able to defend his position, that he doesn't care a whoop in Hades about all this. He can't get away with that. It's the closest, hottest interest he has. It doesn't make any difference whether or not he can sit down to a couple of thousand pages of *The Making of Americans*, any more than it makes any difference whether or not he can read through the pages of the *Congressional Record*. But by God, the results aren't something that he can ignore. If Stein has something, and she has, and if it can be shown that the repellent nature of her page, or the fascination of her page, means a regeneration of the processes of clean thinking and feeling; then it's a man's business to pay attention even when he can't read. And he'd better say, Go to it ol' girl.

The same is true in a different way for the work of Ezra Pound. Literature is right down in among the foundations of the intelligence by its chemistry of words. Difficult to the untrained mind the lines may be. If they're important, and I say they are, the only clue to be got from that is, Learn their significance. It isn't a national matter, as such, any more than "Star Spangled Banner" was of importance to St. Theresa. But just because there is a nation is no reason why works of the intelligence should be systematically excluded from within its confines.

My own feeling is that Stein has all she can do in tackling

the fracture of stupidities bound in our thoughtless phrases, in our calcified grammatical constructions and in the subtle brainlessness of our meter and favorite prose rhythms—which compel words to follow certain others without precision of thought. Thomson's music helps in simulating the next step.

Ezra Pound, in his way, has taken that next step, the step of constructions which are not quite open to Stein. But he is striking, as Stein is, at the basis of thought, at the mechanism with which we make our adjustments to things and to each other. This is the significance of the term culture and an indication of literature's relation thereto.

Pound, in his studious efforts to put us on the track of a released intelligence, a released spirit, a body that can function with what might be health—has dug down into the history of the *mens sana in corpore sano* throughout the ages.

Handball and squash players in the clubs and Y.M.C.A. gyms should take an interest in that. It's at the basis of a good life that the excellence of literature is aimed. You ball-batters don't know what kind of a moral floor you're running around on. If you had any purpose in batting a ball you'd know what excellent writing is about.

And in this latest of Pound's cantos he's come to the administrations of Andrew Jackson and Martin Van Buren. In the history courses at colleges did anyone ever hear of them? Not on your life. They were Presidents of the United States. They had battles on their hands. Oh, is zat so? The same sort of answer they would give to Gert. And if anybody has the itch and doesn't go find out what's causing it we'd call him a damn fool. Well, Jackson fought and won! for awhile, the same kind of fight that's been going on in this country and in every country since the days of the Gracchi, that against the illegal use by private interests of the resources of government. What of it? Nothing, except that it's the *same* fight that's going on today, the same because of the stupidity, the lack of culture, the wordless proneness of the ball-batters, the pseudo-erudite, clever guys, the dumb clucks who haven't enough sense to know what it's all about.

It may be added that both Gertrude Stein and Ezra Pound live in Europe.

Pound's Eleven New "Cantos"

1935

POETRY as daring thought toward a constructive understanding of human destiny—a construction which embodies among its concepts, its words and the form of their composition, the deep and serious aspirations of man, that is, poetry as I understand it, is inherent in these verses.

There is a good deal to say about money in this series, 9 per cent, thousands, millions of cash and the ways of men with it—to the exclusion of love. And love.

That all men are contemporaries, in whatever time they live or have lived, whose minds (including the body and its acts) have lifted them above the sordidness of a grabbing world—would seem to be the general theme of the *Cantos*. Thus, searching among the writings of the American patriots of 1775 and a little later—Adams, Jefferson and some others —Pound has turned up material to add to his list. In most of the new eleven *Cantos* these minds recur, striking sometimes at the imbecility around them, observing, inventing, adding to the impressive monument to intelligence, feeling and imagination which Pound is building against our times.

Usury—the work of double-crossing intellectual bastards in and out of government and the church—rules the world and hides the simple facts from those it torments for a profit. The poet sees, links together and discloses in the symmetry of his work this bastardy of all ages. He gives the names and the manner of that murderous business. And against it one or two men acting here and there—alone.

To the economic philosopher—if possible—today, such a theme is anti-revolutionary. In practice it has never proven

167

so. It is the concentrated essences of power which are explosive, not the nitrates which have been spread in a field. Stirring up a war was one thing but the actual revolution which did take place in America came to effective power first in the minds of a few men.

Then, suddenly, in Canto XXXIX, there is disclosed an unfamiliar magnificence of fornication—the official sin of constituted stupidity. That sex will be accomplished in sin, is the blind behind which venality has worked to undo the world. Kids may go masturbating into asylums but profits must be preserved. But, if the poet has always seen through the absurdity, today he sees more clearly than formerly. Love versus usury, the living hell-stink of today: time-fuses sold in Germany to blow Germans into manure, French cannon to Turkey to blast Frenchmen to scrapple—the Napoleons, the Krupps—Love on a cliff overlooking the sea, an ecstasy.

It is the poet who has digested the mass of impedimenta which the scholar thinks to solve by sinking up to his eyes in it and shouting that he has found it.

It is a God that his rod has generated in her belly. And the little girls may if they wish use their own words to describe what the legal blackguards do foully (exhaustedly) in their beds every night under regulation. Where but in poetry can all things be not only spoken of freely but dwelt upon to the enhancement of the intelligence in possessing the world? Pound has enlarged the scope of poetic opportunity. He has the tact and the daring.

The mind of man is dwarfed by the buggery of professional thought. The understanding thrives on a fornication which bespeaks an escape of the spirit to its own lordly domains. The world is narrowed, penned up, herded to be hog-driven to a very real slaughter pending only the cue to start it at its own throat again—to enrich—whom?

If a nation will master its money.

And those responsible must be named. The *Cantos* should become an Index of the Damned and the Damnable, the anatomized *Inferno* of our lives today.

And so, when a light breaks and penetrates the binding chaos in which we are sweltering—a name such as that of Douglas in England—it is poetry and Pound hails it not from a spirit of partisanship but as it is, a light from heaven.

Technically the present cantos are especially interesting—with reference to the poetic line: what we may expect poetry as it appears on the page to become. There is evident all of Pound's old musical solidity and inventiveness, his verve, a pure lyricism *plus* something else—a new. Valid?

It can at least be said that there is a flatness to most poetic form which needs enlargement in our day. We cannot write well as men wrote well in the past, in all respects, and have what we do hold the modern or the fullest content. Pound has not modified the flavor, the *full* meaning of his colonial matter. That's the first point to notice. He has not "modified" it to fit his preconceived—or any preconceived metrical plan. He has kept his own plan fluid enough to meet his opportunities. He has taken, laudably, the speech of the men he treats of and, by clipping to essentials, revealed its closest nature—its pace, its "meaning." And this is his poetry—in most of these cantos.

The line must be measured to be in measure—but this does not mean disfigurement to fit an imposed meter. It's a matter of technique or the philosophy of poetry. Difficult to find many who will agree about it. With Pound it is in itself a revolution—how difficult to comprehend: unless the term revolution be well understood.

An Incredible Neglect Redefined *

The North American Review, 1936

EXUBERANCE HAS given way to scholarship in this fourth edition of H. L. Mencken's "standard" treatise on the American language. In the preface, marked by a note of self-effacing humility, Mencken himself tells us what has taken place. The whole book has been rewritten, from a changed viewpoint. The ebullient self-assurance of the editions up to the third, that characteristic which seemed to come from the very character of the language itself, is gone. Mencken speaks of himself in the preface as a "lay brother" beside the distinguished philologists with whom he has had to do in this latest and probably last edition of his famous work. To them he gives due credit for much of the encouragement and solid backing which have enabled him to restudy the problems he has had to face anew in such a difficult undertaking.

Our language had no credit with the world until Mencken's time. It was believed, except by a few of the most astute among us, that we still spoke English—though the evidence against such a presumption was historic and overwhelming.

But I do not want to allow myself to be overimpressed by the seriousness of this new sally in defense of our native tongue. It is the subject of the study, the language itself, which surpasses all scholarship, that needs special stressing. And in this I am wondering if the previous edition, the third, had not an advantage over the present one.

Rather than make the book unnecessarily cumbersome cer-

* A review of *The American Language*, by H. L. Mencken, Fourth Edition, corrected, enlarged and rewritten. Alfred A. Knopf: New York, 1936.

tain crudities contained in the earlier editions have been omitted, the text being limited to those parts of the subject of which Mr. Mencken has any knowledge. Too bad it had to be so. The often unsupported surmises, the ill-assorted jumble of some of the matter in the earlier editions had an instinctive justness about them, sometimes, which added zest to the whole. I miss them. They left a jagged edge but so does the American language.

For those who may share this feeling I should strongly advise that the third edition be not completely put aside in favor of the present work. For suppose it be true, which I doubt, that by the very weight of numbers, 125,000,000 people moving more or less as a unit, we drag the English language as spoken in England after us, what of it, anyway? The chief importance to us is American.

What a book! I still say it—in spite of the hankering I feel after the old love with its brashness and Cocky self-assurance. "325,000 words of text running 800 pages, concluding with a full word list and an index. A thoroughly scientific treatise on the development of American-English, it is at the same time an extremely diverting piece of reading, full of odd stuff to be found nowhere else." Very true. "There is no other book on the subject which even remotely approaches the value and scope of this one"—so says the notice on the cover.

The printing is excellent, a clear, open type face, on gloss-less paper slightly off the white. The book opens easily, the pages lying flat in position, either side, when the book is held in the hand.

A wise departure from precedent has been in the present case to do away with the bibliography which occupied a large number of finely printed pages at the end of the third edition and for it to substitute footnotes, "setting up as many guideposts as possible" and have the "references keep step with the text."

But what a piece of genius this is, really! I feel a certain diffidence about attempting to speak of the book at all after no more than the sort of reading I have been able to give it during the last two weeks. Apart from anything else, the scholarship, the reading, the labors in compilation—there is throughout the book a spirit of history, of human aspiration toward self-realization, of love for things of the mind, of color, of people themselves in all their maddening proportions—that has permitted Mencken to maintain among a thousand lists and words and quotations a true style which makes the book a splendid piece of writing. It is something a man has lived with for close to a generation. I feel that I shall go on reading it for the next twenty years.

Certainly a major stroke. Only a person with the effrontery for which Mencken has been known in the years past could have undertaken it and carried it through in the face of the official neglect our language has received at the hands of those who should have known better. Acknowledged abroad, in the previous editions, for the great importance of its subject, it is incredible that the subject being what it is, the incentive being of so urgent a nature—the academic mind in America has not hailed this book with the overwhelming enthusiasm it deserves. It should be required reading in every school and college everywhere among us—especially among those who are condemned to teach us. The very genius of the language itself would seem to demand it. But it's still, as Bill Bullitt would say, not done. Still not done.

The excuse would be, as with Shakespeare in Elizabethan times, that the language is so alive we'd rather, by far, use it than talk about it. Meanwhile, this book, to me one of the most fascinating books in the world.

Beginning with "The Two Streams of English," historically treated from the time of Captain John Smith's "Map of Virginia," 1612, it carries us up through "The Language Today" with all sorts of details, voluminous, deftly linked to support the argument. As in the earlier editions "The Period of Growth" is shown in its character of the unrelenting warfare between England and the United States over a language which had burst the bounds of a narrow world and was spreading helter-skelter over a vast new continent.

To me one of the most important chapters is on "The Pronunciation of American." Here lies the secret, in the monotony of our intonation, of much that we might tell.

But the book is primarily of words, new words, slang, proper names; words having Indian, Spanish, Irish, even Chinese derivations—as if the whole of the words in the world had broken loose from books and come deluging upon us to realize themselves in a new condition, under new circumstances, to form a new language. Which is, with English predominating, exactly what has taken place.

Yet, and in spite of a history of stalwarts, beginning with Noah Webster, who fought for American from the beginning, it is still far more likely that there will be a chair of our language established at Oxford than here. Not a university in America has had the astuteness, the common sense, to reorganize its language departments with American at the head and English and the other languages following.

"Blatant, illogical, elate," "greeting the embarrassed gods" uproariously and matching "with Destiny for beers," our language as well as our people has gone forward getting only such recognition from others as they would render up, we may say, only at the point of the bayonet. But the repercussion on ourselves has been unfortunate—we have become shy in whatever native refinement we possess and not at all sure of ourselves. Mencken's present work should support us ably in a better opinion of ourselves.

It it bred of the bone of the country itself, nurtured from its plains and streams. It is its spittin' self and under that—the rest of it. But we're still a colony as far as our badly tutored minds are concerned. We don't quite dare, do we? to say that we have a language that is our own. Surely, we wouldn't be that vulgar. We might, we just possibly might, come to a realization of ourselves that would blast the very rules of prosody out the window.

We are the most asinine country, in many ways, that the world has ever seen. Out of sheer shyness we have subsidized the world from Vladivostok to Cairo, given billions upon billions in cash, sunk whole navies we had built, not for ourselves, mind you—but for others! our time and thought for mosquito-control work—in Egypt, in the Balkans, yellow fever in Africa and Brazil, our women and their fortunes thrown away to England and France, for nothing, apparently, but shyness. But the worst thing of all is to imagine, as we still do, that we speak English. And be proud of it!

Perhaps H. L. Mencken's new edition of his famous book will help us to adulthood in ways which even he did not imagine would be the case. As my mother once said to me, *Santa Torpesa! ora pro nobis*. St. Stupidity! pray for us.

The Basis of Faith in Art

Not previously published

MY BROTHER, who is an architect, told me recently that his mind had been aflame over the problems of construction to-day more than ever before. Upon what shall we base our judgments? he said to me almost in despair. You are a writer, he said, I'd like to know how you work. What do you find to be of importance? We must both be looking for more or less the same things. Tell me how you go about it.

I just sit down and write.

It must be more conscious than that. You must have some basis for acceptance of a word, a phrase—a general character of composition. I, for instance, after a lifetime of practice, feel that I'm just beginning to sense a few of the underlying movements, call them rules, governing my profession and that all this talk of "old" and "modern" has very little to do with the matter.

That's a large piece of woods, though, to get lost in.

The basis is honesty in construction, that you can do certain things with the material and other things you cannot do. Therein lie all answers.

Yes, if you get it down to a bare hunk of rock, a few tree-length timbers, a bucket of rubble and cement and a bundle of glass. But what are you going to do with them? Isn't that more to the point?

Build a house. A few years ago we began to get first the models and then gradually the local examples of the modernistic small dwelling as originated in France and Germany, the so-called "functional" dwellng. This, we were told, is the future. Everything else is old hat. At last architecture has been freed from its trammels. This is the new.

175

It was intended to be a house though, wasn't it?

Yes, a house; rooms, doors, windows. . . .

Electricity, modern plumbing, refrigeration, autos, twin beds . . . just to emphasize the modern phase.

And very good houses they are too, some of them—by Le Corbusier and the rest. But I always wondered about certain of their structural features, their narrow moldings, etc. Look at them today. They are falling apart. Look. I've been designing a display window for a large manufacturer down South. I've been almost crazy with it. I tried the engineers, the glass makers, everybody, on the proper thickness of the pane, the maximum area and safety factors, the proper anchoring of it. They all say it can't be done. But I've got to do it. Then one day last week, right in the middle of my troubles, I walked out of the office and hadn't gone three blocks when I ran plump into such a window as I had been working on, installed, right in front of me. I couldn't believe my eyes so I went up and put my thumb against the glass and pressed! The whole thing shook as if an earthquake had struck it and almost exploded in my face on the rebound. Such a thing can't stand. It wobbled back and forth even under that slight pressure. That's not architecture.

So we talked along.

On the other hand, he said, look at the new So-and-So building they want to put up in Washington. As if we hadn't had enough stone columns there already, X's idea is to take such and such a perfect example of the Greek—he doesn't even bother to design anything—and tell them to large-scale it in everywhere. I can't do anything better than that, he says, why even try?

The spirit of Phidias, eh?—without Phidias.

Tell me, continued my brother earnestly, what about writing? I'm tremendously interested.

You know how I started to write, I said. I didn't know what I was doing but I knew what I wanted to do.

What, for instance?

I wanted to protest against the blackguardy and beauty of the world, my world.

So you took to poetry.

The only way I could find was poetry—and prose to a lesser extent. So I gradually began to learn, very slowly. If I remember rightly it was more a matter of how I could cling to what I had and not relinquish it in the face of tradition than anything else.

It sounds very simple.

All you have to know is the meaning of the words—and let yourself go.

Then what? What did you learn first?

That it isn't so easy to let yourself go. I had learned too much already, even before I started to write. I ran into good safe stereotype everywhere. Perfectly safe, that's why we cling to it. If I ducked out of that I ran into chaos.

Well?

So I had to begin to invent—or try to invent. Of course I had the advantage of not speaking English. That helped a lot.

And then?

I always knew that I was I, precisely where I stood and that nothing could make me accept anything that had no counterpart in myself by which to recognize it. I always said to myself that I did not speak English, for one thing, and that that should be the basis for a beginning, that I spoke a language that was my own and that I would govern it according to my necessities and not according to unrelated traditions the necessity for whose being had long since passed away. English is full of such compunctions which are wholly irrelevant for a man living as I am today but custom makes it profitable for us to be bound by them. Not me.

I can't tell you anything offhand. I made up my mind that everything must come out of someone and relate to him, first and last. And it had to be for all, whether they liked it or not. *You* ought to know. Houses are to live in, that's one of the finest things about achitecture. You build houses, for people. Poems are the same.

Yes, I know, he said. But I'm sick of this "back to humanity, back to the soil" business. You grow spinach in the soil, you don't grow writing there and certainly it doesn't sprout little new buildings ready-made. Neither does humanity. Architecture is an art and writing is an art also, mossy with tradition.

Who said anything else? What I said was that I go back to people. They are the origin of every bit of life that can possibly inhabit any structure, house, poem or novel of conceivable human interest. It doesn't precisely come out of the tops of their heads like flowers but they represent, in themselves, the structure which art . . . Put it this way: If we don't cling to the warmth which breathes into a house or a poem alike from human need——

The stink, you mean.

——the whole matter has nothing to hold it together and becomes structurally weak so that it falls to pieces.

Possibly but I don't follow you.

Maybe I don't follow myself, it's always a possibility. You began by telling me about a craftsmanlike integrity to one's materials. No lying. But that's no incentive to either build or write—no safe incentive, that is. It would apply just as well if you hung a house from a pole like a bird cage.

It's been done only he put the pole up the center of it. Because of earthquakes.

There you are! Just what I said. I mean you build a house for people, don't you? Then the needs of . . . I mean, the minute you let yourself be carried away by purely "architectural" or "literary" reasoning without consulting the thing from which it grew, you've cut the life-giving artery and nothing ensues but rot.

What we seem to be getting to is that all the arts have to come back to something.

And that that thing is human need. When our manner of

action becomes imbecilic we breed Dada, Gertrude Stein, surrealism. These things seem unrelated to any sort of sense UNTIL we look for the NEED of human beings. Examining that we find that these apparently irrelevant movements of art represent mind saving, even at moments of genius, soul saving, continents of security for the pestered and bedeviled spirit of man, bedeviled by the deadly, lying repetitiousness of doctrinaire formula worship which is the standard work of the day. In my young days it was "English." In your young days it was "Greece," "Rome." But the mind is merely enslaved by these ideals, these ideas, unless we can relate them, here, now, in our environment, to ourselves and our day. This requires invention. . . .

Wait a minute! Wait a minute! You forget you are a writer, I am an architect. You are working with words. I am working with building materials. We have to have rules which shall govern us. I grant you that we have to have universal rules—that will work today just as they worked to produce the marvels of antiquity—but they're rules just the same.

As far as I'm concerned I don't think they're any different from human character in service to the inauguration.

You mean that art should be useful?

Stuck your foot out that time, didn't you? But I didn't trip. Yes, useful. They try to deny it. There's an arrogance in art that likes to set itself up against the world. Don't let it fool you. We know we're rather a small band of gypsies. Some still think we had better be driven out of the towns as the medieval lepers were. But don't forget that in a scientific era like the one now passing, the artist's protest that his art is wholly nonutilitarian has a certain amount of truth in it. It's a wonderful picture of us all. The uselessness of it might constitute its principal use, sometimes. Anger, disgust, defiance to a sordid, scurrilous world drive a man to . . .

Whoa, boy. What I want is cold explanation.

But I insist, yes, that the purpose of art IS to be useful.

Why does a poet write as he does? It may be defiance but it is defiance because he sees something worth having. He must shake himself free, he himself as one man, from the destroying horror of an oppressive existence, but if he write it can only be in the hope that he may gather to himself others with whom he would like to see the world better populated.

But good people are repelled by such an artist's efforts.

Don't let's talk about good people.

But I mean it.

Well, perhaps. All right, good people. A man writes as he does because he doesn't know any better way to do it, to represent exactly what he has to say CLEAN of the destroying, falsifying, besmutching agencies with which he is surrounded. Everything he does is an explanation. He is always trying his very best to refine his work until it is nothing else but "useful knowledge." I say everything, every minutest thing that is part of a work of art is good only when it is useful and that any other explanation of the "work" would be less useful than the work itself. Don't worry, the artist will die and his work be explained later. Then other times will require new artists.

You talk as if art should be a department of government— like public health, etc.

Poetry is a rival government always in opposition to its cruder replicas.

Be that as it may, it seems to me that we have wandered. I'm looking for aid in architectural construction from you, a poet. I am working with building materials. You are working with words. But there should be rules which will guide us, rules which may be interchangeable among all the arts.

I think right here we'd better recognize the difference between architecture and poetry. A poet has a less material tenant for his domicile than does an architect——

Not if you include cathedrals——

Anyhow houses do have to be lived in physically. That makes a big practical difference. But wait a minute, maybe I am the one who should be learning, from you. A man comes to you and wants a house. What happens? Some will belie their materials and do anything the client asks. But you're an architect, what would you do?

I wouldn't sell out, I'd rather lose the commission—and do lose them very often for that reason—rather than lie.

I know. But what would you "do," you, yourself, while the man is still in the act of making his proposal to you? You'd start on the house, in your mind, I mean, constructing it, as it must be FOR CERTAIN REASONS. Isn't that right?

Yes, of course.

Nine cases out of ten you'd have the thing up there inside your head within the first ten minutes.

That's right.

Then so far it's just like a poem. After that, hungry for work, you'd look at the man, inwardly, and size him up as to just what he amounted to in your mind, architecturally speaking.

Yes.

After that you'd go to work on him to get what YOU wanted. Isn't that right?

That's right. I would—with my heart in my mouth.

What else does a poet do? And how can I tell you anything about it? It isn't only the tensile strength of the materials. It isn't just "honesty." It isn't standard lengths and all that. It's everything in the world today. First it's human character that decides. Your character, the quality of your client. The only difference with poetry is that the poet builds for an everybody, any person, while you build for everyone in one person. All the modern necessities, the social needs, the falsification of thought, the constrictions of vile habit. The architect is a rebel just as I am. He should be a philosopher, a sociologist, he must have read Thorstein Veblen. He must know human habits, eccentricities. But above all he must know how to put it over.

Fine! But what "art" means to most seems to be the art of deceit. If they flatter a client and give him what he wants they feel that they don't give up their franchise as an artist. On the contrary, they're doing something human, they're employing their hard-earned structural skill to bring into effect the bare demands he makes of them——

The commercial artist, so-called.

Some are pretty good, too.

Why not? *provided,* they can adapt the client's needs to *their* own necessities. This applies also to propaganda.

I'd solve the problem architecturally till hell freezes over —or not at all.

That's why you're a poor man—and my brother!

And the idea that the government can tell me . . .

Whoa, boy! Now it's your turn to take it easy.

I'd discover a material that would be honestly suited to the structure or change the structure to suit the material that I had.

Not enough. Not enough. Nobody gives a whoop in hell for such a viewpoint.

Nobody but an engineer who has a bridge to build maybe, or an astronomer who has no bridge to build.

True, but it still isn't enough.

They don't lie. Everybody else does.

Why should they lie, nobody expects it of them.

Do they expect *you* to lie, as a poet?

And how! You gotta write propaganda today. You know, yuh gotta "help humanity"——

Now, it seems to me, you're the one that's going in the other direction.

Think so?

Well, aren't you ridiculing the tough-guy party man and his intellectual henchmen? They're the ones who are trying to take you writers over for their own purposes and make liars of you, as you say. What about it?

You know, you've made me think. Propaganda is like a house an architect has to build for people to live in. Maybe your client is a damn fool, maybe he isn't. You've got to argue with him—broadly speaking. That broadens the whole matter, doesn't it? Only we're so damned beset with hangovers and dragbacks. They've got to live in them, the houses, poems, we make—but they don't even know they're houses. Their needs govern it but in such a complex manner that it flies out of the mind and nobody knows what it is about. But we've got to come back to it, from both sides. The poet has to serve and the reader has to—be met and won—without compromise.

But how?

Who's going to decide—as it touches the poet, I mean. That's what we're really up against. They want to kill him, if he's good enough. To laugh at him at the very least, in his time. It's a sign of his excellence in most cases. Then, it's not the people who can decide. Never. It's still got to be the artist, himself.

I see what you mean. What do they make of—Poe, or Whitman, for instance, even today, to say nothing of Stein, eh?

Yes, a man like Poe.

Do you mean Poe was a "necessity"——

Amazingly so.

Well, what then?

If the party man sees a writer whom he thinks he can use, wouldn't he be a fool if he didn't try to corral him and use him? Let him go ahead. All I say is, the artist is a pitiful liar if he allows himself to be used that way. As an artist I'm for the party man, maybe, but as an artist I know how I can work most effectively. And if he doesn't use me, as material, for the things I am best able to perform, my best as an artist, then he's a jackass of a party man and doesn't know his own business. He can take advantage of me temporarily and discredit me momentarily, perhaps, but he cannot destroy my work for *him* unless he succeeds in destroying my integrity as an artist toward my own work. And that he shall never do.

I know what they think. They think that, like Jesuits, the

end justifies the means. They think that *until* something is accomplished it is more economical to join solidly on a single front, skilled and unskilled alike——

By what authority?

Humanity.

Take sides and fight!

You mean try to get a job with one of the official housing corporations?

Boy! Oh boy! the housing problem isn't going to be solved by any of the bureaus but by some bright boy steeped in the best there is in architecture. He'll find it and nobody else will.

Sure, if he goes back to humanity far enough.

He'll find it architecturally, not any other way; without the aid of their damned wasteful propaganda. The answers don't come that way, they come to someone, some ONE, working by the means of his art—alone—in some relative attic somewhere. And that's the only way they'll ever come and ever can come.

Hot stuff! We'll get together yet. What faith is there left to humanity anyway other than its faith in art?

Without faith in humanity, anyhow, there's no faith in art. Put it either way, it amounts to the same thing.

2

Very well, let humanity be your ground, an arterial continuity. . . .

No, no! People, this person and that person, human beings, the ones that get killed by the bombs and ride across the United States on bicycles.

I notice you're not too anxious to be classed among them. You still want to maintain your independence as an artist. You don't want to be told what to do.

On the contrary, I am always looking for someone to tell me what to do.

But you wish to maintain the government. Yet from the people, you say, the artist derives all that he is. Aren't these two viewpoints mutually contradictory? I think they are and I think you're not half the people's man you think you are. I don't think the people in general have a thing to do with the artist or with you.

Continue.

Warmth, yes. That's all right. But what of aspirations? Do you mean to tell me that they arise from the people? No sir. What of dreams? Where are they to come from? Their origin is not in the people but in you. You betray yourself when you reserve to yourself what you call the artist's prerogative to decide. You may be rooted in the people but your aspirations . . .

Come from them also.

Your aspirations are antagonistic to the people's wishes and come from you alone. But you do not believe in the soul.

Why not?

Because you say as much.

I don't say anything.

You believe everything is here and now.

Isn't it?—if it expects to be tomorrow?

In you.

In them. From them to me.

From them?

How?

That's a fair question. Through the independence of the artist.

The unpredictable artist! The people's slave! Go on.

You know, of course, what the usual answer is. Peasants hung from crossbars of telegraph poles in Mexico and Lorca shot by a Fascist firing squad in Granada, his Granada!

What's the connection?

You want me to define the connection between the poet and the mob.

And to show how his aspirations arise from them. Not *for* them, mind you, but from them. I haven't forgotten what we started with. Architecture.

He must maintain his independence——

Which amounts to a divorce from society.

—in order to be able to perceive their needs and to act upon the imperative necessities of his perceptions.

Independent and dependent! you make me laugh.

Independent of opinion, dependent of body. The artist had better be a poor man.

A sort of sleuth, eh? who goes smelling about to unearth social requirements.

Ridiculous, eh?

Absurd. Shouldn't we rather say a rudderless nonentity furiously laboring at random whims, from among whose works, with time, a public takes the initiative to select its equally haphazard choices?

Quite.

Then whose is the government?

The one who most needs.

This is nothing but confusion. Disturbing to good sense.

You wouldn't want to jail me or possibly shoot me for it?

It's an idea.

But an old one. It has never worked—for long.

Antisocial, in spite of all your protestations.

We're attempting to track down the origins of a poet's aspirations, what might be called his soul, his longings toward that as yet imaginative new province to which we shall come —tomorrow! That's where our souls are always living.

Let's stick to facts.

Do you know what they are today, our souls?

No.

Ourselves. That's fact enough, isn't it?

Let's say, ourselves. There are qualities in us thoroughly disassociated from social origins, lonely and forbidding to the mass. The iciness of virtue, the uncompromising recognition of good and evil, heroic self-denial and the tragedy of un-equivocal loss.

Only he is lost who has been cut off from his fellows.

The way you talk nothing is either bad or good so long as the mob sanctions it. Get what you want. Have your cake and eat it at the same time. That's the mob. What principles are there in that——?

As a matter of fact, it's absolutely unprincipled.

Well, what then?

What? Why it's the truth and the truth can't be ignored.

But it's wrong. If you are unprincipled you are evil. You know perfectly well what is bad and what is good. Do you believe in your marriage vows?

Not much.

But you pretend that you're married.

I am married.

But you have no faith in it.

Perfect faith. It's a rock to me.

A rock you say!

That I use sometimes to fling at the birds.

You'll lose it some day.

I always find it again.

No fault of your own.

On the contrary, that which is used is saved—often by dint of considerable effort. But I don't believe in vows.

Then you're just a liar, an evil thing floating about on any breeze that blows.

It had better blow me where I intend to go. If not, I'll go against it anyhow. It's a matter of principle.

A disorderly mind, all you do merely hides for a few years the basic faithlessness of your life. If understanding catches up with you on this track you quickly switch to another. Then when you hear the bloodhounds baying you jump into the water—being sure it is shallow enough!—and run for miles. But you will not be able to throw posterity off your track forever. You will be caught in the end and your work will be found to be empty—without the basis of faith.

That I don't believe. But you mentioned something about order—you said I had a disorderly mind. If to have a mind in which order is broken down to be redistributed, then you are right, not otherwise. I was early in life sick to my very pit with order that cuts off the crab's feelers to make it fit into the box. You remember how Taine left Keats out of his criticism of English literature because to include him would spoil the continuity of his argument? And you recall how, failing to discover the thread of its order, Z. moved from the rigors of a harsh sequence to become part of an order easier of access, an established order to which the access had been made easier by a well-trodden path. But order is in its vigor the process of ordering—a function of the imagination——

But principles . . .

What principles?

Hardihood, honesty, devotion . . .

Those are the nicknames for penury. You asked me about marriage and its vows. Let me ask you, Have vows ever made a marriage?

There is no marriage without them.

But marriages may languish even when the vows are not broken, may they not?

Yes, I suppose so.

Did it ever occur to you that a marriage might be invigorated by deliberately breaking the vows.

That is impossible.

Nothing is impossible to the imagination.

I'm not talking about the imagination but—the basis of faith in art. And I said that without principles . . .

No, you began by objecting to my attachment to people and asked the source of aspiration. You see how confused and foolish we have become. If one were versed in philosophy, eh? How orderly might be one's progress, none of the heat of mere human combat, prejudice . . . How can a man make any progress in his life without philosophy? And yet, one must. But even a peasant may sing and in Spain they, anonymously, indite *coplas* to the expansive mind in all sorts of colors. So that, not having philosophy, nor even a shadow of it, some sort of order still emerges——

What are you getting at?

In the world we are confused, embittered, we lose our sense of order and are likely to cling to death because we fear the apparent disorderliness of our lives. We have no faith so we accuse everyone else of breaking his vows. This is pitiful but who is free either from the sins of commission, of lying or envy? Why, envy is the very backbone of conformity. But there remains the province of art.

I know what's coming. You're going to canonize the artist.

You're mistaken, I detest him. I admire your Savonarolas and Calvins. But I disagree with them. I always agree with the blackguardly artist. Why? Because he lives in a world of the imagination where there is nothing but truth and beauty. It is there, in that Olympus, that all our destinies are solved. It is for that alone that we go to our deaths. In that country nothing detracts a man from following his bent, honestly. He may fail to follow it if he remain too ardently attached to the accidents of the world but up there one flies at enormous speed.

Aren't you getting a little bit off the subject?

Certainly, for there are no name places there. There isn't any language either. But if an obstruction is placed between it and the artist in his function of interpreter a blockade results.

But what about people and blood and all that?

They are attractive to the imagination because of their helpless part in it.

As much to destroy them as to build them into *political* schemes?

History supports you, both things have happened, again and again.

You see there are no principles in matters of the imagination.

No principles save the rediscovery in people of the elements of order.

Rot.

What do you mean rot?

You haven't answered a single one of my questions. Order? Discipline? What possible sense of order can you have when you go on this way?

What way?

Every time I ask you something you sidestep it.

That's an exaggeration.

You run away from it as if it were the devil.

It is the devil.

You're childish.

What do you want me to do, split hairs with you over some asinine pseudo-philosophic imbecility? That would be childish. You ask me about the qualities of the mind and I've told you, the imagination! I'm a man. You can't drag me around by a philosophic beard. I won't have it. I'll cut your damned arm off before I let you try it.

Blah, blah, blah . . .

That's right. Use your imagination.

Now it's order! That too arises from the people, I suppose——

You don't mean you think you can impose it on them, do you?

So everything is from them, aspiration, order——?

From them.

Pitiful. They don't either want or need such things. There's your caviar and bread again. Granted they need bread, shelter and amusement—a cheap car. Sure they want what you have if you happen to have more than they. Listen, in 1929 a Polish miner went into a large store in Scranton. He asked to see some fur coats, he wanted one for his wife. All right, Joe, said the man and steered him to a good quality cheaper coat. Is him best you got? said the miner. What about him over there? What kind of coat that? You don't want that coat, Joe, said the salesman, that's our finest coat. Too expensive. What you call that kind fur? asked the miner. Mink. How much? Fifteen hundred dollars. All right I take him. Wrap him up. Here two hundred dollar. My wife stay here. I go get more money. He came back with the money and paid cash.

He got what he wanted.

Just a damn fool. A year later a friend of mine who told me the story was around to his house and happened to see a bedraggled looking fur coat hanging behind the door in the kitchen. Is that the swell coat you bought for your wife last year, Joe? Sure, that's him. My God, Joe! said my friend, she sure did go through it. Well, what you expect, said Joe, when she wear him to wash and scrub floors, got to get dirty. That's all right. I buy her another coat some time.

What do you deduce from that?

They don't need what you have to give. All this hue and cry about housing and slum clearance. Nine-tenths of it is bunkum. They live in the slums because they like to live in the slums. They don't want to be sick, no, and they don't want to be cold but they haven't the discipline to avoid the things that make them so, they haven't the restraints which you live by and they don't want them. They are different in nature from you and me.

You don't have to tell me how maddening they can be.

They are unfit to live in decent houses. Look what they do to a park, to a whole countryside if you don't put fences up against them. Go to Coney Island if you want to see what they really enjoy. Put them in a clean domicile and in a week it will be a pigsty. They befoul everything. And misuse it. They rip out the plumbing, they steal the electric fixtures, everything that is movable is ripped out, electric bulbs, even tiling from the bathroom walls. They'd steal the eye out of a needle if they could do it. And others of their kind make a business of receiving and selling such stolen goods. You can't change such creatures. They aren't fit to waste our qualities upon. What source for poetry, art of any sort is there in such beasts?

Among them are a few who are not like that.

Yes, of course, the few! Exactly what I am saying: a few rare spirits. But not the mob. All the mob wishes to do is to kill and destroy you because you have ideals which they cannot touch and do not, positively do not, need. I see no reason for dragging the world down to their level from a mistaken sense of pity. Take them out and kill them, that's what I'd do. The world would be better for decent people.

War, huh?

And don't talk to me about education.

No, I won't talk to you about education. We're talking about ourselves and what makes us go, now and here. You know, the matter of better housing is very instructive. Why do we do it?

To get votes.

Architecturally, I mean and poetically. What aspiration makes us want to—How does aspiration arise for our highest achievements in architecture and poetry from humanity—at its worst.

That's what I'm asking you. Why not just fling them a bone?

If you have a bone, why not?

But in an artist what inspiration is there, in humanity in the mass, for those intricacies, refinements, difficulties of your art? What is there in them that stirs you to invention, to the decisions which make you, as it might happen, great? You can't tell me that there is any *need* in the ordinary man for these superb movements of the mind—Why they laugh at you for such things. The need of that is only for the rare spirit which knows——

The appreciation but not the need. It is bread and not caviar. The need is always there.

How? Why is the crowd important to you—at your highest moment of activity.

In an artist it must come from a sense of totality; the whole; humanity as a whole. How can a man be satisfied when he sees another man lacking——

But he doesn't lack if he doesn't need a thing or want it.

He doesn't know he lacks and needs it but *I* know he needs it. I know what he needs better than he and I cannot ignore it.

That is pure arrogance.

That is the source of aspiration, a need which the poet sees and devotes his small life to find and to delineate. You know, He watches the sparrow fall. Everything happens within everything else. There can be no satisfaction to the poet otherwise. What can he be without the mob?

"There is no conflict between the individual and society—unless the individual offend. None but a fool contends that the function of society is to generate surpassing individuals. That is antiquated reasoning. The truth is nearer and harder, merely that society, *to be served*, must generate individuals to serve it, and cannot do otherwise than to give such individuals full play—*until* or unless their activities prove antisocial.

"Society must and will and has always helped its servants to retire at the proper moment—whether it be the defeated general, the discredited statesman, the woman who has lost her beauty or the diseased mind. Heartlessly society discards them, and rightly so—but heaven help the society that fails to discard the heel, the sycophant liar who serves it only to flatter command—and yet does away with the useful dissenter.

"That a wealthy and corrupt society indulges, conceivably, in the purchase of costly art works at the expense of the starving poor has no relation to the aspirations, accomplishments or the importance of the artist himself.

"No matter what happens to his works, the artist is the truthfulest scribe of society that is found when he is left free. And if his works are purchased by corrupt or tyrannical fools or institutions, nevertheless, in those very works of art are likely to lie the disruptive seeds which will destroy the very hosts who have taken them in—and preserved them for society even against their will.

"The artist's success as an individual is to be judged in the end not by the purchasers of his work but inexorably *by society*—by society as a whole, the great being great only as society accepts and enthrones them. For what are men to do with themselves once they have been fed? The artist must be their preceptor.

"It is essential to good government that the poet, as an individual, remain at liberty to possess his talent, answerable to no one *before the act* but to his own conception of truth.

"On the other hand he *is* answerable to society for his survival and he knows it, has no other returns for what he does and is governed thus not indirectly by a political agency before the act but *directly* by society itself after the act. In this men differ from bees and ants since with man society must wait upon the individual and not the other way around. Therefore, Man.

"Who shall tell him how or what he must write? His very function as a servant of society presupposes his ability to see clearly beyond the formulations of his day and to crystallize his findings in a durable form for social confirmation, that society may be built more praiseworthily.

"He will be the critic of government whether the party in power like it or not.

"The process is ancient and dynamic—that is to say, constantly operative under all conditions. All the best has been maintained in spite of government as a limiting power. Not against government, *not* against government but against usurpation of government by a class, a group, a set of any sort, king, bureaucracy or sans-culotte—which would subvert the freedom of the individual for some temporary need.

"The artist, an individual, a worker, the type of a person who is creative, who has something to give to society must admit all classes of subject to his attention—even though he hang for it. This is his work. Nothing poetic in the feudal, aristocratic sense but a breaking down, rather of those imposed tyrannies over his verse forms. Technical matters, certainly, but most important to an understanding of the poet as a social regenerator. The facts are enclosed in his verses like a fly in amber."

That's a long quotation. Where did you get it?

I wrote it myself but for another purpose.

I can't say I've been much enlightened. What, in a word, would you say was the gist of the things you've been talking about? Couldn't you sum the matter up for me in a sentence or two? I thought perhaps you might be able to give me a little help in facing my particular problems as an architect— and an artist. Who, in a word, will be the best designer?

He with the most profound insight into the lives of the people and the widest imaginative skill in its technical interpretation—or any part thereof.

1937(?)

Against the Weather

A Study of the Artist

Twice a Year, 1939

WHAT SHOULD THE artist be today? What must he be? What can he do? To what purpose? What does he effect? How does he function? What enters into it? The economic, the sociological: how is he affected? How does his being a man or a woman, one of a certain race, an American enter into it?

If there were more air smelling of the crispness, the chill, the faint flowerless odor of ice and sunlight that reigns here, March 9, 1938, in the neighborhood of New York City today —I could do, and under like circumstances could always have done, any imaginable thing that might unreasonably be or has been expected of a man. But all days are not like today nor is my mind of a consequence always so moved. Quite the contrary.

I've been writing a sentence, with all the art I can muster. Here it is: A work of art is important only as evidence, in its structure, of a new world which it has been created to affirm.

Let me explain.

A life that is here and now is timeless. That is the universal I am seeking: to embody that in a work of art, a new world that is always "real."

All things otherwise grow old and rot. By long experience the only thing that remains unchanged and unchangeable is the work of art. It is because of the element of timelessness in it, its sensuality. The only world that exists is the world of the senses. The world of the artist.

That is the artist's work. He might well be working at it

during a bombardment, for the bombardment will stop. After a while they will run out of bombs. Then they will need something to fall back on: today. Only the artist can invent it. Without today everything would be lost and they would have to start bombing again as they always do, to hide the lack. If the artist can finish before the attack is over it will be lucky. He is the most important artisan they have.

The work an artist has to do is the most important creation of civilization. It is also its creator.

It is a world of men.

It is not an "essence," a philosophic or physiochemical derivative I am seeking but a sensual "reality." Though it *might* be war, it had better be a work of art.

The artist is to be understood not as occupying some outlying section of the field of action but the whole field, at a different level howbeit from that possessed by grosser modes. The artist is to be conceived as a universal man of action—restricted by circumstances to a field in which only he can remain alive, whole and effective. He is the most effective of all men, by test of time, in proving himself able to resist circumstances and bring the load through. Dig up his carvings in the center of the Sahara Desert, where there was once a lake and forests, his effectiveness remains intact.

He differs from the philosopher in point of action. He is the whole man, not the breaker up but the compactor. He does not translate the sensuality of his materials into symbols but deals with them directly. By this he belongs to his world and time, sensually, realistically. His work might and finally must be expanded—holds the power of expansion at any time—into new conceptions of government. It is not the passive "to be" but the active "I am."

Being an artist I can produce, if I am able, universals of general applicability. If I succeed in keeping myself objective enough, sensual enough, I can produce the factors, the concretions of materials by which others shall understand and so be led to use—that they may the better see, touch, taste, enjoy—their own world *differing as it may* from mine. By mine, they, different, can be discovered to be the same as I, and, thrown into contrast, will see the implications of a general enjoyment through me.

That—all my life I have striven to emphasize it—is what is meant by the universality of the local. From me where I stand to them where they stand in their here and now—where I cannot be—I do in spite of that arrive! through their work which complements my own, each sensually local.

This is the generosity also of art. It closes up the ranks of understanding. It shows the world at one with itself. And it solves, it is the solvent—or it can be—of old antagonisms. It is theoretical, as opposed to philosophy, most theoretical when it is most down on the ground, most sensual, most real. Picking out a flower or a bird in detail that becomes an abstract term of enlightenment.

This paper is full of electricity, I can hardly pick it up or lay it down.

Another characteristic of all art is its compactness. It is not, at its best, the mirror—which is far too ready a symbol. It is the life—but transmuted to another tighter form.

The compactness implies restriction but does not mean loss of parts; it means compact, restricted to essentials. Neither does it mean the extraction of a philosophic essence. The essence remains in the parts proper to life, in all their sensual reality.

The grossly active agent of the moment, possessing the government, less whole than the artist, usually a party—that is to say partial or a part—tries to break the artist from his complete position to make him serve an incomplete function. And the *way* they attack him in order to make him serve their purpose is to accuse him of being inactive or reserved to the aesthetic. To which he can have only one answer which is to be active, to practice his unnicked art. For this they will kill him proving his point—and if they have not been successful in destroying all he has done, which is unlikely, he will end by destroying them.

The extreme example of the principle of sabotage as practiced by parties upon the arts was the destruction of the library at Alexandria. So valuable was the work of the artist there that to this day we unglue the backs of old books and even pick apart the lids of sarcophagi in order to find perhaps one line of Sappho.

What does the artist do? And what has the world of varying events to do with what he does? He attacks, constantly toward a full possession of life by himself as a man. Those who possess the world will have it their way but in the conceit of the artist, generous enough, the actual and necessary government occupies only an incomplete segment of that which is just, in the full sense, and possible.

The artist is, by that, called very often a revolutionist and is threatened, as it may be Shakespeare was threatened by the Protestant power, which he had to please being himself a Papist. At the same time *he wrote plays*. And if, in *The Tempest*, he approached the ideology of his bringing up, during his full intervening years *he still wrote plays*. That is the artist, the man of action, as laid against the man of ideas.

Imagine a world without the effects of art. Take it ten years before Shakespeare wrote a play or Dante placed on paper his *Divina Commedia*. Such a world might well be and was in either case governed by laws, but what should be the general applicability of them if it had not been for works of art existing earlier? Without conceptions of art the world might well be and has usually been a shambles of groups lawful enough but bent upon nothing else than mutual destruction. This comes of their partiality. They lack that which must draw them together—without destruction of their particular characteristics; the thing that will draw them together because in their disparateness it discovers an identity. Nowhere will this be found save in the sensual, the real, world of the arts.

Every masterwork liberates while it draws the world closer in mutual understanding and tolerance. This is its aroma of the whole. For these are the pure characteristics, in tremendous concentration, of the work itself, made, demonstrated, as imitated in the laboratory, in which we believe so much today, by the trivial artist. It is the cement of the sensual world. Or even less destructible, it is more the cementless joining itself of the parts, as in the examples of Inca masonry.

As the world is unimaginable without the effects of art— that is to say without art there would be no Chartres, no Parthenon, no *Oedipus Rex*, no pyramids, *Matthew's Passion*, *Divina Commedia*, *Quixote* or *Lear*—which make it one, so a man walks the streets but he is none without the agency of the artist. He may be a "soul" or a "citizen," a "member of the party," an example of certain philosophic concepts in operation or one of the genus *Homo sapiens* but a MAN— lacking art—never! Only that preserves him in his full sensuality, the man himself.

And today, after the same fashion, he is everything imaginable. There are a hundred names and might just as well be five hundred or a thousand—and the reasons one way or the other are often logical (Why not?), cogent, inevitable and overwhelming. But it has an effect, this positivity. It blinds! It deafens, confuses and destroys. Catholic or Protestant can never be more than half a man in the eyes of the artist—each in himself "perfect." A man, to be, emerges through them into a region common to both. He knows them by what they *do*—in relation to each other—to make up the whole.

2

These are some conditions an artist must face and react to: There are two great Spanish epics that illustrate this life of man preserved in the arts. They will serve as examples. Both the *Poema del Cid* and the *Book of Love* are distinguished and live by what is called the "ethical detachment" of the poet exhibited there. He, the poet, saw a specific action, he experienced and he recorded, as a man of sense, directly after the deed without preconception.

The poet saw a sword flash! It lit the field. He did not see

a CASTILIAN sword flash or a MOORISH sword flash. He
saw a SWORD flash. The effect of that flashing did not immediately concern either Spain or Arabia, it concerned a man.
The sword rose or it fell and the work was done or missed.
The poet recorded it with a power that took it out of the
partial, a power which derived from his passion as an artist
to know, in full. This is good.

With the author of the *Libro de Buen Amor*, the fat archpriest of Hita the same. His work was not war but love, love
of God and love of women—almost indistinguishable to the
poet though he made ample gestures both ways. But the *poem*
was the thing—this was his good—as he confesses very
clearly. He came, this amorous archpriest, of a time when
Moslem, Christian and Jew mingled, as it has been said, in
one great fraternity of mirth and pleasure, whatever ends
each otherwise was also seeking. They mingled without prejudice, a resemblance to the conditions of art. They mingled
and *El Libro de Buen Amor* took it up and lives.

A more complex example than the *Book of Love*, Dante's
Divina Commedia throws into even greater relief this com-
pelling force which takes possession of a man and causes him
to act in a certain manner producing works of art—its conditions and significances. In the *Book of Love*, untouched by
morals, the artist's impulse carries the day unopposed. But
the *Divina Commedia* presents three facts, the moral, that of
formal religion and that other whose character, in itself, I
wish to define. The comment of the artist illuminates the
other two—a good place to witness it at work. Dante upon
Dante.

Full stop.

Nothing is under consideration but the artist's concern in
these things, enlightenment upon the artist's significance. And
the reason for going into such seemingly remote matters (as
the poetry of Dante) in the search for present-day solutions
is the question of origins. As writers we shall find in writing
our most telling answers and as writers it is we who should

uncover them. That is our business. If, as writers, we are
stuck somewhere, along with others, we must go back to the
place, if we can, where a blockage may have occurred. We
must go back in established writing, as far as necessary,
searching out the elements that occur there. We must go to
the bottom.

If we suspect that, in past writing, archaic forms give the
significance a false cast we are under an obligation to go back
to that place where the falsity clings and whence it works.
We must unravel it to the last shred; nothing is more important, nothing must stand in the way and no time that is taken
to it could be better spent. We have to dig. For by repeating
an early misconception it gains acceptance and may be found
running through many, or even all, later work. It has to be
rooted out at the site of its first occurrence.

We know that what we are seeking, as writing, lies in the
form or in the substance or both, of what is before us. It lies
there undeciphered but active, malevolent it may be, and
from it steam up the forces which are obstructing the light.
Furthermore it is quite likely to be defended under the title
of "beauty."

It is distinctly important that in the face of "beauty" we
go in and expose the lesion. Nothing could be more timely.
If we do not take the time for it but think to press on to more
advanced matters we leave a basis for destruction in our rear.
While we are using the old forms we unwittingly do ourselves a damage if they carry over within them that which
undermines our own enlightened effectiveness.

The first and obvious contrast between the *Book of Love*
and the *Commedia* is the scrupulous order maintained
throughout the latter both in content and structure as against
the carefree disorder of the Spanish work. One is closely
clipt within ascertained bounds while the other runs away,
going along from point to point, like a child picking flowers
under a hedge.

This is very bad, this looseness, according to one of the major tenets of art, conscious restriction to prescribed form, and very good according to another—unconfined acceptance of experience. Close order makes for penetration. Looseness is likely to prove weakness, having little impact upon the mind. But it is wise, always, to beware of that sort of order which cuts away too much.

The *Divina Commedia* has since the twelfth century exerted a lasting influence on Western poetry. What sort of influence? Good or bad? Which of the characters it presents has been the most influential? What of it relates to the art and how much masks under the colors of art and to other effect?

This begins to give an inkling of what, to the artist, is meant, as Rembrandt might conceivably have used the term, by "the great tradition"—an inkling of what is good and what is evil relating to his world by which he lives and acts beyond the aesthetic in his person as an artist.

Good and evil are the conjoint theme of the *Divina Commedia*, full of prejudice as between the blessed and the damned and structurally full of the mystical forms of religious ritual—in which it closely resembles Gothic architecture. But it is also a great work of art in that the same lack of ethical prejudice prevails as in the *Book of Love*. The blessed and the damned are treated by Dante, the *artist*, with scrupulous impartiality. The drawing is the same, the intense application toward veracity, the same meticulous care for "the good" whether in heaven or hell, the same address toward the truth—throughout its gamut.

I am comparing two poetical works of diverse character to discover wherein the practices of the artist are significant. These works are not arbitrarily chosen but represent two casts of thought stemming from them which stand confronting each other also today.

But my purpose in contrasting these works is the opposite

of an attempt to weigh one against the other. Rather I want to draw out the same metal from both to see what its influence there is and has been.

Both the *Commedia* and the *Libro de Buen Amor* have love as their theme, earthly and heavenly. But earthly love, in its own right (Paolo and Francesca) is condemned in the *Commedia* and celebrated to the full in the *Book*—free to the winds.

Dante restricts, the archpriest expands. Dante fastened upon his passion a whole hierarchy of formal beliefs. The fat priest slighted the formality of his beliefs in favor of the sensual thing itself to its full length and breadth.

In the structure of their works will stand revealed that they, as artists, conceived of their material. In the structure the artist speaks as an artist purely. There he cannot lie. The artist as a man of action perpetuates his deed and records himself as a reality in the structure of his work—for which the content is merely useful.

The artist addresses himself to life as a whole. By reason of this he is constantly questioned and attacked. He is attacked by the closed lobbies of thought, those who have special solutions. Those who wish to halt the mutations of truth under a single aegis fixing it to a complexion of their private manufacture in search of a way through to order as against the modern lostness and distress.

But the general reason for our distress seems to be that we are stopped in our tracks by the dead masquerading as life. We are stopped by the archaic lingering in our laboring forms of procedure—which interested parties, parts, having or getting the power will defend with explosives—seeking to prevent the new life from generating in the decay of the old.

Those who see it one way call it the defense of tradition. Others see tradition belied in that tradition once was new— now only a wall.

In Dante and the fat archpriest of Hita, two artists look at good and evil; as artist they agree, unbiased. Dante condemned not only usurers and murderers to hell but lovers also unless formally blest. Yet as an artist he seems to pity Paolo and Francesca by the grace with which he has portrayed them.

To the other there are no barriers, only a glowing at the center which extends in all directions equally, resembling in that the grace of Paradise. To Dante the passion was restricted by the narrow corset of the times, the *Commedia* by its constriction to a set of special symbols standing to lose much of its availability as time passes and knowledge increases. Their harsh, restrictive and archaic nature approaches the malevolent today—in face of the great tradition.

There is likely to prove as time passes more good in the *Book of Love* than could ever be contained in Dante's *Paradiso*. That is why the *Paradiso* is so much weaker than the *Inferno*. The artist is belied there. There Dante set himself to limit virtue by a set of narrow symbols.

Just what is wrong with the *Paradiso* becomes clearer when the whole place of the sensual artist in sacred works is better understood. Pan is the artist's patron. How have morality and the Church compromised to bring him in and be saved? It is an unnatural alliance. The structure of the work must reveal it. The structure shows this struggle between the artist and his material, to wrestle his content out of the narrow into the greater meaning.

Dante was the agent of art facing a time and place and enforcement which were his "weather." Taking this weather as his starting point, as an artist, he had to deal with it to affirm that which to him was greater than it. By his structure he shows this struggle.

All I say is that the artist's is the great master pattern which all others approach and that in this Dante and the archpriest are the same. The moral good and bad approach the good and bad of the arts. Formal patterns of all sorts represent arrests of the truth in some particular phase of its mutations, and immediately thereafter, unless they change, become mutilations.

The great pattern is difficult to approach: This is the principal objective of a work of art—to maintain this against the weather of the other conditions—so that though they warp and bend it the effect will be still the supersedure of that above these effects.

And so when a life approaches the conditions of art we have clement weather, when it recedes from them the weather is vile and tormented.

The absolute is art with its sharp distinction of good and bad, the great tradition; nothing is wholly good which has no place for every part.

Dante was a craftsman of supreme skill, his emphasis upon a triple unity is an emphasis upon structure. All his elements are in threes. In the solid structure of the Spaniard, far less skilfully made, it is important to note the flat-footed quadruple rhyme scheme as opposed to the unfinished three of the Italian dogmatist. The emphasis is upon structure, the sensual structure of the verse.

Without such sensuality the dogmatism of the *Commedia* would have killed all attempts at a work of art—as it limits it and, except for the skill of the artist (had the faintest prejudice intervened), would have submerged it. It is only as the artist has clung fast to his greatness in sensual portrayal, without influence from the content of his work, that he is able to give the content whatever secondary value it posseses. The real significance of the *Commedia* today is that it is a work of art—its meaning shifting steadily with time more and more away from the smallness, the narrowness of special pressures of its dogmatic significance. Just as the whole Renaissance has a flavor of fading dogmatism about it, a perversion, that the artist leaning upon Hellenic originals rescued sacrilegiously while painting Christian models.

This must show somewhere in the structure. There is an undercurrent, a hidden—mystical!—quality about the whole

Renaissance. This is the missing part that is not named. In the *Commedia*, Dante, like the painters, fused the two, the Hellenic and the mystic, but in doing so had to seem to sacrifice the wholeness which made pagan art universal, the charge of Pan whom the Church hates.

To realize these two in Dante, as typifying what the artist has to do, to sense the point of fusion and how it tortures the handling (as in El Greco), is to realize the inevitable direction art took following the Renaissance. The archpriest, freed by geography from the dominance of Christian dogma, was closer to the artist of today than the abler Florentine.

Today is the day in question. Does the work of Dante instruct or maim today? He must be split and the artist rescued from the dogmatist first. When this is done he gives life, when we fail to do so he inspires death. The sunnier scatterings of the amorous archpriest at least manure the entire poetic field.

Look at the structure if you will truly grasp the significance of a poem. The dogmatist in Dante chose a triple multiple for his poem, the craftsman skilfully followed orders— but the artist?

Note that beginning with the first line of the *terza rima* at any given onset, every four lines following contain a dissonance. In the *Book of Love* four rhymes are continuous, one piled upon the next four in the manner of masonry. Throughout the *Commedia* this fourth unrhymed factor, unobserved, is the entrance of Pan to the Trinity which restores it to the candid embrace of love underlying the peculiar, faulty love of the great poem which makes remote, by virtue, that which possessed, illuminates the Spanish epic.

This fault, this celebration of denial, that enters into the archaic structure of the Renaissance as against the broader Hellenic which it copies, the necessities of art correct.

It is not until today that we see the full bearing of this, the elemental significance of the work of the supreme artist shouldering through the impediments of his time. For if the poem set out to punish the wicked and reward the virtuous, it had better have been on the basis of fulfilled love than unfulfilled.

All these things, all things relating to the world of art are to be unraveled, not to be swallowed whole with amazed eyes.

Both materials and structure have a meaning that is to be discovered, one in relation to the other, not in an esoteric, special sense but in a general sense hidden by the other, a full sense which the partial, selective sense seeks to hide and is put there to hide.

The natural corrective is the salutary mutation in the expression of all truths, the continual change without which no symbol remains permanent. It must change, it must reappear in another form, to remain permanent. It is the image of the Phoenix. To stop the flames that destroy the old nest prevents the rebirth of the bird itself. All things rot and stink, nothing stinks more than an old nest, if not recreated.

This is the essence of what art is expected to do and cannot live without doing. These are some conditions which an artist must face and react to.

3

How does this apply here, today?

Take America. When America became the escape for the restless and confined of Europe the significance, as a historic moment, was not guessed. It has never been clarified. The commonly accepted symbol for it, naturally enough, was "freedom," in which the sense of an escape from a tyrannical restriction was emphasized. This was inevitable and in the first flush of release seemed thoroughly justified, but it left a great deal to be desired.

Liberty is the better word. It was liberty they needed, not so much liberty for freedom's sake but liberty to partake of, to be included in and to conserve. Liberty, in this sense, has the significance of inclusion rather than a breaking away. It is the correct sense for the understanding of America, a sense which the word has had difficulty to convey and which few properly interpret.

But to have liberty one must be first a man, cultured by circumstances to maintain oneself under adverse weather conditions as still part of the whole. Discipline is implied.

But freedom remained the commonly accepted and much copied cliché, implying lack of discipline, dispersion.

As a matter of fact, men and women isolated in Europe found each other here and banded together to resist official restrictions of the people to join on points of common agreement. The impulse was toward joint action. It was a drawing together.

The real character of the people became their joint and skilful resistance to the weather. Some broke away, but their leaders usually hanged those. They had banded together to resist it in Europe and, in a transmuted form, the same applied here. The real character of the people is not toward dispersion except as a temporary phase for the gathering of power, but to unite. To form a union. To work toward a common purpose—to resist the weather.

For what? On the principle that only in this way can that which is common, commonly possessed—be preserved among differences. Commonwealth Avenue was the center of Boston. The common persists among New England towns.

Man has only one enemy: the weather. It came to America, this philosophy, largely from the northern countries where the weather is bad. Being able to resist individually *taught them* to work toward a stronger union so that they could better resist as a whole. It comes from boats and the sea, from the north, through England to us. It is interesting that the Icelanders who lived in perishable ships should have been among the first to be governed by common councils. It came also from Norway.

There were certain effects.

Braddock in Pennsylvania was advancing down a narrow, wooded road with his men in close formation. They were among the finest troops in the world. Suddenly being picked off panic-stricken from behind trees, they stampeded to the rear until Washington—whose advice had been earlier put to scorn—sick as he was, grabbed a horse, rode up and got his Americans out among the trees to fight the enemy at its own game. He gave each man his liberty, under orders, to look out for himself in open formation. The result was to save the day—to whatever extent it could be saved.

Later when Von Steuben, trained in the army of Frederick the Great, came to drill the American troops at Valley Forge he was not blind to the advantages of certain native tactics. It was he who wrote the first American Manual at Arms, the *Army Blue Book*. When he did so he adopted from America the open formation, theretofore unheard of, now the common usage of all armies of the world and likely to become more and more important as warfare progresses and trees get wings.

The weather changes and man adapts his methods that he may survive, one by one, in order to be there for agreements later. In this sense only is the artist an individualist. The whole material has shrunk back before attack into him. It is with him as with the Chinese today: the front has to be broken up and guerrilla tactics adopted. Let them hunt us out individually and kill us one by one because we carry the destiny of united action within us, action on the plane of a whole man. Not to be alone for individual reasons but only in that it is sheer suicide to advance in phalanx and be destroyed. Disperse and survive.

The artist is the servant of need.

The need is to resist the cracking weather on all fronts. There is more destruction in a pleasant day than in a stormy one because the storm carries a greater emphasis of its intent. We live under attack by various parties against the whole. And all in the name of order! But never an order discovered in its living character of today, always an order imposed in the senseless image of yesterday—for a purpose of denial.

Parties exist to impose such governments. The result is inevitably to cut off and discard that part of the whole which does not come within the order they affect.

By this it is to be observed that even the ordinary political mind finds important what the composition of a work of art may be. It must be measured to the same measure that the political situation calls for or suffer—by which its dangerous interest is made clear.

Then let those who would force the artist to conform to their party—in the broadest sense—but especially let such poets realize, such pretty orderists as seek to impose a fixed order from without, that the acts of today, the brutalities and bigotries of the various segmentary regimes are a direct moral consequence upon their own faithless acts of a generation previous. Of course their affectation is a faith! Faith! Since they are the betrayers of the great tradition nothing but to affect a faith (in *something*) will excuse them.

England has lopped off that Spain where loyalty to the dangerous present is assertive—a Spain that does not fit that "order" which conveniences her, just as Russia periodically lops off those men who do not convenience the party.

Chamberlain had to make a choice, black or white, to defend the best of English tradition fighting for its life in Spain or to defend the British Empire under Tory rule. He chose the latter. This is a choice no artist could make without sacrificing his status as an artist.

There is a sharp cleavage between the true and the false in art; that illustrates it.

The responsibility of the artist in face of the world is toward inclusion when others sell out to a party. Nations may be said to have to take what is and to be convenient liars for a purpose, because they have to do something and only by so doing can they exist. But the artist, for that very reason and all the more so because of it, can never be a liar. He has to perpetuate his trust on an unlying scale. If he fails, the character of his failure lies precisely there, his crime, for which I condemn him to the eighth circle of hell, dry rot. Of all moral hells that of the faithless artist is the worst since his responsibility is the greatest: as England murders Spanish babies, dextrously, behind the back of opinion, and censors the terrors of Disney's *Snow White* from its children.

This is the sort of thing an artist is incapable of performing.

The poet must see before and behind—if he will know what he sees in front of him or comprehend its significance— for the art forms of today open the way to the intelligence of tomorrow.

The understanding of Walt Whitman is after the same nature. Verse is measure, there is no free verse. *But* the measure must be one of more trust, greater liberty, than has been permitted in the past. It must be an open formation. Whitman was never able fully to realize the significance of his structural innovations. As a result he fell back to the overstuffed catalogues of his later poems and a sort of looseness that was not freedom but lack of measure. Selection, structural selection was lacking.

And so about a generation ago, when under the influence of Whitman the prevalent verse forms had gone to the free-verse pole, the countering cry of Order! Order! reawakened. That was the time of the new Anglo-Catholicism.

The result was predictable. Slash down the best life of the day to bring it into the lines of control.

It comes to this: Murder can't be murder—it has to be some special sort of murder—with a quasi-secret, cabalistic significance—not understood by everyone. It has to be murder *in the cathedral*—whose momentum is lost, at the full, except to the instructed few. And instructed poetry is all secondary in the exact sense that Dante's *Commedia* is secondary where it is archaic and fettered against a broad application of the great tradition. Nothing can be simply beautiful, it must be so beautiful that no one can understand it *except* by the assistance of the cult. It must be a "mystery."

Man is mysterious in his own right and does not submit to

more than his common sensual relationships to "explain" him. Anything else approaches the trivial.

He is a man to be judged, to live or die, like other men by what he does. No symbolism is acceptable. No symbolism can be permitted to obscure the real purpose, to lift the world of the senses to the level of the imagination and so give it new currency. If the time can possess itself of such a man, such an actor, to make it aware of its own values to which through lack of imagination it remains blind, amorphous, it can gain such a momentum toward life that its dominance will be invincible.

The imagination is the transmuter. It is the changer. Without imagination life cannot go on, for we are left staring at the empty casings where truth lived yesterday while the creature itself has escaped behind us. It is the power of mutation which the mind possesses to rediscover the truth.

So that the artist is dealing with actualities not with dreams. But do not be deceived, there is no intention to depict the artist, the poet, as a popular leader in the Rousseauian sense. Rather he builds a structure of government using for this the materials of his verse. His objective is an order. It is through this structure that the artist's permanence and effectiveness are proven.

Judged equitably by the great tradition, of which the processes of art are the active front—obviously it is the artist's business to call attention to the imbecilities, the imperfections, the partialities as well as the excellence of his time.

Obviously—all defects are officially neglected by those in power; never studied or even mentioned—for clear reasons!

The trick is delay; to involve the mind in discussions likely to last a lifetime and so withdraw the active agent from performance. The answer is, an eye to judge.—When the deer is running between the birches one doesn't get out a sextant but a gun—a flash of insight with proof by performance—and let discussion follow. If the result is a work of art the effect is permanent.

Meanwhile twenty or thirty generations have died stupe-
fied by it. The genius of the colored would have started singing it off before any one of them was twelve.

Obviously the trick of postponement needs to knock one
leg from under the table so that it will wobble—to keep
everyone scurrying about for a prop instead of sitting down
at the table and eating. Finally they put a living caryatid in
the form of a Mexican-Spanish-Russian-Chinese peasant under the loose corner to take the brunt of it on his shoulders
while SOMEBODY gorges.

Why are we dull other than that the best minds are inopera-
tive, blocked by the half minds.

Obviously—"It's *his* money and a man can do what he
pleases with his own money." "He doesn't really *own* the
money, my dear. After all, you must know *that*. It's really
in all our pockets . . ." and "$500,000 may seem impressive
to you but we are in the habit of dealing with a weekly balance of $35,000,000, or more, so that to me $500,000 might be
something easily overlooked."

Obviously—a man of quite ordinary intelligence sees at
once what is at stake. Somebody ought to offer a prize.

Obviously—the economic imbecilities of the age are reflected in everything save the artist's judgments:

The political, the social. Fascism is helpless without compromise with capital-credit just as Russia is the same. Both
come out of the same pot. The revolution that will be a revolution is still to be made. It will have a complexion of the
great tradition, cannot have any other, which capital-credit
traduces in the name of "masterpieces," to them no more than
conspicuous waste.

"What heavenly blue on those Gutenberg Bibles! We
haven't anything like that nowadays."

Obviously—the Church sold out in 325 A.D. at the council
of Nicaea. The writing shows it—the secrecy and all the rest
of it when compared with the directness and clarity of the

first century. Leo shows his good heart—or showed his good heart in the encyclical *Rerum Organum* addressed to Spain forty years ago, in which he warned of what was to happen, and has since happened! if the peasants were to be continually robbed as they were being robbed at that time under the Church's dominion. Splendid! But it does not for a moment wipe out the systematic economic policy upon which the institution of which A. Vetti is the official head was founded.

Invest in the N. Y. market and count on inside information to get your funds out before the crash without comment on the character of the market. These things are obviously marked with their origin.

Obviously every little cleric who happens to bleat and consider himself an artist because of his association with the Church has no title whatever to consider himself so for that reason. Rather the Church is likely to be a insuperable barrier today if the major function of the artist—to lift to the imagination and give new currency to the sensual world at our feet —is envisaged.

Obviously the artist cannot ignore the economic dominance in his time. He is all but suppressed by it—which should mean something—but never converted. On the contrary he attacks and his attack is basic, the only basic one.

It was not I or even my day that brought the Church into the discussion touching poetry but by their adoption of its authority, those seeking order from it, do not by that remove the question of its revelance there.

Modern painting and the State have divorced themselves from clerical alliances to good effect—good being the inclusive sweep of the great tradition. If poetry is to be tied into it anew it should show in the structural breadth of its receptors—not a narrowing lilt and a content of "mysteries."

All formal religions, in spite of their varieties, embrace one final and damning evil; founded on the immanence of a religious experience, they tend rather to be monopolies using

religion to bring a man under an economic yoke of one sort
or another for the perpetuation of a priesthood—largely
predatory in character.

The simple teaching, "Give all thy goods to feed the poor"
was in spite of great examples, such as that of St. Francis,
turned into—the draining of every cent from the Russian
serfs, the Mexican peon and the Spanish peasantry to their
everlasting misery and impoverishment—murders, wars. No
wonder they hate the Church.

When Chamberlain in England—while the poor man, poor
in ways not to be more than half-guessed, starves—plays for
the dominance of the banking class before the obvious
dread that were Italy and Germany and Franco, *not*-trium-
phant England must, of necessity, reform her internal economy. To which the Church supported by the Bishop Man-
nings of America in pay of those who have to build his heap
of stone—sends out a large mouthed, Aye!

A curious anomaly is the suppression of the Jew for practical reasons—on borrowed ethical grounds—today in Germany as throughout past history. But a Jew as a Jew does not
exist. He is a man, an oriental somewhat characterized by
certain manners and physiologic peculiarities perhaps, but no
different from any others in that. But a Jew as party to a
tribal-religious cult is something else again. Judaism in *that*
sense, he must not forget, is precisely the equivalent of *that*
aspect of Fascism today.

Communism is the obverse of that facet. And in spite of the
poetic and theoretical solidity of Marxist teaching the effects,
so far, do not warrant unthinking obedience to it.

How will the artist show the side he has taken? as a man?
By subjecting himself, like Lorca, to attack—to be dragged
gutless through Granada and burned with his books on the
public square? Or to be an exile like Thomas Mann?

All I say is that, unless all this is already in his writing—in
the materials and structure of it—he might better have been a
cowhand. The effect of the aristocratic revolution that the

artist knows is necessary and intended—must be in his work, in the structure of his work. Everything else is secondary, but for the artist *that*, which has made all the greatest art one and permanent, that continual reassertion of structure, is first.

The mutability of the truth, Ibsen said it. Jefferson said it. We should have a revolution of some sort in America every ten years. The truth has to be redressed, re-examined, re-affirmed in a new mode. There has to be new poetry. But the thing is that the change, the greater material, the altered structure of the inevitable revolution must be *in* the poem, in it. Made of it. It must shine in the structural body of it.

There is a bookish quality too patent in Communism today, taken from a book that appears not to have been properly related to its object—man. Raw. And I'll back, as I regret, the faces of some of my young compatriots, with scars on their backs and faces, from policeman's fists and clubs, showing the part they have taken in strikes. They've seen the froth at the mouths of the men who club women in the belly with night sticks and seen how they bare their upper teeth as they attack. But—when I look at their poems, I wonder. The structure is weak.

The poet is a special sort of fool. He only has the one talent in most cases which can't be spent to effect but once.

Think of a work of art—a poem—as a structure. A form is a structure consciously adopted for an effect. How then can a man seriously speak of order when the most that he is doing is to impose a structural character taken over from the habits of the past upon his content? This is sheer bastardy. Where in that is the work, the creation which gives the artist his status as a man? And what is a man saying of moment as an artist when he neglects his major opportunity, to build his living, complex day into the body of his poem?

Unless he discovers and builds anew he is betraying his contemporaries in all other fields of intellectual realization and achievement and must bring their contempt upon himself and his fellow artists.

Who cares anything about propaganda, about alliances with the broad front of a life that seeks to assert itself in any age when lived to the hilt—unless the best thought is built newly, in a comprehensive form of the day, into the structure of the work? And if such a basis is accepted then, indeed, propaganda can be thoroughly welcomed. Built into the structure of a work, propaganda is always acceptable for by that it has been transmuted into the materials of art. It has no life unless to live or die judged by an artist's standards.

But if, imposing an exposed, a depleted, restrictive and un-realized form, the propagandist thinks he can make what he has to say convincing by merely filling in that wooden structure with some ideas he wants to put over—he turns up not only as no artist but a weak fool.

Whitman, a key man to whom I keep returning, was tre-mendously important in the history of modern poetry. But who has seen through his structure to a clear reason for his values and his limitations? No one that I have encountered. They begin to speak of his derivations, of his personal habits, of his putative children. For God's sake! He broke through the deadness of copied forms which keep shouting above everything that wants to get said today drowning out one man with the accumulated weight of a thousand voices in the past—re-establishing the tyrannies of the past, the very tyran-nies that we are seeking to diminish. The structure of the old is active, it says no! to everything in propaganda and poetry that wants to say yes. Whitman broke through that. That was basic and good.

But Whitman was a romantic in a bad sense. He was the peak, in many ways, of his age but his age has passed and we have passed beyond it. His, his own, structure has to be re-realized. He composed "freely," he followed his untram-meled necessity. What he did not do was to study what he had done, to go over it, to select and reject, which is the making of the artist.

Whitman took in the good and the bad in structure merely because he "felt" it and himself made it. He composed beautifully but he revised—or failed to revise—like a politician, not an artist. He did as much as he could maybe. But we have to do better, we have to look, to discover particulars and to refine.

Thus, from Whitman, we draw out—what we have to do today. We don't have to discover it from Whitman but we may discover it from Whitman if we want to. It is, not to impose the structures, the forms of the past which speak against us in their own right but to discover, first, by headlong composition perhaps, what we can do. Then to study what we have put down, as he seems not to have done, and to take out of that what is useful and reject what is misleading.

It is structure that we must invent by the use of every bit of clear-mindedness, courage, perception we own. When we find that, the rest hardly matters—we can be what we please in our day.

Federico García Lorca

The Kenyon Review, 1939

In 1936 Lorca was dragged through the streets of Granada to face the Fascist firing squad. The reasons were not obvious. He was not active in Leftist circles; but he was a power—he was a man of the people. His books were burned.

There are two great traditional schools of Spanish poetry, one leaning heavily upon world literature and another stemming exclusively from Iberian sources.

Lorca was child of the latter, so much so that he is often, as if slightly to disparage him, spoken of as a popular poet. Popular he was as no poet in Spain has been since the time of Lope de Vega. He belonged to the people and when they were attacked he was attacked by the same forces. But he was also champion of a school.

The sources whence Lorca drew his strength are at the beginnings of Spanish literature. In the epic conflict which the Spanish maintained in over four thousand battles for the reconquest of the peninsula from the Moors, there stands out an invincible leader who was, and continues to be in the memory of the people, the great national hero: Rodrigo Diaz de Vivar, called *El Cid Campeador*. His popularity is justified not only by reason of his qualities as a man of audacity and power but also for his having been the champion of popular liberties in face of the kings, one who disdained and despised their sovereignty under the dictates of reason and protected the people. The periods of the greatest deeds of this hero make up the *Cantar de Mio Cid* or *Poema del Cid*, the oldest work that survives in the Castilian tongue. The types are intensely human, the descriptions rapid and concrete:

> *Martin Antolinez mano metio al espada:*
> *Relumbra tod' el campo.*

The flash of a sword lights the whole field.

This *Song of My Cid* was written, tradition says, by one of his loyal followers, not more than forty years after the death of the hero it celebrates: and there Spanish literature gives a first and striking proof of its ability to make poetry out of the here and the now. This quality it has never lost. Lorca knew it in his *Lament for Ignacio Sánchez Mejías.*

Not only is *Poema del Cid* the first preserved to the Castilian language but it sets at once the standard in point of form for all Spanish poetry to follow. Sometimes out of favor but always in the background, its meters have become imbedded inextricably in the songs of the people—and there is no Western poetry in which the popular has a greater bulk and significance than the Spanish. Its line is famous. It is of sixteen syllables assonanced sometimes for long periods on the same vowel. This line, divided in half as usually written, becomes the basis for the *romance* or ballad, many of the *romances viejos* being, in all probability, as old as *Poema del Cid* itself or even older. It was a form much used by Lorca whose reassertion of its structural line, unchanged, forms the basis for his work.

Writing in the old meter eight hundred or a thousand years perhaps after its invention, García Lorca was pleased, as he stood in the street one night before a wineshop in Seville, to hear the words of a *copla* which he himself had written sung word for word by an illiterate guitarist, syllable for syllable in the mode of the twelfth-century epic.

And I remember one night in 1910 in Toledo listening in the same way before a cubicle opening onto one of the plazas where a few men were sitting drinking. One of them was singing to the beat of a guitar. I went in, a young man not very familiar with the language and an obvious stranger, but they became self-conscious so that I took my drink and left soon after. They looked like the shepherds I had seen coming in that afternoon across the narrow bridge with their big wolfish dogs.

Toward the middle of the thirteenth century Alfonso X, called the Wise, first gave due honor to the language of the country by ordering all public documents to be written in the common tongue rather than in Latin as formerly. It is typical of Spain that many blamed precisely this change for the disorder and disasters which followed. It was Alfonso who, in 1253, gathered a whole book of *cantigas* or *letras* to sing in the *dialecto gallego*. He was dethroned by his own son and driven an exile to die neglected in Seville, after which for close to a hundred years, "in that miserable epoch," so it is said, "the men of Castile seemed to possess hearts only to hate and arms only with which to kill."

Yet it was appositely enough during this distressed period that there appeared the second of Spain's great early poems, *Libro de Buen Amor*, the Book of Good Love, the work of that most arresting personality in Spanish medieval literature: Juan Ruiz, archpriest of Hita. This is the portrait he gives of himself among the many contained in his famous work: corpulent, a big head, small eyes under heavy eyebrows black as coal, a big nose, the mouth big also, thick lips, a short, thick neck, an easy gait—a good musician and a gay lover.

If Lorca has rested his poetic inspirations firmly in the structural forms established by *Poema del Cid*, much of his mood and spirit can be discovered in the nature of the old reprobate archpriest of Hita.

Juan Ruiz was a priest of that disorderly type which his time tolerated, his favorite company the people, always the people, and particularly that part of the Spanish population, says Madariaga, "which it is so difficult to imagine today, in which Jews and Moors and Christians mixed in an amiable fraternity of mirth and pleasure." Such a population is perhaps less difficult to imagine today in the South, where Lorca was at home, than those not fully initiated might have supposed. For it is the home of the Andalusian folksong which Lorca so ably celebrated, that curious compound of the "philosophical desperation of the Arab, the religious desperation of the Jew, and the social desperation of the gypsy." With these elements he was thoroughly familiar.

The major work of the fourteenth century in Spain, Ruiz' *Libro de Buen Amor* is in reality a picaresque novel in verse and prose, much of it in dialogue full of laughter, full of movement and full of color, a vast satirical panorama of medieval society. The poet, for all the faults and indignities of the priest, is a great one. He knows the secrets of that direct plunge into action which is typical alike of *Poema del Cid*, of Spanish *romances* no less than of Spanish comedies, and, nowadays, of popular song, to all of which Lorca owes much of his inspiration.

To understand fully all that is implied in Lorca's poetic style, what he rejected and what he clung to, the development of Spanish poetry subsequent to the work of the early masters must be noted. There was a sharp revulsion from the "old taste" which they exemplified up to the time of Juan de Mena. As always in matters of this character geography must be recognized as playing a leading part.

Spain is a peninsula dependent from the extreme lower corner of Europe, cut off from Europe by the Pyrenees which make of it virtually an island. It is, besides, far to the west of all direct European influences. From the South the Moorish invasion, with its softening influences, failed, being driven back after four centuries of temporary supremacy into Africa whence it had come, though its mark remains still in a certain quarter of Spanish and all European thought. Lorca, whose home was Granada, knew this inheritance. The Moorish invasion stopped short and receded while Latin thought, following the tracks of Caesar, had in the main gone east of Iberia up the Rhone valley through France to the north. Thus the flexibility and necessitous subtlety of the French, their

logic and lucidity of ideas, remained unknown to Spain. Enclosed within themselves, Spaniards have remained basically
limited to a reality of the world at their feet from which there
was no escape (save across the sea, which failed them) and
that second steep reality of the soul in whose service they
have proved themselves such extravagant heroes.

Little affected by the Renaissance and not at all by the
Reformation, early Spanish literature reached a stop, just
prior to the discovery of America, in the work of Juan de
Mena (1411–1456). For two hundred years thereafter, during
the fifteenth and sixteenth centuries or until the time of Góngora, the "old taste," characteristic in its resources, limited in
its means, succumbed, and the influence of Italy held an ascendancy. As Quintana says in the introduction to his *Poesías
Selectas Castellanas* (1817), "The old assonanced versification
of octosyllabics, more suited to the madrigal and the epigram
than to more ambitious poems, could not be sustained without awkwardness and crudeness—as Juan de Mena had
found. It was unfit for high and animated conceptions.
Force of thought, warmth of feeling, harmony and variety,
without which none can be considered a poet, all were lacking." But Cristóbal de Castillejo in a violent satire "compared
these novelties of the Petrarquistas, as he called them, to those
Luther had introduced into the Christian faith."

Great names abounded in Spanish poetry following this
breakdown of the old modes, some of the greatest in Spanish
literary history, all under the newer influence, all working as
they believed to enlarge and enrich the prosody and general
resources of the language. Fernando de Herrera celebrated
the majesty of Imperial Spain. There was the mystic Fray
Luis de León and among the rest Saint Teresa, that greatest of
Spanish mystics, whose few poems, not more than thirty in
all, ignoring grammar, logic, ignoring everything but the
stark cry of the spirit, wrung direct from the heart, make
them seem its own agonized voice crying in our ears. It is the
same recurrent, unreasoning note found in the strident, bright

colors and tortured lines of El Greco. Escape! As ideas come into Spain they will stop and turn upward: "I proceed," Unamuno says still in the twentieth century, "by what they call arbitrary affirmations, without documentation, without proof, outside of modern European logic, disdainful of its methods."

But toward the end of the sixteenth century the typically Spanish reaction occurred. It is curious and interesting to note how the otherwise mildly acquiescent Quintana responds to it, how for the first time he really warms to his subject and his style glows when he records: "At this time (1570–80) corresponding with the youth of Góngora and Lope de Vega it happened that a new interest began to appear in the old *romances*. . . .

"Stripped of the artifice and violence which the imitation of other modes had necessitated; its authors caring little for what the odes of Horace or the *canciones* of Petrarch were like; and being composed more by instinct than by art, the *romances* could not possess the complexity and the elevation of the odes of León, Herrera and Rioja. But they were our own lyric poetry; in them music found its own accents; these were the songs one heard at night from windows and in the streets to the sound of the harp or the guitar. . . .

"There are in them more beautiful expressions and more energetic, ingenious and delicate sallies than in all our poetry besides. But curiously enough in a few years this revival of a taste which popularized poetry, and rescued it from the limits of imitation to which the earlier poets had reduced it, served also to make it incorrect and to break it down, inviting to this abandon the same facility as in its rehabilitation." Góngora was the man!

It was Luis de Góngora who as a lyric poet brought the new adventure to its fullest fruition and then attempted to go away, up and beyond it—to amazing effect.

Góngora is the only Spanish poet whose inventions, at the beginning of the seventeenth century, retain a lively interest

for us today, one of the few poets of Spain of world reputation and lasting quality of greatness. Look at his picture: chin
deep in his cravat, his forehead a Gibraltar, the look on his
face slightly amused but formidable, not to say invincible, his
person retracted into an island of strength resembling nothing
so much as the map of Spain itself. There you have the spirit
that sustained Lorca in our day.

A master in his *romances*, one of the greatest masters of the
burlesque and the satire, Góngora had already established a
redoubtable reputation when toward the latter part of his life
he set out to elevate the tone of Spanish poetry, illustrating
it with erudition and new conceptions, enriching the language with those tones and turns which distinguish it from
prose. It was the same ambition which had inspired Juan de
Mena and Fernando de Herrera; but Góngora lacked, as they
said, the culture and moderation possessed by those predecessors.

Be that as it may Góngora, who to the end of his days continued at times to write his lovely *romances*, "developed a
style—turgid and difficult, infuriating his age, which became
known as *Culteranismo*. And inasmuch as Góngora was the
great representative of *Culteranismo* it became known as
Góngorismo."

What else but the same escape upward! As in the poems of
Saint Teresa! When Góngora found himself confined by the
old, unwilling to go back to the borrowed Italianate mode, he
sought release in an illogical, climbing manner, precursor of
today. He could not go back to Latin, to Greek or the Italian.
Never to the French—so he went up! steeply, to the illogical,
to El Greco's tortured line. So that when Luzán and those
other humanists (who after a century were restoring good
taste) applied themselves to destroy the sect and its consequences—denouncing its founder—they took Góngora and
detestable poet to be one and the same thing.

It was for Federico García Lorca, in our day, to find a
solution. Like the young Góngora, Lorca adopted the old

Spanish modes. I have taken his book *Llanto por Ignacio Sán-chez Mejías* (*Lament for the Death of a Bullfighter*) to be touched upon for the conclusion of these notes.

There has always seemed to be a doubt in the minds of Spaniards that their native meters were subtle enough, flexible enough to bear modern stresses. But Lorca, aided by the light of twentieth-century thought, discovered in the old forms the very essence of today. Reality, immediacy; by the vivid-ness of the image invoking the mind to start awake. This peculiarly modern mechanic Lorca found ready to his hand. He took up the old tradition, and in a more congenial age worked with it, as the others had not been able to do, until he forced it—without borrowing—to carry on as it had come to him, intact through the ages, warm, unencumbered by draperies of imitative derivation—the world again under our eyes.

The peculiar pleasure of his assonances in many of the poems in this book retains the singing quality of Spanish poetry and at the same time the touch of that monotony which is in all primitive song—so well modernized here: In the first of the *romances* which make up the book's latter half, *La Casada Infiel*, the play is on the letter o; in *Preciosa Y El Aire* upon e; in *Romance de la Guardia Civil Española* upon a; etc., etc. This is straight from *El Cid;* but not the scintillat-ing juxtapositions of words and images in the three *Romances Históricos* (at the very end), where the same blurring of the illogical, as of refracted light, suggests that other reality—the upward sweep into the sun and the air which characterized the aspirations of St. Teresa, of El Greco and the Góngora whom none understood or wished to understand in his day, the "obscurities" which Unamuno embraces with his eye to-ward "Augustine, the great African, soul of fire that split it-self in leaping waves of rhetoric, twistings of the phrase, antitheses, paradoxes and ingenuities . . . a Góngorine and a conceptualist at the same time. Which makes me think that

Góngorism and conceptualism are the most natural forms of passion and vehemence."

The first stanza of Lorca's greatest poem, the lament, has for every second line the refrain: *A las cinco de la tarde*—"at five in the afternoon."

That refrain, *A las cinco de la tarde*, fascinated Lorca. It gives the essence of his verse. It is precise, it is today, it is fatal. It gives the hour, still in broad daylight though toward the close of the day. But besides that it is song. Without reading Lorca aloud the real essence of the old and the new Spanish poetry cannot be understood. But the stress on the first syllable of the "CINco" is the pure sound of a barbaric music, the heartbeat of a man's song, *A las CINco de la tarde*. What is that? It is any time at all, no time, and at the same time eternity. Every minute is eternity—and too late. *A las CINco de la tarde*. There is the beat of a fist on the guitar that cannot escape from its sorrow, the recurring sense of finality translated to music. The fatality of Spain, the immediacy of its life and of its song. *A las CINco de la tarde*, Mejías was killed! was killed on a bull's horns. *A las CINco de la tarde*, he met his end.

This is the brutal fact, the mystical fact. Why precisely *a las CINco de la tarde?* The mystery of any moment is emphasized. The spirit of Góngora, the obscure sound of the words is there.

Much in the examples of Lorca must have been in the mind of the elder poet when he strained at the cords of the old meter, the old thoughts, refusing to adopt the Italianate modes of his immediate predecessors until the words broke like a bridge under him and he fell through among fragments—wisely.

Two years after the event the Spaniard takes a man killed in action—a bullfighter killed in Mexico—for his theme. No matter what the action, he was a man and he was killed: the same ethical detachment and the same freedom from ethical prejudice which characterized *El Cid* and the *Book of Good*

Love. The same power also to make poetry of the here and the now. The same realism, the same mounting of the real, nothing more real than a bullfighter, mounting as he is, not as one might wish him to be, directly up, up into the light which poetry accepts and recasts. That is Lorca.

In the *Romance of the Faithless Wife* is reflected the same aloofness, the same reality, the same reserve—not the superficial passion that is surface only: The gypsy takes the woman, the ecstasy he wins from her and of which she speaks to him are real, but she made him believe she was a virgin and he found that she was married. So he enjoyed her realistically and paid for it, like a gypsy, but he would not love her thereafter—just as in a song from the high valleys of the Asturian Pyrenees, a man sings:

> *Una niña bonita*
> *Se asomó a su balcón.*
> *Ella me pidió el alma,*
> *Yo lo di el corazón,*
> *Ella me pidió el alma,*
> *Y yo la dije adiós.*

He gave her his heart but when she asked for his soul he said good-bye.

In reading Lorca the whole of Spanish history must be borne in mind, Saint Teresa with her bodiless thrust of soul, the steadfastness, the chastity—*but* also the reality of the Spaniard. Spanish poetry, says Madariaga, is both above and below the plane of thought. It is superficial to talk of Lorca as a sensualist. He is a realist of the senses and of his body but he is far from the common picture of a sensualist. The cold and elevated plateau which has bred the chastity of the *copla*, such as that quoted above, enters into all of Lorca's work. Read carefully, the icy chastity of Spanish thought comes through the reality of the event from which the man does not flinch—nor does he flinch before the consequence. He will give the body, yes, but the soul never! The two realities, the earth and the soul, between these two the Spaniard swings, firm in his own.

These are the influences that made Lorca. The old forms were bred of and made for song. The man spent his life singing. That is the forgotten greatness of poetry, that it was made to be sung—but it has been divorced from the spoken language by the pedants.

Lorca honored Spain, as one honors a check, the instinctive rightness of the Spanish people, the people themselves who have preserved their basic attitude toward life in the traditional poetic forms. He has shown that these modes, this old taste, are susceptible of all the delicate shadings—without losing the touch of reality—which at times in their history have been denied them. In such "obscurities" of the words as in the final *romances* in his book, the historical pieces addressed to the saints, he has shown how the modern completes the old modes of *The Cid* and *The Book of Good Love*. He has carried to success the battles which Juan de Mena began and Góngora continued.

Federico García Lorca, born in 1899 in the vicinity of Granada, produced a number of outstanding works in lyric poetry, drama and prose between his eighteenth year and the time of his death in 1936 at the age of thirty-seven. He was a pianist, the organizer of a dramatic troupe, and a distinguished folklorist of Spanish popular songs of great distinction.

Many stories are told of him. He was loved by the people. His murder by the Fascist firing squad in Granada is perhaps as he would have wished it to be: To die on the horns of the bull—if a man does not put his sword first through its heart. Like most men of genius he went about little recognized during his life but he has left us a weapon by which to defend our thought and our beliefs, a modern faith which though it may still be little more than vaguely sensed in the rest of the world is awake today in old Spain, in proud defiance of destruction there. By that Lorca lives.

Introduction

Charles Sheeler—Paintings—Drawings—Photographs, 1939

HERE FOR the first time, I think, the paintings of Charles Sheeler have been assembled for a complete retrospective view giving him and others an opportunity to witness them as a whole. This is an important moment for contemporary painting. Apart from the enjoyment received, it provides a means for the study and evaluation of the work in all its phases as well as a cross-check on painting generally today.

The catalogue details elsewhere a chronological list of the exhibits. No comment on the individual pieces will be made nor does it seem appropriate to more than mention the biography so ably covered in previous publications. All that is intended is a bird's-eye view of the exhibit and a quick pencil sketch of some of its features and implications—as they appeal to one who is not a painter, a bad thing perhaps, writers incline to be gassy.

I think Sheeler is particularly valuable because of the bewildering directness of his vision, without blur, through the fantastic overlay with which our lives so vastly are concerned, "the real," as we say, contrasted with the artist's "fabrications."

This is the traditional thin soup and cold room of the artist, to inhabit some chance "reality" whose every dish and spoon he knows as he knows the language that was taught him as child. Meanwhile, a citizen of the arts, he must keep his eye without fault upon those things he values, to which officials constantly refuse to give the proper names.

The difficulty is to know the valuable from the impost and to paint that only. The rest of us live in confusion between

231

these things, isolated from each other by the effects of it, a primitive and complex world without air conditioning. It is the measurable disproportion between what a man sees and knows that gives the artist his opportunity. He is the watcher and surveyor of that world where the past is always occurring contemporaneously and the present always dead needing a miracle of resuscitation to revive it.

More and more alone as time goes on, shut off from each other in spite of facile means of communication, we shrink within ourselves the more, the more the others strike against our privacy. We cannot be forced to love and talk, the gangsters are right—I should say they are the mirrors. Nor can it be told by looking into a man's face what he is thinking or in what hovel-sized confinement he exists. But the monasteries of our thoughts have walls like any others for paintings to carry us beyond them to reality. Lucky the man who can dispel them with a Sheeler.

And let it be strictly noted, the arresting thing is that this world of the artist is not of gauze but steel and plaster. It is the same men meet and talk and go to war in. Pictures are made with paint and a brush on canvas.

Any picture worth hanging, is of this world—under our noses often—which amazes us, into which we can walk upon real grass. It's no "fabrication," we realize that at once, but what we have always sought against that shrunken pulp (from which everyone is running faster nowadays than ever) called, monstrously, "the real."

Charles Sheeler give us such a world, of elements we can believe in, things for our associations long familiar or which we have always thought familiar.

Driving down for illumination into the local, Sheeler has had his Welsh blood to set him on. There is a Sheelerville, Pa., up in the old mining district. The Shakers express the same feeling in maple, pine and birch, pieces which Sheeler out of admiration for what they could do with those materials keeps about him.

But the world is always seeking meanings! breaking down everything to its "component parts," not always without loss. The arts have not escaped this tendency, nor did Sheeler whose early work leaned toward abstraction, in the drawing and composition, the familiar ironing out of planes. Something of it still lingers in his color.

Later Sheeler turned, where his growth was to lie, to a subtler particularization, the abstract if you will but left by the artist integral with its native detail.

The tree grows and makes leaves which fall and lie in the swampwater. The ages change, as the imagination changes, and of the resultant coal we draw off an electric fluid. But for the artist, for Sheeler as an artist, it is in the shape of the thing that the essence lies.

To be an artist, as to be a good artisan, a man must know his materials. But in addition he must possess that really glandular perception of their uniqueness which realizes in them an end in itself, each piece irreplaceable by a substitute, not to be broken down to other meaning. Not to pull out, transubstantiate, boil, unglue, hammer, melt, digest and psychoanalyze, not even to distill but to see and keep what the understanding touches intact—as grapes are round and come in bunches.

To discover and separate these things from the amorphous, the conglomerate normality with which they are surrounded and of which before the act of "creation" each is a part, calls for an eye to draw out that detail which is in itself the thing, to clinch our insight, that is, our understanding, of it.

It is this eye for the thing that most distinguishes Charles Sheeler—and along with it to know that every hair on every body, now or then, in its minute distinctiveness is the same hair, on every body anywhere, at any time, changed as it may be to feather, quill or scale.

The local is the universal.

Look! that's where painting begins. A bird, up above, flying, may be the essence of it—but a dead canary, with glazed eye, has no less an eye for that well seen becomes sight and song itself. It is in things that for the artist the power lies, not beyond them. Only where the eye hits does sight occur. Take a cross-eyed child at birth. For him to see at all one of the eyes must go blind, he cannot focus it. But let him look past the object to "abstraction" long enough and soon the other eye will follow.

The exhibits date back approximately a quarter of a century, but their quality is singularly uniform, lucid and geometric from the first. It was an early perception of general changes taking place, a passage over from heated surfaces and vaguely differentiated detail to the cool and thorough organizations today about us, familiar in industry, which Sheeler has come more and more to celebrate.

Sheeler had especially not to be afraid to use the photographic camera in making up a picture. It could perform a function unduplicatable by other means. Sheeler took it that by its powers his subject should be intensified, carved out, illuminated—for anyone (I don't know that he said this to himself) whose eyes might be blurred by the general fog that he might, if he cared to, see again.

It is ourselves we seek to see upon the canvas, as no one ever saw us, before we lost our courage and our love. So that to a Chinaman Sheeler at his best should be a heartfelt recognition, as Sheeler, looking at some ancient Chinese painted screen, would hope fervently to see himself again. A picture at its best is pure exchange, men flow in and out of it, it doesn't matter how. I think Sheeler at his best is that, a way of painting powerfully articulate. But after all, so is all good painting.

The Tortuous Straightness of Chas. Henri Ford *

IN READING these poems through, from beginning to end, at one long stroke, a special condition of the mind is generated which to me seems the gist of the poems and the only way to understand them particularly or generally. They form an accompaniment to the radio jazz and other various, half-preaching, half-sacrilegious sounds of a Saturday night in June with the windows open and the mind stretched out attempting to regain some sort of quiet and be cool on a stuffed couch. . . . The poems form a single continuous, running accompaniment, well put together as to their words, to a life altogether unreal. By retaining a firmness of extraordinary word juxtapositions while dealing wholly with a world to which the usual mind is unfamiliar a counterfoil to the vague and excessively stupid juxtapositions commonly known as "reality" is created. The effect is to revive the senses and force them to re-see, re-hear, re-taste, re-smell and generally revalue all that it was believed had been seen, heard, smelled and generally valued. By this means poetry has always in the past put a finger upon reality.

This sort of particularly hard, generally dreamlike poetry is inevitable today when the practice of the art tends to be seduced by politics. As always you find the foil immediately beside the counterfoil. Poetry must lie against poetry, nowhere else. So that this book can be enjoyed immediately beside whatever hard-bitten poet of "the revolution" it is

* Introduction to *The Garden of Disorder* and Other Poems, by Charles Henri Ford, New Directions: Norfolk, Connecticut, 1939.

desired to place it and there fecundate—in active denial of all the unformed intermediate worlds in which we live and from which we suffer bitterly.

To me the sonnet form is thoroughly banal because it is a word in itself whose meaning is definitely fascistic. To use it subverts most intelligences. I object to its use even here, as I always object to its use other than for doggerel. But for Ford's sake I am willing to ignore the form as unimportant and look for the small excellences of tenuous but concretely imagined word appositions which are contained in them They can be read in that way.

What I like best are his "Late Lyrics." For in every man there must finally occur a fusion between his dream which he dreamed when he was young and the phenomenal world of his later years if he is to be rated high as a master of his art. In these later lyrics it seems to me that Ford shows evidence of this important fusion—sometimes with loss of his keenest intuitions where his sympathies have been too roughly roused—but then again with all his best faculties retained. I always look for such lines as these—"I, Rainey Betha, 22,—from the top branch of race-hatred look at you." That's hard material to handle. It tests every resource of a poet to do it well. Ford's method of handling it is interesting. One should look for these differences of handling of the to-day conventional theme—as one looks at the handling of the Crucifixion—by Bellini, Raphael and El Greco.

But in the last poem of the book Ford seems to return to something he had begun to forget—a fantastic drive out of, while in the very process of entering the banal: using the banal to escape the banal—and by this, placing accurately a value upon that which is excellent and good.

1939

A Letter

Furioso, 1940

DEAR WHITTEMORE:

I've got a subject, you write, that I don't know anything about. It may have been covered a lot before, but it certainly should be covered right now in *Furioso*. Propaganda in Poetry. Poetry that tries to influence people. In other words, just what is the function of poetry? What has a poetry magazine to do with a war, with a country's policy, with a new bunch of quintuplets, etc.? In publishing *Furioso*, I think that's one of the things we've been trying to find out, and so far I haven't found out anything. Pound says that everything he's written has economic implications. Everything (nearly) that Genevieve Taggard writes says "better read Marx." In other words most of the modern poets *think* they're pointing toward something which they believe is right. And I want to know if they've picked the right medium. Why not write an article for *Liberty*? My idea is that poetry deals with the generalities of human conduct, with questions that are important for more than ten minutes, with movements greater than the French occupation of the Saar Basin. Then all I can do is say, So what? I wonder what's the good of writing an article for *Liberty* either, except that we're still a neutral country. . . . I've read several poems of yours that are precisely about what I'm trying to get at, etc., etc.—To all of this my answer would be, Yes.

Take an extreme case, take the concepts that walk around as T. S. Eliot. We know they are completely worthless so that aside from Eliot's being a poet we do not have to pay much attention to him. He is strictly limited even as a poet, but for

237

all that we may speak of him as a good poet, good, that is, far beyond his other limitations.

That, I think, if true, would leave a certain irreducible minimum which we may designate as the poetic quantum.

Taggard may entertain certain concepts but these do not by any stretch of the imagination make her a good writer. Pound, you say, believes that all his writings have an economic implication. So, by the way, does the peanut vendor at a ball game. It is obvious that unless Pound's writings have other implication, the poetic quantum, he would be of far less use to us as Pound than a lucid text on the subject he believes he is expounding, the lucid text he is always dreaming of. Should his concepts ever clarify themselves, that is to say, his economic concepts, and he be able to transcribe them . . . it might be the end of him. Horrible thought.

Peter Cooper said a number of years ago, Exorbitant rent (commonly called interest) silently but surely devours the substance of the people.—I think this, in one sentence, says more succinctly than Pound ever dreamed, everything he ever conceived of economics. But Peter Cooper was not a poet, Pound is a poet, so we forgive him.

We all like to believe that we are master minds. But what men seldom seem to learn is that the end of poetry is a poem; I don't know a thing about the value of a poem as such or of a hunk of gold as such or of a man himself as such, but I do know *that*.

Some exposure to the sharp edge of the mechanics of living —such as blindness, political exile, a commercial theatre to support and be supported by, a profession out of necessity, dire poverty, defiance of the law, insanity—is necessary to the poet. It doesn't matter what the form is, these are all of a class, to give the poet his sense of precision in the appreciation of values, what is commonly spoken of as "reality." They force him to observe and to weigh, they prompt his choice of the means of expression and give his words pungency and a charge. In themselves they have nothing to do with poetry.

Notice clearly, this is the sole use of these focusing stimulae; they are not in any way related to the poet's function as a poet. He must know this without possibility of a doubt. The end of poetry is something apart from all that.

A blind singer for bed and board, an altar thief, a starveling —if they for one moment forget, prodded as they may be by death, disease or economic pressures, that their work as poets is completely alien to all that—if they permit themselves to be caught in the snare of their own lives and let that affect their decisions touching their workmanship in the faintest possible manner—they are lost. It is a balance as to the push of reality's either stimulating them to excellence or killing them outright—but they must never forget that the real significance passes beyond such incidentals. It lies imbedded indestructibly in the body of the poem itself, if . . . !

This being true, the poet who mistakes the function of the propaganda he practices, taking it overzealously to heart, is his own dupe. Let's have no more jerked measures. To the poet it is plain that all stimulae are and must be one, he is the Jesuit of his own mind, the end always justifies the means if he produce a good poem. But he must be more resourceful than all that, he must still remain a Jesuit even in giving up the Church. No matter what the propaganda and no matter how it touches him, it can be of no concern to the poet. To hell with it as soon as he has finished with it, when it's worn out he'll find some other propaganda.

Be the Shakespeare of your own day, write well, skilfully, covertly, deceitfully, with every faculty under a hood or blanket concealed from public view, write of that which is nearest to the skin (to hell with the heart!) but write well.

So what, huh? After all, man being human must believe himself at times a great conceptualist (read your Spanish lit.: "just savages" E. P.), at least for home consumption, or lie down and die of disgust at the sights he sees about him. I don't blame anyone for wanting to teach his fellows to "blow hard" when Papa wields the rag. 's O.K. by me.

Then occasionally we get someone who can write. It's a *double entendre* that goes something like this:

> See the little angels
> Ascend up! ascend up!
> O! see the little angels
> Ascend up to Heaven!

There's something deeper to it than most people imagine. Ha!

Midas: A Proposal for a Magazine

Now, 1941

A CERTAIN NUMBER of refugees from the Death in Europe, revolutionary in the full sense, have met others here who welcome them to this country. Together they propose to continue an advance into the present and to publish from time to time a bulletin of their interest.

In the present emergency, the revolutionary element in thought and in life will continue their concern; to preserve and to elevate to its proper place before the mind everything constructive, aggressive, of radical power in art as in the physical sciences today. If the concern be painting, to celebrate what new thrusts will stand upon the shoulders of surrealism and to discern a new horizon beyond that; to raise woman from her proposed servitude to the state; to announce the new cure for cancer when it comes; the poem that shall be actually new.

One of the purposes of the Death among us is to terrify the world, to use a destructive ideology to push our culture so far back that it will take a full generation, another crop of flesh and mind, before it can begin to regenerate. Then another war will be upon us to drive the mind from its advances, this shuttle to go on in perpetuity. We are never to be allowed to catch up, to regain our equilibrium for a permanent arrest of the Destroyer.

But we on our part will stay on the heels of the Death, baying and snapping, never giving it a moment's rest, driving it among the rocks, to keep it there at bay. So that at the moment of respite, the instant war has finished its last ravages, its strength spent, THE VERY NEXT INSTANT, we may

241

spring forward to enhearten and supply the elements of a peace—not where it left off but still further advanced above what it had been formerly. We propose without pretense to publish a bulletin of our activities, if any, and to notice the work of creative agents in other fields.

War elevates the artist, the builder, the thinker to the peaks of the stars, trebles his significance. In times of peace he is, at best, a humdrum worker not because he must be so, but because he is perpetually laboring under weights to inflame and to magnify. But in times of war—helplessly split off in the cyclotron of the times—he becomes inevitably king of men. By his very existence, woman blossoms from her imposed shell, man, older than the stones, rears himself and reaches out into the unknown.

We address ourselves not to the poet, the scientist, the sociologist separately—rather to the fertile subject itself which we intend to transform and to magnify: not to man so much as man as he is the product of time. Who am I that exist now and existed then? Not merely a man, surely, but far more complex than that, the summation of all men that preceded me and their very genius to push themselves forward—in me! That is where I exist, in that inheritance.

Everything which advances the understanding of this subject, this "thing" which makes new sallies into time—comparable in its movements precisely to geography in the era of Vasco da Gama, the arts in the twelfth century, psychiatry in the later years of the nineteenth century, astrophysics, organic chemistry; French painting since 1820—anything which pushes an advance, a tenable new position into that substance which is not merely "man" but which includes also his image in time; in sum, everything which constitutes the province of the poet (who encloses the whole materium and continuum in his concept) in its revolutionary grasp, we conceive as our business.

The poem alone focuses the world. It is practical and comprehensive and cannot be the accompaniment of other than an unfettered imagination. It cannot exist other than as revolutionary attribute of a free people—wherever they may be by twos and threes. To limit is to kill it. It comes when the climate permits or its does not materialize. But if it does not appear, then the plant has never blossomed. That climate which gives it life to expand is love, as gold, its symbol, is most gold when it is given freely to the beloved.

It is the striking gesture of the arm of a man wherever employed. Chop off the arm, the gesture is taken up by other arms intact. Deny a people its arms in time of persecution, as the people of Spain were, actively or passively, left armless by the great niggardly peoples of the earth, the tragic poetry of it is still unaffected. You can't prune that. You can't destroy gold. Gold may destroy you, for you can't eat it, any more than you can eat the arts. It is to give away, essence of the poem. These are the prizes of free men—murderous in intention if thwarted—the prizes of love.

Modern poetry is a definition, in the radical speech patterns of the day, asserting our development and elevation of thought above that of the ancients.

Not that there are not defects. America as an asylum is in many ways not a good one. Man has been mother to woman so long in America that he has forgotten her function (and his own) in large measure. This "protection" by men has produced an effect as when any culture touches a product—to improve it. But the producer is haggard at the termination of his labors. Man somewhat as a consequence has lost his revolutionary character, touching woman and going on from there. This is an effect in America productive also of a matrix of undifferentiated thought, inimical to complete contacts as a general thing—with a throwback of female elements in the arts and in affairs: anti-revolutionary, complacent, quilted.

The attack upon the basic problem goes on underneath the shows of the surface one. It is always basically, in all the variation, one, with its apex on the moment, in the sciences as well as the arts: one. Thus and only thus may highly divergent appearances coincide, be conceived to unite and be understood as related to effects of varying orders. And thus only will such a concept as surrealism find a common ground, no matter how antagonistic it may seem to be, with the advance of thought and effort in America where it has no such original basis as existed in France yesterday. That is only when a profound enough basis is discovered here in our own lives—on which we can meet others.

That basis is the Midas touch, the alchemy of the mind which cannot be seduced by political urgencies—but makes all into gold: the COM radical; com-bined; com-plex; com-plexion; com-prehensive; reaches out, takes hold. We are united in our hatred of the Terror, the negative, the Death.

We seek as far as we are American to take in the difficult "foreign," identical with us in the GOLD of it no matter how the ornament is shaped or what may be the purpose to which it seems to be put. To reject the spurious, i.e., war, fake. To reveal the rare and the curious relationships which are the mind's true business.

We deal with the truth which we KNOW. We are NOT in doubt. We interpret ALL GOOD in ANY form and show its revolutionary value even in revolution itself—where it is churned up in the general pell-mell and the virtue of it disguised by accident: to dig under where, hidden in the soil of the mind, divergent excellences may be found stemming from the same pure stem of gold.

For if money is the symbol of collective effort, gold, by its indestructibility by air or acid, its malleability, its color and its sheen, is the symbol toward which money looks in its turn. And there is nothing that can take its place as an uncounterfeitable, readily available, though rare enough, object of value to pass thus symbolically from hand to hand. The old originators didn't select gold arbitrarily to be their standard of exchange. But gold, that is to say "gold," by confusion has come to be taken as identical with money in some languages. We do not fall into that error.

We accept it for granted, then, that the complexion of our minds, Americans and those who come to us with their gold is the same, we who have not yet been attacked directly and those who have newly retreated before the Terror. We know the gold and its identity with the living but have no desire to eat it—only the mad do that.

What are we to do in this complex of difficult understanding? Certainly, if we retreat it is only to lay the ground for a final revolutionary advance: the ideogram of George Washington's retreat across Jersey to win in the end is neither quaint nor untimely in this context.

War is a bastard agent. It eats its young, it creates only to mutilate and swallow its own offspring. It fertilizes the body of its continental flesh, the female carcass that it cynically urges to new bursts of labor, with glee, offering a prize (literally!) to its women that she may exceed herself; then piglike it crunches her shoats in its jaws while pushing her into the trough, finally eating her also—thus becoming sterile! War feeds on lies of deception, on the confusion of the woman, on pushing indignities upon her and then robbing her piecemeal. She is suppressed, her aphrodisiacs taken away from her and her reproductive wiles crushed to the features of a sausage machine—the sacks of flesh shooting into his gullet as fast as produced. He swallows and belches—while she serves him in his disgusting trade.

The arts of war! There are no arts of war but sterility and deceit. There is no art of shoat swallowing. There are arts but they are only bastardized after their theft by war. The arts create, war destroys. The sciences are! but they have not a single character which war can claim as its own but their undoing.

Make no mistake, war releases energy, so far it is good—but it has no art of its own, no authentic character but mud, exhaustion and—heroism which is never more heroic than when it throws its life away for nothing at all—that might not have been had casually from love for the mere asking.

The tradition is that the art of war is to have the most men on the field first. But that's the art of painting, before the on-rushing impetus of the idea, when it is ravishing the mind. What's peculiar to war in that? Not a single thing. War has no art to create anything, only to degrade and destroy. But the artist pauses, disciplines the fury and translates it to the eye. War creates nothing but stinking corpses and the perversion that makes leaders. Leaders! sucked out of men, eating others because of their own poverty. There are no arts of war. Everything is stolen there—except the energy released which is not its own and badly used by it.

This must be returned to creative forces by revolution, there is no other way, no other incentive sufficiently violent to overtake it, claim it and carry it away. It must be returned to the correct complexion of the imagination, will use it generatively—with a fury war only imitates, second-hand, and at once before it is dissipated completely.

The revolution must capture from the Terror this power it makes available. Only peace as it might be conceived in all its controlled violence can capture this initiative from destruction and build it directly into mechanisms for our use. Now woman is honored and fertilized as creature of the imagination, nor merely her carcass doubled or trebled by a kind of fission. War's lies, leeches that they are, sprinkled with salt, let go our flesh and fall off. We must ferret out those lies no matter where the trail leads. We shall be surprised or not, no matter, the objective is to capture the initiative for the creator everywhere, the artist, the scientist—the running animal; un-deceive the puppet-makers concerning the true nature of the revolutionary St. Francis—whom they recaptured and subjected to their rule.

Nothing but war HAS made America the battleground of intelligences. These things do not come from nowhere. But war released badly what might have been released well. It released at least what was needed here—and gained, perhaps, something for them there. War has brought together, by release, divergent intelligences for new trial and opportunity, let us acknowledge it.

But these intelligences and initiatives, it must be clear, have nothing to do with the Death, the Death has been only the dispersing agent. It has released energy, created nothing. The same thing might have happened to better advantage in times of peace, when life was predominant. But it didn't happen. It was stalled by stupidity. The energy was lacking, but only the energy locked them from our use. In desperation now before the Death, life begins to move violently.

The doing away with the slum districts of London is an excellent thing. War has begun the demolition of the slum districts of London. But this is not an act to be credited to war as an agent but to the release of energies consequent upon war. The necessary destruction could have been better done, more economically, with less collateral waste through the agency of peace but only a violent peace dominated by revolution. The means were locked up in stupidity, war released them.

And here that which has been hog-tied, condescended to, shoved about and set to watch honors being given to plaster casts—gets a backing that will set it up to new sallies of its own.

We must know. We must say what we know. We will not be defeated or bemused. But the artist not only knows and reveals, he proves the reliability of his contentions by his works. As with geometry this is the basis of art; the diagram is not didactic. It is fact, proof of the existence of creative man—signed by the creator.

What shall follow surrealism? Picayune question—though there is a way by which the issue can be predicted. But that something equally pregnant must follow it, consequently, we are set to prove, as that nothing could have escaped it, at its major moment, no matter how vitiated that thrust developed to be in some hands. For nothing but surrealism, as it has turned out, preceded, foretold and so sapped the war of all intellectual strength before it started. And the best of art is

always so. Surrealism took all the war's identity, predicted
and emasculated it by the same stroke—sucked it dry and was
its plain Bible to read in—if it hadn't frightened so many.

Thus, plainly, none but the poet holds it in his secret power
to tell, in terrific, frightening concentration what the consequences of those forces which make this war its plaything
will be. This will be the successor to surrealism.

The idiotic belief that the arts must be put aside for arms—
UNTIL a time of peace (as if they needed coddling and were
perishable) must give way to a triple fury of activity, to steel
the released energy for constructions.

We proclaim the occasion of our intent to drive the program (of fertility and construction) home.

A living and secret activity, as of fetation, has been undertaken. We do not overlook the fact that nothing but a gnat is
born the week following its conception. A time of considerable length must often pass before parturition. But, under
cover, the activity is there madly, as at no subsequent period
during life, overwhelming changes compressed to a matter of
hours—whereas later years will go by in comparative un-
productivity. Unless the arts attack by revolution and at once
the offspring of this energy, released by war, will all be bastards.

In short it is to legitimatize the products of that power released by the Death and induct it into the services of life that
the arts are addressed and we are its servants.

There I might end but there is a codicil of specific direction: We are offered the "normal and healthy" as a corrective
to our perverse habits, inviting us to "purify" our minds of
"degenerate" art, to wean ourselves from its corrupt interests, the degradation inherent in woman and to fall in love
instead with "nature"—after all somewhat too palpable and
childish a deception. We are to gape heroically at mountains,
peer down into mines, whence they would get the materials
we are thus induced to dig for our own destruction, and love
it! the great "outdoors"!—all such lies carefully ornamented

to our tastes, for deadly profit. In truth, the great "outdoors," "joy for health" and all such crap (because a covered lie) we are determined shall give way before the far greater mountains, the far greater depths of the imagination.

We have no interest in that "normal" art which is a subterfuge, using "nature" and its flesh to hide the deceptive sterility of a cringing imagination—asking us to be passionately attached to a cylinder (of hollow steel, mind you!) because of its classic proportions. Lies! They mean deceit of the most formal diplomatic sort. They mean trickery with a purpose to undermine and destroy. It is the Death in whatever form they present it.

An Afternoon with Tchelitchew

Life and Letters Today, 1937

A HOT JUNE afternoon, 1937. East 57th St., N. Y., studio apartment, 5th floor, rear. 5 P.M. The model about to leave, waiting, before going home to her husband, to pour tea for us.

Any who would know and profit by his knowledge of the great must lead a life of violent opposites. The deeper at moments of penetration is his mastery of their work, the more vigorously at other moments must he fling himself off from them to remain himself a man. But if he himself would do great works also only by this violence, this completeness of his wrenching free, will he be able to use that of which their greatness has consisted.

The failure to understand this condemns the perennial student who has, in short, by a sort of sluggishness shown himself to have succumbed to the effects of former greatness and not profited by it to establish his own mastery. This is the banality of the academic, maliciously called the cultivation of "tradition," maliciously because under it is implied an attack upon the "radical" who does not submit himself to such respectable negation.

A man must know but he will not be told how he must know nor submit to the terms of those who make knowledge no more very often than self-denial in subservience to honorific symbols by which they seek to maintain dominance over him while he is seeking the substance. But it is man who must be achieved.

These convictions had come to life in the presence of Tchelitchew's canvasses. Not a very "good" painter. He was saying so himself, in deep respect for the deftness of the Spanish and French moderns among his friends. He only wished he might be able to handle his materials with their ease, their amazing facility. He referred to the new sensations, to Dali especially.

They are my good friends, he said. Dali is a jeweler in paint. And he sees everything. He has eyes that stick out, like the eyes of a crab. And he eats the world of the eyes, like a crab. Numb, numb, numb, numb! And T. brought the fingers of both hands up before his mouth rapidly wiggling them toward his moving lips as if it was a crab or a lobster jiggling his mandibles and feeding. It is very beautiful, he said. But what are they doing? Sucking it in and passing it out again, their charming compositions. What do we care? They have eaten. We are very glad. There is nothing they do not eat, there is nothing they do not see. Such eyes! They make very fine compositions. That is the French influence.

Yesterday, he said, there was a woman here in the studio. A very rich old woman. Ooo! I did not dare offend her. She had on a hat with feathers and ribbons like—I can't describe it. Many many different colors. Like a parrot. And a dress! with a piece of lace, a piece of silk, a piece of blue, green—anything you can imagine. And she talked, cha, cha, cha, cha, cha, cha! all the time. Like a parrot. She was a parrot. Perfect.

It was amazing. It was bewildering. You would not believe there could be such a person. And she was interested. She wanted to see.

So I showed her the big canvas I am working on. This here. She looked and in her voice, like a parrot, she said, Oh Mr. Tchelitchew! you paint nothing but monsters!

The painting was before us. I looked at it for a long time. Nothing but human monsters of one sort or another. It was a canvas of perhaps eight by twelve feet. It wasn't finished, though most of it had been drawn in. Figures of all sorts filled it, of all sizes, spreading out upon a background of mountain, classical ruin and Mexican adobe house, with sea and sky going off toward the top and back. Small in the center was the face of an old woman, a tormented, wrinkled face—as if under a lens; above that a tennis court with naked figures on it below a glacier prospect made of ice-heads, infants packed in as though they were rounded ice cubes in a modern refrigerator——

To the left, the signature, a man with one enormous foot, the back of Diego Rivera it may be, painting the wall of a house. Siamese twins, women with six breasts, acephalic monsters, three-legged children, double-headed monsters, sexual freaks, dwarfs, giants, achondroplastic midgets, mongolian idiots and the starved, bloated, misshapen by idea and social accident—of all the walks of life.

In the foreground was a surf with a girl in a pink bathing suit. They ask me if it is surrealist! What do you think? he looked at me.

As a physician, no, I answered. And why not? Because these things are drawn from life, I said. You see that, you see that! he was delighted. Of course, you are a doctor. That is beautiful. He was delighted.

What is surrealism? Anybody can do that. What a lot of fooling nonsense.

As a fact every monster in the picture was authentic. It was actually what is found in life. He has taken things which do occur every day for his mirror. It is a mirror, he added, for them to see themselves.

Our life is horrible, he said. We are monsters. We hate each other and we try to destroy everything that is lovely. And we hide it. No. We *are* beasts—I beg pardon to the beasts. Even our language is distorted, we say we are like "beasts" who are lovely. But we are disgusting. And when I show them how disgusting they are they say, He only wants to paint monsters!

I don't want to paint monsters. Pretty soon I will be tired of monsters. I want to communicate with people. That is painting. The ancients knew what painting was. It is to say

something. It is to communicate. It is to use beautiful colors
because we love them. We enjoy what is lovely and we paint
to speak of it. Because we want to tell somebody that we like
this and they must see it because we like it.

That is why I want to paint everything soft. Because I love
feathers and pearls and fluffy things that hold the light and
split it into rainbows. I am a very poor painter. I cannot paint
like those Spaniards. I work very hard but I go very slow.
When I have filled these spaces—pointing to unfinished
places on the picture—then I will work to get the texture I
desire. I want to make it beautiful, everything the most delicate shading of the colors, light as a feather. That is why I
have painted it as a double rainbow. Because the rainbow is
phenomenal. It is charming to me. I like it. I will paint it that
way.

Indeed all the figures in the picture, the monsters waiting
to be beautified of the softness and the colors were, as they
occurred in various parts of the picture, either green or red
or purple or blue—but the colors quite realistically modu-
lated. As if they had been seen toward evening here, at noon
there, and at sunrise there, before a storm, as it might be.

What do they mean by composition? There are half a
dozen compositions. Everybody knows them. What is that?
They balance here, there. What does it mean? Cezanne!
Pooh. Yes, he could paint a good composition. He knew how
to paint colors. But what is it? Another tree. Another orange.
Another table with flowers. What does it mean? Always the
same. I am tired of that.

That is enough of that. He turned the big picture to the
wall. Let me show you some portraits.

Do you like this one? I paint my portraits all after I have
made the sketch, a year afterward perhaps. When I feel what
I wish to see and I know how to do it. This morning I painted
this face of Edith Sitwell all over. I could finish it today.
What do you think?

It was a white-looking woman in a nun's habit. She was

sitting as if in a straightback, medieval chair completely self-absorbed, ascetic, severe. It was a shock to me after what I thought I had known of the woman's verse.

She is like that, he said. A very beautiful woman. She is alone. She is very positive and very emotional. She takes herself very seriously and seems to be cold as ice. She is not so. I wanted to paint her as I know her. What do you think?

I am glad to know her. I didn't know her. Never thought much of her verse.

Oh, you don't know her then, he said. This will be your introduction. You will see if I am not right. An amazing woman.

And these—this is Ford and his sister. He showed me the portraits of the two young Americans. Their faces were made to radiate the opalescent colors he loves. I looked back at the Sitwell again. Her face I saw now was not white but all the colors of the rainbow minutely blended, not *pointilliste*, but soft as feathers, as down.

You have seen enough paintings, he said, for one afternoon. Next year you shall see the big one—when I have been able to finish it. You will see the difference. Every part of it must be done as I have done the face of Edith Sitwell—this morning. Delicate and soft, with all the colors of the rainbow. You will like it then.

Author's Introduction

The Wedge, 1944

THE WAR IS the first and only thing in the world today.

The arts generally are not, nor is this writing a diversion from that for relief, a turning away. It *is* the war or part of it, merely a different sector of the field.

Critics of rather better than average standing have said in recent years that after socialism has been achieved it's likely there will be no further use for poetry, that it will disappear. This comes from nothing else than a faulty definition of poetry—and the arts generally. I don't hear anyone say that mathematics is likely to be outmoded, to disappear shortly. Then why poetry?

It is an error attributable to the Freudian concept of the thing, that the arts are a resort from frustration, a misconception still entertained in many minds.

They speak as though action itself in all its phases were not compatible with frustration. All action the same. But Richard Coeur de Lion wrote at least one of the finest lyrics of his day. Take Don Juan for instance. Who isn't frustrated and does not prove it by his actions—if you want to say so? But through art the psychologically maimed may become the most distinguished man of his age. Take Freud for instance.

The making of poetry is no more an evidence of frustration than is the work of Henry Kaiser or of Timoshenko. It's the war, the driving forward of desire to a complex end. And when that shall have been achieved, mathematics and the arts will turn elsewhere—beyond the atom if necessary for their reward and let's all be frustrated together.

A man isn't a block that remains stationary though the

psychologists treat him so—and most take an insane pride in believing it. Consistency! He varies; Hamlet today, Caesar tomorrow; here, there, somewhere—if he is to retain his sanity, and why not?

The arts have a *complex* relation to society. The poet isn't a fixed phenomenon, no more is his work. *That* might be a note on current affairs, a diagnosis, a plan for procedure, a retrospect—all in its own peculiarly enduring form. There need be nothing limited or frustrated about that. It may be a throw-off from the most violent and successful action or run parallel to it, a saga. It may be the picking out of an essential detail for memory, something to be set aside for further study, a sort of shorthand of emotional significances for later reference.

Let the metaphysical take care of itself, the arts have nothing to do with it. They will concern themselves with it if they please, among other things. To make two bald statements: There's nothing sentimental about a machine, and: A poem is a small (or large) machine made of words. When I say there's nothing sentimental about a poem I mean that there can be no part, as in any other machine, that is redundant.

Prose may carry a load of ill-defined matter like a ship. But poetry is the machine which drives it, pruned to a perfect economy. As in all machines its movement is intrinsic, undulant, a physical more than a literary character. In a poem this movement is distinguished in each case by the character of the speech from which it arises.

Therefore, each speech having its own character, the poetry it engenders will be peculiar to that speech also in its own intrinsic form. The effect is beauty, what in a single object resolves our complex feelings of propriety. One doesn't seek beauty. All that an artist or a Sperry can do is to drive toward his purpose, in the nature of his materials; not to take gold where Babbitt metal is called for; to make: make clear the complexity of his perceptions in the medium given to him by inheritance, chance, accident or whatever it may be to work with according to his talents and the will that drives them. Don't talk about frustration fathering the arts. The bastardization of words is too widespread for that today.

My own interest in the arts has been extracurricular. Up from the gutter, so to speak. Of necessity. Each age and place to its own. But in the U. S. the necessity for recognizing this intrinsic character has been largely ignored by the various English Departments of the academies.

When a man makes a poem, makes it, mind you, he takes words as he finds them interrelated about him and composes them—without distortion which would mar their exact significances—into an intense expression of his perceptions and ardors that they may constitute a revelation in the speech that he uses. It isn't what he *says* that counts as a work of art, it's what he makes, with such intensity of perception that it lives with an intrinsic movement of its own to verify its authenticity. Your attention is called now and then to some beautiful line or sonnet-sequence because of what is said there. So be it. To me all sonnets say the same thing of no importance. What does it matter what the line "says"?

There is no poetry of distinction without formal invention, for it is in the intimate form that works of art achieve their exact meaning, in which they most resemble the machine, to give language its highest dignity, its illumination in the environment to which it is native. Such war, as the arts live and breathe by, is continuous.

It may be that my interests as expressed here are pre-art. If so I look for a development along these lines and will be satisfied with nothing else.

Shapiro Is All Right *

(Editors' Note: *William Carlos Williams is treated
by Shapiro as an "objectivist" poet, in part as follows:*

*And (if this is not irrelevant) I for one
Have stared long hours at his discoveries
That seem at times the germs of serious science,
At times the baubles of the kaleidoscope.
A red wheelbarrow, a stone, a purple plum,
Things of a fixed world, metaphysics strange
As camera perception, in which no change
Occurs in any image. And prosody yields
To visible invariables; motion fails,
And metric, a fallacy in a static mold
Freezes itself to dazzling shapes, grows cold.*)

Kenyon Review, 1946

SUPPOSE ALL WOMEN were delightful, the ugly, the short, the
fat, the intellectual, the stupid, even the old—and making a
virtue of their qualities, each for each, made themselves available to men, some man, any man—without greed. What a
world it could be—for women! In the same figure take all the
forms of rime. Take for instance the fat: If she were not too
self-conscious, did not regret that she were not lissome and
quick afoot but gave herself, full-belly, to the sport! What
a game it would make! All would then be, in the best sense,
beautiful—entertaining to the mind as to the eye but especially to that part of a man which we call so mistakenly the
intellect. It is rather the whole man, the man himself, alert.
He would be analyzed by their deportment and enriched in

* A review of *Essay on Rime*, by Karl Jay Shapiro. Reynal & Hitch-
cock: New York, 1945.
258

the very libraries of his conscience. He would be free, freed
to the full completion of his desires.

Shapiro speaks lovingly of his "rime," which he defines
here and there in his poem—variously, as it should (not) be
defined. It is the whole body of the management of words to
the formal purposes of expression. We express ourselves there
(men) as we might on the whole body of the various female
could we ever gain access to her (which we cannot and never
shall). Do we have to feel inferior or thwarted because of
that? Of course not. We do the best we can—as much as the
females of our souls permit. Which isn't much generally.
Each man writes as he is able under the circumstances under
which he exists.

The trouble with this exercise of Shapiro's is that it is so
damned easy to read, so interesting, such a pleasure. One can
sympathize with a man sitting down in a "camp" somewhere,
bored stiff by removal from his usual environment and playing (*in vacuo*, so to speak) with the problems he must someday face in practical work. He doesn't solve much, he doesn't
expect to solve much, he wants only to clarify, to make a
definite distinction between the parts of the great body that
presents itself to him for his enjoyment. He attacks it bravely.
She lies back and smiles—not with any intent to intimidate.
She is very definitely sure of herself and—friendly. Whether
she will be stirred to passion by his attack is a question. But he
is young and that's a lot.

Well, you don't get far with women by quoting Eliot to
them. Maybe the Sacred Hind means something to them—
and wistfulness is dear to the female heart but I don't believe
it beyond a certain point. She gets tired of being tickled
merely.

However, we're talking of the art of writing well in a modern world and women haven't much to do with that, I guess.
Not directly. America is still too crude for that. I don't think
any place is much better. Not France. Not England—so far
as I know. And not Russia. Of course it's ridiculous to think

of any land, as a land, in this respect. Women are as various (and as rare) as men.

What Shapiro does point out however is that—

> No conception
> Too far removed from literal position
> Can keep its body.

I imagine that will put a quietus on the "abstractionists" so far as writing (with words) is concerned. It's all right to make Maltese crosses of poems and use words as pigments—but, well . . . Women want men to come to the point. Writing, too, is like that. At least I think that is what Shapiro means, relative to the prosody. If so I agree with him.

I admire his respect for Milton (*pace* Winters) especially with reference to the amazing transition Milton effects between the dialogue and the chorus in *Samson*. But I am especially interested in the view he takes of Milton the craftsman, to whom he calls strongest attention—though I must say it would have been better if he had a little stressed the necessity Milton was under in achieving his effects to distort the language in ways we may not descend to. He however ignores, as what craftsman must not, the mere subject of Milton's major poem. Lesser critics do not get beyond that.

Shapiro intimates the *formal* importance of Whitman—another thing nobody notices. Nobody notices enough, that is.

Oh, well, I've only read halfway through his poem as yet. I think it is illuminating in its summations of the field, the large expanse of what we must approach to be masterful.

I came at the book with positive aversion. What the hell! But he has won me. I think Shapiro may very well—at least I permit him to go on writing. He isn't a liar, he isn't an ape, he isn't just sad over the state of the world and the stars, he doesn't even bother to concern himself with humanity, or economics, or sociology or any other trio.

He's almost painfully interested in writing as it has been, masterfully, in the world and as it may be (under changed

and changing conditions) in the world again. He keeps on the
subject. And that's rare. More power to him. I hope he finds
her rarest treasures—I am not jealous.

Beginning toward the last thousand lines I find—

> But grammar
> like prosody is a methodical afterthought,
> A winter flower of language.

There are many such successful aphorisms among the two
thousand lines, not the worst part of the poem—good summations of fumbled concepts we all play at remembering.

Then he goes off on A. It may be a personal matter with
him but I don't know one man writing in America today who
ever reads A. or so much as thinks of him or his work when
writing. I may be uninformed, I merely mention what to me
is a commonplace. Vazakas once went to see A. at Swarth-
more and found him a nice boy, still, and very kind—but I
didn't discover that he came away with any broader impression—and with the next sentence we were talking of other
matters. This infatuation I think reveals Shapiro's faulty objective in some of his work. A. seems frankly to be desper-
ately fumbling with a complicated apparatus—to find, to find
—could it possibly be something not discoverable here? That
would really be too bad.

We haven't half enough translations. How can Shapiro say
historians will discover we've had too many? I am sure Ezra
Pound will be known principally for his translations, the most
exquisite in our language. Of bad translations, yes, we've had
too many—and of translations of bad poetry, popular at the
moment, far, far too many. Rilke and Rimbaud *ad nauseam.*
Why don't we read *them* at least in the originals? Every
translation I have ever read of either painfully stinks.

Yop. "And less verse of the mind."

I can't agree on Hart Crane. He had got to the end of his
method, it never was more than an excrescence—no matter
what the man himself may have been. He had written it right

and left, front and back, up and down and round in a circle both ways, crisscross and at varying speeds. He couldn't do it any longer. He was on his way back from Mexico to—work. And couldn't work. He was returning to create and had finished creating. Peggy said that in the last three hours he beat on her cabin door—after being deceived and thrashed. He didn't know where to turn—that was the end of it.

That he had the guts to go over the rail in his pyjamas, unable to sleep or even rest, was, to me (though what do I know —more than another?) a failure to find anywhere *in his* "*rime*" an outlet. He had tried in Mexico merely to write—to write anything. He couldn't.

Yes, love might have saved him—but if one is to bathe to satiation in others' blood for love's sake . . . ?

Belief would be marvelous if it were not belief but scientific certainty. But you can't go back and believe what you know to be false and no belief has ever existed without holes in stones that emit smoke—to this day. Belief must always for us today signify nothing but the incomplete, the not yet realized, the hypothetical. The unknown.

Where then will you find the only true belief in our day? Only in science. That is the realm of the incomplete, the convinced hypothesis—the frightening embodiment of mysteries, of transmutations from force to body and from body to —nothingness. Light.

The anthropomorphic imaginatives that baffle us by their absence today had better look to Joyce if they want a pope and endless time.

Anyone who has seen two thousand infants born as I have and pulled them one way or another into the world must know that man, as such, is doomed to disappear in not too many thousand years. He just can't go on. No woman will stand for it. Why should she?

We'll have to look to something else. Who are we anyhow? Just man? What the hell's that? Rime is more.

Lower Case Cummings

Wake 5, 1946

To ME, of course, e. e. cummings means my language. It isn't, of course, mine so much as it is his, which emphasizes the point. It isn't, primarily, english. It isn't at all english. Not that superb inheritance—which we both, I am sure, stand before in amazement and wonder, knowing the dazzling achievements of which it is the living monument. We speak another language; a language of which we are so jealous that we won't even acknowledge that we hold it in common.

Esoteric is the word the englishers among us would give to the languages we americans use at our best. They are private languages. That is what cummings seems to be emphasizing, a christian language—addressing to the private conscience of each of us in turn.

But if, startlingly, each should disclose itself as understandable to any great number, the effect would be in effect a veritable revolution, shall we say, of morals? Of, do we dare to say, love? Much or even all cummings' poems are the evidences of love. The french say you can't translate his poems into french: just so many words. A curious sort of love, not at all french, not at all latin. Not, above all, anything even in the faintest degree resembling the english.

I think of cummings as Robinson Crusoe at the moment when he first saw the print of a naked human foot in the sand. That, too, implied a new language—and a readjustment of conscience.

We are inclined to forget that cummings has come *from* english to another province having escaped across a well defended border; he has remained, largely, a fugitive ever since.

I don't think he should be held too closely to account for some of his doodles, his fiddling with the paraphernalia of the writing game. He has been for a good part of the last twenty years like the prisoner in solitary confinement who retained his sanity by tossing a pin over his shoulder in the dark and spending long hours searching for it again.

Without the least question cummings is a fugitive; a fugitive from the people about him whom he irritates by telling them they are human beings subject to certain beauties and distempers they will not acknowledge; a fugitive as well from the university where the bait of official recognition has brought down many of his former fellows.

cummings, who is not robust, is positively afraid of physical violence if he goes out of his rooms. For a species of americans and certain other wild animals are prone to attack a man going alone. Imagine the armed bands of the intelligentsia which roam Greenwich Village by day and night—the belligerently convinced—that a poor lone man like cummings would have to face to survive if he went so much as to the baker's for a dozen breakfast rolls. It is frightening. Important. But he hasn't run away. Just the opposite.

It would be all right if e. e. were himself more gregarious, more, what shall we say, promiscuous—at least less averse to the pack—even to very nice packs certified by the very best teachers in the very best schools here and abroad. But he isn't. He feels that among those curious things called americans there isn't one, in this inarticulate jungle, to whom he can say more than—How do you do? Was that your footprint I saw in the sand this morning?

Imagine if the startled black should turn on him and say in reply, Swing low sweet chariot! That wouldn't be it. That wouldn't be it at all. cummings would be completely defeated, and cummings cannot afford to be defeated! why he's a member of the strongest nation on earth—bar none. He's in a very tight squeeze every day of his life, Year in, year out, holding to his supplies, finding what shelter is possible to him. Writing. Isn't that the thing to do? Write.

He paints also—but I don't like his painting. I think it represents the worst of his style; an insistence that any artist will fall into when he is sick of his proper medium and of those defects which he, better than anyone else, is conscious of, and which yet he tries still to put over by a shift in direction to flout the world. But maybe he paints just because it rests him —a minor matter.

Words are his proper medium, the specific impact of words, which give them in his work such a peculiarly un-historic, historical new world character. A toughness which scorns to avoid fragility.

When I say "new world" I do not mean american. That is just what cummings says over and over again, that's what he lives; that, too, is what makes him solitary. Not "american," sensual. I almost want to say, that that which deprives him of academic as well as popular understanding or effectiveness in argument makes him at the same time a good deal like the steeple of one of those New England churches facing the common up there, so strangely remote an effect. I avoid speaking of the clipper ships. I avoid speaking of Moby Dick.

No, it is something very much older and very modern too. Cotton Mather? Yes, he had a library. If it goes back to the King James version of the Bible, and it does, it goes there solely for what that *says* to the Christian conscience. It says, Ignore the dress in which the Word comes to you and look to the Life of which that is the passing image.

cummings is the living presence of the drive to make all our convictions evident by penetrating through their costumes to the living flesh of the matter. He avoids the cliché first by avoiding the whole accepted modus of english. He does it, not to be "popular," God knows, nor to sell anything, but to lay bare the actual experience of love, let us say, in the chance terms which his environment happens to make apparent to him. He does it to reveal, to disclose, to free a man from habit. Habit is our continual enemy as artists and as men. Practice is not a habit though it must be watched lest it become so.

The drunk, the whore, the child, are typical cummings heroes. (Is that Deacon Cummings speaking? Probably.) At the start, right out of the Greek of his college days, he threw the whole of the english department armanentarium out the window—a sort of Cambridge Tea Party.

Then he began to speak of rabbits, mice, all the sprites of the native pastures—as though he had just got sight and were afraid he was going to lose it again—with infinite tenderness, with FEELING. He wanted to feel. He wanted to see, see, see! and make the words speak of what he saw . . . and felt. For it must not be forgot that we smell, hear and see with words and words alone, and that with a new language we smell, hear and see afresh—by this we can well understand cummings' early excitement at his release. If a woman came into the picture early she vanished in favor of women: he got them badly mixed up. He didn't know what the thing meant —much. It wasn't, in effect, art. He was sure of that.

Now women, that's different. That's a subject that has some meat to it. You can love women. But how in almighty heaven can you love a woman and be free to embrace the world in new and unaccepted terms?

Then he left his entire early mountain world. Went to France and landed—*The Enormous Room*. That doesn't need explanation; but it is, for cummings, today, an annoyance. There he was and he wrote what he had to say about it, superbly. One remembers (if vaguely now) those spirits, ghosts —lost souls—victims of whom do you think? The Japs? No, by God, the French! Can you imagine the impertinence of smelling a french stink? But cummings merely smelled it.

Finally he came, with finality, to New York. The express elevators ran up and down inside him for a while—until they busted and—stopped.

To adopt the ballad forms of nursery rhymes—merely emphasizes in a primary manner . . . the continued necessity for reappraisals in the arts: and the pre-eminence of the lyric. The best of cummings' lyrics seem as if they had been taken from something else, a series of fantastic plays which he never wrote—for it would have represented an actual world which never existed save in his imagination. It is a new world—the only clue to its substantiality being the language cummings uses. It may have been Atlantis—which he knew to exist since he could tell very definitely that his father had been there also.

He lives today in a second Enormous Room, this time of the imagination—so real it is.

I don't see how you can avoid speaking of cummings in this way, dangerous as it surely is. You are likely to go off into a Never-Never Land which is so much froth. But if we lay the fact of cummings against that background we see better than in any other way how bitterly he has persisted with his revolution in the language and to what planned effect.

He has fixed it, too, that he can't be imitated. You've got to learn the *basis* for his trapeze tricks. When you have done that you'll be able to do tricks of your own—as the masters did in the past. Not before. In that he's our best schoolmaster in the language; the kind that you just don't avoid.

What fools critics are who try to make him a painter with words. With cummings every syllable has a conscience and a specific impact—attack, which, as we know now—is the best defense.

Perhaps, at some time in the future, though it is extremely unlikely, we'll be able to shed the lower case and embellish the new language with Caps. But for the moment cummings has the right idea.

Revelation

Yale Poetry Review, 1947

THE OBJECTIVE in writing is, to reveal. It is not to teach, not to advertise, not to sell, not even to communicate (for that needs two) but to reveal, which needs no other than the man himself. Not even, after all, to invent except that to reveal one must reveal something, not nothing—even though that would be better.

Reveal what? That which is inside the man. That is why the "stream of consciousness" idea was recently so correct and will be so again in another ten years more or less: it revealed . . . heaven knows what it revealed, at least it was properly directed. It put aside "composition," empty as "perspective" in painting. It went to the basis of the matter, it wanted to let out something even if it didn't know what— that was its weakness, that it didn't know what. But it was properly aimed toward revelation, without let, without impost; it wanted to open up the hide.

The "philosophy of writing" one might say. Pathetic. Everyone writes to reveal his soul, what's that? Souls are a dime a dozen today. Even idiots have souls with a cash value to someone, someone important! Guess who? Even monsters . . . for the cash value. Not really? You don't mean . . . Or do you? Probably.

The fact is that in the head there is a lightning calculator, you know, the thing that made Shakespeare seem an intellectual. It worked. Watch it work, that's all there is to writing (if it works). Turn it loose. Let it turn itself into a codex on the page. That's writing, revelation. . . . it doesn't have to be too compact. But it usually is, at its best, the most complicated formulas worked out (by it) in a few seconds and set down: the mind racing at top speed to touch and decipher. Put a situation, a proposal in at the hopper-end and watch it come out at the other—in "beautiful" formality. The non-rational, shall we say? The revealing, perhaps what Randall Jarrell calls the "romantic" as against the classical approach, the leap to the answer as against lapidary work.

What it is actually is the depth of the brain at work, up and down, tapping the deeper veins, not merely the interrelationships of the conscious surfaces. Or, better, the conscious surface as it relates itself to the deeper brain, back and forth at lightning speed, governed by the profundities. It is what is "inside" that does the work and it is "work" that it does, giving answers. It often gives unwelcome answers.

Take the newspapers or a salable novel or a play. They reveal nothing whatever, for they only tell you what you already know—you wouldn't recognize it otherwise. That would be too expensive a proposition. They tell you "all about a murder" which you have committed fifty times in your own mind. Is that revealing? Silly. Or they tell you in "mystery" stories the same thing (it has to be the same to be soothing to presidents and stenographers) they tell you the completely unrevealing things, the Churchill and Stalin speeches and all the other claptrap of the conscious mind, the prepared thought, the rehearsed concept.

Imagine a proselytizing sermon! One that "moves" you. It sets out to be a revelation! Why, the only reason you were moved is that you weren't there. You weren't watching it. It was directed at you. You were unaware but it was watching you. It had you spotted. It was (in its sense) lying in wait for you and, as you turned toward it, pop! you were caught. Nothing has been revealed, rather veiled—of a purpose to catch you, idiot!

But revelation, when it perceives you, turns away—in the opposite direction. You cannot snare it by deception. The difference between the revealer and the others is that he reveals HIMSELF, not you.

Thus the birth of every baby, whatever its quality, is a revelation. But the moment it is christened, circumcised or indoctrinated by other means into whatever sect or clan will delimit it from others of its generation, revelation is at an end. It may defy its circumscribers later and maintain whatever is left of its first or "original sin" against them to some degree as best it may, but that will be its measure.

We must recognize, of course, that the attack of "interests" will come. But it seems fairly well established that when through fortuitous circumstances, the child, escaping the imperfectly armed adults about, who would twist the sprout into the way it should, by their reason, grow, when he by some accident can preserve some rare, unblemished area of the first revelation hidden in his secret heart, it is there that he will live and most beautifully blossom. It is there he will be revealed the agent for discoveries largely lost where he has been pretwisted in the underlying depths of his brain. It is in fact the history of everyone that his whole infancy is spent in a mad attempt to rescue what he can for himself from his first revelation. Every infant will do his best, if he is let decently alone (under adult guard) to rescue himself in secret, there to live his life through.

The attack must come, the attempt to "school" the unhappy child, but nothing is more revolting to decency than to hear the adult say that if he can catch the young before the age of six, is it? or younger? he doesn't care what shall happen to him later. Nothing, to my mind, so reveals the essential depravity, the basic starvation of the adult mind as that common saying and what is behind it. It comes of the wasted revelations known and lost to us for the most part in early youth.

We are like clams that close their shells at the approach of a direct attack—but cannot protect themselves against the boring worm that penetrates the heaviest shell. We are deformed also, as are they, when spawned between two stones and must grow there.

Suddenly there is a revolution! Immediately, without

change in ourselves, we take that shape (our minds take the shape of the revolution), we are perhaps deformed into that shape (or its opposite). That is no revelation. Rather than released we are, as I pointed out years ago in the case of the Puritans, shut about by danger and contract in order to be able to survive under the new order. To survive means everything to us, as it does to a clam in the mud or a woman before the invention of contraceptives—or permission for their use. Contraceptives have altered the entire concept of women. They have proven a revelation concerning her. She was thought to be essentially modest, retiring, the weaker vessel but all this was a false appraisal induced entirely by her fear of pregnancy. She was as a consequence ideologically shrunk up to be contained in a narrow case, only the very powerful and hazard-loving could manage to break away. Thus and because of that we had the history of the Abelards and Heloises, the Paolos and Francescas, the Romeos and Juliets, a whole literary genealogy to be swept away.

I am advancing no brief for immorality, rather the opposite. I am speaking of the necessity for revelation in order that we may achieve morality. In order, briefly, to get at the actual values that concern man where they frequently lie buried in his mind. Only through a loosening of the reins, the escape of the child from the mother and father, the escape of woman from the domination of childbearing—can that loosening that allows any depth of penetration of thought to occur in our minds can we get to the revelations which will restore values and meanings to our starved lives.

Proust dug back into his mind for something, something lost, mind what I say, something lost. It was lost and he did not, definitely he did not, find it any more than Rousseau found it in his *Confessions*. Both men are moralists, they tell you, don't let it happen as it happened to me or to Swann or to Thal. They are saying as any sensible man must say: Stop maiming the times! Fear deformed us and we reveal to you the depths of our deformity. We do not like our deformity. Look what might have been!

Carl Sandburg's Complete Poems

Poetry: A Magazine of Verse, 1951

CARL SANDBURG has been around a long time. In that period, during which modern art has celebrated some of its greatest triumphs, he has accumulated a mass of poems which have now been published as a single volume. Because of the man's name, his position and the conclusion forced on us that here summarized is the work of one of our best known poets, we should give the book major attention.

Search as we will among them we must say at once that technically the poems reveal no initiative whatever other than their formlessness; there is no motivating spirit held in the front of the mind to control them. And without a theory, as Pasteur once said, to unify it, a man's life becomes little more than an aimless series of random and repetitious gestures. In the poem a rebellion against older forms means nothing unless, finally, we have a new form to substitute for that which has become empty from the exhaustion of its means. There never has been any positive value in the form or lack of form known as free verse into which Sandburg's verse is cast.

That drive for new form seemed to be lacking in Sandburg. We must never make the mistake of trying to substitute the materials of a new territory for the great and universal power of the art itself. The vigor of new forms demands its own prerogatives but only to increase the range and break through the restrictions of the old. We have, for instance, recently come to realize that there is a new bible left us by the highly cultured tribes of the New World, representing a memory, an orderly record of an all but vanished race. It is called the

Popul Vuh. It is a new set of terms which the old wished to but could not quite destroy.

But if it failed seriously to move him that doesn't mean that we shouldn't be animated by it when we look at his work. He put it down ten years ago. It was an accumulation, it did not develop—faded off rather for lack of structural interest on his part, nothing to inform it, nothing to drive it forward. The theory, the active worm in the fruit, the thing that corrupts a man, kills him if you will; the sick (if you will) intelligence that got Socrates poisoned because he would not let go of the logic but drove it forward until either he or it should be annihilated, wasn't there. Sandburg didn't feel that way about his verse but the damning material he collected is still valuable. It is up to us to discover (as he couldn't) what in that may be picked up and carried forward, a great mass of evidence which he painstakingly gathered.

There are those all too ready to take the opportunity of Sandburg's comparative failure to reject the whole that he represents—which at least ran synchronously with the upsurge of the modern impetus—ready at any excuse to reject the whole new configuration at sight of any flaw. They're delighted to be able to snigger behind their hands and, throwing him out, profit by the occasion to rush back to their old and respectable deadness. Sandburg may not have known what he was doing, it may never have entered his mind that there was anything significant to do with the structure of the verse itself, but the best of him was touched with fire.

Carl Sandburg petered out as a poet ten years ago. I imagine he wanted it to be that way. His poems themselves said what they had to say, piling up, then just went out, like a light. He had no answers, he didn't seek any. Without any attempt at the solace which the limitations of art (as with a Baudelaire) might bring, the formlessness of his literary figures was the very formlessness of the materials with which he worked. That was his truth. That was what he wanted truthfully to make plain, that was his compulsion. That form he could accept but at a terrible cost: failure deliberately invited, a gradual inevitable slackening off to ultimate defeat.

"Chicago," his first brilliantly successful poem, should have been his last. Between the writing of that and "Number Man" (*for the ghost of Johann Sebastian Bach*), one of his latest, occurs the mass of his work. It is that bulk that makes up the book with which we are dealing, pushing it on our attention. The devotion he has spent on it, the painstaking and voluminous notes he has gathered, the indignation it has caused him—tripped him up. He refused to lie, or was incapable of taking his eyes away from what he saw. Nor could he be neat, or choosy, or selective about it. It overwhelmed him. He couldn't get over it. He let it dictate its own terms, he was willing to go under with it. He must have looked occasionally at some pleasant guys and the way they could train the words to stand on tubs and jump through hoops. He kept wandering off behind the scenes to talk with the hands who set up the props.

There is a lot of talk of "kings who shall no longer be kings, nor the sons of kings become kings." But the language generally is just talk, the sort of reporting that never gets over straight in newspapers and never can. It's always bitched up in the magazine section on Sunday; it's always slanted with maddening implications, made nauseating at the editor's desk, in the slicks and true-stories magazines. This is the subtle censorship which Sandburg tried to avoid. Without art it is a task almost impossible to accomplish.

It goes on and on from the Swede in the flat below, through railroad men, the farmer reaping his acres, the Texas ranger, slum dwellers, women, pimps playing the piano in whorehouses, back to the salesgirls in department stores in the big cities. In the end he sums it up, *The People, Yes*, and lets it go at that.

For twenty years he kept this up with diminishing force, book after book, *Chicago Poems*, 1916, *Cornhuskers*, 1918,

Smoke and Steel, 1920, *Slabs of the Sunburnt West,* 1922, *Good Morning America,* 1928, and *The People, Yes,* 1936. In *Cornhuskers* occurs a different sort of poem from his usual wont, it was called "Ashurnatsirpal III" (*From Babylonian tablet, 4000 years before Christ*) and shows a more indirect approach to the theme from that which Sandburg usually exploited. Had he followed that lead the man's natural love of violence, so wonderfully exhibited at the start of his career in the poem "Chicago," might have carried him on to great distinction. But the theme remains neglected.

He seems to have lost hope finally at directly invoking the imagination by aid of poetic invention in favor of a single image, Abraham Lincoln, which he exploited in prose. That he used indirectly, as an image; he meant it to carry the whole burden of what he had been saying directly in his human catalogues. Here it is, he seems to tell us. This is what I have been talking about, these Hunkies, these gals on the back streets. But by then the poetry was gone. He put it deliberately aside.

It was a magnificent conception. He had documented a thousand examples of that which the pinching poets with their neat images, take e. e. cummings for instance in comparable passages, have merely brushed upon in passing. Sandburg has piled them up as if by the sheer mass of them he would call attention to their significance, forcing them on us —as if in amazement that we should, any of us, be so blind as not to see, *see*, SEE! what it is that we should be thinking of winter, summer, day and night, waking, sleeping, eating, drinking, bathing, lying dirty in our rags, burying our dead —to the exclusion of all other sensible things—this colossal image! You cannot ignore such a man.

To him it is an image, a magnificently effective image. But he couldn't hold the figure he'd begun, he couldn't hold it off. He fell into the facts themselves. He couldn't limit himself to being a mere poet, the facts were too overpowering, he himself was swept off his feet by their flood.

There is a steady diminution of the poetic charge in his

verses from about the period of *Cornhuskers* to *The People, Yes*. He seems to have lost the taste for it. When Picasso became a Communist, convinced that that was his human duty, it did NOT alter his dedication to his task as an artist. And the official Communist blackguards were forced to accept his point of view, not he theirs. They did NOT suppress him.

But Sandburg, convinced that the official democracy he was witnessing was rotten, abandoned his art to expose it. He suffered the inevitable results. He knew what he was doing. To have persisted as a pure poet would have maimed what to him was the outstanding thing: the report of the people, the basis of all art and of everything that is alive with regenerative power.

He didn't see that the terms the people use are so often the very thing that defeats them. It is by his invention of new terms that the artist uniquely serves. The process is much more complex than Sandburg realizes. It is not, as between the mob and supremely sensitive man, a direct process though its incentives are no less simple for that. The most inspired artist is moved by SIMPLE designs dormant in the very "people" of which Sandburg speaks. It doesn't matter how compelled to distortion their inventions may appear on the canvas or the page, in fact it is the very character of distortion which has shaped their truth.

The poet in himself, tormented by the things which Sandburg evinces, dissatisfied with mere repeated statement, over and over reiterated but undeveloped, digests that powerful incentive and puts it out as imaginative design, a new thing that embodies all their timeless agonies. It may not seem as effective to the active tormented man as the direct outcry— of an Okie in the desert, as Sandburg envisions him—but it has far more carrying power.

It is shocking for the uninformed to look at a Picasso or to pick up a poem by Rosalie Moore. He can't understand them. He will never understand them until he has CHANGED within himself. When he does that he will change what he performs. He will no longer be the same man. He will be MOVED by those works of art more than he is by all the piling up of images that Sandburg has ever assembled. Because the instances Sandburg has piled up merely say to them, "somebody" is responsible. But it is never they themselves whom they consider responsible (though they are directly responsible for their own comparable misfortunes). But if they face and are faced by the canvas and the page of which I have spoken they will not be able any longer glibly to accept the facts Sandburg has so assiduously assembled. They will be changed as the facts could never change them, they will have been acted on by a new principle and they will in turn act on their part.

To maintain the force of his assault the artist will remain remote from the field. He deals in stratagems. This detachment gives brilliance to his effects. The surgeon does not feel the cuts he makes, so it must be with the poet. The killing in the *Iliad* takes place in the open air, it is an air we can breathe, almost taste—after all these years. It is the poet's detachment that is the spring, Homer himself is unaffected. He can show Achilles to have compassion knowing himself doomed but he, Homer, remains the mere accurate teller of the tale. For him to wince in the slightest degree would make him a cad and a liar, he shows no sign of it. His senses remain unclouded so that ours too may remain unclouded—as our hearts are wrung.

In this massive book covering a period of close to forty years the poems show no development of the thought, in the technical handling of the material, in the knowledge of the forms, the art of treating the line. The same manner of using the words, of presenting the image is followed in the first poem as in the last. All that can be said is that a horde walks steadily, unhurriedly through its pages, following without affection one behind the other.

It is a monstrous kind of show. It isn't even a pageant, it

might be a pilgrimage. It comes off best as a pilgrimage, but look at Chaucer's varied art. That is all the unchanging meaning to be got, a massive pilgrimage: good and bad, male and female, the sheer weight of numbers going in one direction (the same as the sun) they seem unable to turn right or left and never back. Its unchanging burden, unchangeable it seems as we read, is the failure to find happiness. The theme of happiness in Sandburg is always something remembered and lost. Even the hope for it is lost. There is only a pressing forward (without understanding), pressing forward, an unrelenting drive, oxlike you might almost call it. That is the great image Sandburg draws.

It is hopeful, it is massive, it is impressive—but not for itself. Fatigue is the outstanding phenomenon as it affects the characters, they walk as if doped. The ideal for the self seems very nearly that of Eastman, spoken of in one of the poems, a man knowing himself doomed who shoots himself, through a wet towel, in the heart, after carefully putting his will in order so that it may have the exact effect he has planned.

Nowhere among the poems will you find anything that you can speak of as a recurrence: nowhere a rhyme, a stated line, a recognizable stanza, it is one long flight. This could not be different. It is the very formlessness of the material, its failure to affirm anything formal, the drift of aimless life through the six hundred and seventy-six pages that is the form. It had to be shapeless to affirm what was being said: persistence in change.

Of Sandburg himself there seems to emerge more in *Cornhuskers* than the other books. One catches glimpses of a half-hidden figure that looks at you a moment with questioning eyes before disappearing again in the crowd. I was struck by such poems as "Roses," "Horses " "Joliet," "Knucks," "In Tall Grass," "Mammy Hums" and "Bringers." But they are lost in the drift of all that surrounds them.

For it is formless as a drift of desert sand engulfing the occasional shrub or tree and as formed. The *Collected Poems* make a dunelike mass; no matter where you dig into them it is sand. (Sandburg! I didn't think of that. It seems as if the name itself has gotten into it.) His characters, a drift of people, a nameless people for the most part, are sand, giving the wind form in themselves until they lie piled up filling his pages.

The Poem as a Field of Action

Talk given at the University of Washington, 1948

LET'S BEGIN by quoting Mr. Auden—(from *The Orators*): "Need I remind you that you're no longer living in ancient Egypt?"

I'm going to say one thing to you—for a week! And I hope to God when I'm through that I've succeeded in making you understand me. It concerns the poem as a field of action, at what pitch the battle is today and what may come of it.

As Freud says bitterly in the first chapter of his *The Interpretation of Dreams*, speaking of the early opposition to his theory:

> —the aversion of scientific men to
> learning something new

we shall learn that is a characteristic quite as pronounced in literature—where they will *copy* "the new"—but the tiresome repetition of this "new," now twenty years old, disfigures every journal: I said a field of action. I can see why so many wish rather, avoiding thought, to return to the classic front of orthodox acceptance. As Anatole France put it in Freud's time, *"Les savants ne sont pas curieux."*

It is next to impossible to bring over the quantitative Greek and Latin texts into our language. But does anyone ever ask *why* a Latin line in translation tends to break in half in our language? *Why* it cannot be maintained in its character, its quantitative character as against our accented verse? Have *all* the equivalents been exhausted or even tried? I doubt it.

I offer you then an initiation, what seems and what is actually only a half-baked proposal—since I cannot follow it up with proofs or even *final* examples—but I do it with at least my eyes open—for what I myself may get out of it by presenting it as well as I can to you.

I propose sweeping changes from top to bottom of the poetic structure. I said structure. So now you are beginning to get the drift of my theme. I say we are *through* with the iambic pentameter as presently conceived, at least for dramatic verse; through with the measured quatrain, the staid concatenations of sounds in the usual stanza, the sonnet. More has been done than you think about this though not yet been specifically named for what it is. I believe something can be said. Perhaps all that I can do here is to call attention to it: a revolution in the conception of the poetic foot—pointing out the evidence of something that has been going on for a long time.

At this point it might be profitable (since it would bring me back to my subject from a new point of view) to turn aside for a brief, very brief discussion (since it is not in the direct path of my essay) of the materials—that is to say, the subject matter of the poem. In this let me accept all the help I can get from Freud's theory of the dream—as a fulfillment of the wish—which I accept here holus-bolus. The poem is a dream, a daydream of wish fulfillment but not by any means a field of action and purposive action of a less high order because of that.

It has had in the past a varying subject matter—almost one might say a progressively varying choice of subject matter as you shall see—I must stress here that we are talking of the *recent* past.

And let me remind you here to keep in your minds the term reality as contrasted with phantasy and to tell you that the *subject matter* of the poem is always phantasy—what is wished for, realized in the "dream" of the poem—but that the structure confronts something else.

We may mention Poe's dreams in a pioneer society, his dreams of gentleness and bliss—also, by the way, his professional interest in meter and his very successful experiments with form. Yeats's subject matter of faery. Shakespeare—the butcher's son dreaming of Caesar and Wolsey. No need to go on through Keats, Shelley to Tennyson. It is all, the subject matter, a wish for aristocratic attainment—a "spiritual" bureaucracy of the "soul" or what you will.

There was then a subject matter that was "poetic" and in many minds that is still poetry—and exclusively so—the "beautiful" or pious (and so beautiful) wish expressed in beautiful language—a dream. That is still poetry: full stop. Well, that was the world to be desired and the poets merely expressed a general wish and so were useful each in his day.

But with the industrial revolution, and steadily since then, a new spirit—a new *Zeitgeist* has possessed the world, and as a consequence new values have replaced the old, aristocratic concepts—which had a pretty seamy side if you looked at them like a Christian. A new subject matter began to be manifest. It began to be noticed that there could be a new subject matter and that that was not in fact the poem at all. Briefly then, money talks, and the poet, the modern poet has admitted new subject matter to his dreams—that is, the serious poet has admitted the whole armamentarium of the industrial age to his poems—

Look at Mr. Auden's earlier poems as an example, with their ruined industrial background of waste and destruction. But even that is passing and becoming old-fashioned with the new physics taking its place. All this is a subject in itself and a fascinating one which I regret to leave, I am sorry to say, for a more pressing one.

Remember we are still in the world of fancy if perhaps disguised but still a world of wish-fulfillment in dreams. The poet was not an owner, he was not a money man—he was still only a poet; a wisher; a word man. The best of all to my way of thinking! Words are the keys that unlock the mind. But is that all of poetry? Certainly not—no more so than the material of dreams was phantasy to Dr. Sigmund Freud.

There is something else. Something if you will listen to many, something permanent and sacrosanct. The one thing that the poet has not wanted to change, the one thing he has clung to in his dream—unwilling to let go—the place where the time-lag is still adamant—is structure. Here we are unmovable. But here is precisely where we come into contact with reality. Reluctant, we waken from our dreams. And what is reality? How do we know reality? The only reality that we can know is MEASURE.

Now to return to our subject—the structure of the poem. Everything in the social, economic complex of the world at any time-sector ties in together—

(Quote Wilson on Proust—modern physics, etc.)

But it might at this time be a good thing to take up first what is spoken of as free verse.

How can we accept Einstein's theory of relativity, affecting our very conception of the heavens about us of which poets write so much, without incorporating its essential fact —the relativity of measurements—into our own category of activity: the poem. Do we think we stand outside the universe? Or that the Church of England does? Relativity applies to everything, like love, if it applies to anything in the world.

What, by this approach I am trying to sketch, what we are trying to do is not only to disengage the elements of a measure but to seek (what we believe is there) a new measure or a new way of measuring that will be commensurate with the social, economic world in which we are living as contrasted with the past. It is in many ways a different world from the past calling for a different measure.

According to this conception there is no such thing as "free verse" and so I insist. Imagism was not structural: that was the reason for its disappearance.

The impression I give is that we are about to make some discoveries. That they will be far-reaching in their effects.—

This will depend on many things. My address (toward the task) is all that concerns me now: That we do approach a change.

What is it? I make a clear and definite statement—that it lies in the structure of the verse. That it may possibly lie elsewhere I do not for a moment deny or care—I have here to defend that only and that is my theme.

I hope you will pardon my deliberation, for I wish again to enter a short by-path: It may be said that I wish to destroy the past. It is precisely a service to tradition, honoring it and serving it that is envisioned and intended by my attack, and not disfigurement—confirming and *enlarging* its application.

Set the overall proposal of an enlarged technical means—in order to liberate the possibilities of depicting reality in a modern world that has seen more if not felt more than in the past —in order to be *able* to feel more (for we know we feel less, or surmise that we do. Vocabulary opens the mind to feeling). But modern in that by psychology and all its dependencies we *know*, for we have learned that to feel more we have to have, in our day, the means to feel *with*—the tokens, the apparatus. We are lacking in the means—the appropriate paraphernalia, just as modern use of the products of chemistry for *refinement* must have means which the past lacked. Our poems are not subtly enough made, the structure, the staid manner of the poem cannot let our feelings through.

(Note: Then show (in what detail I can) what we may do to achieve this end by a review of early twentieth-century literary accomplishments. Work done.)

We seek profusion, the Mass—heterogeneous—ill-assorted —quite breathless—grasping at all kinds of things—as if— like Audubon shooting some little bird, really only to look at it the better.

If any one man's work lacks the distinction to be expected from the finished artist, we might well think of the *profusion* of a Rabelais—as against a limited output. It is as though for the moment we should be profuse, we Americans; we need to build up a mass, a conglomerate maybe, containing few gems but bits of them—Brazilian brilliants—that shine of themselves, uncut as they are.

Now when Mr. Eliot came along he had a choice: 1. Join the crowd, adding his blackbird's voice to the flock, contributing to the conglomerate (or working over it for his selections) or 2. To go where there was already a mass of more ready distinction (to turn his back on the first), already an established literature in what to him was the same language (?) an already established place in world literature—a short cut, in short.

Stop a minute to emphasize our own position: It is *not* that of Mr. Eliot. We are making a modern bolus: That is our somewhat undistinguished burden; profusion, as, we must add in all fairness, against his distinction. His is a few poems beautifully phrased—in his longest effort thirty-five quotations in seven languages. We, let us say, are the Sermons of Launcelot Andrewes from which (in time) some selector will pick *one* phrase. Or say, the *Upanishad* that will contribute a single word! There are summative geniuses like that—they shine. We must value them—the extractors of genius—for what they do: extract. But they are there; we are here. It is not possible for us to imitate them. We are in a different phase—a new language—we are making the mass in which some other later Eliot will dig. We must *see* our opportunity and increase the hoard others will find to use. We must find our *pride* in *that*. We must have the pride, the humility and the thrill in the making. (Tell the story of Bramante and the building of the dome of the Duomo in Florence.)

The clearness we must have is first the clarity of knowing what we are doing—what we may do: Make anew—a re-examination of the means—on a fresh—basis. Not at *this* time an analysis so much as an accumulation. You couldn't expect us to be as prominent (as *read* in particular achievements—outstanding single poems). We're not doing the same thing.

We're not putting the rose, the single rose, in the little glass vase in the window—we're digging a hole for the tree—and as we dig have disappeared in it.

(Note: Pound's story of my being interested in the loam whereas he wanted the finished product.)

(Note: Read Bridges—two short pieces in the anthology: 1. The Child 2. Snow.)

We begin to pick up what so far is little more than a feeling (a feeling entirely foreign to a Mr. E. or a Mr. P.—though less to them than to some others) that something is taking place in the accepted prosody or ought to be taking place. (Of course we have had Whitman—but he is a difficult subject—prosodically and I do not want to get off into that now.) It is similar to what must have been the early feelings of Einstein toward the laws of Isaac Newton in physics. Thus from being fixed, our prosodic values should rightly be seen as only relatively true. Einstein had the speed of light as a constant—his only constant—What have we? Perhaps our concept of musical time. I think so. But don't let us close down on that either at least for the moment.

In any case we as loose, disassociated (linguistically), yawping speakers of a new language, are privileged (I guess) to sense and so to seek to discover that possible thing which is disturbing the metrical table of values—as unknown elements would disturb Mendelyeev's table of the periodicity of atomic weights and so lead to discoveries.

And we had better get on the job and make our discoveries or, quietly, someone else will make them for us—covertly and without acknowledgment—(one acknowledges one's indebtedness in one's notes only to dead writers—preferably long dead!).

We wish to find an objective way at least of looking at verse and to redefine its elements; this I say is the theme (the radium) that underlies Bridges' experiments as it is the yeast animating Whitman and all the "moderns."

That the very project itself, quite apart from its solutions, is not yet raised to consciousness, to a clear statement of purpose, is our fault. (Note: the little Mag: Variegations) But one thing, a semiconscious sense of a rending discovery to be made is becoming apparent. For one great thing about "the bomb" is the awakened sense it gives us that catastrophic (but why?) alterations are also possible in the human *mind*, in art, in the arts. . . . We are too cowed by our fear to realize it fully. But it is *possible*. That is what we mean. This isn't optimism, it is chemistry: Or better, physics.

It appears, it disappears, a sheen of it comes up, when, as its shattering implications affront us, all the gnomes hurry to cover up its traces.

Note: *Proust:* (Wilson) He has supplied for the first time in literature an equivalent on the full scale for the new theory of modern physics—I mention this merely to show a possible relationship—between a style and a natural science—intelligently considered.

Now for an entirely new issue: Mr. Auden is an interesting case—in fact he presents to me a deciding issue. His poems are phenomenally worth studying in the context of this theme.

There is no modern poet so agile—so impressive in the use of the poetic means. He can do anything—except one thing. He came to America and became a citizen of this country. He is truly, I should say, learned. Now Mr. Auden didn't come here for nothing or, if you know Auden, without a deep-seated conviction that he *had* to come. Don't put it down to any of the superficial things that might first occur to you—that he hates England, etc. He came here because of a crisis in his career—his career as a writer, as a poet particularly I should say. Mr. Auden may disagree with me in some of this but he will not disagree, I think, when I say he is a writer to whom writing is his life, his very breath which, as he or any man goes on, in the end absorbs *all* his breath.

Auden might have gone to France or to Italy or to South America or following Rimbaud to Ceylon or Timbuctoo. No! He came to the United States and became a citizen. Now the crisis, the only crisis which could drive a man, a distinguished poet, to that would be that he had come to an end of some sort in his poetic means—something that England could no longer supply, and that he came here implicitly to find an answer—in another language. As yet I see no evidence that he has found it. I wonder why? Mind you, this is one of the cleverest, most skilled poets of our age and one of the most versatile and prolific. He can do anything.

But when he writes an ode to a successful soccer season for his school, as Pindar wrote them for the Olympic heroes of his day—it is in a classic meter so successful in spite of the subject, which you might think trivial, that it becomes a serious poem. And a bad sign to me is always a religious or social tinge beginning to creep into a poet's work. You can put it down as a general rule that when a poet, in the broadest sense, begins to devote himself to the *subject matter* of his poems, *genre*, he has come to an end of his poetic means.

What does all this signify? That Auden came here to find a new way of writing—for it looked as if this were the place where one might reasonably expect to find that instability in the language where innovation would be at home. Remember even Mr. Eliot once said that no poetic drama could any longer be written in the iambic pentameter, but that perhaps jazz might offer a suggestion. He even wrote something about "My Baby," but it can't have been very successful for we seldom hear any more of it.

I wish I could enlist Auden in an attack, a basic attack upon the whole realm of structure in the poem. I have tried but without success so far. I think that's what he came here looking for, I think he has failed to find it (it may be constitutional with him). I think we have disappointed him. Perhaps he has disappointed himself. I am sure the attack must be concentrated on the *rigidity of the poetic foot*.

This began as a basic criticism of Auden's poems—as a reason for his coming to America, and has at least served me as an illustration for the *theory* upon which I am speaking.

Look at his poems with this in view—his very skill seems to defeat him. It need not continue to do so in my opinion.

Mr. Eliot, meanwhile, has written his *Quartets*. He is a very subtle creator—who knows how to squeeze the last ounce of force out of his material. He has done a good job here though when he speaks of developing a new manner of writing, new manners following new manners only to be spent as soon as that particular piece of writing has been accomplished—I do not think he quite knows what he is about.

But in spite of everything and completely discounting his subject matter, his *genre*, Eliot's experiments in the *Quartets* though limited, show him to be more American in the sense I seek than, sad to relate, Auden, with his English ears and the best will in the world, will ever be able to be.

It may be the tragedy of a situation whose ramifications we are for the moment unable to trace: That the American gone over to England might make the contribution (or assist in it) which the Englishman come to America to find it and with the best will in the world, is unable to make.

Thus the Gallicized American, D'A——, according to Edmund Wilson in *Axel's Castle*, with the iambic pentameter in his brain, was able, at the beginning of the symbolist movement in Paris to break the French from their six-syllable line in a way they had of themselves never been able to do. There is Ezra Pound also to be thought of—another entire thesis— in this respect. I see that I am outlining a year's or at least a semester's series of lectures as I go along.

Now we come to the question of the origin of our discoveries. Where else can what we are seeking arise from but speech? From speech, from American speech as distinct from

English speech, or presumably so, if what I say above is correct. In any case (since we have no body of poems comparable to the English) from what we *hear* in America. Not, that is, from a study of the classics, not even the American "Classics"—the *dead* classics which—may I remind you, we have *never heard* as living speech. No one has or can *hear* them as they were written any more than we can *hear* Greek today.

I say this once again to emphasize what I have often said—that we here must *listen* to the language for the discoveries we hope to make. This is not the same as the hierarchic or tapeworm mode of making additions to the total poetic body: the mode of the schools. This will come up again elsewhere.

That being so, what I have presumed but not proven, concerning Auden's work, can we not say that there are many more *hints* toward literary composition in the American language than in English—where they are inhibited by classicism and "good taste." (Note the French word *tête*, its derivation from "pot.") I'd put it much stronger, but let's not be diverted at this point, there are too many more important things pressing for attention.

In the first place, we have to say, following H. L. Mencken's *The American Language*, which American language? Since Mencken pointed out that the American student (the *formative* years—very important) is bilingual, he speaks English in the classroom but his own tongue outside of it.

We mean, then, American—the language Mr. Eliot and Mr. Pound carried to Europe *in their ears*—willy-nilly— when they left here for their adventures and which presumably Mr. Auden came here to find—perhaps too late. A language full of those hints toward newness of which I have been speaking. I am not interested in the history but these things offer a point worth making, a rich opportunity for development lies before us at this point.

I said "hints toward composition." This does not mean realism in the language. What it does mean, I think, is ways of managing the language, new ways. Primarily it means to me opportunity to expand the structure, the basis, the actual making of the poem.

It is a chance to attack the language of the poem seriously. For to us our language is serious in a way that English is not. Just as to them English is serious—too serious—in a way no dialect could be. But the dialect is the mobile phase, the changing phase, the productive phase—as their languages were to Chaucer, Shakespeare, Dante, Rabelais in their day.

It is there, in the mouths of the living, that the language is changing and giving new means for expanded possibilities in literary expression and, I add, basic structure—the most important of all.

To the English, English is England: "History is England," yodels Mr. Eliot. To us this is not so, not so *if* we prove it by writing a poem built to refute it—otherwise he wins!! But that leads to mere controversy. For us rehash of rehash of hash of rehash is *not* the business.

A whole semester of studies is implicit here. Perhaps a whole course of post-graduate studies—with theses—extending into a life's work!! But before I extol too much and advocate the experimental method, let me emphasize that, like God's creation, the objective is not experimentation but *man*. In our case, poems! There were enough experiments it seems, from what natural history shows, in that first instance but that was not the culmination. The poem is what we are after.

And again let me emphasize that this is something that has been going on, unrecognized for years—here *and* in England. What we are at is to try to discover and isolate and *use* the underlying element or principle motivating this change which is trying to speak outright. Do you not see now why I have been inveighing against the sonnet all these years? And why it has been so violently defended? Because it is a form which does not admit of the slightest structural change in its composition.

Marianne Moore

Quarterly Review of Literature, 1948

THE MAGIC NAME, Marianne Moore, has been among my most cherished possessions for nearly forty years, synonymous with much that I hold dearest to my heart. If this invites a definition of love it is something I do not intend to develop in this place. On the contrary I intend to describe, very briefly and indirectly, a talent.

It is a talent which diminishes the tom-toming on the hollow men of a wasteland to an irrelevant pitter-patter. Nothing is hollow or waste to the imagination of Marianne Moore.

How so slight a woman can so roar, like a secret Niagara, and with so gracious an inference, is one with all mysteries where strength masquerading as weakness—a woman, a frail woman—bewilders us. Miss Moore, in constant attendance upon her mother the greater part of her life, has lived as though she needed just that emphasis to point up the nature of her powers.

Marianne Moore (whom for no adequate reason I always associate in my mind with Marie Laurencin who may be the size of a horse for all I know) once expressed admiration for Mina Loy; that was in 1916, let us say. I think it was because Mina was wearing a leopard-skin coat at the time and Marianne had stood there with her mouth open looking at her.

Marianne had two cords, cables rather, of red hair coiled around her rather small cranium when I first saw her and was straight up and down like the two-by-fours of a building under construction. She would laugh with a gesture of withdrawal after making some able assertion as if you yourself had said it and she were agreeing with you.

A statement she would defend, I think, is that man essentially is very much like the other animals—or a ship coming in from the sea—or an empty snail shell: but there's not much use saying a thing like that unless you can prove it.

Therefore Miss Moore has taken recourse to the mathematics of art. Picasso does no different: a portrait is a stratagem singularly related to a movement among the means of the craft. By making these operative, relationships become self-apparent—the animal lives with a human certainty. This is strangely worshipful. Nor does one always know against what one is defending oneself.

I saw yesterday what might roughly be referred to as a birthday card—made by some child a hundred or so years ago in, I think, Andover, Massachusetts. It was approximately three inches in its greatest dimension, formally framed in black, the mat inside the frame being of a particularly brilliant crimson velvet, a little on the cerise side and wholly undimmed by age. This enclosed a mounted bouquet of minute paper flowers upon the remnants of what had been several artificial little twigs among greenish-blue leaves.

There were in all three identically shaped four-petaled flowers, one a faded blue, one pinkish and one white, perfectly flat as though punched out of tissue paper. At the bottom of the bouquet, placed loosely across the stems under the glass, was a slightly crumpled legend plainly printed on a narrow half-inch strip of white paper:

"Walk on roses."

I never saw a more apt expression. Its size had no relation to the merits of its composition or execution.

I don't know what else to say of Marianne Moore—or rather I should like to talk on indefinitely about her, an endless research into those relationships which her poems, her use of the materials of poetry, connote. For I don't think there is a better poet writing in America today or one who touches so deftly so great a range of our thought.

This is the amazing thing about a good writer, he seems to make the world come toward him to brush against the spines of his shrub. So that in looking at some apparently small object one feels the swirl of great events.

What it is that gives us this sensation, this conviction, it is impossible to know but that it is the proof which the poem offers us there can be little doubt.

A Beginning on the Short Story (Notes) *

THE PRINCIPAL feature re the short story is that it is short—and so must pack in what it has to say (unless it be snipped off a large piece of writing as a sort of prose for quality of writing which might be justifiable).

It seems to me to be a good medium for nailing down a single conviction. Emotionally.

There's "Melanctha" (and there are the Poe stories), a means of writing, practice sheet for the novel one might *discover*, in it. But a novel is many related things, a short story one.

Plato's discourses: the *Republic*, a walk up from the port of Athens, the stopping with a friend and talking until morning. Socrates as a hero.

You can't "learn" to write a short story—either from De Maupassant or Henry James. All you can learn is what De M. or H. J. did. Or take a reader of the short story like Charles Demuth—and observe what he *did* in the way of painting following the texts.

It isn't a snippet from the newspaper. It isn't realism. It is, as in all forms of art, taking the materials of every day (or otherwise) and using them to raise the consciousness of our lives to higher aesthetic and moral levels by the use of the art.

As in the poem it must be stressed, that the short story uses the same materials as newsprint, the same dregs—the same in fact as Shakespeare and Greek tragedy: the elevation of spirit that occurs when a consciousness of form, art in short, is im-

posed upon materials debased by dispirited and crassly cyn-
ical handling. What the newspaper uses on the lowest (sentimental) level, the short story had best elevate to the level of
other interests.

This should make apparent that a mere "thrilling" account
of an occurrence from daily life, a transcription of a fact, is
not of itself and for that reason a short story. You get the
fact, it interests you for whatever reason; of that fact you
make, using words, a story. A thing. A piece of writing, as in
the case of De Maup't, "A Piece of String."

In plainest words, it isn't the mere interest of the event that
makes the short story, it is the way it raises the newspaper
level to distinction that counts.

This is not easy. At first or perhaps at any time, it won't
sell. Hemingway's "Two Fisted" or "Two-hearted River"—
was that way. And to *make* a story of any sort, short or long,
we use words: writing is made of words—all writing is made
of words, *formal things.*

We have Kipling's famous short stories, we have Gogol,
we have Dickens' "Christmas Carol."

We also have agents who, seeing some spark of novelty
(but a big slab of conventionality) in some recent graduate—
will teach her to write *Ladies Home Journal* or *Sat. Eve. Post*
—at the rate of $200 to $2000 a throw. And do it every day,
more or less. We also have the picture of an "accepted"
writer, someone known by her style, that she will not offend
or shock us, who long after her final deterioration (repeating
the same stock) will go on selling the *Delineator* (note the
use of "selling") for $50,000. A THROW. (There's a good
story with that, the mag saying the price is too high, dropping the serial or whatever and getting another "good" writer
to take on the stint for $25,000. The only trouble was that
they, the mag, lost money on the deal, made more money by
hiring the first lady at $50,000 to write for it. Except that
after that experience her fee went up to $75,000. And they
paid it!)

I should think, for myself, that the short story is the best form for the "slice of life" incident. It deals with people and dogs and cats, sometimes horses—those creatures who are the commonest sublimation of man's sexual approaches to woman: Big eyes, magnificently curved haunches and slender ankles, the mane, the dilating nostrils—how exquisitely Shakespeare sketched one in the *Venus and Adonis*—like Dürer at his best. They top monuments and sometimes cathedrals—as at St. Marco in Venice. Kafka and the cockroach.

It is for all that man (as man and woman) from the "Boule de Suif" to the "Murders in the Rue Morgue," a trait of some person raised from the groveling, debasing as it is debased jargon, fixed by rule and precedent, of reportage—to the exquisite distinction of that particular man, woman, horse or child that is depicted. The finest short stories are those that raise, in short, one particular man or woman, from that Gehenna, the newspapers, where at last all men are equal, to the distinction of being an individual. To be responsive not to the ordinances of the herd (Russia-like) but to the extraordinary responsibility of being a person.

Can we not anticipate and look forward with eagerness amounting to despair to the time (past most of our lives) when there will appear those journals, those poems and short stories, being written underground now in Russia as in Ireland of this century by the literary heroes of the future? For it has to be so. And the Russians of all people will be the most persistent, the bravest and the most, I think, brilliant. Any nation that has braved Siberia for eight generations and survived to catch a glimpse of freedom so often dragged, as it has been today, from before their eyes, will be writing the masterpieces of the future.

As we write for the magazines today so they write, officially, for the Politburo. But the real writing, the real short story will be written privately, in secret, despairingly—for the individual. For it will be the individual.

Thus and for that purpose, the great writer will use his materials formally, in his own style, the words, the choice and the mode of his words—like Boccaccio, Stein and Faulkner.

But what right have I who never wrote a successful, that is to say salable, moneymaking short story in my life, to speak to you in this way? I feel like an impostor. I'm just a literary guy, not *practical*—like a one-time atomic physicist. Even a poet, of all things. What a nerve to come to a going institution of learning to teach you how to write?! Even to sell? Why, you might as well have an Einstein. HE at least can play the violin, this is, fairly well.

There's something to it. And so I object also.

But Hemingway did at first sit at the feet of Gertrude Stein and Ezra Pound. They taught him a lot. And then he went out and capitalized on it—to at least *her* disgust, so they say. And she had written at least one magnificent short story. Pound not even one. But then again Hemingway's not a bad poet and might have been a better one.

So if they did that may we not, conceivably, do this? I'll go the limit, as far as I know any limit. From me perhaps you'll pick up a point or two and make use of it. At the worst we'll fool the trusting faculties who invited me here while you get a laugh.

Nobody knows who's going to be successful. Moreover nobody knows who's going to be good. Now it's Paul Bowles.

So let's look at short stories and see what CAN be done with them. How many ways they CAN be written, torturing the material in every way we can think of—from that YOU draw what you want to.

The art would be, by the style, to wed the subject to its own time and have it live there and then. Have it live.

Take one of Kipling's best tales. Can we learn anything from it for our use today? Take O. Henry's ending. They are out of date "an O. Henry ending." Obviously not. Take a Gogol story, the woman who ran wild and naked at night baying like a dog on her hands and feet through the country. I speak of this from memory. Take a Kafka story more recently dead—the sliding of consciousness, a lateral slip that stands up to nothing but fantasy and is yet firm.

What is the common quality in all these changing styles? Not a stereotyped snaring of the interest, a filling in of necessary documentary details and a smash finish. That is merely the cheap surface of the ten-cent customers. What about Hemingway's "Short Happy Life"? or Poe's "Gold Bug"?

They all have a frame—like a picture. There is a punch, if you like. But what *is* that punch? What kind of a punch do you want: philosophic as Plato's *Republic* and—what in a woman shooting her husband's head off with an elephant gun? What in "The Gold Bug?" Murder is nothing at all but death—and what's new about death? Violence is the mood today. Now it's something if a son cuts his mother's throat as in the Agamemnon. Maybe Plato was a bit fed up on the Sophocles. His endings are arguments: that he did give Socrates the hemlock (and a termagant for a wife) finally: who could even outtalk her.

What today will be the punch paragraph or maybe today we'll shift the emphasis and get a punch from having no punch. Maybe the buildup and the documentation will be merely hinted. The rough stuff (lying usually) or the capitalizing of the Negro comic (so-called) at a dime a throw—to flatter a certain snob sense of fixed values? To flatter a buyer—in good old 6th Avenue style? Oh, but don't let's be so vulgar!

In other words when you begin to write a short story you should really know what you're writing about—because, if you write skillfully enough, sooner or later someone is going to find it out and judge you as a man for it.

Oh, but am I making a mistake? Perhaps all you want is to write a story and not be judged a liar because you lie. I'm really afraid I'm in the wrong bin. I'm taking the art of the short story seriously.

What will it *do?*

For instance—what was my problem or urge or opportunity for realization of my insights in 1932?

What was going on?

How did I solve it? Why did I choose the short story and how much must it have been modified from a stereotype to be serviceable to me?

(I do not mean to imply that the choice was a conscious one altogether. I mean, looking back upon it, what were the elements involved in my coming upon the short story as a means?)—that is during the Depression?

Answer: The character of the evidence: to accommodate itself to the heterogeneous character of the people, the elements involved, the situation in hand. In other words, the materials and the temporal situation dictated the terms.

I lived among these people. I know them and saw the essential qualities (not stereotype), the courage, the humor (an accident), the deformity, the basic tragedy of their lives—and the *importance* of it. You can't write about something unimportant to yourself. I was involved.

That wasn't all. I saw how they were maligned by their institutions of church and state—and "betters." I saw how all that was acceptable to the ear about them maligned them. I saw how stereotype falsified them.

Nobody was writing about them, anywhere, as they ought to be written about. There was no chance of writing anything acceptable, certainly not salable, about them.

It was my duty to raise the level of consciousness, not to say discussion, of them to a higher level, a higher plane. Really to tell.

Why the short story? Not for a sales article but as I had conceived them. The briefness of their chronicles, its brokenness and heterogeneity—isolation, color. A novel was unthinkable.

And so to the very style of the stories themselves.

This wasn't the "acceptable," the unshocking stuff, the slippery, in the sense that it can be slipped into them while

they are semiconscious of a Saturday evening. Not acceptable
to a mag and didn't get into them.

To continue our study:

What sort of a short story must a Gogol have written or a
Kipling in India—in their time?

And so, practically speaking, what sort of short story must
be written in the U. S. or the Northwest today? I use the
word *must*, I don't ask what you would care to do. Each man
or woman is born facing a *must*. Who will drive it through or
even see it? The one who will, will be at least justified and
happy in his own eyes doing it. But he will know what he
must do.

In other words, to write a short story of parts one must
know what he is writing *about*, see it, smell it—be compelled
by it—and be writing what ordinarily one doesn't want to
hear.

Is that extraordinary?

We forget the meaning of art. Art means the skillful lie—
what doesn't exist—as Aristotle pointed out.

To be an artist, one must deceive, make up a story. One
must get the punch in, the shocking punch so skillfully that
no one will suspect it. The art covers that. The shock is necessary. Necessary to make them stop, look, listen—in other
words, read and say, 1) how awful, and 2) how fascinating.
What a wonderful writer!

The artist always has his tongue in his cheek.

It must be so artful with the truth that above and beyond
anything else its beauty of style or accurate statement will
negate all its petty and thoroughly excusable lies. For its lies,
never of statement, originate from its affection.

It must be written so well that that in itself becomes its
truth while the deformity informs it.

I say a man must know what he is writing *about* but the
short story, as a form, must be demanded.

Down to your own Jack London: what do Jack London's stories *mean?*

They mean, as far as I can tell,—take "To Build a Fire," they mean, the impact between civilization and the wild. For, note, that he isn't interested in the pioneer who goes native and survives fairly well. He means (when he is any good at all and not a pure sentimentalist) the terror and lonesomeness of the wilderness in its impact on civilized man. That, as far as I can see, is the best of him.

His failure?

When he tries to talk big—which reveals no more than his littleness.

12/22

So how shall we write today (unpredictable—or to predict the genius who will answer) of what shall we write today? Let us try to predict. What will the short story consist of and what will be its terms?

The hero? Who is a hero? The peasantry? There is none. Men and women faithful to a belief? What belief?

One thing I found out for myself by writing a short story once that almost broke up the faculty of Arizona University and was finally published obscurely in Berkeley, Calif. It is this:

Most of us are not individuals any more but parts of something. We are no one of us "all" of anything. It is too big for us. So why not write of three people as one? That's what my story tried to do, make itself more than one, three in one. Imagine a woman looking at herself three ways. Wouldn't that break up the faculty of any university?

I cannot tell you how to write a short story, I can only tell you how you must write it.

It is not to place adjectives, it is to learn to employ the verbs in imitation of nature—so that the pieces move naturally— and watch, often breathlessly, what they *do.*

That is the enlargement of nature which we call art. The *additions* to nature which we call art.

You do not *copy* nature, you make something which is an *imitation* of nature—read your Aristotle again.

That is the *work* of the imagination, as the late Virginia Woolf pointed out. You have to work, you have to imagine the character, which is for your mind to *be* the creator.

Arrived at that condition, the imagination inflamed, the excitement of it is that you no longer copy but *make* a natural object. (Something comparable to nature: an other nature.) You yourself become the instrument of nature—the helpless instrument.

You must tell the truth. You can't lie because the moment you attempt to fall off you destroy yourself.

It *is* nature. I don't think you know in a short story what's coming out. That is the excitement of it.

Take "Death in Venice," take "Boule de Suif," take "Melanctha." They are creations. Natural objects. Not copying. But by housing a spirit, as nature houses juice in an apple, they live.

It is perhaps a transit from adjective (the ideal "copy") to verb (showing process).

There are no beginnings and ends in nature—except birth and death—which are meaningless to us. Religion imitates nature with the imagination—a once moving fable—which we have to know is a lie before we can believe it.

There is only, we might say, flux in nature.

But there is also an apple, a flower and a man.

The artist adds, "There is also a work of art." Now how absurd it is to dwell upon cherries so real that the birds peck at them (I knew a man who had a whole canvas full of cherries in a heap which to him was art). How absurd it is to make a statue so copied that it is mistaken for a woman: The story of Pygmalion and Galatea is merely a best seller—a very second-rate fable for jokesters.

The secret lies elsewhere—in the *marble* of it. If it is merely mistaken for a woman it is senseless: a copy.

But as an *imitation* of nature (not a mere woman's body) it becomes something a woman never was, something a woman at her best may imitate—a work of art. A work of man to lay beside nature and enlarge it. Engrandize it. Make a Caesar greater than Caesar or, if not that at least a Caesar, an undying Caesar whose other works have crumbled—a *completion* of his greatness. It is what the imagination *adds* to the woman that makes the statue great.

Something of this sort is what Oscar Wilde must have meant when he said, "God created man, then woman, then the child and finally the doll. And the greatest of these was the doll."

Carnal desire for a statue is for adolescents and senility if not the pathological (at least the stupid). But to take decay, despair and elevate the details to an action, to greatness as in "Death in Venice"—to make by an action a thing that is deformed clean, salutory—*that* is an addition to nature.

To take a lump of fat and transform it by imitating nature —goes beyond copy—to transform a cockroach, the same— into a work of illuminating penetration—gives us a glimpse of the process.

Braque would take his pictures out of doors and place them *beside* nature to see if his imitations had *worked*.

So you see how it opens up sculpture, painting and writing. In the Greek tragedies the imitation of the gods.

The short story is no different.

(I didn't say not to copy, not, for instance, accurately to observe conversation. But I did say that *that* is not the short story. It *might* be, but only when there is something else as well.) A view, a room with a view, something heard through a knothole—a secret.

Now what are some of the advantages of the short story as an art form—bearing what I have said, in mind.

It should be a brush stroke—as compared with a picture.

One chief advantage as against a novel—which is its nearest cousin—is that you do not have to bear in mind the complex structural paraphernalia of a novel in writing a short story and so may dwell on the manner, the writing. On the process itself. A single stroke, uncomplicated but complete. Not like a chapter or paragraph.

Thus, bearing a possible novel in mind, if you will, you can play with the words as materials. You can try various modes of writing—more freely.

Try all sorts of effects. The short story is a wonderful medium for prose experimentation. You may, economically, try devices—varied devices—for making the word count toward a particular effect. I'd say write a story—as Joyce did. *Dubliners* to *Stephen Hero* to *Ulysses* to *Finnegans Wake.* I say that it took off from the short story. It makes a delightful Field of Mars—for exercises in the Manual of Arms. I think that's its chief value.

And be careful not to imitate yourself—like how many others. Remember: the imagination! The short story has all the elements of a larger work—but in petto. Dash off a story in an evening—any old way, trying to follow the action of some characters you can *imagine*. Sit down blind and start to fling the words around like pigments—try to see what nature would do under the same circumstances—let 'em go and (without thinking or caring) see where they'll lead you. You may be surprised—you may even end up as a disciplined writer.

12/23/29

Crawl into the man's head and how get inside a woman's head, being a man? That is the *work* of the imagination (of which V. Woolf speaks). This is where the *imitation* of nature takes place. There is no copying here.

You *are* now nature: given a set of circumstances—a woman: a man—names:

What is there to do?

Now go ahead and do it. Name the actions and perform them—yourself.

This is something that you yourself (as "Jim Higgins")

have very little to say about (you become a nonentity, like Shakespeare). You are in the creative process—a function in nature—relegated to the deity.

You have now entered what is referred to as the divine function of the artist.

Let's keep away from frightening words and say you are nature—in action.

It is an action, a moving process—the verb dominates; you are to *make*.

And who are you, anyway?—with your small personal limitations of age, sex and other sundry features like race and religion?

Unimportant.

You, even you are at the moment—the artist, good or bad —but a new creature.

You must let yourself go—release it and be that transcendence (but in control by your technique which you have learned—like the voice of an opera singer) but inside that frame of reference you must *release* yourself to act.

How, in *The Sheltering Sky* (a novel) is Bowles going to get the girl undressed. He is going to *act* to do it.

By setting the imagination to *work*. WORK. The artist is now a woman, a particular woman. He is therefore bound by her conditions and so he works at it. And in this case what comes out?

The woman is going to be undressed *willingly*—within a time limitation of a train schedule. She will *want* to be undressed even while she fights against it—by running out.

So he gets her soaked to the skin. But on a train? in Africa. How?

Read it. Lesson No. 1.

December 30/49

It is the transit to the imagination from the plebeian plodding of ordinary consciousness which is the important thing

—the sometimes impossible thing for any of us, the always impossible thing for many of us—or so it seems. To take to the imagination is the first requisite.

How does one take to the imagination? One may recognize its approach in that its first signs are like those of falling asleep —which anyone may observe for himself. It is likewise governed by the conditions of sleep.

At first all the images, one or many which fill the mind, are fixed. I have passed through it and studied it for years. We look at the ceiling and review the fixities of the day, the month, the year, the lifetime. Then it begins; that happy time when the image becomes broken or begins to break up, becomes a little fluid—or is affected, floats brokenly in the fluid. The rigidities yield—like ice in March, the magic month. They coalesce and, finally, merciful sleep intervenes. Sleep is black. But before we awaken it begins again, in reverse—with dreams. Ending in waking and we return to consciousness, refreshed. By the imagination?

That is the way sleep goes. But we are now looking for cues to something else, we are speaking of the resemblance between falling asleep and the awakening of the imagination that sometime impossible step to be taken before the writing begins (tho' it is wavelike and even during the writing, of many qualities, it rises and falls—tho' it remain of the same texture).

Possessed by the imagination, we are really asleep tho' we may awake: it explains much bravery. We do not hear what is said to us, we do not see the danger.

Kenneth Burke once said to me that the way to write or perhaps to learn to write is to sit down and to begin to write. Write down anything that seems pertinent to the subject or to no subject. Get into the fluid state, for unless you do, all you will say will be valueless. Continue to write until you have begun to say what you find to be necessary to the subject. Tear up the first eight to twenty pages and you have made a start!

Arrived! we think on a different plane. All the lines—the complex arrangement of reins lie free in the hand.

What distresses can happen in the effort to let go! to release ourselves to the imagination, with this we are all familiar. It is because we are really afraid. We can be struck to the ground by a realization of how we have been conditioned in our lives. The realization of it may be a terrific blow. In all our conscious lives we stick to what we call standards—to precepts—to those bulwarks against quicksands—so we say. Think of Rimbaud etc.

Then to reverse the process: Where might we not land? What fences we put up in the past are precisely our stumbling blocks now. I once wrote down: How did Shakespeare become great? By begetting twins, abandoning his wife, running away to London and falling in love with men. In other words—to let go the imagination.

I don't especially recommend it. How can I?

I am now stressing the diseases. We get fixed in squirrel cages of thought. Everyone does. Drink, drugs—anything you can think of is practiced to escape. The Yeats story about his London lecture.

All I am trying to point out is that it is all the effort to take that step into the imagination. Queer dress. Nocturnal habits like Balzac who went to bed at 10 A.M. etc. Do not forget the tremendous advantages of prison and far greater Cervantes wrote *Don Quixote*. The imagination is freed. To raise the heat of the brain to bring it oxygen.

March 26/50

We speak of a man's "mettle"—it might better be metal. It is as with other metals, when it is heated it melts. It is when the metal is fluid the imagination can be said to become active; it is the melting, the rendering fluid of the imagination that describes the mind as entering upon creative work.

It must be melted to create; fluid, unfettered by anything.

The characteristic of being melted is for the object to have lost the form it was in. It can be played with, made into a new form as we desire.

With the short story as with any sort of creation, I am trying to say, the imagination (that is the mind in a fluid state or a melted state) has to be given play.

Now, we know by knowledge of the physiology of the brain that it acts only when it has been supplied oxygen in abundance. So it glows and sweats when it is active—as with anything else.

What is the origin of that heat? Something has stirred us, some perception linked with emotion. We are angry, we are committed to something in our lives, as with the poem. It doesn't matter what it has been—anything. We heat up. This incentive is usually secret, it is guided by our fears perhaps. But we are heated and (if we can get quiet enough, as in jail, or running away—finally) we melt and the imagination is set to flow into its new mold.

April 24/50

What shall the short story be written about. Obviously not, if it is serious, the mere sentimental characters. How write about a poor Wop, a Polish gal in her kitchen, a foreign peasant who is barely articulate.

What then? Something that interests the writer seriously, as a writer (not necessarily a man for in that case the interest would be moral and perhaps best NOT as a short story). It is the way his interests, as a writer, impinge upon the material— graphically told.

The result is life, not morals. It is THE LIFE which comes alive in the telling. It is the life under specified conditions— so that it is relived in the reading—as it strikes off flashes from the material. The material is the metal against which a flint makes sparks.

Anything, thus anything can be used without fear of sentimentality. The THING we are writing, directing all our wit, our intelligence to discovering and setting down—is revealed as it hits against anything at all. That's the modern under-standing—and I guess it is pretty hard to realize. Whatever that may be for each man who writes. What good are you? Prove it. Or what do you see, young as you are? Do you think a prostitute is "bad" because she's a prostitute. And yet how shall you show her "good" except by speaking of her in the conditions of her prostitution. By using that material, graphically, specifically you must learn to tell all you want to tell—whatever YOU want to say. That is the art.

December 15, 1949

Foreword

The Autobiography of William Carlos Williams, 1951

NINE-TENTHS of our lives is well forgotten in the living. Of the part that is remembered, the most had better not be told: it would interest no one, or at least would not contribute to the story of what we ourselves have been. A thin thread of narrative remains—a few hundred pages—about which clusters, like rock candy, the interests upon which the general reader will spend a few hours, as might a sweet-tooth child, preferring something richer and not so hard on the teeth. To us, however, such hours have been sweet. They constitute our particular treasure. That is all, justly, that we should offer.

I can't tell more than I know. I have lived, somehow, from day to day; and so I describe it, from day to day, as I have struggled to get a meaning from my failures and successes. Not that my conclusions have been profound. But even the most trivial happenings may carry a certain weight.

I do not intend to tell the particulars of the women I have been to bed with, or anything about them. Don't look for it. That has nothing to do with me. What relations I have had with men and women, such encounters as have interested me most profoundly, have not occurred in bed. I am extremely sexual in my desires: I carry them everywhere and at all times. I think that from that arises the drive which empowers us all. Given that drive, a man does with it what his mind directs. In the manner in which he directs that power lies his secret. We always try to hide the secret of our lives from the general stare. What I believe to be the hidden core of my life will not easily be deciphered, even when I tell, as here, the outer circumstances.

Such an autobiography as this could stretch into a thousand pages. All I should have to do would be to keep on writing. No doubt I could hold the general interest even so. But stretching the story out, padding it up a bit, putting in a few more stories of some of my contemporaries, wouldn't help much to clarify it. It might make a far more amusing book than it is likely to be in its present proportions, but nothing thereby would be added to its worth—if it has any worth beyond that lent to it by the interest of a few friends.

I have not even attempted to include a full list of my friends. I have paid no attention to lists of any kind. All that I have wanted to do was to tell of my life as I went along practicing medicine and at the same time recording my daily search for . . . what? As a writer, I have been a physician, and as a physician a writer; and as both writer and physician I have served sixty-eight years of a more or less uneventful existence, not more than half a mile from where I happen to have been born.

Because Flossie, my wife, and I have never moved, 9 Ridge Road has become a landmark for many friends who, though they have seldom or never visited us, have at least known where we lived. They have written many letters, all of which I have answered; that has been one of my major occupations over the years. I am surprised that I have not mentioned such names as Ed Corson, Arthur Noyes and Bert Clark, among my old classmates at medical school; they are old friends. Wallace Stevens is another scarcely mentioned, though he is constantly in my thoughts. And the late Alfred Stieglitz. None of these ever has been to see me in Rutherford. There is a great virtue in such an isolation. It permits a fair interval for thought. That is, what I call thinking, which is mainly scribbling. It has always been during the act of scribbling that I have gotten most of my satisfactions.

For instance, I'd go to see Alfred Stieglitz. I did this fairly regularly at one time. There'd be no one at all in the gallery.

He'd recognize me, and after I had a chance to look around he'd come out from behind his partition and we'd begin to talk. We'd talk about the pictures, about John Marin and what he was doing then. Or another day it would be a Hartley show or a visit to the Portinari show at the Modern Museum. Or we'd have been to hear Pablo Casals. Or we'd visit the tapestries at The Cloisters. After that, I'd come home and think—that is to say, to scribble. I'd scribble for days, sometimes, after such a visit, or even years, it might be, trying to discover how my mind had readjusted itself to its contacts.

Or sometimes, not often enough, we'd get in the car and go forty miles into the country to visit my fellow Jerseyite, Kenneth Burke, and his family. The life he has led on his old abandoned farm in Andover has always fascinated me. I approve of it. I admire the mind that conceived and carried out such a life. We'd meet there Peggy Cowley who'd be bitten by a rattlesnake and yell for me before she'd be taken to the hospital to be cured, Mattie Josephson, Malcolm Cowley, Gorham Munson, in striped pants and carrying a cane in that country place. All afternoon would be spent in argument, we hugging our glasses of applejack. Reactivated, I'd go home to the eternally rewarding game of scribbling. Thought was never an isolated thing with me; it was a game of tests and balances, to be proven by the written word. Then would come the trial. The poem would be submitted to some random editor, or otherwise meet its fate in the world. I would observe that fate and so come to judge the intelligence of my contemporaries. Once, in great excitement, we took the train for Philadelphia late in the day to be present at a performance of *Lysistrata* before it could be censored.

When and where, after such forays, did I or could I write? Time meant nothing to me. I might be in the middle of some flu epidemic, the phone ringing day and night, madly, not a moment free. That made no difference. If the fit was on me— if something Stieglitz or Kenneth had said was burning inside me, having bred there overnight demanding outlet—I would be like a woman at term; no matter what else was up, that demand had to be met.

Five minutes, ten minutes, can always be found. I had my typewriter in my office desk. All I needed to do was to pull up the leaf to which it was fastened and I was ready to go. I worked at top speed. If a patient came in at the door while I was in the middle of a sentence, bang would go the machine —I was a physician. When the patient left, up would come the machine. My head developed a technique: something growing inside me demanded reaping. It had to be attended to. Finally, after eleven at night, when the last patient had been put to bed, I could always find the time to bang out ten or twelve pages. In fact, I couldn't rest until I had freed my mind from the obsessions which had been tormenting me all day. Cleansed of that torment, having scribbled, I could rest.

We have lived by the seasons. It is in winter that illness occurs here, mostly. It is then that a physician's services are in greatest demand. But it is then that the going is hardest. I have never taken a winter vacation. Perhaps the time is coming when that will have to be changed. Winter is a tough time for a doctor. But in spring the world is altered for us. The small world of the patch of ground that I call my yard has always been of tremendous importance to me. Henri Fabre has been one of my gods. Not that I have followed his scientific example, though at one time I might have done so and perhaps been a happier man, but his example has always stood beside me as a measure and a rule. It has made me and induced in me a patient industry, and in spite of my insufficiencies, a long-range contentment. What becomes of me has never seemed to me important, but the fates of ideas living against the grain in a nondescript world has always held me breathless.

"Parade's End" *

Sewanee Review, 1951

EVERY TIME we approach a period of transition someone cries out: This is the last! the last of Christianity, of the publishing business, freedom for the author, the individual! Thus we have been assured that in this novel, *Parade's End*, we have a portrait of the last Tory. But what in God's name would Ford Madox Ford be doing writing the tale of the last Tory? He'd far rather have tied it into black knots.

In a perfectly appointed railway carriage, two young men of the British public official class, close friends, are talking quietly together. Back of their minds stands Great Groby House, the Tietjens' family seat, in Yorkshire, the north of England—its people, neighbors, and those associated with them just prior to the beginning of the First World War. It was a noteworthy transition period. It would be idle of me, an American, to try to recreate so highly flavored an atmosphere as that represented in this railway carriage. One of the speakers is Christopher Tietjens, younger son to Groby's ancestral proprietor; he is a blond hulk of a man, a sharp contrast to his companion, MacMasters, dark-haired and with a black pointed beard, a smallish Scotsman for whom the Tietjens family has provided a little money to get him through Cambridge and establish him in town.

Sylvia, young Christopher's beautiful wife, has four months previously gone off to the Continent with a lover. She has sickened of him and wants to be taken back. The two men on the train, thoroughly well bred and completely Brit-

* A review of *Parade's End*, by Ford Madox Ford. Alfred A. Knopf: New York, 1950.

ish, are discussing the circumstance and its profitable outcome
—Christopher, defending his wife, has consented to let her
do as she pleases. There begins now to unravel (you might
almost say it is Christopher's ungainly bulk itself that is un-
raveling) as intimate, full, and complex a tale as you will find
under the official veneer of our day.

Four books, *Some Do Not, No More Parades, A Man
Could Stand Up,* and *The Last Post,* have been for the first
time offered in one volume as Ford had wished it. The title,
Parade's End, is his own choosing. Together they constitute
the English prose masterpiece of their time. But Ford's writings have never been popular, as popular, let's say, as the writings of Proust have been popular. Yet they are written in a
style that must be the envy of every thinking man. The pleasure in them is infinite.

When I first read the books I began, by chance, with *No
More Parades;* as the story ran the First World War was in
full swing, the dirt, the deafening clatter, the killing. So it
was a little hard for me to retreat to *Some Do Not,* which
deals with the social approaches to that holocaust. At once,
in the first scenes of this first book the conviction is overwhelming that we are dealing with a major talent. We are
plunged into the high ritual of a breakfast in the Duchemin
drawing room—all the fine manners of an established culture.
There's very little in English to surpass that, leading as it
does to the appearance of the mad cleric himself, who for
the most part lies secretly closeted in his own home. Beside
this we have the relationship of the man's tortured wife with
Tietjens' friend MacMasters; the first full look at Valentine
Wannop and of Tietjens himself before he appears in khaki
—the whole rotten elegance of the business; Sylvia, at her
best, and the old lady's "You are so beautiful, my dear, you
must be good." Then it shifts to Christopher and the girl,
Valentine, in the fog, linking the land, disappointment, the
yearning for fulfillment and—the ten-foot-deep fog itself
covering everything but the stars of a brilliant sky overhead;

we see Christopher in the carriage holding the reins, Valentine leaping down to find a road sign and disappearing from his view. Only the horse's head, as he tosses it, reappears to Christopher from time to time as the man sits there alone. Following that is the restraint and hatred in the scene between husband and wife, Christopher and Sylvia. He at table in uniform, she standing behind him, bored. Casually she flings the contents of her plate at the back of his neck, glad she hadn't actually hit him—but the oil from the dressing dribbled down on his insignia. He didn't even turn. It is their farewell as he is about to leave for the front.

This is the first of the four books. The war intervenes. *No More Parades*. The war ends. Tietjens is invalided home, his mind half gone. Valentine lives for him and he recovers. Mark, the present heir to Groby, the Correct Man, represents the family and England as a family. Living with his French mistress he suffers a cerebral hemorrhage and lies, during all of *The Last Post*, in a sort of summerhouse, where with his last breath, and as he holds the pregnant Valentine by the hand, the saga comes to an end.

Sylvia, through all the books, in her determination to destroy her husband, does everything a woman can, short of shooting him, to accomplish her wish. From start to finish she does not falter.

This is where an analysis should begin; for some, who have written critically of *Parade's End*, find Sylvia's extreme hatred of her husband, her inexorable, even doctrinaire hatred, unreal. I think they are wrong. All love between these two or the possibility for it was spent before the story began when Christopher lay with his wife-to-be, unknowing, in another railway carriage, immediately after her seduction by another man. It made an impossible situation. From that moment all that was left for them was love's autopsy, an autopsy and an awakening—an awakening to a new *form* of love, the first liberation from his accepted Toryism. Sylvia was done. Valentine up! A new love had already begun to shimmer above the fog before his intelligence, a new love with which the past was perhaps identical, or had been identical, but in other terms. Sylvia suffers also, while a leisurely torment drives her to desperation. It is the very slowness of her torment, reflected in the minutiae, the passionate dedication, the last agonized twist of Ford's style, that makes the story move.

In his very perception and love for the well-observed detail lies Ford's narrative strength, the down-upon-it affection for the thing itself in which he is identical with Tietjens, his prototype. In spite of all changes, in that, at least, the Tory carries over: concern for the care of the fields, the horses, whatever it may be; the landed proprietor must be able to advise his subordinates who depend on him, he is responsible for them also. That at least was Tietjens, that too was Ford.

When you take those qualities of a man over into the new conditions, that Tietjens paradoxically loved, the whole picture must be altered—and a confusion, a tragic confusion, results, needing to be righted; it is an imperative that becomes a moral duty as well as a duty to letters.

Ford, like Tietjens, paid attention to these things. I'll not forget when he came to visit me in Rutherford, a town lying in the narrow sun-baked strip of good soil, land which the Dutch farmers cultivated so well in the old days, between the low Watchung Range and the swampy land of the Hackensack Meadows. It is one of the best tilled, you might almost say currycombed, bits of the Garden State, as New Jersey is still called. Old Ford, for he was old by that time, was interested. He asked me to take him out to see the truck farms. We spent the afternoon at it, a blistering July day when the sprinkler system was turned on in many of the fields, straight back into the country, about three or four miles, to the farm of Derrick Johnson, who personally showed us around. I was more interested in the sandpipers running through the tilled rows—birds which I hadn't seen up to then other than running on the wet sand of beaches as the water washed up and retreated, uncovering minute food. But on the farm they were nestling, here their eggs were laid and hatched in the heat between the beet rows on the bare ground. But Ford, who was looking around, questioned the farmer closely about the cultivation of the lettuce, carrots, dandelion, leeks, peppers, tomatoes and radishes which he was raising. It was all part of his understanding of the particular—and of what should properly occupy and compel a man's mind. He might have been Tietjens.

So far I have spoken in the main of Christopher and Sylvia, their relationship, their positions and their marriage. But there are other characters as important in the argument as they. Mark, Christopher's elder brother, the one man whom Sylvia has never been able to impress, should be put down as the first of these—as Ford, I think, recognizes, when he makes him the key figure of the entire last book, *The Last Post*. Mark, the perfectly cultured gentleman. Professor Wannop, old friend of the family, a studious recluse who has brought up his daughter, Valentine, in his own simple and profound ways, is gone. And there is, of course, Valentine herself, though she appears, generally speaking, little. She fills, however, a dominant place. *A Man Could Stand Up* is her book. General Campion, official England, is another to be named. He will carry off the girl, old as he is, at the close. At every turn he appears, often as Sylvia's instrument to thwart Christopher, triumphant officialdom.

But greater than he, Tietjens, are the men in the trenches, his special responsibilities, over whom he pains, a bumbling mother, exhausting himself to the point of mental and physical collapse.

Few could be in the position which Ford himself occupied in English society to know these people. His British are British in a way the American, Henry James, never grasped. They fairly smell of it. The true test is his affection for them, top to bottom, a moral, not a literary attribute, his love of them, his wanting to be their Moses, to lead them out of captivity to their rigid aristocratic ideals—to the ideals of a new aristocracy. Ford, like Tietjens, was married to them, and like Sylvia they were determined to destroy him for it. Even when he could help them, as Tietjens helped MacMaster, Ford got kicked for it and was thrown out of the paradise of their dying ideas—as much by D. H. Lawrence on one side, the coal miner's son, as by the others. He helped Lawrence but Lawrence soon backed out. And still no one grasps the significance of Tietjens' unending mildness, torn between the two forces—no one, really, but Valentine and Mark in the last words.

Sylvia's bitter and unrelenting hatred for Tietjens, her husband, is the dun mountain under the sunrise, the earth itself of the old diabolism. We sense, again and again, more than is stated, two opposing forces. Not who but *what* is Sylvia? (I wonder if Ford with his love of the Elizabethan lyric didn't have that in mind when he named her.)

At the start her husband has, just too late for him, found out her secret; and feeling a responsibility, almost a pity for her, has assumed a superior moral position which she cannot surmount or remove. She had been rudely seduced, and on the immediate rebound, you might almost say with the same gesture, married Tietjens in self-defense. She cannot even assure her husband that the child is his own. She cannot be humble without denying all her class prerogatives. Christopher's mere existence is an insult to her. But to have him pity her is hellish torment. She is forced by everything that is holy to make him a cuckold, again and again. For England itself in her has been attacked. But Valentine can pick up her young heels, as she did at the golf course, and leap a ditch, a thing impossible for Sylvia unless she change her clothes, retrain her muscles and unbend.

But there is a deeper reason than that—and a still more paradoxical—in that Tietjens forced her to do good; that as his wife she serves best when she most hates him. The more she lies the better she serves. This is truly comic. And here a further complexity enters. Let me put it this way: If there is one thing I cannot accede to in a commonality of aspiration, it is the loss of the personal and the magnificent . . . the mind that cannot contain itself short of that which makes for great shows. Not wealth alone but a wealth that enriches the imagination. Such a woman is Sylvia, representing the contemporary emblazonments of medieval and princely retinue. How can we take over our *Kultur*, a trait of aristocracy, without a Sylvia, in short as Tietjens desired her? What is our drabness beside the magnificence of a Sistine Chapel, a gold salt cellar by Cellini, a Taj, a great wall of China, a Chartres? The mind is the thing not the cut stone but the stone itself. The words of a Lear. The sentences of *Some Do Not* themselves that are not likely for this to be banished from our thoughts.

Ford gave the woman, Sylvia, life; let her exercise her full range of feeling, vicious as it might be, her full armament of woman. Let her be what she *is*. Would Tietjens divorce her? When there is reason yes, but so long as she is truthfully what she is and is fulfilling what she is manifestly *made* to be, he has nothing but respect for her. Ford uses her to make a meaning. She will not wobble or fail. It is not his business. This is a way of looking at the word.

Ford's philosophy in these novels is all of a piece, character and writing. The word keeps the same form as the characters' deeds or the writer's concept of them. Sylvia is the dead past in all its affecting glamor. Tietjens is in love the while with a woman of a different order, of no landed distinction, really a displaced person seeking replacement. Valentine Wannop is the reattachment of the word to the object—it is obligatory that the protagonist (Tietjens) should fall in love with her, she is Persephone, the rebirth, the reassertion—from which we today are at a nadir, the lowest ebb.

Sylvia is the lie, bold-faced, the big crude lie, the denial . . . that is now having its moment. The opponent not of *le mot juste* against which the French have today been rebelling, but something of much broader implications; so it must be added that if our position in the world, the democratic position, is difficult, and we must acknowledge that it is difficult, the Russian position, the negative position, the lying position, that is, the Communist position is still more difficult. All that is implied in Ford's writing.

To use the enormous weapon of the written word, to speak accurately that is (in contradiction to the big crude lie) is what Ford is building here. For Ford's novels are written with a convinced idea of respect for the meaning of the words —and what a magnificent use they are put to in his hands! whereas the other position is not conceivable except as disrespect for the word's meaning. He speaks of this specifically in *No More Parades*—that no British officer can read and understand a simple statement unless it be stereotype . . . disrespect for the word and that, succinctly put, spells disaster.

Parenthetically, we shall have to go through some disastrous passages, make no mistake about that, but sooner or later we shall start uphill to our salvation. There is no other way. For in the end we must stand upon one thing and that only, respect for the word, and that is the one thing our enemies do not have. Therefore rejoice, says Ford, we have won our position and will hold it. But not yet—except in microcosm (a mere novel you might say). For we are sadly at a loss except in the reaches of our best minds to which Ford's mind is a prototype.

At the end Tietjens sees everything upon which his past has been built tossed aside. His brother has died, the inheritance is vanished, scattered, in one sense wasted. He sees all this with perfect equanimity—Great Groby Tree is down, the old curse achieved through his first wife's beneficent malevolence, a malevolence which he perfectly excuses. He is stripped to the rock of belief. But he is not really humiliated since he has kept his moral integrity through it all. In fact it is that which has brought him to destruction. All that by his upbringing and conviction he has believed is the best of England, save for Valentine, is done. But those who think that that is the end of him miss the whole point of the story, they forget the Phoenix symbol, the destruction by fire to immediate rebirth. Mark dead, Christopher, his younger brother, has got Valentine with child.

This is not the "last Tory" but the first in the new enlightenment of the Englishman—at his best, or the most typical Englishman. The sort of English that fought for and won Magna Carta, having undergone successive mutations through the ages, has reappeared in another form. And this we may say, I think, is the story of these changes, this decline and the beginning of the next phase. Thus it is not the facile legend, "the last Tory," can describe that of which Ford is speaking, except in a secondary sense, but the tragic emergence of the first Tory of the new dispensation—as Christopher Tietjens and not without international implications. *Transition* was the biggest word of the quarter-century with which the story deals, though its roots, like those of Groby Great Tree, lie in a soil untouched by the modern era. *Parade's End* then is for me a tremendous and favorable study of the transition of England's most worthy type, in Ford's view and affections, to the new man and what happens to him. The sheer writing can take care of itself.

In a Mood of Tragedy:

"The Mills of the Kavanaughs"

New York Times Book Review, 1951

IN HIS NEW BOOK Robert Lowell gives us six first-rate poems of which we may well be proud. As usual he has taken the rhyme-track for his effects. We shall now have rhyme again for a while, rhymes completely missing the incentive. The rhymes are necessary to Mr. Lowell. He must, to his mind, appear to surmount them.

An unwonted sense of tragedy coupled with a formal fixation of the line, together constitute the outstanding character of the title poem. It is as though, could he break through, he might surmount the disaster.

When he does, when he does under stress of emotion break through the monotony of the line, it never goes far, it is as though he had at last wakened to breathe freely again, you can feel the lines breathing, the poem rouses as though from a trance. Certainly Mr. Lowell gets his effects with admirable economy of means.

In this title poem, a dramatic narrative played out in a Maine village, Mr. Lowell appears to be restrained by the lines; he appears to *want to* break them. And when the break comes, tentatively, it is toward some happy recollection, the tragedy intervening when this is snatched away and the lines close in once more—as does the story: the woman playing solitaire in the garden by her husband's flag-draped grave. She dreams of the past, of the Abnaki Indians, the aborigines, and of how, lying prone in bed beside her husband, she was ravished in a dream.

Of the remaining five poems, "Her Dead Brother" is most succinct in the tragic mood that governs them all, while the lyric, "The Fat Man in the Mirror" (after Werfel) lifts the mood to what playfulness there is—as much as the mode permits: a tragic realization of time lost, peopled by "this pursey terror" that is "not I." The man is torn between a wish and a discipline. It is a violently sensual and innocent ego that without achievement (the poem) must end in nothing but despair.

Is the poet New England—or what otherwise is his heresy (of loves possessed only in dreams) that so bedevils him? At the precise moment of enjoyment she hears "My husband's Packard crunching up the drive." It is the poet's struggle to ride over the tragedy to a successful assertion—or is it his failure?—that gives the work its undoubted force.

Shall I say I prefer a poet of broader range of feeling? Is it when the restraints of the rhyme make the man restless and he drives through, elbows the restrictions out of the way that he becomes distinguished or when he fails?

It is to assert love, not to win it that the poem exists. If the poet is defeated it is then that he most triumphs, love is most proclaimed! the Abnakis are justified, their land repossessed in dreams. Kavanaugh, waking his wife from her passionate embraces, attempts to strangle her, that she, like Persephone, may die to be queen. He doesn't kill her, the tragedy lying elsewhere.

The tragedy is that the loss is poignantly felt, come what may: dream, sisterhood, sainthood—the violence in "Falling Asleep Over the Aeneid"; "Mother Maria Theresa";"David and Bathsheba in the Public Garden," excellent work. What can one wish more?

Dylan Thomas

1954

STRANGE TO SAY I remember Dylan Thomas better as a prose writer than a poet. His *Portrait of the Artist as a Young Dog* and the short accounts and stories written at that time made a great impression on me. I was not then familiar with his poetry. I see in retrospect a view of an English sea resort inhabited by real enough young women and men who lived in boarding houses of the cheaper sort and there carried on their reckless lives. There were views of the sea itself and of a carnival spirit that led to violence and in the end to an amnesic sequence where the author was left going up and downstairs in pursuit of a girl whom he never found. It is an impression of Dylan Thomas which has colored all that I have learned of him subsequently.

There is another view of him that I have kept when he spoke of himself as a half-grown boy perpetually in trouble over stolen fruit, trespasses beyond walls and troubles of every sort.

The poem must have been, as it is for such young men, an escape. Being a Welshman it had to take the form primarily of a song, which for any man limits it to his youth. But if a man can sing, and Dylan Thomas could that with distinction, what else matters? Not old age, Dylan Thomas appeared never to think of old age and need not have thought of it. It is as if he always meant to escape it and now without any loss to his lasting fame he has done just that.

Reading over his collected poems I have thought of what chances he had to enhance his fame by thinking again and perhaps more profoundly of what he had in mind. But what can be more profound than song? The only thing that can be asked is whether a man is content with it. It is not a drawing-room atmosphere that produced the tragedy of King Lear. Wasn't Lear himself a Welshman? But was Dylan Thomas capable of developing the profound attitudes of a Lear? If he was and his scholarship gave evidence of it, he might have gone on to write a verse tragedy—though the times are all against it.

Politer verse, more in the english style, appears to have been impossible for Thomas, it's a constitutional matter, in which a man has no choice. At least I don't think it was a choice that was open to him. Thomas was a lyric poet and, I think, a great one. Such memorable poems as "Over Sir John's Hill" and, even more to be emphasized, "On His Birthday," are far and away beyond the reach of any contemporary english or american poet. Not only in the contrapuntal metaphors which he uses, the fuguelike overlay of his language does he excel but he is outstanding in the way he packs the thought in among the words. For it is not all sound and image, but the ability to think is there also with a flaming conviction that clinches each point as the images mount. The clarity of his thought is not obscured by his images but rather emphasized.

The wind does "whack" as the hawk which is "on fire" hangs still in the sky. This devotional poem which in its packed metaphors shows a man happy in his fate though soon to die shows Dylan Thomas in a triumphant mood, exultant. What else can a man say or be? He carries the image through to a definite conclusion and as a lyric poet at his best does show the sparks of light which convinces us that he means what he says. He includes the whole world in his benisons.

The second poem, "Poem on His Birthday," is demonic, you have to chortle with glee at some of the figures. But it is the way the metaphors are identified with the meaning to emphasize it and to universalize and dignify it that is the proof of the poet's ability. You may not like such poems but prefer a more reasoned mode but this is impassioned poetry, you might call it drunken poetry, it smacks of the divine—as Dylan Thomas does also.

The analytic spirit that might have made him backtrack and reconsider, building a rational system of thought and technique, was not his. He had passion and a heart which carried him where he wanted to go but it cannot be said that he did not choose what he wanted.

Painting in the American Grain *

Art News, 1954

How *not* to begin an article on American primitives in painting: You don't begin speaking about Giotto and Fra Angelico or even Bosch, but of a cat with a bird in his mouth—a cat with a terrifying enormous head, enough to frighten birds, or of a six-foot Indian in a yellow breech clout. . . . Washington, apart from its official aspect, is a quiet, old-fashioned city, fit home, the only fit home for a collection of primitives such as this that smacks so of the American past.

As you enter the gallery—there are a total of 109 paintings of all sizes—the first thing that hits your eye is the immediacy of the scene, I should say the color! They were putting down what they had to put down, what they saw before them. They had reds to use and greens and flesh tints and browns and blues with which they wanted to surround themselves in shapes which they recognized. A beloved infant had died. If only they could bring it to life again! An artist was employed to paint a counterfeit presentment of the scene as the child stood in the garden by a tombstone near a weeping willow and a cat with arched back. It would bring comfort to the bereaved parents. That is how the artist painted it.

No matter what the skill or the lack of it, someone, somewhere in Pennsylvania—all trace of the painters that we may identify them has been lost—wanted on his walls a picture of Adam and Eve in the garden before the Fall. There is no serpent here, no sign even of God, just the garden and its

* *Art News* asked Dr. Williams to write on the unusually large collection of American primitive paintings presented by Col. and Mrs. Edgar W. Garbisch to the National Gallery in the Spring of 1954.

329

bountiful blessings. Wild beasts are at Adam's feet or at least one panther is there. The sky is luminous, this was not painted in a potato cellar. The vegetation is luxuriant, huge grape clusters hang from the trees and there at their ease sit together our primordial parents, naked and unashamed, bathed in sunlight. Who shall say the plenty of the New World so evident about them was not the true model that has been recorded?

A head, a head of a young woman in its title designated as "Blue Eyes," caught my eye at once because of the simplicity and convincing dignity of the profile. The hair was black and chopped off short to hang straight at the neck line. The complexion was clear, there was a faint smile to the lips, the look, off to the right, was direct, but the feature of the portrait was for me not the blue eyes but the enormous round chin perfectly in proportion that dominated the face and the whole picture. No one can say that chin was not real and that it was put down to be anything else. It is a world, not a chin that is depicted.

A record, something to stand against, a shield for their protection, the savage world with which they were surrounded; color, color that ran, mostly, to the very edge of the canvas as if they were afraid that something would be left out, covered the whole of their surfaces. One of my first views of the show was of the "Sisters in Red." Both my wife and I were amazed. They were talking to us. The older girl, not more than six, had dark hair and, looking at us directly, was the most serious, even slightly annoyed. The younger sister, holding a flower basket, a blond with wavy hair, wore an alert and daring expression of complete self-assurance, the mark of a typical second-child complex, which made her to me a living individual. I fell in love with her. The brilliant red dresses from which decently projected the snow-white pantalettes, ironed no doubt that morning, and dainty slippers completed the arresting picture.

A view of the burning of Charlestown by the British, with Boston untouched across the harbor, once again emphasized the importance for these people of the recording of events. Titles in this case were superimposed upon the canvas, Charlestown on one side and Boston on the other and between them, incongruously, Bunker Hill. Smoke was billowing to a sky already filled with masses of round clouds that rose above the flame and smoke in the distance.

Intimate scenes of rural life, a scene showing a side view of four cows and two horses, the barn and beyond that a house, a clapboard house, painted white. An obvious pride of possession and of the care which are owed such things.

There is a different pride in a grouping that fills one canvas, again to the very edge, called "The Plantation." Apparently it is near the sea, for a full-rigged ship occupies the foreground. Above rises a hill. The theme is formally treated and not without some skill. The perspective is elementary. Clusters of grapes larger than the ship's sails come in from the right meeting two trees, one on each side, that reach the sky framing the plantation house, with its garden, in the center distance toward the picture's upper edge. Birds are flying about, and down the hill nearer the foreground, linked by paths, are the farm buildings, and at the water's edge a warehouse.

A portrait of a woman past middle life attracted me by the hollow-cheeked majesty of its pose. A plain bonnet from which the two white strings lie symmetrically on either side of her flat breast completes the whole. There is a single tree, formally pruned and cut off only partially shown above her left shoulder. There is a companion portrait of her husband. They are serious individuals; the principal interest for me, apart from the impression they give of pride and reticence, is the colors the unknown artist has used. Nowhere except in El Greco have I seen green so used in the shadows about the face.

You will find here another of Hicks's "Peaceable Kingdom," but that hardly needs further comment. The same for "Penn's Treaty with the Indians."

Henry James said it is a complex thing to be an American. Unconscious of such an analysis of their situation, these artists as well as their sitters reacted to it nevertheless directly. They scarcely knew why they yearned for the things they desired, but to get them they strained every nerve.

The style of all these paintings is direct. Purposeful. The artist was called upon to put down a presence that the man or woman for whom the picture was painted wanted to see and remember, the world otherwise was for the moment put aside. That dictated the realist details of the situation and also what was to be excluded.

The kind of people that called for the paintings determined their quality. They demanded something to stand against the crudeness that surrounded them. As Wallace Stevens put it:

> I placed a jar in Tennessee,
> And round it was, upon a hill.
> It made the slovenly wilderness
> Surround that hill.
>
> The wilderness rose up to it,
> And sprawled around, no longer wild.

These were talented, creative painters. They had to be. They had no one to copy from. They were free as the wind, limited only by their technical abilities and driven by the demands of their clients. The very difficulties, technical difficulties, they had to face in getting their images down only added to the intensity of their efforts and to the directness of the results. It gave them a style of their own, as a group they had a realistic style, direct and practical as Benjamin Franklin. Nothing was to daunt them.

The circumstances surrounding the painting of Abraham Clark and his children, 1820, are known. Mr. Clark had just lost his beloved wife. He had gone into his garden with his six small children to read for them from the Bible. There he instructed the artist to paint him with the remainder of his family about him. The father, in profile, his thumb in the Bible no doubt at the passage from which he had been reading, sat to the right under the trees. The boys closely grouped, the baby on the knee of the oldest bareheaded before him. They all look alike, an obvious family. All are serious as befits the occasion. One leans his elbow against the tree. Their colorful faces stand out, no doubt in the clear light of the Resurrection, upon the forested and carefully painted background. The fifth son carries a pet hen in his arm. We are deeply moved by the intimacy.

Across the room is a large portrait of a young woman, Catalynje Post, 1730, wearing a flowered apron. She has a white lace cap on her head. Her arms are bare halfway to the wrist. She wears a low-necked dress and a necklace of pearls. Her hands, crudely painted, are placed one at the waist upon the hem of the colored apron, the other at the throat playing with an ornament which her fingers find there. A four-petaled flower and some carefully placed roses are seen in the background. But the feature of the ensemble is the slippered feet, standing at right angles before the eye; they have high heels and pointed toes and were no doubt the pride of their possessor. The artist had difficulty with the nose, which is presented full face or almost full face; his struggle to master it has not prevented him however from presenting an engaging and realistic portrait of a young woman.

There are still lifes which I wish there were room to comment upon. Fruit, in one case a watermelon with its red flesh, attracts the eye and the palate. One group symmetrically arranged on an oblong table, recognizably Shaker, particularly fascinated me. Curtains hang, always symmetrically, across the top. At either side are plates, with fruit knives. A bowl, it might be that of which Wallace Stevens speaks, stands in the exact center of the picture making of it an obvious decoration, with melons, grapes, apples, perhaps an orange, peaches and pears.

It was the intensity of their vision coupled with their isolation in the wilderness, that caused them one and all to place and have placed on the canvas veritable capsules, surrounded by a line of color, to hold them off from a world which was most about them. They were eminently objective, their paintings remained always things. They drew a line and the more clearly that line was drawn, the more vividly, the better. Color is light. Color is what most distinguishes the artist, color was what these people wanted to brighten the walls of their houses, color to the last inch of the canvas.

It was so with the portrait painted in 1800 of the Sargent family, artist unknown, the gayest and one of the largest pictures in the exhibition. It is the portrait of a cocky little man, in an enormous—to make him look tall—beaver hat (you can't tell me that the artist was not completely wise to the situation), surrounded by his wife and little daughters in white and flouncy dresses. The wife is sitting, sideface, with a new baby in her arms. The room is suffused with light. A toy spaniel frisks joyfully upon the hooked rug, the canaries singing—at least one of them is—in their cages between the pictures on the gaily papered walls. The paneled door is open. Every corner of the painting is distinct and bathed in light. It is a picture of a successful man.

There are in the same gallery two pictures, among the earliest of those shown, 1780, two large canvases of men heavily clad and in top hats, coursing hounds in the half-light of dawn and near sundown: the "Start" and "End of the Hunt." True to the facts the light in both cases is dim, which presented practical difficulties to the artist. These pictures are among the most crudely painted of those shown, but the record they present is filled for all that with something nostalgic and particularly moving. It brings to mind, as it was meant to do, another day which even then was fast vanishing. The artist was faced by the facts and the difficulties they made for him, but he faced them in the only way he knew, head on.

There is also a picture, undated, titled "The Coon Hunt." That, too, presented a scene which must have been familiar to the men of that time. It is moonlight. Half the party, carrying a lighted lantern, is approaching through a forest of partly felled trees; the quarry is on a high limb above their heads. The dogs are bounding into the air at the tree's base. The other half of the party is resting.

It is all a part of their lives that they had to see re-enacted before them to make it real that they could relive it in memory and re-enjoy it and it must be depicted by the artist so that it could be recognized—awkward as he may be.

In the middle gallery, apart from two Rembrandt-like portraits of an ageing burgher and his comfortable and smiling wife, among the best portraits in the exhibition, are two of the most interesting, imaginative pictures of all. I don't quite know what they meant, but suspect that the intention is to represent the travels of a man who has seen much of the world, has made money, perhaps retired from his labors and come home to rest and enjoy his memories. Each of the pictures presents, one overtly, a volcano in the distance, in the background a range of high mountains, perhaps the Andes, before a foreground crowded with all the appurtenances of a commercial civilization to the minutest detail, in the fullest light. The artist means to have you see into every part of his canvas; cities, factories, virtual palaces, railroad trains, alas, giving out smoke, rivers with waterfalls are prominently displayed. It is a pride of wealth which must have decorated a great house now all forgotten.

Many more such pictures showing the lives of the people of the period are displayed in this noteworthy collection. I must not forget to mention a picture labeled "Twenty-two Houses and a Church," depicting just that. The outlines of the buildings, covering several acres, are shown with their surrounding fences, painted white except in the foreground where a darker color is used—the only art displayed aside from the spacing of the buildings. Light, as in all the primitives, is everywhere. Not a single human figure is to be seen in the village, the buildings alone are recorded. The paintings have a definite style of their own which gives them a marked distinction as forthrightness, a candor and a practical skill not to be gainsaid and separate from European schools of painting with which they had not the time or the opportunity to acquaint themselves. So that, collectively, they represent not individual paintings so much as a yearning in the new country for some sort of an expression of the world which they represent.

It was a beginning world, a re-beginning world, and a hopeful one. The men, women and children who made it up were ignorant of the forces that governed it and what they had to face. They wanted to see themselves and be recorded against a surrounding wilderness of which they themselves were the only recognizable aspect. They were lonely. They were of the country, the only country which they or the artist knew and so represented.

This is a collection of paintings, lovingly assembled by a couple, Colonel and Mrs. Edgar William Garbisch, for their home on the eastern shore of Maryland. They found almost at once that the scope of what they had to choose from far exceeded their plans. They are called "American Primitives," the work of gifted artists whose names are largely lost in the shuffle of history.

On Measure—Statement for Cid Corman

Origin, 1954

VERSE—we'd better not speak of poetry lest we become confused—verse has always been associated in men's minds with "measure," i.e., with mathematics. In scanning any piece of verse, you "count" the syllables. Let's not speak either of rhythm, an aimless sort of thing without precise meaning of any sort. But measure implies something that can be measured. Today verse has lost all measure.

Our lives also have lost all that in the past we had to measure them by, except outmoded standards that are meaningless to us. In the same way our verses, of which our poems are made, are left without any metrical construction of which you can speak, any recognizable, any new measure by which they can be pulled together. We get sonnets, etc., but no one alive today, or half alive, seems to see anything incongruous in that. They cannot see that poems cannot any longer be made following a Euclidian measure, "beautiful" as this may make them. The very grounds for our beliefs have altered. We do not live that way any more; nothing in our lives, at bottom, is ordered according to that measure; our social concepts, our schools, our very religious ideas, certainly our understanding of mathematics are greatly altered. Were we called upon to go back to what we believed in the past we should be lost. Only the construction of our poems—and at best the construction of a poem must engage the tips of our intellectual awareness—is left shamefully to the past.

A relative order is operative elsewhere in our lives. Even the divorce laws recognize that. Are we so stupid that we can't see that the same things apply to the construction of

337

modern verse, to an art which hopes to engage the attention of a modern world? If men do not find in the verse they are called on to read a construction that interests them or that they believe in, they will not read your verses and I, for one, do not blame them. What will they find out there that is worth bothering about? So, I understand, the young men of my generation are going back to Pope. Let them. They want to be read at least with some understanding of what they are saying and Pope is at least understandable; a good master. They have been besides scared by all the wild experimentation that preceded them so that now they want to play it safe and to conform.

They have valid reasons for what they are doing—of course not all of them are doing it, but the English, with a man such as Christopher Fry prominent among them, lead the pack. Dylan Thomas is thrashing around somewhere in the wings but he is Welsh and acknowledges no rule—he cannot be of much help to us. Return as they may to the classics for their models it will not solve anything for them. They will still, later, have to tackle the fundamental problems which concern verse of a new construction to conform with our age. Their brothers in the chemical laboratory, from among whom their most acute readers will come if they know what is good for them, must be met on a footing that will not be retrograde but equal to their own. Though they may recognize this theoretically there is no one who dares overstep the conventional mark.

It's not only a question of daring, no one has instructed them differently. Most poems I see today are concerned with what they are *saying,* how profound they have been given to be. So true is this that those who write them have forgotten to make poems at all of them. Thank God we're not musicians, with our lack of structural invention we'd be ashamed to look ourselves in the face otherwise. There is nothing interesting in the construction of our poems, nothing that can jog the ear out of its boredom. I for one can't read them.

There is nothing in their metrical construction to attract me, so I fall back on e. e. cummings and the disguised conventions that he presents which are at least amusing—as amusing as "Doctor Foster went to Gloucester, in a shower of rain." Ogden Nash is also amusing, but not amusing enough.

The thing is that "free verse" since Whitman's time has led us astray. He was taken up, as were the leaders of the French Revolution before him with the abstract idea of freedom. It slopped over into all their thinking. But it was an idea lethal to all order, particularly to that order which has to do with the poem. Whitman was right in breaking our bounds but, having no valid restraints to hold him, went wild. He didn't know any better. At the last he resorted to a loose sort of language with no discipline about it of any sort and we have copied its worst feature, just that.

The corrective to that is forgetting Whitman, for instinctively he was on the right track, to find a new discipline. Invention is the mother of art. We must invent new modes to take the place of those which are worn out. For want of this we have gone back to worn-out modes with our tongues hanging out and our mouths drooling after "beauty" which is not even in the same category under which we are seeking it. Whitman, great as he was in his instinctive drive, was also the cause of our going astray. I among the rest have much to answer for. No verse can be free, it must be governed by some measure, but not by the old measure. There Whitman was right but there, at the same time, his leadership failed him. The time was not ready for it. We have to return to some measure but a measure consonant with our time and not a mode so rotten that it stinks.

We have no measure by which to guide ourselves except a purely intuitive one which we feel but do not name. I am not speaking of verse which has long since been frozen into a rigid mold signifying its death, but of verse which shows that it has been touched with some dissatisfaction with its present state. It is all over the page at the mere whim of the man who has composed it. This will not do. Certainly an art which implies a discipline as the poem does, a rule, a measure, will not tolerate it. There is no measure to guide us, no recognizable measure.

Relativity gives us the cue. So, again, mathematics comes to the rescue of the arts. Measure, an ancient word in poetry, something we have almost forgotten in its literal significance as something measured, becomes related again with the poetic. We have today to do with the poetic, as always, but a *relatively* stable foot, not a rigid one. That is all the difference. It is that which must become the object of our search. Only by coming to that realization shall we escape the power of these magnificent verses of the past which we have always marveled over and still be able to enjoy them. We live in a new world, pregnant with tremendous possibility for enlightenment but sometimes, being old, I despair of it. For the poem which has always led the way to the other arts as to life, being explicit, the only art which is explicit, has lately been left to fall into decay.

Without measure we are lost. But we have lost even the ability to count. Actually we are not as bad as that. Instinctively we have continued to count as always but it has become not a conscious process and being unconscious has descended to a low level of the invention. There are a few exceptions but there is no one among us who is consciously aware of what he is doing. I have accordingly made a few experiments which will appear in a new book shortly. What I want to emphasize is that I do not consider anything I have put down there as final. There will be other experiments but all will be directed toward the discovery of a new measure, I repeat, a new measure by which may be ordered our poems as well as our lives.

1953